Under the Moonlit Sky

Moonlit Sky

Nav K. Gill

D1269766

Napoleon

Cover art by François Thisdale, design by Emma Dolan

Le Conseil des Arts
du Canada | The Canada Council
for the Arts

Canada

We acknowledge the support of the Canada Council for the Arts for our publishing program. We acknowledge the financial support of the Government of Canada through the Book Publishing Industry Development Program (BPIDP) for our publishing activities.

Napoleon Publishing
an imprint of Napoleon & Company
Toronto, Ontario, Canada
www.napoleonandcompany.com

Mixed Sources
Product group from well-managed forests, and other controlled sources
FSC www.fsc.org Cert no. SW-COC-002358
© 1996 Forest Stewardship Council

Printed in Canada

Library and Archives Canada Cataloguing in Publication

Gill, Nav K., 1983-
    Under the moonlit sky / Nav K. Gill.

ISBN 978-1-894917-99-5

        I. Title.

PS8613.I45U64 2010   jC813'.6   C2010-900763-8

Dedicated to the memory
of my late Father, Nazar Singh Gill,
whose love and encouragement dared me to dream.
The first four chapters were written in his presence,
while the rest of the novel was completed in his memory.

To my mother—if anything is possible,
it is because of you and your strong belief that there
are no limits in life and that dreams can come true.
You inspire me.

To Sony and Harry—you stuck with me
from the beginning and made sure I got here.

There is wisdom in every story told,
every experience shared;
a wisdom that can become a beacon
for hope and change for the future.
But first, we must listen.

PROLOGUE

November 1st, 1984

The air is polluted. Instinctively I bring my hand over my mouth and nose, but I can still feel it seeping into my lungs. My heart is racing and my legs are tired, but I've kicked into survival mode, and I know that right now it's the only thing that is keeping me alive.

"Chase her! Don't stop until you get her! Remember, blood for blood!"

"Blood for blood! Blood for blood!"

I can hear the chants of the mob chasing after me as I force myself to continue. *Keep running, Esha. Just keep running!*

The streets are tight and the gates to the houses are either shut or have been broken down by the angry mobs. With the shouts getting louder, I race on, trying not to pay too much attention to the charred and dismembered bodies lying in the streets. Up ahead, the road breaks off into two. I decide to go right, and as I turn the corner, I immediately trip over a body and crash to the ground, scraping my knees. Covered with blood, not my own, I can smell the stench of death. It hovers in every street and alley. A reality that, just one day earlier, I would never have imagined possible.

The footsteps of men can be heard clearly now as their pace quickens. I don't have much time. If I am to survive, I must press on. I gather what strength I have left, stagger to my

1

feet and start running again. I can sense the fear sitting deep within me, waiting to get loose and take over. It is a fear that I can't afford to entertain, for if I do, then I'll definitely fall victim to the mob's hunger.

Hope quickly slipping away and my legs feeling heavier by the second, I begin to tremble. How is it possible to reach such a hopeless moment?

I remember the beautiful, bright and sunny morning, the laughter in the house. I remember thinking that it was going to be a nice day. But the screams of innocent victims and roars of angry mobs took control. As much as I tried, I could not force myself to stop thinking, stop remembering what I'd seen. How could I? I was still here, running to survive with nowhere to go.

Had I known what my decision was leading me into, I would never have taken such a risk. I would never have boarded that flight, and I would never have come to Delhi.

"Never lose sight of who you are," my grandma had told me. This exact phrase has been repeated to me over and over again, but it has never taken on the significance that it does now.

These words are at the very core of identity. This damn word, *identity*, has haunted me for months, and now suddenly it has tipped the scale between life and death. I don't even belong here, but still they chase me, because to *them* I am a Sikh.

Now, as I fight to keep ahead of the pursuing mob, I realize that this struggle with *identity* has become my story…and ultimately landed me in this hell.

Part One

Discovery

ONE

May 1984

I felt a tingle go down my spine. *Am I sweating? If so, can he tell?* His scent was getting stronger. It was a mix of leather and the fruity shampoo he used in his hair. Usually his fruity smell was the butt of my jokes whenever I was close to him. But this moment was different. He was closer now...much closer. He looked me dead in the eyes, oh, with those gorgeous blue eyes. He brought his left arm to the small of my back and pulled me closer.

"Johnny!" I gasped.

"Esha, I've wanted this for a long time now."

My heart was beating rapidly. As he leaned in, I held my breath. I couldn't function well enough to breathe. This was *Johnny*! My friend, but also the guy I had been crushing on for a very long time. He came closer and closer, and I could feel him breathing now...here it goes...and...

"ESHA! Hey! There you are! It's our song! Come on!" Johnny and I almost tripped over ourselves. A blonde girl in a leather jacket, fishnet stockings and a black skirt, the ultimate Madonna groupie, was standing in the doorway.

"Mandy, wait!" I protested as she grabbed hold of my arm and pulled me away. Johnny looked on in confusion. It was too late, and the moment was lost.

Mandy pulled me along a hallway filled with guys and gals

4

who were either busy with a bottle or busy with each other. I could hear the beat pumping now as she pulled me into the large living room that we had transformed into a makeshift dance floor.

"Mandy, do you realize what you just interrupted?"

"Oh, don't worry, you got all summer to get hot and heavy with Johnny Boy. Tonight you party with the girls! Hey, Jason! Put it up! Esha's here!"

"No problem, Mandy, this one's for you girls! Enjoy!" As Jason began to spin Cyndi Lauper's current hit, Mandy and I joined our girlfriends on the dance floor.

"Girls, here it comes...get ready for the chorus!" Mandy yelled as she threw her hands up into the air.

"Girls just wanna have fuh-un...whoa-o-o..."

"Esha! SHOTS!" Mandy yelled as she grabbed my arm for a second time.

"No, Mandy! I think I'm good for the rest of the night."

"Oh, stop complaining," said Carrie, the sweetest and usually most level-headed girl from our group. "We've graduated university! We're finally done with exams, studying and all of that stress. Come on! Celebrate! We don't know when we'll be able to party like this again."

"Carrie, we party every weekend!" I pointed out.

"Pleeeeeeease," pleaded Reet. Throughout my whole life, Reet had been my only friend from another Punjabi family. She was stuck in the same tug-of-war as I was between our parents and our lifestyles.

"Reet! What happened to your shoes? And you're soaking wet!" I cried out. Reet was standing on her tiptoes with her legs crossed at the ankles, as if she were hoping that no one would notice her bare feet. Her tank and skirt were drenched, and her hair was a tangled ball of wet curls. The three of us stared at Reet from head to toe before bursting into laughter.

"Honestly, Reet, what the hell did you do now?" Mandy laughed.

"Nothing, really... Well, Chase was chasing me—"

"Ooooo, Chase was *chasing* you!" we teased in unison.

"Oh, stop it! But really, so Chase and I were just joking around outside by the water, and we sorta ran into the water, and then a wave came...and...when I ran out...I was... slipper-less," Reet said, shrugging.

"You sure you were only *slipper-less*?" Mandy said as we all continued to laugh.

Reet's predicament didn't surprise us. She was known to get herself into tricky situations that were embarrassing for her but absolutely hilarious for us. Chase, her boyfriend of one year, had quickly grown accustomed to her unpredictable behaviour. From sleeping in on exam day to driving off with her soda can still on top of her car, it could be anything, but definitely worth a laugh. That was our Reet.

"Oh, shut up! Now, people, can we continue with our shots?" Reet demanded.

"Oh, right! Esha, come on!" Mandy said, quickly shifting her focus to me. All three pouted on cue. Together they made puppies look like bulldogs.

"Uhh...okay...okay, OKAY! Bring it on! Why the hell not?" I conceded.

"YES!!!!"

Mandy placed a tray full of dirty whiskey shots in front of us, while I tried not to think about the insanely huge headache I was definitely going to have the next morning.

"What should we toast to?" Carrie asked in her usual soft tone.

"Esha?" Mandy raised her eyebrows at me.

"Um, okay, how about to living life on the edge and never forgetting your girls."

"Cheers!" We all tipped our heads back and downed the shots. I closed my eyes as the golden liquid burned through my body. I basked in the immediate warmth it offered, something I couldn't find anywhere else.

"Okay, enough of this. Let's go party it up on the dance floor, ladies. Follow me!" Mandy proclaimed as she led the way back there.

It was quite crowded now. Everyone was making their way into the centre of the room. We were hitting the three a.m. mark, which meant that everyone was pretty much drunk or high. School was done, summer was starting. A whole new path stood out before us. We were young, and we wanted to party and let loose. Sensing this feeling, Jason chose to feed the crowd what it was yearning for, the hottest track of the year, "Thriller" by Michael Jackson.

I became lost in the music. People around me were letting go, singing along with the song, being free and just simply moving to the music. For a short while on the dancefloor, you can actually convince yourself that you don't have a care in the world. You're numb to pain, you forget your troubles, and there are no parents, no pressures, no family concerns or secrets. We all understood each other once we were on that dance floor together. We were all there for the same reason— we needed to be free. This was what parents didn't get. They didn't understand the inspiration and the comfort of being around people who were at the same level as us. We all shared the same uncertainties about life, and we were all trying to find a way to stall the process of having to grow up. Right then, none of it mattered; not my frustrations about my mother's weaknesses, and especially not my father's behaviour. That night I was free.

*   *   *

"Eshaaa! Wake up! It's almost noon!" My mother's voice startled me from my drunken sleep.

"Stop bugging meeeee!" I yelled as I toppled to the floor of my bedroom. My nose was flat against my rug, which from this angle looked like it needed a good vacuuming. Right now, my only concern was my throbbing headache. "Oh man, this is gonna hurt," I said, holding my head as I looked up at my bed. It seemed I had been sleeping on the very edge. I guessed I'd been too out of it last night to see where I'd landed. My room was just as I had left it. The numerous outfits I had tried on last night were still strewn across the floor and over the desk, which sat across from my bed. Sunlight poured in from the many windows that lined my L-shaped room. I had graciously been given the best bedroom at the back of the house, with my sister's old room situated across the hall from me. Each morning I rose out of bed to the scenic view of the mountains, and in summer the clear blue sky and the bright sun. Normally it was a welcome view to begin a fresh new day. Today, however, the bright sunlight only worsened my headache.

Lying on the floor of my room, I could still hear my mother venting her frustration downstairs as she prepared lunch. She was complaining, as usual, about the young generation growing up in the West and breaking away from Indian culture and traditions.

"What is it with these kids these days?" she complained. "Why are they always after ruining the peace and happiness of their mothers? Stay out all night and then don't wake up in the morning. What is this nonsense? In my days, and in my Punjab, we girls would *never ever* think of doing such things! And now look at these new-age girls! Waheguru, forgive me. My child has lost her way!"

Why must these Indian women always yell?

My mother was very much a typical Punjabi mother living in the West: overbearing, talking non-stop about the way things had been in the old days in India, and above all else, constantly trying to force her children to conform to the "Indian" way of life. I fought back nausea each time she insisted on drawing comparisons with me.

Every morning on her way to work, she would stop off at the local Sikh temple, called a Gurdwara. This was her daily routine, and of course she had done her best to force me to adopt this particular ritual, but I had happily resisted with equal force. Eventually, however, she had given up. I think she was finally reaching the point of exhaustion in her efforts to change me. Yet the loud wake-up calls persisted, and I didn't expect those to go away any time soon. To be honest, I understood that as a mother, she was full of love and just wanted the best for her kids. What that precisely entailed was where we differed in our opinions.

Sadly, my older sister had fallen into that trap. She'd grown up making Mom and Dad quite proud. Upon completing her university studies, she'd gone out into the professional world, gotten a good job, then married and settled down, as she was expected to do. I, on the other hand, still carried my dreams of becoming a celebrated athlete. I was a competitive soccer player, and I was quite good. The only problem was that women's soccer was still struggling to achieve the recognition it deserved. For that reason, I was expected to find a "more suitable" career, according to my parents.

My family had moved out west to British Columbia in the late 1960s, and that is where I was born. Dad had made a good living from working in the mills, and we enjoyed a comfortable life. I had just reached my twenties, and for a tall, slim, dark-haired female, life was just beginning, but every time I stopped to take in the breathtaking view of the Rockies surrounding our small town, I felt suffocated. It was a strange feeling to overlook such a vast, open environment and yet to feel utterly stifled. I blamed the fact that I felt stuck between two cultures: that of the West, where I was born and raised, and the other that of my parents and their conservative cultural ideals. I guess it wasn't entirely their fault. The Indian community here had made a point of carrying over their Indian culture. The only problem was that they all persisted in shoving it down my throat, and I wasn't too sure I wanted to accept it. I didn't feel like I belonged to it.

To my mother's dismay, I continued to resist their efforts to make me adopt their Sikh identity as well. I always wondered why it was such a big deal to them. After all, it was just another label, one among many, and unfortunately for my parents, it didn't fit too well in my life. And so every Saturday morning, after a night of partying, I was thrust back into reality with a loud mother who complained relentlessly about my behaviour.

Accepting my fate that morning, I finally pushed myself off the floor and stepped into the bathroom to freshen up. I examined my reflection in the mirror. I was happy with my looks and compliments were never scarce, in fact quite abundant. I was thankful to my parents for that much. I got my large light-brown eyes from my mother and my striking jawline and smile from my father. Whenever I smiled, someone would tell me how much I resembled him.

"Oh my dear, just like her father. Mirror image," I would hear the group of Punjabi women exclaim whenever they managed to corner me at a family gathering.

I must admit that being reminded of how much I resembled my father did not sit well with me any more. Once upon a time, I would have been overjoyed to receive such a compliment. I would have been proud to carry on any attributes that remotely resembled the strong, dedicated father I knew. Things, however, were different now. And just as our relationship had changed, so too had my level of pride.

At this moment, however, I wasn't too proud of myself either. As I lowered my gaze, I saw a bright, reddish mark on my neck. "Oh shit…a hickey! Shit, it can't be! Mom's gonna kill me!"

Before I could figure out how to cover the damn thing, my phone rang. I ran to answer it. It was Carrie.

"Carrie, thank god! Girl, I have a hickey! How do I get rid of it? I don't even remember getting one!"

"Chill out, Esha!" she laughed. "It's not a hickey, or at least I don't think it is, because I never saw you with anyone. It's probably a bruise."

"A bruise? From what?"

"You honestly don't remember? Girlfriend, you decked Skanky Rachel, then she lunged at you."

"What? Oh shit," I cried, trying to remember the details.

"You caught her with Johnny. Sorry about that, by the way, but I guess everyone was a tad overboard last night. It was a hell of a party. We gotta hand it to Tiffany. She may be an annoying

11

little rich twit, but she can still throw some crazy parties."

"Yeah, it was pretty insane. But...Johnny... I'm sorta remembering it, but everything's still fuzzy. Maybe it'll get sorted out later. I just got a crazy headache right now. Gonna go nurse it. I'll catch you later?"

"Yeah, that's fine. I just called to remind you of tonight's plan. We're meeting at Mandy's later then heading to the bonfire. Don't be late!"

"Sounds good, take care," I replied, hanging up.

Damn that Skanky Rachel. She really couldn't keep her hands off any guy. I couldn't believe I'd gotten into it with her, but Johnny had surprised me even more. I'd really thought we had something going, but I guessed I'd been wrong. Though it was funny to think that I must have bruised up Skanky Rachel; funny enough to at least put me in a better mood.

* * *

I finally managed to come downstairs while the aroma of my mother's cooking was still fresh in the air.

"It's about time, Esha. Are you not hungry?"

"Famished," I replied, quickly loading up my plate with mom's homemade yogurt and Indian *parotas*, which were really just fatter versions of roti jacked up with a lot of margarine. Nothing cured a hangover like my mother's parotas.

"Esha, my child, you must really not stay out so late at night," she began. She was warming up to lecture me again. I thought it best to stop her before she got too far.

"Mother, please. Let's not start this again, okay? I just graduated, so I went out to celebrate a little with friends. I did nothing wrong, so *please* don't grill me. Not today," I pleaded.

"Fine then, if not safeguarding your future, let's talk about something else," she said, sounding annoyed.

"Good. Glad to hear you say that. So tell me, what's on your mind, mother dearest?" I asked between mouthfuls.

"You and your father."

Oh, how I dreaded this topic, and my loud sigh reflected that. I would rather have listened to another lecture on partying too late. "Mom, you know I have nothing more to say on that subject."

"But I do, Esha. He is your father, and today we are going to discuss it," she said, sounding very adamant. I opened my mouth to object, but she held up a hand and continued. "He has worked hard his entire life so that he can give you a life without complaints. He deserves your respect, and I wish that you would show him some."

"But that's just it, Mom. I *do* have complaints against him. Many complaints! He isn't the man I grew up thinking he was. We've lived in ignorance. *I've* lived in ignorance. If I hadn't found that picture, I probably would have continued to live in ignorance. It's humiliating, *he's* humiliating!"

"Esha! Watch your language! He is your father! Like it or not, that is the truth!"

"No! That is not the truth!" I slammed my fists on the table as I stood up. The anger was rising within me. I could barely control my voice. Just thinking about it made my palms sweaty, my insides jittery. This always happened, and she just could not let it go. Today I had to let my thoughts out. I could not continue with the stress of burying my true feelings. If she insisted on bringing up this subject, then today I was going to give her what she wanted. "The truth, Mother, is something that you know very well, and that I had to find out by sheer coincidence. Apparently, you didn't find it necessary to fill me in on Daddy's little secret."

"Watch what you say!"

"Why? Huh? Why, Mom? What difference does it make? The truth is still what it is. My *father* still has *another* family!" I spat the words out. It was revolting to think about, let alone to say it out loud. "So really, it doesn't matter what I say or how I say it. In fact, let's just put it out there today. He has us here, while he keeps a wife and son in India! And what drives me insane is that you don't object to it. Why is that? Why are you quiet about his indecency? I don't understand why Indian women lack all self-respect!"

Ouch. There it was. Clearly, I had finally managed to hurt my mother's feelings with my last remarks. Her eyes watered, and she turned away from me. I regretted that remark the moment I let it escape my lips. As much as it pained me to think about what my father had done, a part of me still felt sorry for my mother.

"Esha, enough is enough." She spoke ever so softly now. "If you knew the whole truth, you would not feel this way. He…" She quickly cut herself off, as if she had said something she did not intend.

"What are you talking about? What do you mean by 'if you knew the whole truth'?" Suddenly my mom's gaze was concentrated on her hands, and I could see that she was struggling with her thoughts. Yet I still could not calm my own anger. Discussing my father was an explosive issue for me. "I don't know if I can hear any more. Just leave it alone."

"This you must, Esha. This you must." Her voice was almost as low as a whisper now, but she continued. "I have been bound by a promise I made to your father before you

14

were even born. I cannot bear to see your relationship with him deteriorate any further. I cannot bear to hear you say such horrible things about him, treat him with the neglect that you show him every single day then watch him weep at night, unable to correct the image that you have of him. I think that it is time I told you the whole truth."

I sat back down in my chair and braced myself. My mother's truth, however, went no further that day, as we were interrupted by the ringing of the telephone.

TWO

I never really knew what the nurse said to my mother over the phone, or what she heard as she desperately clutched the receiver. All I heard were two words that kept replaying over and over again in my head as we burst through the doors of the hospital emergency room: "…terrible… accident…"

We later found out there had been a collapse at the mill. As his colleagues tried to explain the scenario, I sat quietly overwhelmed with disbelief and with fearful thoughts rushing through my mind. I only managed to pick up a few words that were being said. Something about a stack of logs, "Hit his head…trying to save our lives…very brave…"

These words became jumbled in my head, and I became even more confused. I was lost. I had no clue what I was to do, what to expect, or how I was to behave. All I knew was that the man I called "Daddy" was lying in a room, not knowing if he was going to live or die. Doctors were claiming that they could do no more.

The man that I had barely said two words to in months was now disappearing rapidly before my eyes, and I could only sit there, trembling with fear and plagued by memories of our past. I could feel the fear slowly taking control of me. The terrifying sensation made its way up from the tip of my toes, flowing up through my legs, then it was in my arms, my stomach and my chest. Soon I couldn't breathe. I was silently drowning in fear.

I didn't notice when my mother came out of the room

and sat down beside me. Nor did I notice when my sister and her husband came running down the corridor. I only snapped out of my shocked state when my mother covered my hands with hers and said, "Esha, it's time you spoke to him." Her voice was soft, yet it carried a firm and urgent undertone.

I didn't have the courage to look at her, but I nodded and patted her hands. I got up and slowly forced one foot in front of the other, making it through the doorway and finding my way to his bedside.

His hands were bandaged, and his face was badly swollen. It was an incredibly scary sight at first. He was marked by nasty cuts and bruises, and his body looked broken. As I studied his face closely, I could barely find traces of the man I knew to be my father.

"Daddy?" It was hardly a sound. Less than a whisper, but it was all I could manage at first. I held his hand and said it once more, trying hard to find my strength. "Daddy, it's me, Esha. It's your Esha, Daddy… Aren't you going to open your eyes for me?"

I felt his hand twitch. He slowly moved his eyelids until he finally managed to open them. For a moment, I almost thought I saw him attempt a weak smile. Perhaps it was just a wince from the pain he must have been feeling.

"Daddy, do you hear me?" He nodded and tried to speak, but at that point the pain was clearly visible on his face. I hushed him softly and told him not to push himself. "You have to rest. Don't try to speak."

Seeing him in this state made our problems seem almost trivial, but I still could not forgive him. He very well could be on his deathbed, and the horrible truth of his past had kept us apart for months. So much time had been wasted between us.

"Daddy, there's so much to say, yet I'm finding it difficult to find the right words." He gently squeezed my hand, giving me courage to continue. "No matter the reason, I am sad that we have lost out on so many months together. Seeing you here like this, Dad… makes me realize how much…how much…" My words lost their strength, and I sobbed quietly. I now felt the enormity of the situation. He squeezed my hand tighter this time, but instead of just being an encouraging gesture, it felt rushed, as if he was trying to tell me to hurry. So I obliged. "Daddy, I realize how much…I love you and need you. I'm sorry, so sorry that I've shut you out of my life this past year. Please forgive me." There, I'd finally said it. Moments earlier, I had been questioning whether or not I could forgive *him* for his secrets, and now I had just asked him to forgive *me*.

He opened his mouth to speak, and his pain was terribly evident. Despite my attempts to persuade him to stay quiet, he eventually found his own words through his pain. "Forgiveness…is what I must…ask for from you, my child. I have not been honest with you." He squeezed my hand again. "Esha, there is much that I must say to you, and so little time. So I'm going to just get this out as quick as I can.

"The choices that you make when faced with a crisis determine just how good of a human being you really are. Remember that, child. I have made some choices that have affected my loved ones, my family. Were they the right choices? I don't know. I suppose God will have to decide now, as I sense we shall be meeting very soon."

"Daddy, don't say that, please!" I cried.

"I never ever wanted to hurt you. You are my little princess. Always have been and always will be. I love you dearly. When you were born, I was so happy. People said to me 'aw, another

18

girl,' but I was so proud. You were so beautiful, and you had such a peaceful glow in you. And I am sorry for the hurt that you have felt, all because of the choices that I have made. But you must understand the reasons that led me to those choices."

With every word he spoke, his breathing became heavier, and I could see that he was struggling to remain calm in front of me. I placed a soothing hand over his and wiped the sweat off his forehead with my other hand. I looked deep into his eyes and tried to return his reassuring smile.

"I realize, child," he continued, "the difficulties you have had and the hesitations you have demonstrated in accepting your identity as a Sikh, as an Indian. But this is who we are. You may say that you are not an Indian, but the truth is that I am. You may battle demons inside of you, refuse to accept that you are a Sikh, but I accept and recognize my religion. I have never tried to force it upon you. Rather, I have always secretly prayed that one day you would find your way to accepting it as a part of your identity."

"Daddy, why are you saying this to me now? What difference does it make?"

"It matters, Esha dear. It matters. The way I have lived my life is a reflection of how important being a Sikh is to me. It is a way of life. It does not define who you are in the beginning, rather it helps you to find out who you want to become. It continues to guide you, until one day you can look at yourself in the mirror and embrace who you are. When you are able to embrace it in front of all others, irrespective of the outcome, then you will have fully embraced your identity. Be proud, Esha, and live without fear."

"Is this how you rationalize your choices?" I questioned with a hint of sarcasm, which I immediately regretted.

"Call it what you may, but it has been my chosen way of life. It is what I see to be right and just."

"I'm sorry, but you're not making much sense, Daddy. Forgive me, but I'm having a very difficult time understanding how this 'chosen way of life' has led you into having two families. The absurdity of it makes me want to yell to the world that my whole life has been a lie! Dad, it's a total soap opera, one that I never thought would become a part of my reality. How in the world does someone rationalize *that*?"

"No one can, my princess, no one. But at the same time, you are not completely correct when you assume that this tale has become part of your reality."

"I don't understand." I lowered my gaze as my eyes welled up with tears again, and I shook my head. "I'm tired with all of these lies and half-truths. Please, just tell me straight, what is the true story behind this family in India and their connection to you? I have to know."

"Listen to me carefully now." His discomfort was becoming more and more evident now. His breathing became heavier with every word. "I know your mother tried to tell you the truth. She was bound by a promise that I forced her to make years ago. Despite what you have heard and what many have been led to believe all these years... I was never the rightful husband, nor the biological father to the family in India. I simply...answered...God's call."

My mouth went dry as I became numb. In the few moments of silence that passed between us, I tried to absorb what he was trying to tell me, but it made no sense. I tried to react, but all I could muster was, "What?"

"That is the truth, Esha. And...all I can do right now is seek your forgiveness, and in time, your understanding." He closed his eyes, and my heart skipped a beat as I feared the worst, but he kept speaking. "God will now help me to see whether my choices were in fact right or wrong, but I keep my faith… I love you, my princess."

He opened his eyes again and gave another weak smile. I returned his affection with a kiss on his forehead. "Daddy, I love you." My voice croaked, and I looked away, fighting back the tears. This was getting to be too much.

My mind was racing with so many contradictory thoughts. First, I'd been led to believe that the family in India belonged to him, and now I was being told otherwise. I'd spent a year being angry with him, and now I was frustrated. I couldn't deal with it, because here he was, lying before me all bruised and broken and talking about his faith in God and his identity as a Sikh. What the hell was going on? I had so many questions for him, but he was too weak for a long discussion. In the meantime, I was going crazy. I had to get out. I needed air.

"Daddy, I'll see you a bit later. I'm just going to go get some air."

As I let go of his hand, I had a strange feeling that I was letting go of a part of me. I could sense an empty feeling creeping up from within. I turned and looked at him once more from the doorway. *This can't be it. Surely, I'll see him again. Don't be so scared, Esha.*

Taking a deep breath, I turned on my heels and walked out the door. I tried to focus on happier moments to come, like bringing my father home and making up for lost time. I convinced myself there was still time. Life couldn't be that cruel. *Could it?*

Later I realized that life has a mind of its own. It doesn't pay any heed to the ways in which we try to convince ourselves that we have control over it. I wanted more time, because *I* wasn't ready to let go of my father. I thought I had it.

He never came home from the hospital, and we didn't make up for lost time. I never saw my father breathe, smile, talk, or open his eyes again. He passed away in my mother's arms. She soothed his pain and watched him go. Where was I? When my father needed me most, I wasn't there. Instead, I was out in the parking lot secretly having a cigarette, convincing myself that I had more time, because I wasn't ready to let go. The more I thought about it, the more I couldn't decide whether life was cruel, or I was.

THREE

After my father's death, I found solace by sitting in my room and gazing out the window in complete silence. How many mourners visited the house, telephoned, or stood watching me as I sat in solitude, I never noticed. I allowed myself to become lost in my own quiet world of grief and regret. Memories of my father circulated in my mind constantly and pushed away all notion of sleep. Whenever I was lying in my bed, I half-expected him to come open my door as he always had when I was younger. It was a small knock, followed by a light whisper: "Esha, you awake yet?"

Maybe this is what that "phantom" feeling was all about. I had heard people describe such a feeling after they had lost something, like an arm or a leg. They had a hard time letting go of the expectation that it was still there. That's how I felt now in my father's absence.

Following that night at the hospital, I did my best to avoid my mother. I'm not sure if it was guilt or regret about the conversation we'd had right before we got the call about the accident, but for some reason I couldn't bring myself to look her in the eye. So I avoided her altogether, until finally, one day, she came to my room.

I was once again perched up against my window, looking out at the mountains where they lined the clear blue sky, caught up in my own thoughts. She laid a hand on my shoulder and squeezed it slightly. Her touch brought me back into the room, and I slowly tilted my head towards her.

She was dressed in a white salwar-kameez, a simple Indian suit, with a shawl covering her from her waist up. Her face was pale and swollen. Her eyes were severely reddened from weeks of crying and sleepless nights. She had aged rapidly. Her once bright and striking appearance was nowhere to be seen.

"Esha," she began, "our lives have changed a lot in the past few weeks. Waheguru only knows what the coming days will be like. No matter what, we must be a family."

Hearing her use the word "family" brought tears to my eyes. I turned towards her, sinking my head into her stomach as she wrapped her arms around me. Feeling her warmth made me realize how lonely I had felt. Her warmth filled the longing I had been battling since the moment I had left my father's bedside. She offered reassurance, comfort and love, and I accepted.

"I feel lost without Daddy," I confessed. "I don't know... anything any more. How I should behave, what I should do, who I should be...I'm lost." I could no longer hold back my emotions. I felt a surge of energy and rage come from within, and this time I let it flow out. "I just feel so horrible. The things I said about him, those words, those feelings, they haunt me every moment, but... at the same time, it still doesn't make any sense, Mom."

"What doesn't?"

"Everything! What's true, what's not, the things Daddy said to me before he... It's too much!"

"Perhaps it is, but life does not stop moving because things get to be too much, Esha. Time does not stop. We have to pick up the pieces."

"Why does everyone keep saying that? Life isn't moving for me. Everything has stopped moving, everything..."

"Your father was a good man. He had a lot of respect and admiration for the people in his life, and he received just as much in return. Most important, he loved his kids very much. I hope you will remember that always."

I nodded as she continued. "What you have heard about this...this other family in India...is partly true and partly fictional. The time has come for you to know everything."

I looked up as she finally started to address a topic that was very disturbing for me. She turned away and walked over to my bed, where she sat down and gently folded her hands in her lap, staring at them intently. Perhaps she didn't have the courage to look me in the eye as she spoke of this secret that obviously had been a burden on her marriage for years.

"You and your sister are not aware of this, but your father once had a brother. He was only one year younger than your father, but they were like twins, always together. Your father loved him very much, the whole family did. All the neighbours in the village would comment on how proud he would make the family one day. He was bright, handsome, and full of life."

"Why haven't we been told about him before? Why didn't Dad ever say anything about a *brother*?"

"Because the family cut all ties with him not too long after your father and I married. It was agreed that we would never mention him again. Even now, I am not sure how to tell you about him."

"Just say it, Mom. From the beginning," I said eagerly.

"Okay, well," she began, "he was a very carefree young boy, someone who was praised by his peers and adored by the elders. Like most boys, he was always up to some mischief, but

25

never anything serious, and he could almost always get away with it. After your father and I married, he did his very best to make me feel comfortable within the family. We got along very well. He would come running to me and plead with me to calm your father and smooth things over whenever he was caught cheating on his school papers."

"So what happened?" I asked. My curiosity was becoming unbearable.

"It was the evening of Diwali. The house was lit up with candles, and it looked beautiful, just like every year. The house was filled with people preparing for the evening's festivities. Your grandfather was really particular about celebrating special occasions with family and friends. Diwali was always a very special day for him. Your father had just returned from the bazaar with sweets, and I was rushing him into the bedroom, pleading that he get dressed quickly so we could go outside and join everyone else. I was walking out to the courtyard when I heard it..."

She trailed off, and I hesitated a moment before pushing her to keep going. "Heard what, Mom?"

"A noise... It sounded like muffled screams. I looked around and tried to determine if what I heard was real or just in my head. So I stopped and listened carefully. Then I heard it again, and this time I followed the voices in the direction of the servants' quarters. No one else was in the house, as most were either out in the courtyard, or just making their way back from the Gurdwara. We had given the servants the evening off to go and be with their families, so the noise immediately aroused my curiosity.

"As I made my way to the back, I saw a dim light emerging from the storage room, located by the servant quarters, and

I heard it again; a faint scream and cries that could only belong to a female. I could hear a shuffling noise, which I later attributed to the struggle that was going on inside."

"Struggle? Oh, Mom...what did you see?" My heart pounded as I made my way closer to where she was seated.

"I crept to the door and slowly pushed it open," she continued with her eyes still carefully averted away from my curious gaze. "The door creaked a little, and I remember trembling at that moment. I was nervous and almost afraid to step inside. When I looked up, I was instantly filled with terror. The scene before me was...it was...to this day I cannot put it out of my mind. There he was...the pride of our family, the joy of the village... forcefully on top of an innocent girl. Her hands were pinned high above her head with his. Tears were streaming down her face, and her legs were pinned beneath his weight. Her clothing had been stripped off...the sight was so disgusting, I screamed and I screamed. I yelled at him to let her go. I was so shocked and so hurt to see him in such an act. I could not believe what was happening right before my eyes."

"Oh my god...oh my... Mom, what did you do?"

"What else could I do but try and stop him? I ran to him, and I started pushing him away. I just threw myself at him. I was hysterical. I cannot forget how he just looked at me. There was no sadness or remorse; he just stared at me as he blocked my attacks. Eventually, he managed to push me aside, got up and walked away. He never once turned around. He just simply *walked away*."

"What about the girl? What happened to her?"

"I took her in my arms, and I alerted your father about what had happened. He was furious. I could never have imagined the anger that I saw in his eyes that night. He decided that his father, your grandfather, should be notified and left in charge of the situation.

"In the end, it was decided that Jeet would marry that poor girl. She was so traumatized by what had happened. It was clear that she was terrified about the uncertainty of her future. She was scared, as most women back then were. There weren't many options for female victims of rape then. Her life was ruined by Jeet's moment of lust and insanity."

"I can't even begin to imagine what she was experiencing, but *marry*?" I said. "Forcing her to marry her rapist is even worse! What about the cops? What about charging his ass with rape, dumping him in jail and tossing away the key?" I found it absolutely absurd that they didn't jump to the obvious remedy.

"Oh, Esha, back then things were done differently," she replied, waving a hand. "Families tried to salvage what they could of their honour. The girl's father was worried that no man would marry her if the ordeal was made public. Also, a few weeks later, it was learned that she was pregnant. Marriage was the only way to save both families."

"I seriously don't agree, but, okay, what happened next? I imagine things didn't go as planned, otherwise why would I find a wedding picture of Dad and that woman? That was her, wasn't it?"

"Jeet wasn't pleased with the idea of marrying her. He protested against the will of the family, and the night before the wedding, he ran away."

"*He ran away?*"

"Yes, and this posed a serious problem for your grandfather. The girl's father was very upset and decided that since the truth would now most likely leak out, he would take things into his hands. He threatened to cause a public stir and defame the entire family. Your father could not stand by and watch the family suffer for a sin that Jeet had committed. So he announced that he would stand in Jeet's place, that he would marry the girl."

"How was that possible? He was already married to you."

"Yes, legally he was my husband, and he had already filed immigration papers to come to Canada. No outsiders were invited. Just the family conducted a small ceremony to give satisfaction to the girl and her father that her child would have a name. It was done to give her some peace of mind after such a traumatic experience. The villagers didn't even know what had happened. So to keep the secret, your grandfather shifted the entire family to Delhi. When your father received his immigration to Canada, he left India and never went back, but continued to send money. Papers were doctored to show that Jeet had in fact married her, and the child was his."

"Wow, that's…that's…that's really messed up."

"It's a lot to understand. I had a tough time dealing with it, but I had seen the state that the poor girl was in. I understood why your father did what he did. I never had any complaints against him. If he hadn't married her and made sure that she would be taken care of, then God only knows where she would have ended up, or if she and her child would have survived."

"But why was a picture taken of Dad and her? I mean, if Dad just stepped in, why the photo?"

"It was leverage. The girl's father wanted it taken, in case our family backed away from carrying out our promise to care for her and her son and giving them the family name."

"I wish you had told me this sooner, Mom. It would have

prevented my hostile behaviour towards Dad this past year. It would have helped if you had said something sooner."

"I realize that, but I took an oath that I would never say a word unless your father deemed it necessary."

"So why now? What difference does it make? He's already gone. I can't correct what's happened in the past year, the way I attacked him and cut him out of my life. "

"It matters now, Esha, because your father wanted you to know. He…" Her voice trailed away as she got off the bed and walked carefully over to the window, staring off into the vast landscape that surrounded us. After a short silence, she continued. "Before he left us, your father made a request."

"What kind of request?"

She turned around to face me now. "He wished that I tell you the truth regarding the family in India. He wished that you be the one to travel back with his ashes. He wished that you discover the family in India, and that along with the son, you travel to Kiratpur, the sacred place for Sikhs, and that you pour his ashes into the river as it has been done for countless Sikhs, including several of our Gurus. Esha, your father wished that you try, at least once, to discover what it is to be a Sikh."

That sounded like more than just one request, and what was this about "learning to be a Sikh?" What did she mean? Travel to India? Me? The idea was laughable at best. I wasn't sure I even wanted to meet that family.

"Mom, this is too much!" I finally objected. "What am I going to do in India? And it's such a big responsibility to…to… well, the ashes thing. I've never been to India, I barely visit the Gurdwara here, so what do I know about doing stuff like that? I can't do it, no way! And that family, I'm not even sure I want to meet them. I mean, you just told me all of this stuff now; I haven't even begun to process it. It's too soon, and what about my soccer season? I can't just abandon the team…and—"

"This is your father's dying wish, Esha! Can't you even *try*?" she said, cutting me off. "Just once, try to do something for the father who spent *his* life working hard to give you this life; for the father who held your small hands and taught you how to walk; for the father who died waiting for his daughter to return…from…from what? What were you doing when your father was in his last moments, waiting and hoping that his youngest daughter would be by his side, huh? Where? I imagine you were out on a cigarette break? Right? What, you think I don't know what you are up to?"

She knew!

"Don't jump to conclusions, Mom! I was not having a cigarette. I don't smoke!" I lied. "And don't try to change the subject here. Honestly, you know I can't go to India. I can't do this!"

"Esha." She walked towards me and placed her hands on my shoulders. I could sense she was shifting her strategy, but I wasn't going to give in. "Your father and I have tried not to force you to live life the way we wish you would. Instead, we have always secretly prayed that one day you would find your way back to us. This is the time to carry out your responsibility. You are his daughter. Your father has passed on, but he has made one last request. It is your duty to follow through on that request.

"You have a whole life ahead of you. This is your only chance to discover that other part of you, discover the part that you have shut up and put away all these years. You are a Sikh. You may not care, but it was an important part of who your father was. He wants you to discover why. Think of it as a challenge or an adventure, but please do this one thing for him, child."

She held my gaze for a long time, then she patted my cheek ever so softly before she walked away. *Damn that guilt trip!*

"Mom," I called out in defeat just as she reached the doorway.

"Yes?"

"What's his name?" I asked.

"Who?"

"The son in India, what's his name?"

"His name is Ekant, Ekant Singh."

FOUR

"Esha, I still can't believe you're going through with this," Mandy said as she paced around my room. "I mean, India, it's so…so…"

"Exotic?" Carrie offered.

"I doubt it's exotic, Carrie," Reet replied.

"Yeah, but so Third World, no? I mean, what are you going to do there, and can you even speak their language? How long will you be gone?"

"Mandy's right, and dude, just think how annoyed we get here when we have to attend Indian stuff. Now you'll be surrounded by it with no escape!" added Reet.

"Okay, calm down! And thanks for pointing that out, Reet. But, honestly, I don't know how long, and I have no clue what it'll be like. Trust me, this wasn't my idea. As for the language, my father made sure long ago that my sister and I learned how to speak Punjabi, so I doubt that'll be a problem."

I was just finishing up my packing. The girls had been over since the previous night. They were dreading the idea of summer without me, but at the same time they were very excited over the prospect of me trying to survive on my own in India.

"So why are *you* going? Why can't your sister or your mother go?" Mandy asked as she stood with her hands on her hips. She always was a bit overprotective with her girlfriends.

"Mands, you know why. It was my father's wish. Besides, my

33

sister is pregnant. She can't travel, and Mom isn't in any shape to travel either, and I don't think in her state she should be getting more stressed out by having to face that family in India."

"Oh yeah, I almost forgot about your brother…or…cousin…whatever. Dude, that's messed up. What do you think he'll be like?"

"I have no clue, but I'm sure I can handle him. I'm more concerned about carrying out my father's request. Going to an unfamiliar place, carrying out these last rites, it's totally not my scene. But…I feel terrible for the way I handled things with him," I admitted. I put down the books I had spent the past half hour searching for and slumped onto my bed. "I mean, I wasn't even there when he was…you know…in the end. I was too caught up in my own fear and denial."

"Esha," Carrie said as she placed a comforting hand on mine, "if you aren't ready to do this, maybe you should wait a bit."

"No. It's already been a month," I replied, getting back up. "I've thought about this a lot, and I have to make it up to my dad. I *have* to do this. I mean, I just have to go there, meet this son, go spread the ashes, then I can catch a flight back home. I'll get out of there as soon as I can. It can't be too hard, right?"

"I hope not! We're going to miss you!" Mandy cried as she wrapped me in her arms.

"Wait! Me too!" Carrie threw her arms around both of us.

"And me!" cried Reet as she joined in.

"I'm going to miss you so much," I said, as I thought sadly about the dreary weeks ahead of me while my friends enjoyed the wonderful summer weather in B.C.

"Summer's going to suck without you, Esha. You better get your ass back here as soon as possible," Mandy whined.

"You gotta do one thing for me, though," I said as I broke away from the group hug.

"Sure!" she exclaimed with eyes wide.

"Promise me you'll make Skanky Rachel's summer hell and keep her away from Johnny!"

"For sure! She's going down!" yelled Mandy with a stern face.

We all burst into laughter. I really was going to miss them.

"Esha, you ready?" My sister was standing in the doorway.

"Uh, yeah, just about, Sandeep. I'll be right down," I replied as I returned to my luggage.

"Hurry then, and meet us outside. We still have to go pick up the ashes from the funeral home," she said as she turned around and went back downstairs.

"Okay, let's jam, girls. Help me take this down."

We each grabbed a bag and made our way downstairs. My sister, her husband, and my mother were just making their way out the front door. I threw on my shoes and gave the house a quick glance. It was time to go.

As I made my way to the door, I suddenly gave a very loud and unexpected sneeze. "Wow, sorry about that," I said as the girls giggled.

"Oh no, Esha!" my mom yelled, running back into the house. "You sneezed before leaving! That's a bad omen. Oh, Waheguru. Back into the house, everyone!"

"What? Wait. Mom, don't be so superstitiously Indian! We can't waste any more time. Come on, don't believe this nonsense." I grabbed my bag and walked out the door and started loading my things into the jeep.

"Esha, please, child, this is true. We cannot leave the house after someone has given a single sneeze. It is a bad omen!"

"Mom, I don't believe that. Now I'm ready to go. Are you guys coming?"

My sister and her husband hesitated for a moment and exchanged worried glances before following me to the jeep. After a long time contemplating her options, my mother reluctantly joined us.

With the smile of victory on my face, I turned my attention to the girls, who looked somewhat bewildered by my mother's weird reaction to the sneeze. "So I'll see you when I get back then? Take care, have loads of fun, but try not to get into any trouble without me," I said as I hugged all three.

"Oh, Esha, we'll do our best," Carrie reassured me with her usual comforting smile.

"Exactly babe, we'll be fine. Just take care of yourself and write us a letter or something. They do that in India, right?"

"Oh, shut up, Mandy. I'll try to call you if I can."

"Be careful, and don't let those people get you down," advised Reet.

"Forget me. I'm more worried about you! Try to stay out of trouble," I teased.

"Bye, Esha," Reet said with a sigh. Even my teasing wasn't going to put her in a cheery mood today. It was disconcerting to see her so down.

After one last hug, I turned away and climbed into the jeep. I waved goodbye to my three best friends as we drove away. As the image of Mandy, Carrie and Reet became smaller and eventually disappeared, I was struck by an unsettling fear.

Up to this point, travelling to India had been an idea, then a discussion. Later it had become a topic of great curiosity for my friends. Now, with no discussion, no friends and no humour, the reality of the situation began to set in. I was going through with it. I was really going to India.

I was going to be with the family that had been at the root of my fights with both of my parents for the past year. I was going to meet the family that had been created by a malicious attack, carried out by an uncle who until recently I didn't even know existed. My every instinct screamed that I wasn't prepared for what awaited me on the other side. This was going to be one hell of a trip.

"Shit," I said out loud.

"Esha, this is not the time to swear," my mother scolded. "This is the time to pray to Waheguru that you have a safe trip to India, and that your father's last wish is realized. After which, you will once again join us. Waheguru, look over my sweet daughter."

"Oh, Mom." I swung my arm around her and smiled. "I'll be just fine. You should feel sorry for the poor Indians that are going to have to put up with me. I'll be back in no time, just you wait and see."

She returned my smile, but as her eyes met mine, I saw her fear. I guess mothers never can stop worrying.

Indians.

I took a deep breath and looked out at the passing mountains. My whole life, I had been surrounded by the beauty of these very mountains. It saddened me to think I wouldn't be waking up to them for the next few weeks.

Don't worry, mountains; I'll be back very soon.

Part Two

Journey

FIVE

June 1984

L adies and gentlemen, please take your seats and fasten your seatbelts. We will begin our descent to the Palam Airport in New Delhi shortly. Thank you."

My stomach tightened as the airplane descended. So far the flight had been unbearable, and as the plane now began its landing, my impatience grew. Massaging the back of my stiff neck didn't do much for the discomfort. It must have been over sixteen hours since we'd departed. Thankfully, I had a window seat with no one beside me. The flight wasn't as packed as I had feared it would be.

"Shit—I hate planes. Why did I have to come all this way?" I complained as I stretched out my arms. The answer, however, was resting on my lap. "Oops. Sorry, Daddy. I didn't mean to swear again. I can't wait to get off this plane. You know how I…" my voice trailed off.

I realized that I wasn't speaking to a real person. Instead I was speaking to a box of ashes. It had been a painful experience collecting his urn from the funeral home. My mother's strong façade had fallen apart as soon as she'd laid eyes upon the urn. Soon after, both my sister and mother had become faint, and so of course, swallowing my emotions, I'd stepped forward and completed the formalities.

Now, however, as I held my father's urn, I couldn't help but remember a man who had chased after me during my toddler days; a man who'd picked me up and carried me on his shoulders when I couldn't walk any further; a man who was very much alive and excited for life and his children. That man was now nothing more than ashes, tied in a bag, secured in a wooden box and placed in a suede emerald sack.

"You did love us, right, Daddy? But, then why did you lie all of these years? And especially when you knew I had found that photo. Why didn't you say anything then? It would have changed things, changed the way I ended things…"

A sea of lights lit up the late-night cityscape below. As the plane glided towards the runway, the crowded streets became more visible. The plane gave a bit of a jolt as it touched down on the tarmac. Just as it came to a stop, I took a deep breath. *Here we go.*

As soon as I stepped off the plane, I was engulfed in thick smog that carried a rank smell, as if there were month-old dirty socks in every pocket of Delhi. If that wasn't bad enough, the heat was excruciating. It was like walking into an oven.

Well, this is going to take some getting used to! I thought as I made my way towards the baggage collection area.

While collecting my bags, I noticed that I was being stared at quite a bit. Walking towards the exit, I realized I was still drawing a lot of attention. I usually am quite pleased to attract attention, but the constant stares were admittedly a bit unnerving. I looked down, trying to see if there was something wrong with my clothes or if something was out of place, but there wasn't, so I just moved on. I desperately hoped my ride was waiting for me.

Once outside, I scanned the curious faces in the crowded

gated area through which all arrivals had to pass after collecting their bags. It was mostly men in the crowd. I could barely spot any women. They were shouting out names, smiling and waving at their relatives. Eventually my gaze landed on a short, skinny, dark-complexioned man with large round eyes. He was holding a sign that read: *Esha Kaur Sidhu—Canada.*

"Kaur? Great, I'm not even out of the airport yet, and they're already turning me into a full-fledged Sikh...Indian... whatever!" I walked up to the man with the sign, and he looked relieved that he had finally found me. I smiled and offered my hand. "Hi, I'm Esha. Just simple Esha, not EEE-sha, but like the sound of an 'a', okay, Esha. And please no Kaur, okay?"

He eyed my offered hand nervously, simply nodded and said, "Hello, ma'am. I am Chotu, the family driver."

"Chotu? Is that your full name?" I asked in Punjabi as I took my hand back. As expected, he didn't speak English.

"No, ma'am. It is Chandrasheiker Singh. Everybody calls me Chotu, well, because as you can see, I am not so very tall. It is since childhood. Just Chotu," he said smiling, clearly pleased that I had taken interest in his name. I followed him to a medium-sized white car in the airport parking lot. The stares from passersby still had not ceased.

"So, Chotu, why is it that wherever I pass, people are staring at me?"

Chotu found this funny. "Oh, ma'am, do not worry too much about it. You are a very fair-looking young woman. It is only normal that they will stare at a foreigner such as yourself."

"I see. So, uh...where's the family? I mean, I thought Ekant would come to collect me."

"Sir was busy with business, so he sent me to receive you. The family is eagerly awaiting your arrival at home. It is the

41

first time we are having a foreign guest visit. Everyone is very excited to see you, but also very sad to hear about your father." Chotu lowered his gaze to the urn held tightly in my hands.

"Yeah, me too," I sighed as I climbed into the backseat and he loaded up my baggage.

The drive to the house didn't take very long. After the time it had taken to get through customs, collect my bags and exit the airport, it had gotten pretty late, almost midnight. Therefore, as Chotu explained, the streets now were clear for a smooth, traffic-free drive.

I rolled down my window, hoping to feel a breeze. The humidity was making my hair frizz, so I tied it back. The last thing I should do is show up looking like a crazy bag lady. I straightened my clothes and tried to make myself look presentable. I did the best I could from the backseat of the car and in such poor light. A spritz of perfume and the cool feel of lotion on my arms and face was incredibly refreshing, especially in this smoggy atmosphere.

Besides the smog, New Delhi didn't appear to be so bad. It was quite dark, but the roads were paved, and there were traffic lights, even though I realized my driver wasn't exactly paying any attention to them, or to the speed limit, if there was any. As yet, I hadn't seen a sign with a limit on it.

"That, ma'am, is India Gate. Many foreigners come here to take pictures of it." Chotu pointed towards a massive arch-like monument that had been erected in a spacious road crossing. It really did look like a gate, but it was enormous. It was lit up in the dead of night. Such a simple structure, yet so beautiful.

"What's this gate for, Chotu?" I asked, curious to know why anyone would want to build a gate as a monument.

"It is actually a war memorial for the Indians who gave their life in the First World War and in the Afghan wars. It is a good thing to remember those who have died to protect others."

"It's beautiful," I replied as it fell behind us in the distance.

A few more minutes passed, then we pulled into a different neighbourhood. Each house had a gate in front, and each was different from the next in both size and shape, but it was difficult to see them properly in the dark. The bright city lights had disappeared, and right now the only source of light was from the moon. Chotu stopped in front of a double gate and honked the horn until there was movement behind it, and eventually it swung open. Once in the courtyard, he cut the engine. Slowly climbing out of the car, I examined my surroundings. It was an open courtyard with a balcony running all the way around the second floor of the house. The ground was cement, as were the walls. There was a combination of screen doors and wooden doors on every side, leading to what I assumed were bedrooms and sitting areas. Right by the front gate, however, a strange dark shadow caught my eye. As I looked closer I realized it was…a…a cow. Why was there a *cow* in the courtyard of the house?

"Chotu! Chotu, you have returned safely?" A slightly overweight old woman of medium height was slowly making her way through one of the doors to the right. She was wrapped in a white shawl that she had also draped over her head. She had half-moon spectacles on, but her extremely fair complexion was visible underneath, even in the dark. I carefully examined her before recognizing her from the photo my mom had shown me. She was my grandmother; my Dhadhi. She moved slowly, with a slight limp, but she kept her gaze steady as she smiled and made her way towards me.

"Ah, my child! My Dilawar's daughter! Let me look at you!" She rested her hand on my cheek and analyzed me from top to bottom, after which she settled her gaze once again upon my face. Her smile grew wider and wider with each passing moment, but after the long look, tears slowly began to roll down her face. "You remind me just of your father. He was very handsome when he was your age. You have his face." She threw her arms around me and wept softly.

I didn't quite know what to say in return. My father's urn was still in my hand. I tried to balance it with my left hand while I wrapped my right arm around her.

"Dhadhi, I'm very happy to finally meet you. Dad always talked a lot about you. The family misses you very much." I repeated what my mother had told me to say and hoped that it would offer her some comfort.

I had never known the love of a grandmother. My mom's parents had both passed away when I was just a baby. I used to ask my father why his parents didn't live in Canada with the rest of us, and of course he had always just shrugged it off.

"Oh, is this him? Is this my child?" Dhadhi asked, looking at the emerald sack held in my hand.

"Yes, it's Daddy's...well, yes," I stammered, holding it up for her to see properly.

"May I?" she asked softly, her eyes firmly fixed on the object before her.

"Of course, I mean, you are his mother," I answered carefully as I moved it in her direction. I feared triggering any further emotion in her. I wasn't new to seeing Indian women grieve. The days and weeks immediately following my father's passing were still fresh in my memory. The women were uncontrollable in many respects.

She hesitated for a moment as tears continued to stream down her fair but aged face. She held up her hands and caressed it before taking it into her grasp. She then removed the green sack, kissed the top of the wooden box and held it tightly against her bosom. I stood watching her as she wept harder and cried out for her son, whom she had not seen for almost thirty years. I felt a cold chill go down my neck as I watched the immensely emotional and tragic interaction of a mother searching for the warmth of her son in a wooden box of ashes. As disconcerting as the image was for me, I couldn't help but feel sad for her. My face began to feel hot, and my vision blurred, enough for me to realize that I too had tears streaming down my face.

As I watched her cry, I felt a fire burn within me. My stomach felt like it was doing flip-flops, and my breathing became heavier. I couldn't bear seeing her in this state of despair. I wanted to hug her and tell her that everything was going to be all right. I wanted to reassure her that she was loved. All the feelings that I had for my mother were now being directed towards this old woman whom I had never known or met until this moonlit night.

Was this the love between a grandparent and a grandchild? What I had missed my entire life until now? Perhaps it was mere pity or a reflection of my own sadness at losing my father?

As I stood debating my feelings, another woman came through another one of the doors and made directly for Dhadhi, where she wrapped her arms around her and told her what I could not. "Dhadhi, calm yourself. Have faith in Waheguru. Everything will be made all right by Him."

"Yes, child, you are right," Dhadhi replied as she wiped her tears and placed the urn back into the rich emerald sack.

"You must be Esha," the woman said as she looked my way with a smile, then pulled me into a gentle embrace. She stood as tall as me and wore a traditional salwar-kameez, with a shawl draped around her. Her thick black hair was tied back into a neat bun. She too had a fair complexion that was visible under the moonlight. There was a glow in her large round eyes that hinted at a warm and kind-hearted character.

"Yeah, I'm Esha. I just got here."

"I am Jas! Well, Jasdeep, but no one calls me by my full name. I am Ekant's wife! So that makes me your sister-in-law!" she said with a wide smile, showing that she was genuinely excited at the prospect of our relationship.

"Wow, wife, eh? I didn't know Ekant was married," I blurted out, not knowing how foolish I might seem in front of her, not knowing such an important thing about my own family.

"Really? Well then, there is a lot you do not know, but it is a good thing you came. We can now become better acquainted," she replied, still smiling. "However, I am very sorry to hear about your father. Even though he was Ekant's uncle, Ekant has always viewed him as his own father." Her gaze fell to the urn. There was an awkward silence as she continued to look at it, as though she were lost in deep thought. The sudden silence made me uncomfortable.

"So, um…where is Ekant?" I asked in an effort to change the subject. I was curious to meet him and to find out why he hadn't come to collect me from the airport himself. I felt he could have *at least* made the effort.

"Oh," Jas said, "he was called away by one of his business associates. Some business matter."

"This late at night?" I asked.

"Well, time is not really an issue," she replied. "I am sure it was important, otherwise he would not have left, especially when you were due to arrive. Now, come on in. We've spent way too long standing out here. You must be tired. Allow us to get you settled in." She began to shuffle about, checking the car to make sure I hadn't left anything, then she led me to a nearby door.

Watching her closely, I could sense that she was making a concerted effort to make it appear as if there was nothing fishy about Ekant's absence. Perhaps it was just business, but at *midnight*? I had flown thousands of miles with my father's ashes. It was the first time I was to meet this mysterious son of the family, and he wasn't here. A little voice in my head kept telling me that things might not be so smooth after all, and that made me nervous.

I followed Jas and Dhadhi into what appeared to be a living room. The light was quite dim. The room was simple, yet colourful and spacious. Yellow glass adorned the windows directly opposite to where I was standing in the doorway. Sofas with green fabric and wooden frames were set up in the middle of the room, along with black chairs and a red rug beneath them. There was a wooden desk, and bookshelves were scattered along the walls. The opening behind the living room revealed a dining area, and there were doors leading outside and doors on the left and right, which I figured were for other rooms in the house. The family wasn't much for decorating, though. None of the furniture matched, really. There were just simple wooden things thrown together to fill the space.

"Esha, this is the sitting room, and the kitchen is through the door on the right, just behind the dining table," Jas said as she pointed to yet another brown wooden door on the right.

"I'll show you your room, where you can freshen up, unpack, then you can eat. You must be hungry."

"I actually had dinner right before the plane landed, so I'm okay. I'm just very tired, but thanks."

"Esha, child, you must eat something. You have travelled so far," insisted Dhadhi.

"No, Dhadhi, it's okay. I'm fine. I just need to sleep; it's been a long trip. Where is everyone else though, I mean, Ekant's mother, is…"

"She is no longer with us," Jas said quickly, cutting me off. "Um…sadly she passed away three years ago."

Ouch, way to go, Esha!

"Oh…I'm…I'm really sorry. I wasn't told," I mumbled in embarrassment.

"That's okay. Well, follow me," Jas replied as she led the way through the hallway on the left.

I followed her up a small set of cement stairs to the second floor and into a large, dark bedroom, as Dhadhi trailed behind us. There was a stale smell in the room, indicating that it wasn't used very often.

"Sorry, the electricity in the area has been acting funny all day," Jas explained as she lit a lamp on the dressing table. "This should help out for tonight. I placed new clean sheets on the bed. The nights can be chilly, so I put a blanket out as well for you just in case. As you can see, Chotu has already brought up your suitcases. This room has a washroom connected to it, and it is all yours, so please feel at home. Dhadhi Ji's room is right next to yours on the left, if you need anything, and Ekant and I are just down the hall. Are you sure you do not want anything to eat?"

"Yeah, don't worry. I'm fine," I said impatiently. All I

wanted was a shower and to get out of my sweaty clothes.

"Here, child," came Dhadhi's voice as she held up the emerald sack. She had been so quiet that I had almost forgotten she was still in the room with us, holding the urn. "This belongs to you, keep it safe."

I gently retrieved the urn from her trembling hands and placed it on the dressing table before turning to my newfound family members and bidding them good night.

"We will see you in the morning, Esha!" Jas called out as she guided the weeping Dhadhi out of the room. "Dhadhi Ji, you must control your emotions," I could hear her say as they made their way down the hallway stairs.

Alone at last!

"Ugh! I'm so tired and hot!" I complained as I threw off my pullover. "I can't believe Mom made me wear this thing in this heat."

"Don't go showing off those arms and bare skin when you arrive in Delhi," she had said as we raced towards my gate in the airport. "Make sure you cover up! It is not Canada over there!"

"I'd like to see her wearing a sweatshirt in this heat," I said as I turned my attention to the room I was going to be sleeping in for the next week.

The bed was quite large, possibly a king size. There was only one mattress on it, which was draped in a red sheet. Jas had placed a thin white blanket on top. Similar to the living room, the furniture was wooden. The left side of the room consisted of a wooden dresser and cabinet, and to the right was a painted blue door leading to the washroom. There was a framed painting on either side of the washroom door. The left one had two young boys standing in front of an incomplete wall. They were clad in orange garb and stood side by side with one arm raised. I figured it had to be some kind of revolutionary Indian thing.

The painting on the right, however, was that of a male and was much more familiar. My mother had a similar painting back home. It was of some Sikh Guru, whose name I couldn't really remember at the moment. This particular one was clad in a yellow and blue robe with a gold turban. A red feather ran along the top of the turban, while a smaller peacock feather stuck out in front. His right hand held up a sword with a golden handle, while the left arm held onto the reins of a white horse. These too were painted in gold. It wasn't your typical saintly photo. This Sikh Guru, with the extravagant attire and largely defined eyes, looked like a determined prince riding out to battle.

My attention was suddenly diverted by movement in my belly. I hadn't gone to the washroom since my connection in London. I quickly stepped into the washroom and hit the light.

"What the…where is the…" Words escaped me as I turned my head in every direction, seeking a toilet. I scratched my head in confusion. There was no toilet! There was a shower head on the left and a small white sink on the wall in the middle, but no toilet.

"Great! Where am I supposed to go now?" I cried out as I held onto my stomach, which was now becoming more and more impatient. Just as I turned to leave, I noticed a glimmer in the right corner. It was a chain. My eyes trailed the length of the chain, and I realized it was attached to a small, thin pipe that ran along the ceiling and down the back wall. As I looked down, I noticed a hole. There were tiles in place, outlining the oval shape; a shape that looked very much like…like the seat of a toilet.

"Ugh! This can't be it. *This* cannot be the toilet!" I said, looking around the washroom again, hoping that a regular, civilized toilet would just magically materialize and save me. No such luck.

"Okay, Esha pull yourself together," I said as I tried to calm myself, "and face the fact that you have to go, even if it's… it's…on…or…in…this *thing*. But first, I have to be sure."

I grabbed a hold of the chain, took a deep breath and gave it a yank. There was a gurgling sound, followed by the sound of water. I looked down at the hole and saw that a small wave of water had splashed into it, and hopefully retreated as well.

"I guess I have no choice," I concluded as the moans from my stomach grew louder by the minute. I had to go badly. With a sigh, I closed the washroom door behind me and locked it. The last thing I wanted was to be caught with my pants down squatting over a hole on my first night in India. First I bent down and took a long careful look at the hole, just to make sure that nothing was lurking inside it. I shuddered at the thought of a snake slithering up. I shook my head and tried to breathe. Finally, confident that the coast was clear, I stood up and planted my feet on either side of the hole. I pulled down my pants and squatted.

"Oh, no!" I cried out, standing up before anything started. "Toilet paper!" I looked around once again and found nothing. So I ran back into the bedroom and threw open my suitcase. There lay a half-dozen rolls of toilet paper. Thinking back, I felt stupid that I had made fun of my mother when she was loading these rolls into my suitcase. She had insisted that I would have use for them, and I'd thought she was just wasting precious luggage space. Why wouldn't they have toilet paper?

"Thanks, Mom!" I said as I ran back into the washroom. I

locked the door once again and took my position above the hole. I have to admit, it wasn't as uncomfortable as it had appeared it would be, but it took a lot of concentration and aim. After a few minutes, I stood up and retreated. I yanked the chain, eagerly waiting for the water to splash away the remains, but nothing happened. I yanked the chain even harder, but again nothing happened.

"This is just freakin' great! Now what?" I was beginning to panic. "Please, please, please, oh wonderful Mr. Chain, just flush!" I begged. I held onto the chain once again and pulled it down hard, only this time I held it down for a while longer. After what seemed like an eternity, the gurgling sound appeared, and water began to splash into the hole. "Yes! Thank you, thank you, thank you!" I cried as I made my way to the sink to wash my hands then ran out of the washroom, closing the door behind me.

I looked at my watch; a half hour had passed. With slightly sore legs and a nauseous feeling, but with relief that it was behind me, I fell onto the bed and closed my eyes. I was exhausted.

SIX

The breeze was warm and inviting. The light from the red sun was slowly fading away, casting a shadow on the mountains and hilltops. The grass was soft, just like Johnny's hands, which now rested upon my own. As I laid my head against his lean shoulders and watched the sun dip lower and lower, I noticed how gentle the atmosphere was.

"What a beautiful day, isn't it, Johnny?" I whispered.

"Just like you, Esha," he replied.

"Oh, Johnny," I sighed.

"Who's Johnny?" a high-pitched voice bellowed in my ears.

"Esha, did you hear that?" Johnny asked as he turned his head in every direction.

"Ignore it, babe," I answered as I held on tightly to his arm, refusing to lift my head off his strong, welcoming shoulder.

"Okay, let's just enjoy this beautiful day."

"Yes," I agreed, "let's enjoy this day. I'm happy wherever you are, babe."

"Babe? Who is babe?" the mysterious voice appeared again.

"Stop it! Who is that?" I questioned as I lifted my head. When I looked again, Johnny was gone. "Johnny? Johnny? Where'd you go? Johnny!"

"Esha Puah!" screamed the mysterious voice just as I felt a sharp pain pierce my arm.

"OUCH!" I yelled as I sat up, grabbing my stinging arm. I rubbed my eyes and realized I was still in bed. I dropped my shoulders as reality settled in. I was in India, *not* in B.C. with Johnny. It was just a dream. I looked down at my arm and saw a bright red mark. Someone had pinched me.

"Sorry, Esha Puah, but you were talking funny."

"Puah?" I repeated quickly. Curious to know who would address me as their aunt, I looked in the direction of the voice.

Standing before me was a skinny little boy. He had on blue trousers with a matching blue shirt and black sandals that were a bit tattered at the edges. He could not have been more than six or seven years old, yet the manner in which he stood, with his back straight, smiling widely with hands firmly on his hips, gave him an air of maturity. Also, his pointy blue turban added a few extra inches to his height.

"Esha Puah!" the boy said, breaking my concentration.

"Huh…what?" I struggled.

"Why are you so quiet? And who is Johnny and Babe?" the wide-eyed boy asked.

"What? Johnny? Here? Wait, wait, forget that. First, who are you? And why are you in my bedroom?" I was slightly embarrassed that I had been talking about Johnny in my sleep.

"*Me*? Ha! I am Bhagat, your nephew!" he exclaimed as he jumped onto the bed and threw his arms around me.

"What is it with your family and hugs?" I complained under my breath.

"What, Esha Puah?" the boy asked.

"Uh, nothing. So we're, uh, family? That's cool," I muttered as I pulled him away and sat him up on the bed. "So wait a minute, who taught you English?"

"Everyone in school knows English." He giggled as if I had

54

said something silly. "I'm so happy I have a puah! I could not sleep last night, but you came so late!" the boy shouted.

"Yeah, about that, why do you keep calling me puah?"

"My daddy is your brother," the boy replied with an even larger smile.

"You're Ekant's son?"

"Yes! My name is Bhagat Singh, like the proud warrior! I'm going to be like him when I grow up!"

"That's interesting," I said, pretending I knew who or what he was talking about. "Okay, Bhagat, how about you go downstairs while I wash up, and I'll see you a bit later?"

"Okay, Esha Puah. I'll tell Mummy you are awake." He jumped off the bed and bolted out the door.

I got out of bed and walked over to the mirror to brush my hair. *Ekant has a son.* The thought kept running through my mind. I was feeling more and more out of place in this house now. I couldn't believe that this whole family had existed all these years, and I didn't even *know* them. Bhagat was my nephew, Jas was my sister-in-law, and I hadn't even met Ekant, a man who saw my father as his own. And what about Dhadhi, my grandmother? She was my father's mother, and I was seeing her for the first time. It made me uncomfortable to think about how I might appear to them. They seemed to be quite excited thus far, but the question was, how did they really feel?

I just hope we can do this final rite thing quickly so that I can go home, I thought as I made for the washroom.

Getting dressed took longer than I had anticipated. I struggled to find a suitable outfit. I had packed a couple of tank tops, figuring it would be hot, but my mother was adamant that I stick to something more conservative and not "show my skin," as she phrased it. However, the heat proved to be unbearable. I finally settled on a white t-shirt and a pair of blue jeans that had torn patches at the knees. I also settled for flip-flops instead of runners, as the idea of wearing socks made me feel even hotter. Studying my hair, I concluded that it was an absolute frizz-ball, which had to be tied back. I wondered if they had any suitable salons in the area.

Jas already had breakfast waiting for me by the time I made it downstairs. Sunlight poured in from the many windows, but no breeze accompanied it. Instead, fans were placed in each room to combat the humidity. Bhagat could be seen through the screen door playing in the courtyard with two other little boys.

"Dear, what happened to your pants? Come here, quickly, I will fix it!" Dhadhi exclaimed as she entered the room.

"What? Where?" I asked, examining my pants from every angle possible.

"Your jean is ripped!" she cried out. She had made her way to the sofa and was patting the cushion next to her, motioning for me to join her. "Come here, let me fix it. I will sew it up."

"Sew it? What…oh!" I finally realized that she was referring to the tears at the knees. "Dhadhi, they're supposed to be like this. Don't worry, they're fine."

"Fine? What fine? Come here. Your knees are showing," she persisted.

"No, Dhadhi, I did this myself!" I said in a raised voice, since she clearly wasn't getting the point. "I did this, they're fine. It's the style of the jeans."

"Style? And you did this? Crazy children these days. You are ruining your pants. When you decide to fix it, come find me. I am going out to the courtyard to rest," she answered as she made her way outside.

"Okay, see you later," I said, relieved that she was leaving. I didn't exactly enjoy having to justify my choice in style to an old Indian woman who'd probably never worn a pair of jeans her whole life.

"Esha, come eat," Jas said, appearing from the kitchen. I nodded and joined her at the table as a slim, boyish looking servant placed two platefuls of *parotas*, yogurt and two cups of tea before us. In daylight, I was now able to see her clearly. Again she had on a plain green salwar-kameez, her hair tied back in a bun and no trace of make-up on her face. She was adorned with only a pair of gold hoop earrings.

Jas's simplicity, however, did not take away from her beauty. She had a creamy complexion, large, round and surprisingly green eyes and a perfect smile. Ekant had definitely chosen well. Speaking of which, where was Ekant? Noon was approaching, and still I had not seen any hint of him around the house.

"Esha, you haven't touched your food. Is everything okay?" Jas asked, interrupting my train of thought.

"Huh, oh, yeah, everything is fine. I was just wondering if Ekant will be joining us."

"Oh! He...he was here this morning. He already left," Jas answered in a slightly shaky voice. "Another meeting. Work can get busy sometimes, you know," she continued with a weak laugh. "He is anxious to see you. Tonight for sure, uh, but first eat, then you should also call home to Canada and notify your mother of your arrival."

I nodded and smiled, turning my attention to the plateful of food before me. I hadn't called Mom yet. She would be worried, as usual. Right now, what concerned me more was the eerie feeling I was getting regarding Ekant. I'd met the other members of this family, but the main person was still missing in action. Perhaps he really was busy, but still something just didn't feel right.

After breakfast, Jas was kind enough to give me some time alone in the living room so I could use the only phone in the house. It was refreshing to hear Mom's voice on the other end of the line.

"Esha dear, how are you? How was the flight? Did you sleep, did you eat? Are you sick?" She was shooting off one question after another, and I'd barely had a chance to respond to one yet.

"Mom, Mom…Mom! Calm down, let me speak!" I pleaded.

"Sorry dear, I am just so happy to hear your voice. It feels like it has been so long. You cannot blame a mother, can you?"

"Of course not, mother dearest. Now, to answer your questions, yes, I am fine, the flight was okay. It was just very tiring and looong. But I'm okay, you don't have to worry, it's not that bad."

"And how is your Dhadhi ji?" she asked in a slightly lower tone.

"Oh, she's good. She was quite sad last night when she saw Dad's…well, you know, but she's okay."

"And how…how is everyone else?" I could tell by her tone that it was getting uncomfortable for her to talk about the other family.

"Okay. Ekant has a wife and a son, and they're both cool. I actually haven't seen Ekant yet. Apparently he's been busy with work. I guess I'll see him tonight."

"A wife and son? That's wonderful," she replied, her tone lightening again.

"Yeah, but Mom, there's something you should know. Ekant's mother…well, she's not here. I mean, she's already

58

passed away," I said. I didn't know how else to tell her. It was best that I just come out with it now. Perhaps it would make her feel more at ease that she wouldn't ever have to face that woman again.

"Oh no! That's terrible, Esha, when did that happen?" she asked, sounding genuinely hurt.

"Actually, Mom, it's been a couple of years. I ended up asking Ekant's wife, Jas, where his mother was. It was so damn embarrassing! I'm surprised you didn't know," I answered.

"Esha, you know there was very little communication all these years between us. I don't know, perhaps your father knew."

"Well, it doesn't really make a difference now. I already made a total fool out of myself. Anyway, do me a favour and let Mandy and the rest know that I've arrived," I said, changing the subject.

"Yes, I will. Those girls are driving me crazy asking about you. By the way, your sister is doing great, in case you are wondering!"

"Of course she is, Mom, she's always all right. I'm the one roasting here in this heat," I muttered.

"I am going to pretend I did not hear that. So, tell me now, have you all discussed when you will be leaving for Kiratpur?"

"No, nothing yet. I got in pretty late last night, knocked out, and now I've just had breakfast. Plus, Ekant hasn't shown up yet, remember. I have to wait for him to make the arrangements, right?"

"Yes, but be polite, Esha. Try not to be bossy and so headstrong," she warned.

"Mom! I'm not stupid! I think I can handle some Indians. I was raised by you, wasn't I?" I countered.

"You know how you can get sometimes. I'm just telling you that they are family, but you are in India, and you are a girl. You cannot go bossing people around. There is a way to do things over there. Just take care and speak to Ekant. I'm sure he will make the proper arrangements soon. Stay close to Dhadhi ji and don't wander off. I miss you very much, my child."

"Miss you too, Mom. Anyways, I should go now. Take care and talk to you soon. Bye," I said before hanging up. *Try not to be bossy? Oh, please!* Above all else, my mother always made it a point to criticize me. "Don't be like this and don't be like that." It was annoying. I wasn't a child any more, yet she never stopped.

The day continued with little excitement. Dhadhi wouldn't let me leave the premises, because she said it was "dangerous for a girl like me to walk around alone in the streets." So I just wandered about inside the house.

I discovered a stairway leading to the open rooftop, which provided an extraordinary view of the surrounding city. The houses were extremely close to one another in both proximity and height, so I could see far into the distance on every side. On the rooftop were chairs and hammocks and tables. I brought up some of my magazines and settled into a chair by the doorway.

Every now and then, neighbours would come and stand and stare at me from their own balconies. It was odd that they found me so interesting. I mean, Delhi was the capital of the country. Many foreigners must come through these streets, but these people behaved as if they were seeing a foreigner for the first time. I felt like I was on display, and I soon realized that I could do nothing about it except ignore them until they disappeared.

Slowly but surely, the day passed by, and the sun began to set. Evening prayers from the nearby Gurdwara could be heard through loudspeakers. The day was coming to an end, and Ekant still had not shown up. As nightfall approached, I ventured downstairs to escape the mosquitoes and lizards that were starting to appear. Jas and Dhadhi were in the living room, and Bhagat sat at a desk doing his school work.

"Esha! Come sit with us," Jas said, smiling up at me as she patted the seat next to her.

"Thanks," I said, walking over.

"How was your reading?" she asked.

"It was fine. The rooftop is quite comfortable, and the heat wasn't so deadly today," I answered, stealing glances around the room as I looked for evidence of Ekant's return. This was getting to be too much. I had planned on travelling to Kiratpur within a day or two of my arrival so that I could return quickly, but the man that was supposed to help me wasn't showing up! "Dhadhi," I said, looking in her direction.

"Yes, child."

"I need to travel to Kiratpur soon. Do you think we can start making the travel plans?" I said plainly. I figured Dad's mother would be concerned about his last rites.

"Oh yes, you do need to travel there soon," she agreed, "but…you will need Ekant's assistance. I am sure he will have some time tomorrow to discuss the plans with you."

Sure he will.

"Are you sure he'll…" I trailed off as a loud bang came from the front gate. Someone was here. Perhaps Ekant had finally decided to come home.

I stood up and walked over to the screen door. I peered through the dark, trying to see who had arrived as Chotu opened the gate to let the visitors through. In walked two women, both draped in shawls and wearing of course the traditional salwar-kameez. What was it with these women and their shawls in the deadly summer heat? The woman in front was heavy and swayed from side to side as she walked. Behind her was a much thinner and younger girl.

"Chotu! Who is at the door?" Dhadhi called out.

"It is Rano ji and her daughter," Chotu replied.

"Ah, Rano! Come to the living room, dear. We are here."

I stepped away from the screen door as the two females approached. The mother slowed as she reached me and pulled down her glasses to the tip of her nose, scanning me from head to toe. I matched her stare at every point until she pushed up her glasses and marched on towards Dhadhi and Jas. I watched her quietly, noticing her repeated glances in my direction.

While the mother had already been annoying, the daughter was quite different. After saying hello to both Dhadhi and Jas, she had quietly taken a seat in a chair at the far corner of the room. She was keeping herself busy with a book that she had picked up from a nearby shelf. Was she shy? Had she not noticed me? Perhaps she did not care to notice.

"Rano, this is my granddaughter, Esha. My Dilawar's youngest," Dhadhi said proudly in Punjabi. "She has come from Canada."

"Really, all the way from Canada, hmm? It is nice to finally see someone from your son's family. How long will she be staying?" Her tone was careful and inquisitive. I already didn't like her.

"She is to travel to Kiratpur. After that we will see. So how is everyone at home?" Dhadhi asked.

"Oh, it is wonderful!" Rano exclaimed. "My daughter has received a magnificent proposal for marriage. Sardar Dalip Singh has asked for her hand for his son, Daya."

"Really, our young Daya?" Dhadhi said without much surprise. She flashed the daughter a look that suggested she had already been expecting this proposal. Ignoring Dhadhi's response, Rano carried on.

"Oh, Dhadhi, Daya is such a striking young man now. My daughter will go into such a rich and respected family. My heart is filled with joy!"

As the mother continued in her praise, the daughter carried on reading. She paid no attention to the ongoing discussion regarding her marriage. Meanwhile, Rano once again shifted her focus to me. She pulled her glasses down again to the tip of her nose and stared at me.

"And…what of your granddaughter, Dhadhi?"

"Esha?" Dhadhi looked at me. "Oh, she is young. I am sure her time will come when it is right."

"I see," replied Rano. "Well, she still has time then to fix herself up."

Fix myself up?

"Excuse me?" I asked, deciding that it was time I spoke up.

"Oh child, you know you are so thin. Do girls in Canada eat anything? And look at your hair! If you are to be a beautiful Indian bride, you must grow that hair. Now, just look—"

"Oh, we cannot criticize children who have been raised in different countries," Jas interrupted. "Besides, I am sure that Esha and her family can decide what is right for her. You need not worry."

Just as I was about to add my two cents, Jas gave me a stern nod, suggesting I should let the moment pass. I clenched my teeth and suppressed the harsh words that were sitting impatiently at the tip of my tongue.

"Of course," Rano sighed. "Well, we should get going. It is

late. I just wanted to inform you of our wonderful news."

"Oh, Rano, you have not had anything to eat or drink yet. How can you go like this," Dhadhi said without much force.

"No, no, Dhadhi, next time. Come, Sumedha dear. Say bye to Dhadhi and Jas."

The mother left without another look at me, and I didn't mind at all. The daughter, surprisingly, stopped at the screen door and nervously turned in my direction. She had a tanned brown complexion, but her most extraordinary feature was her clearly defined unibrow.

"I am sorry about your father," she said in perfect English. Her voice was so soft that I almost had to strain my ears just to hear her. "Jas told me about his passing."

"Yeah, I'm sorry too," I replied.

"My—"

"Sumi! Where have you gotten stuck? Come on!" Rano barked in the distance. The daughter gave a nervous smile and hurried out the door to catch up with her mother. I was surprised at how different the two were. One was obnoxious and rude while the other was timid and sweet.

"Esha," called Dhadhi, making her way towards the staircase. "Do not listen to that Rano. She talks more than she thinks."

"Yeah, I can tell," I replied, following her upstairs.

"Good. But her daughter is a very sweet child. She is your age. Her name is Sumedha, but we lovingly call her Sumi. While you are here, you should spend some time with her, to be around kids your age. If you are with Sumi, then I will not worry about you. Okay?"

"Sure," I said, though I had no real intention of hanging around very long in the city.

"Good. Now, get some rest. See you in the morning," she

said as she turned into her bedroom.

"Goodnight, Dhadhi," I replied as I made my way into my own room. I went straight for the bed and fell back onto it. A whole boring day had passed, and I still had not seen Ekant.

"Oh, I miss you, Canada, my girls, B.C., fast food, pizza, my bed…Johnny…" As I counted away my sorrows, my eyes became heavy, and I slowly dozed off.

*   *   *

The next morning, when I opened my eyes, I found a hot cup of tea next to the bed. I picked it up, wondering why anyone would serve me in bed while I slept.

"Ma'am, have you finished tea?" asked a small, quivering voice. "Um, would you like more?"

I followed the voice to the foot of my bed. There stood a short, dark-skinned, skinny little girl. Her gaze was lowered and fully concentrated on the floor, as though staring at her feet was the most important thing in the world. Her hands were behind her back, and she didn't make a move until I responded.

"Excuse me?" is all I could come up with.

"More tea, ma'am?" she asked again without moving her gaze away from her feet. She looked absolutely terrified of me. I didn't get it. I mean, I was pretty fit as an athlete, and I was known to get into a few rough situations on the field, but off the field no one had ever reacted to me in fear.

"Oh! No, no, thank you. I'm, uh, going to get up actually and shower and stuff," I said, quickly sipping the warm tea and placing the cup back where I had found it.

"Okay, I will leave you alone then and make sure that food is ready for you," she said quickly, turning to leave.

"Hey, wait!" I called out.

"Yes?"

"Who are you?" I asked. "I mean why are you serving me tea in my room? Why don't you look at me?"

"My name is Sheila," she replied, still refusing to look at me. "I work in this house. Dhadhi ji has ordered that I look after your needs in this house. I...I am sorry, ma'am, if I have upset you."

"No, no, don't worry about it. So why haven't I seen you before now?" I asked.

"I had gone home to Calcutta to see my family. I just came back this morning, ma'am."

"I see... Now, tell me, why aren't you looking at me directly?" I lightened my tone and tried to sound a bit more welcoming. Her fear was discomforting.

"Ma'am...I—"

"Oh, come on, raise your gaze...that's it...higher...don't worry, there's nothing exciting going on with your feet or this floor, for that matter. Now, looking at me, there's excitement!" I said, smiling.

"I am sorry, ma'am. For the first time I will be working for a NRI. You are from Canada, yes? I was not sure if you would appreciate me looking at you—"

"Sorry, NRI?" I asked, cutting her off.

"Oh yes, Non-Resident Indian, NRI," she replied.

"Let's get one thing straight, Sheila. I'm not Indian. My nationality is Canadian, okay?"

"Sorry, ma'am, I just—"

"And look me in the eyes when you speak to me. Don't be so scared. It's weird."

"Yes."

"All right, I should, uh, get dressed. You can relax. I don't really need anything, but thanks for the tea?"

"Yes, ma'am."

I headed for the shower as Sheila collected my teacup and quietly made her way to the hallway. A servant? Hmmm…I could get used to that.

When I walked into the dining room, a plateful of food was of course waiting for me. Sheila was very efficient. Jas walked in and out of the kitchen, as usual, preparing meals for the day, while Bhagat and his school friends met up in the courtyard. Dhadhi was doing her prayers in the living room, but today there was an addition. Beside Dhadhi sat a tall individual in brown sandals and white pants and shirt. The morning paper was obscuring the top half of the person. However, the large muscular arms and legs hinted that whoever was behind that paper was definitely a man. Suddenly I felt like Sheila, but why should I? My heart started racing. Could it be Ekant?

Uncertain if I should approach Dhadhi and the stranger or sit quietly and wait until I was noticed, I stood in the same position and tried to get a glimpse of the man. Probably it *was* Ekant. It would be about time that he showed up.

"Esha?" Jas was standing over the table, holding a plate of food. "What are you doing standing there? Come join me."

I quickly turned on my heels and followed suit. As I walked towards the table, I could hear the rustle of the newspaper behind me, yet no voice followed.

"Did you have a good sleep?" Jas asked.

"Yeah, it was fine," I replied.

Throughout our meal, I glanced back and forth between Jas and the stranger, yet she made no attempt to introduce me to him. Dhadhi continued her prayers, and the strange man continued reading his paper. It was only after Dhadhi put down her prayer book that she called out and broke the silence.

"Esha! Esha child, come here quick!" I walked over and stood behind the sofa that she was seated on. "Ekant," she began, "put that paper down and meet your sister."

It *was* Ekant. He slowly lowered his newspaper and revealed his face to me. I was shocked to see how closely he resembled my father. He was a big, muscular man. He had a black beard that reached down to his chest, and he too wore a turban. His long and narrow nose, large round eyes and thin lips all contained traces of my father. The resemblance was uncanny.

"Esha, this is Ekant. I am so happy that you two are finally meeting!" Dhadhi continued, with a smile stretching from ear to ear.

"Hi," I said, offering my hand.

He studied me for a while, then instead of shaking my hand, he folded his hands before him. "In India, we greet people with respect and in our traditional way of putting our hands together. I guess they do not teach you this in Canada?" His voice was deep as I had imagined it to be, but I sensed the disapproval in his tone, and that didn't sound the least bit comforting.

"Last time I checked, a handshake was considered quite respectful," I retorted as I withdrew my hand.

"Hmm…" is all Ekant mustered before he opened up his paper once again and became lost in the day's news, as though the little exchange between us had never happened.

Was this it? This was how we were going to meet for the first time ever? Was this all he had to say to me? Weeks of wondering what this moment would be like, what we would say to each other, and this was it. We had a brief and rude exchange on the correct method for greeting someone, then silence. He had made no mention of my father; no show of emotion or grief over his passing. Then again, why would he? Dad was his uncle in reality, and Ekant was a son born out of the crime of rape. But hadn't Jas mentioned that Ekant viewed my dad as his very own father? So really, what was with the attitude? In any case, it didn't matter. I was here for a reason, and I had to accomplish my task regardless of what he might think.

"So, when can we set out for Kiratpur?" I asked, pretending that his rude behaviour had gone unnoticed.

"Kiratpur?" he asked, almost sounding surprised.

"Uh, yeah, Kiratpur. You know, for Dad's ashes," I replied.

"Impossible."

"What is?" I asked, confused by his curt response.

"Travel to Kiratpur is impossible at the moment."

"What? How come?"

"Kiratpur is hours away. There is no safe passage right now. Travel is not an option."

"So what if it's hours away? We jump in a car and drive there. Simple. I don't see the big problem," I said, growing impatient with this sudden refusal. No one else had mentioned anything regarding unsafe passage to Kiratpur in the last couple of days. It was hard to believe that Ekant knew more than anyone else did.

"It has only been a few weeks since Operation Bluestar. Travelling to Kiratpur right now is not safe. The social and political climate is too fragile. It's just not safe to travel, so I'm sorry if you—"

"Wait, what is Operation Bluestar?" I asked innocently.

Ekant abruptly put down his paper. "What is Operation Bluestar?" he asked, mocking my voice. He stood up and looked at me with what appeared to be pure disgust. What had I said?

"*What* is Operation Bluestar?" he repeated. "Dhadhi! Are you sure she is Dilawar uncle's daughter? Are you sure Chotu didn't make a mistake? Is she even Sikh?" he questioned, glaring at Dhadhi then again at me.

I just stood and watched in confusion as his anger grew with each passing moment. His sudden reaction was alarming and didn't make any sense.

"What's the problem?" I asked, getting defensive. "So I don't know what it is. Why are you getting so angry? I don't understand what this Operation Bl…uh…Blue…shit…Blue—"

"Bluestar! BLUESTAR!" he roared. "Every Sikh knows what Operation Bluestar is. It is a mark on our heritage, on our very foundation! How dare you be so ignorant?"

"Chill out! So this is some religious nonsense? Now what does that have to do with *me* going to Kiratpur, then getting back to Canada?" I asked, still not sure what his exact reservation was.

Instead of enlightening me, however, Ekant crumpled up his morning paper and tossed it onto the table. It was unbelievable. He was actually fuming. If I looked closer, I thought I might see steam escaping from his ears. But I didn't really care. I just wanted to get to Kiratpur, so I just stared blankly at him. He turned around and stormed out the screen door, mumbling something under his breath. I watched in surprise as he paced back and forth outside in the courtyard, spitting out words. To an outsider, he would have looked like a psych ward patient. Jas simply shook her head and sat down beside me. I looked at Dhadhi, hoping for an explanation.

"This is a very sensitive subject for Ekant," she said. "It is for all of us."

"For the family?" I asked.

"No child. It is for all Sikhs," she answered.

"What is Operation Bluestar, Dhadhi?"

"On June fourth, just a few weeks ago, the Indian Army attacked our Harmandir Sahib, or as many call it, the Golden Temple, in Amritsar. Thousands of pilgrims were there, and most were killed. The holiest shrine for Sikhs has been nearly destroyed. People say the complex still stands, but it is no longer what it was. Gunfire, tanks, cannons, all have ripped it apart. Our most respected and comprehensive library containing many original scripts from our Gurus has burned down. What is worse, the oppression continues. The army still maintains its control over it."

"There must be a reason for all of this?"

"The government and army argue that they had no choice. They say they needed to bring out 'terrorists' who had taken refuge in the Complex. The problem is the army wasn't clear on who it considered a terrorist. Some call the men under Sant Jarnail Singh Bhindrawale, who was a spiritual leader for many Sikhs, terrorists, but they never harmed anyone. Under him, many Sikh people became baptized. He brought back people's devotion to the religion in a healthy manner. In the end, politics is politics," she said with a loud sigh. "All this talk about terrorists and separation it is to make Sikhs seem like the aggressors. They are making it appear like something that it is not. Punjab needs better representation and an equal share of the resources *it* provides to the rest of the nation. Along the way, it turned into a discussion about a new Punjabi homeland. Sikhs led the fight, and somehow it all turned upside down. Regardless of how it happened, I am sure that there was a choice."

"How can you be sure?" I persisted. I was baffled at how a simple question had turned into a political discussion.

"Sikhs are warriors, Esha. We have fought many wars during the time of our Gurus, and we make strong, principled soldiers. But we fight for justice. It is a cardinal rule for our religion. So it is understandable why the so-called militants devoted to Sant Bhindrawale persisted for their cause. Now, not every Sikh agrees with that. What matters most is the principle that builds the foundation of a Sikh's fight or cry for battle, and that is justice. So I strongly believe that no Sikh would willingly sacrifice a holy shrine like the Harmandir Sahib without leaving a choice. That Sikh, like every Sikh, has to answer to God one day or another."

"But maybe there really wasn't a choice."

"There is always a choice," Dhadhi said, quickly cutting me off. "Can you imagine anyone carelessly attacking the Muslim holy shrine in Mecca or the Roman Catholics' Vatican in this day and age? This was not just a golden complex. It was the heart of millions of people; it was the soul of a great doctrine. It survived British rule and Partition. When there are political disagreements, you do not attack the ancient foundation of a world religion. You do not burn scriptures that have a place in civilization. You do not mercilessly kill thousands of innocent pilgrims. It is a sin; a sin that was committed for what? Land, resources, pride?" Dhadhi dropped her shoulders and clutched the prayer book in her hands. "When will man give more importance to the soul of a human being?"

"But Dhadhi, to allow a completely new territory, a Punjabi homeland, I mean that would have shaken up the country, no?" I pointed out.

"Would it really? A separate Punjab was already promised during the time of Partition. India just has not delivered on that promise. But of course they do not want to give up that land now. Besides, separation is not what Punjabis or Sikhs were calling for. Later, it turned into a separatist discussion, because the central government had already painted Sikhs as separatists. The demands were for greater equality, to address diplomatically the issues that concerned the land. For example, Sikhs are not even legally recognized. We are still categorized as Hindus. Reforms were needed, but through discussion and appeals, as was the initial course of action. However, the government did not allow it."

"Why not?"

"Because Punjab feeds this country, that's why!" yelled Ekant. He had ventured back into the room and was standing over the table with his arms firmly crossed over his chest. "Punjab is rich in resources," he continued. "The vast and bountiful farmlands, the five rivers that run through it, the clean air, the beautiful climate. The rest of India is heavily polluted or barren compared to Punjab. There is no way the central government will give up its control. Instead, they want to keep a tight leash over it, subjecting Punjabis and farmers to an unequal status. But all of this could have been debated. It was not a reason to attack Amritsar. Debate, discussion and choice are supposed to be the core of any democratic nation."

"So why attack Sikhs by destroying their holiest shrine?" I asked. I wanted to know more. Ekant's erratic behaviour suddenly made me very interested in the topic.

"Because they want to completely destroy the morale and the soul of Sikhs. Under Sant Bhindrawale, Sikhs were becoming unified. Since the day of the attack, reports have been coming in of forced disappearances. Sikhs are being randomly picked up, jailed and beaten. Innocents are being branded as 'terrorists', regardless if they are ten years old or fifty.

The social and political climate is too unpredictable. If we set out on a long journey to Kiratpur, there is no telling what could happen. We are safe in Delhi, as long as we stick to our business. So, until I decide otherwise, you will remain in this house and only travel about in the city during daylight hours."

"But how long—"

"Until I say so!" Ekant shouted.

"You really love to shout, don't you?" I snapped, but Ekant didn't reply. He turned around and left the room. I looked to Dhadhi for support, but she just patted me on the shoulder.

"I agree with Ekant, dear. It is not safe," she said and walked off.

I turned to Jas, hoping she could see reason, but she only shrugged and disappeared into the kitchen. Now, *this* I wasn't expecting. I quickly ran to the phone and dialled home. For sure my mother would find a way out for me.

"Mom, you have to help me!" I cried into the phone as she picked up.

"Esha? Are you okay, child? What's wrong?"

"I'M STUCK!" I yelled into the phone.

"Esha, calm down. Tell me, what has happened?"

"Ekant says it's too dangerous to travel. Some attack on the Golden Temple. Why didn't you think of that, Mom, before sending me here?"

"Oh child, I was so caught up in the grief of your father that I was not watching the news when it happened, but these past few days, I have been seeing the sadness and frustrations in the community here. It is a terrible, terrible thing that has—"

"I know, I get it, Mom. I wasn't asking for a lecture on politics, I'm getting enough of that here!" I said, cutting her off. "But what do I do now? I can't just stay here. Who knows how long it'll take, and Ekant didn't seem like he's in any hurry."

"Oh! You met him! How is he?"

"Very rude," I replied.

"Rude? Oh come on, Esha, do not be so negative all the time."

"I'm not being negative, Mom; he *is* rude!"

"What does he look like?"

"Actually, a lot like Dad," I muttered. I was quickly beginning to despise the fact that he resembled my father so much.

"Really? Oh, well then, you two must really look like brother and sister, right?"

"Unfortunately, but who really cares. Stop changing the subject and let's solve my problem! I think I should come back home. I can come back to India and go to Kiratpur some other time. I mean nothing is happening to Dad's ashes in that box."

"No, Esha! You cannot leave your journey incomplete! You made a promise. Besides, it will be a very bad omen if you leave. One cannot desert their journey to perform the last rites once they have already set out on it. You have to complete it, only then can you return."

"But Mom, what am I going to do here? I've really had it with all of your bad omen talks. Everything is a bad omen for you!" I snapped. Her reaction was more frustrating than Ekant's!

"We are talking about your father's soul, Esha! This is not a trip to the mall or one of your parties that you can just leave when you have had enough. Why must you always leave when things get tough?"

"What do you mean? When do I do that?" I demanded. I hadn't been expecting her to attack me in return. She was supposed to be on *my* side.

"Every time—at home, in the hospital and even now, you

want to give up. I understand you do not like it, but damn it, child, you made a promise, and those ashes belong not only to your father but to my husband. You will not leave India until you have put his soul to rest. Do you understand?"

As much as I hated to admit it, she did have a point. I had made a promise, and it *was* for my father. "Okay...fine... fine! I won't return until I take Dad's ashes to Kiratpur. That doesn't mean that I'm just going to wait around here forever for Ekant to finally decide he's not a coward."

"Just do not cause any trouble, please?" she pleaded.

"Yeah, whatever,"

"Esha, take care of yourself. I love you."

"Bye, Mom," I said, hanging up. So much for helping me. Now, I really *was* stuck.

SEVEN

August 1984

The next few weeks were insufferable. I spent the better part of each day just sleeping. The rest of the day was spent reading. At first I went through all three books that I had brought along and read them repeatedly until each chapter and paragraph was embedded in my memory, and I could bear them no longer. Thankfully, before I could tear my hair out or claw at the walls, Jas located a bookstore that carried titles by American authors. The selection was quite decent, and I was able to find enough books to occupy my time. So while I waited for Ekant to give the green light for travel, I dove into the suspense, drama and romance of American culture.

Eventually I expanded my list of activities when I found one of Bhagat's neglected soccer balls. When I wasn't reading or sleeping, I focused on my training, using the courtyard as my makeshift field. It was a relief to find something to do during the long, sweltering summer days. I quickly found that I couldn't visit the rooftop balcony during daylight hours without attracting the curious stares of the strangers who surrounded me. The neighbourhood was disgustingly cluttered and busy. From one roof, you had a front row view of the entire neighbourhood. They could spy on me, just as easily as I could spy on them. It was infuriating at first, but in due course, they grew bored of me. Still, I did my very best to avoid people.

Sumi had become a regular visitor. She came by each day, looking to spend time with me, but I never had much to say to her in return. I mean, what could we possibly have in common? However, Dhadhi insisted that she visit. So she sat quietly and either flipped through her own books as I sat and read my own or watched me train in the courtyard. Our only real exchanges came when we listened to the news.

I listened and watched daily to various news broadcasts in order to monitor the ongoing political situation in Punjab and the surrounding areas. The reports were quite extensive at first. June and July were consumed with protests, police raids and heated discussions between political analysts, government officials and even literary critics. The army maintained a considerable presence in the region and in the Golden Temple Complex. Mass arrests were taking place all over Punjab.

Each day, I desperately sought a report that would give some indication that things were stable or even remotely safe. However, for weeks, there were constant rumblings from the authorities regarding possible Sikh terrorist retaliation following Operation Bluestar. In contrast to those reports were the ones coming from families who complained of wrongful arrests, police beatings and forced disappearances of male Sikhs.

One day Dhadhi returned in tears from one of her daily visits to the local Gurdwara. When I asked her the reason, she revealed that her friend's fifteen-year-old son had been arrested during a trip to Punjab. He'd been picked up in a small village in the district of Moga. He'd repeatedly cried out, asking for the cause of his arrest, but the police had simply locked him away for five days and beat him regularly. When his mother travelled to the police station demanding answers, she was snubbed. After two days of waiting and refusing to leave the station, the inspectors yelled at her, calling her son a "terrorist". Eventually, they did set him free.

There was never a trial, not even a formal charge for a crime. He wasn't booked for anything. Worst of all, Dhadhi revealed that he was no longer able to walk. Five days. In just five days, the police had roughed him up so much that he wouldn't be able to walk, perhaps for the rest of his life. Ekant used Dhadhi's tale as a further example of why he was right not to travel. I simply sneered at him as he recounted the story each and every night, explaining that it would be "foolish" to attempt any type of travel outside of the city.

Then, one surprisingly cool August day, it went quiet. There were no reports regarding any agitation in Punjab, the surrounding areas or anywhere, for that matter. Instead the news focused on the future of the congress government, the development measures Prime Minister Gandhi was taking in Delhi, and some western writer who was preparing a biography on her. Entertainment and gossip from Indian cinema became headline news. The following day, all was quiet again on the political front. On the fourth day, I decided to approach Ekant with the idea that it was time to carry out our plans for Kiratpur.

I woke up at the crack of dawn so that I could catch him before he left for work. He had just finished his morning prayers and was sitting down for breakfast when I joined him.

"You're up early," he said without even a glance. "I thought you foreigners valued your sleep. What happened? Too hot, is it? Did a lizard crawl into your bed?" As expected, he was indulging in his usual condescension. Today, however, I couldn't fight back with smart remarks. I needed him to be in a good mood.

"No, no, I just thought I'd join you for breakfast, that's all," I replied, attempting a warm smile. When he didn't reply, I suppressed my angry thoughts reminded myself of why I had to put up with his obnoxious behaviour. I took a long deep breath and concentrated on the task at hand.

"Esha! You are up early today. Is everything okay?" Jas asked as she emerged from the kitchen.

"Yeah, totally. Why is everyone so surprised?"

"You never wake so—"

"Jas, I woke up early and…I guess I couldn't go back to sleep, so I came down to join you for breakfast. No big deal, I can go back upstairs if I'm interrupting something," I offered, standing up.

"Please, do not be silly. Sit back down. Can I get you some tea?" she asked, changing the subject, much to my delight.

"Yes, please," I replied, taking my seat opposite Ekant. Once Jas disappeared through the kitchen door, I decided to break the ice with him on a friendlier note. "So, um, how's business going?" I asked, trying to sound as genuine as possible.

"Fine," he grumbled.

"Okay. Well, what is it that you do exactly? I mean, I've been here for…how long? Well June, since June, and I don't even know what you do."

"Transport."

"Transport? Cool. Like what kind of—"

"Trucks, and I also handle distribution," he said rather curtly.

"Interesting. Does it get busy? I mean, how many people work for you?"

"Enough. Why? Tell me you are not trying to get me to take you along, because that would be rubbish. It's no place for a girl like you."

"A girl like me?"

"Yes."

"What does that mean?" I demanded. I was starting to lose my cool.

"You probably never had to work a day in your life. What would you know about hard work? You have probably never gotten grease or dirt on your hands."

"Those are a lot of assumptions. I've spent the past four years working hard for a degree in International Relations. On top of that I follow a very strict and demanding athletic schedule for my soccer training. Living in Canada isn't a piece of cake either, okay? Everyone works."

"I am sure that they do, but I am highly doubtful about you," he said rudely.

"What *is* your problem?"

"You have been here two months, and you have yet to lift your hands and help out around here," he said, looking directly at me this time. I was shocked at the sudden attack and couldn't think of what to say next. His eyes were so fierce and contained in them such loathing, that if he continued to stare at me like this, he'd burn a hole right through me!

"Ekant," came Jas's soft voice, "stop hassling Esha. There is no need for her to do any work around here. She is visiting us, and we have servants who are paid to help out. Esha, here is your tea, and please do not mind him. Ekant can get carried away at times."

I quietly took the teacup from Jas as she gave Ekant a stern look. This guy couldn't even have one decent conversation with me. It was time now to be direct, so I put down my cup and looked at him again. However, before I could even open my mouth, Ekant tossed his spoon on the table, pushed his plate away and stormed out of the room. This guy was impossible!

"What in Waheguru's name is going on here so early in the morning?" Dhadhi asked as she carefully made her way into the room.

"Oh, Dhadhi ji, nothing to worry about. Just some talk between a brother and sister," Jas explained, fetching tea for Dhadhi.

It was more like an attack on a sister.

"Esha, you are awake early today? Are you okay, child?" Dhadhi asked feeling my forehead.

"I'm fine, I just thought I'd ask Ekant today about travelling to Kiratpur. I've been listening to the news reports, and for days now, it's been really calm. I think it's safe, but before I could even bring up the topic, Ekant got all worked up and stormed outta here." I slumped back into my chair and drew a long breath. "Dhadhi, that guy has some serious issues. I think he hates me."

"He does not hate you," Dhadhi reassured, caressing my cheek. "He is your older brother. It is expected that he will behave in an overprotective manner."

"He wasn't being overprotective, Dhadhi. He was being plain rude!" I cried out.

"Now, Esha, I am sure it was not his intention. So you say that things seem safe now?"

"Yes."

"Then I will speak to Ekant, okay?" she offered.

I could feel my eyes widening. "Thank you, thank you, thank you!" I exclaimed. I was relieved she would be taking

82

over what had become a most stressful task.

That night, she waited until everyone had completed dinner and gathered in the living room. I was snuggled up in the corner chair, hiding behind one of my books. Ekant was helping Bhagat with some of his school work when Dhadhi decided to bring up the subject of Kiratpur.

"Ekant, I have been thinking," she began.

"Yes, Dhadhi?"

"Things have appeared quite calm for the past week or so. No more incidents are being reported in the news that would cause alarm for any type of travel. I have also not heard anything lately from any of the folks."

"But, Dhadhi—"

"Ekant, let me finish. Three months have come and gone since my son Dilawar's death. His ashes lie in a wooden box waiting for the day when they will be immersed in the holy river at Kiratpur, giving him eternal peace. Each day that goes by, my heart aches, knowing that this last rite remains incomplete."

"I am sorry that you are going through such pain, Dhadhi," Ekant said.

"He was like your father. He *was* your father. Jeet was just—"

"Do not say that man's name!" Ekant snapped, holding up his hand. Suddenly things didn't seem to be going so smoothly any more. Bad decision, Dhadhi!

"Sorry, Ekant," she apologized.

"Dilawar uncle was less an uncle and more of a father to me. He gave Mother and I what no one else could. Our relationship may only have existed through letters and a rare phone call, but I can appreciate him more than anyone else, perhaps even his own children."

My book fell from my hands as I glared at him. I was amazed at how he repeatedly insulted me, regardless of who was listening. No one had ever attempted such a thing. Now I was forced to put up with this treatment because of my father. Ekant was my ticket to Kiratpur, and going to Kiratpur was my ticket to going back home where things were normal, fun and made sense. So I pursed my lips together and pretended they were glued shut.

"Then you must not delay any longer," Dhadhi continued. "Things seem to have calmed down. You will be travelling with ashes. No one will doubt the reason for your travel. I think it is safe now to complete Esha's journey."

"Complete Esha's journey?" Ekant repeated, sounding baffled. "Of course, now I understand. Of course it is about *her* and *her* comfort. She cannot tough it out here, is that it? I should put us in danger, risk getting abducted by the police, beaten, and maybe even killed because of *her* comfort?"

"It is not like that, Ekant—"

"I am a turban wearing Sikh, Dhadhi!" he yelled. "They will spot me from far away and will not hesitate even for a second to arrest me without cause, and they will thoroughly enjoy beating me until I can no longer walk. You *know* this!" Dhadhi lowered her gaze to her hands and said nothing. We were losing the battle. "I have a family," he continued. "Dilawar uncle is already gone. It hurts to admit it, but he is gone! Your son is gone, Dhadhi. His ashes can wait awhile longer. If it were just me, and if it were for an immediate cause, then I would not hesitate, but I have a family to take care of, and I will not take any unnecessary risks when it is dangerous to do so all because our *dear Esha* is anxious to return to Canada where all is comfortable for her!"

"Ekant, try to see reason," Jas pleaded.

"No, Jas! For the sake of our son, you will not intervene!" Ekant's eyes were wide with anger now, and his bottom lip was trembling. His thundering voice sent a cold chill down my spine, and his impassioned behaviour was troubling. Poor Jas stopped in her tracks and sat back down on the sofa. "This is the end of this discussion. We will travel when I feel it is right to do so. Until then, no one will speak of it. Esha can wait it out. I am sure she can do that much for her father," he said, looking directly at me.

I matched his glare, doing my best not to let on that I was even remotely affected by his display of patriarchal authority. After he left, I walked over to Dhadhi and thanked her for trying.

"I am sorry, Esha, but do not misunderstand Ekant. He is a good person, and he respects your father. If he wishes to wait, then there is cause for it, I am sure. Just hang in a little longer, child."

"He didn't really leave me any choice, now did he?" I muttered.

"Have patience," Dhadhi said with an attempt at a reassuring smile.

I sulked back up to my room. Being faced with the grim reality of staying here longer made me increasingly homesick. I took out the picture that Carrie had given me before I had left for the airport.

"So you won't forget us," she had said.

Carrie, Mandy and Reet were perched up on a rock, beaming into the camera. I had taken the photo during one of our weekend trips to Stanley Park. We would laze around in the sun gossiping about guys, who was dating who, what girls we hated, what concert we were going to check out next. We would wander around eating ice cream and having drinks.

Those were our best times together. Watching them stare back at me now in the photo awakened a gloomy feeling. I was alone, and I longed to go back to my home and to my friends. Tears streamed down my cheeks as I thought about what they must be doing and what I was missing out on. I hated this place, and I hated the impossible situation that my father had gotten me into.

* * *

"Esha Ma'am, Esha Ma'am!"

"Hmmm…"

"Esha Ma'am, wake up!"

I opened my eyes to see Sheila standing over me.

"What is it, Sheila? Why are you disturbing me so early?" I grumbled, pulling the sheets over my head.

"Esha Ma'am, you must wake up. There is a telephone call for you from Canada."

"Call from Canada?" I cried, thrusting the sheets off me. "Why didn't you tell me sooner?"

"I tried, ma'am."

I quickly jumped out of bed, threw on my slippers and ran downstairs. Sheila followed closely behind. Jas was holding the receiver when I entered the living room. I quickly grabbed it. I was hopeful that my mother had found a solution for me.

"Mom?" I shouted into the phone.

"No silly, it's us!" screamed three very different but excited and familiar female voices.

"Oh, shit! Is it really who I think it is?"

"Esha, have you already forgotten your girls?" came Carrie's sweet voice.

"Carrie, how can I forget you?" I replied.

"Hey, what about me?" Reet cried out.

"You? Excuse me, what about me?" cried the loudest of them all, which was of course Mandy.

"Wait! Wait! Chill out, you three. Of course, I haven't forgotten any of you. I totally miss you! You have no idea what..." I cut off, realizing that Jas and Sheila were still in the room with me. "Hey, hang on a sec," I told the three girls and turned to Jas and Sheila. "Um, Jas, do you think you could make me some tea?"

"Oh dear, of course! You have had nothing to eat! I will prepare breakfast. Sheila?"

"Yes, ma'am, coming," Sheila said, following Jas into the kitchen. Now I was alone.

"Esha, you still there?" asked Reet.

"Yeah, sorry about that. I just wanted to make sure we were alone."

"So, how's it going over there?" asked Mandy.

"Yeah, tell us everything! How are the people? What's it like? Do anything cool yet?" All three started shooting out endless questions.

"Nothing's gone the way I had planned," I said, bringing their questions to a halt.

"What do you mean?" asked Carrie.

"Well, I thought I'd land here, go to Kiratpur, maybe take a trip to the Golden Temple like mom said dad would have wanted, then hop back on the plane and come home."

"So what's the hold-up?" asked Mandy.

"A bunch of stuff. Firstly, Ekant, the so-called brother—"

"Oh, yeah! What's he like?"

"Mandy, he's horrible. He's stubborn, rude and obnoxious. I think, no wait, I *know* he hates me."

"Serious? No way!"

"I don't know what his problem is. First he was, like, MIA. I didn't even see him. Then he finally shows up, and when I brought up travelling to Kiratpur, he shot me down, saying it wasn't 'safe' and shit."

"Safe? Why not? What happened?" Carrie asked, clearly worried.

"Some political stuff is going on in Punjab. There was an attack on the Golden Temple. I don't really understand it all. The reports were pretty messed up. There was a woman here whose son was arrested for no reason apparently. He was just picked up off the street and beaten by the police."

"You know, people here have been very vocal about that stuff," Reet said. "It was all over the news back in June. All the Sikhs were in an uproar over the attack. But that was, like, more than two months ago. So, why are *you* still stuck?"

"Because Ekant says that it's still unsafe," I answered with a loud sigh.

"What does the news say there?" asked Mandy.

"For a while, there were lots of reports, but for the past week it's been calm. There's no mention of agitation or arrests, nothing."

"So what's his problem then?" she demanded.

"I don't know! He got so mad when we brought it up with him yesterday. He was acting all tough and yelled that he'll decide when we go, and that no one is to bring up the subject until he does. And what's worse is that he had the nerve to suggest that my sister and I don't care about our father."

"No way!" they all exclaimed together.

"Yeah! Can you believe it?"

"So, he's not a fan of yours, that's pretty much clear,"

Mandy concluded. "Well, who cares anyway what he says or thinks. After you leave that place, you'll never see him again."

"I can't wait for that day," I added.

"Aw, but they're your family, Esha," Carrie said.

"Oh, stop it, Carrie. He hates her, and he's being unnecessarily difficult," Mandy retorted.

"Well, maybe it *is* dangerous," pleaded Carrie. "Maybe he does care for Esha, and he just doesn't know how to express it."

"Okay, well forget him, Esha. Do you really need him to travel to Kiratpur?"

"I guess. I mean, Mandy, how else would I go there?"

"How far is it?"

"I dunno, a few hours," I answered.

"Hmmm…well, India's got trains and buses, doesn't it?" Mandy's voice had a familiar tone in it now. It was a calculating tone, one that she only used when she was planning something.

"I guess so. I mean, yeah, of course. Not that I've been out much. I barely step out of the house. All the neighbours start staring at me, plus I don't really have much interest. Gosh, I'm so bored here!"

"Wow, Esha, you should at least try to find something to do around there. I mean it is Delhi, there's got to be something," said Reet.

"Yeah, I agree," added Carrie.

"I read, I train a little, that's about it. I've got some books, and they carry some magazines over here too, but I really miss the music. What's going on over there? Anything new come out?"

"There's a new track called 'Just Do It' hitting the airwaves. They're a group from England. All the parents are really pissed about it," Carrie explained.

"How come?" I asked.

"Because it's about sex, of course," she answered.

"Aren't they all, though? What's so new about this song? Conservatives just need something to complain about," Reet added.

"Okay, all of you, quiet!" Mandy demanded. "I have an idea!"

"What kind of idea?" I asked wearily. Mandy's ideas had been known to get us into trouble in the past. We had long ago learned to proceed with caution anytime she devised a new plan.

"Look, Esha, you're a grown person, and you're smart and independent. I know you love your father very much, despite the crap you've been through in the past year. We all know you'd do anything for him; that's why you're burning in that heat right now. So, three things are needed: you, your dad's ashes and Kiratpur."

"And a way to get there, smartass," I pointed out.

"Public transportation!" Mandy yelled. "Hello, it's like the most obvious thing. Check the routes for the trains and the buses. Is there anyone there that you can trust to make the arrangements?"

"Wait, wait, wait, Mandy, this is crazy!" Carrie said. "Esha, you can't risk it!"

"Yeah, I don't know how good I'd feel with you taking Indian public transportation all by yourself," added Reet.

"Yeah, Mandy, I'm not sure I can do that, and besides, no one in this house will let me," I said, lowering my voice in case anyone was within hearing distance.

"So don't tell them," Mandy answered.

"Are you suggesting that she…she *run away*?" Carrie asked. I could picture the shock on her face.

"Technically—"

"No, Mandy!" Carrie's tone was unusually firm.

"Oh, stop being such a goody-goody," Mandy snapped. "Do you have a better idea? Esha, listen to me. It's not that big a deal. You're in Delhi, for crying out loud. That's the capital of India! There's got to be a way to travel. My advice is that you find it, and you finish what you went there to do. So, is there someone you can trust?"

"Hmmm…oh! Well, it can't be Jas, because yesterday Ekant made her swear she wouldn't get involved."

"He made her *swear*?" Reet asked.

"Yeah, on their kid. I told you, the guy is intense."

"Is there anyone else?" Mandy persisted.

"I have a personal servant, Sheila."

"Wow, a servant!" they all said mockingly.

"Shut up. She could do it, but no wait, she's always so scared of everyone. Of course! There's Sumi, but…would she do it?"

"Who's Sumi?" Mandy asked.

"She lives in the neighbourhood. Her name is Sumedha. She comes over every day and just hangs around. She's our age, seems pretty cool, but I dunno. What if she freaks out and exposes me?"

"Well, she must like you if she makes the effort to hang out everyday. I think you should ask her."

"I dunno, Mandy."

"No, just listen to me. Just try asking her. You got two options: either melt away in that heat while you wait for this Ekant to grow a backbone, or run off and do what you have to, so you can come back home to us."

"Sounds tempting," I said.

"No, Esha!" Carrie pleaded. "Stay and wait."

"How long is she supposed to wait?" Mandy demanded.

"I dunno, but doing it alone isn't the way," Carrie replied.

"Yeah, I think Carrie's right," Reet added.

"Esha, what do *you* think?" Mandy asked.

"Um, I'm not sure. I mean, travelling on my own and all..."

"Esha, babe, just think about it," Mandy pleaded.

"Okay. I'll think about it," I said. Mandy was very persistent, and I knew she wouldn't take no for an answer.

"Esha, no!" Carrie and Reet screamed together.

"Girls, I'm going to think about it! I'm not running off on my own right now. Come on, let's talk about something else. How's everyone else? How's Johnny?" I asked, changing the subject.

"He's all right," Mandy replied.

"What about Skanky Rachel?"

"You mean are they... Don't worry, everything's cool. Since that night, Johnny caught her with someone else," Mandy answered.

"Actually, he kept catching her with someone else each week," laughed Carrie.

"Well, we didn't name her Skanky Rachel for nothing!" Reet added as she laughed along with Carrie.

"That's for sure. But Esha, Johnny really regrets what happened at that party. He also said for us to tell you he's sorry and he misses you," Mandy said more seriously.

"I'm sure he does. I mean, who wouldn't miss me, right?" I said jokingly.

"Absolutely!" Mandy replied. "It's a shame, though. He's so hot!"

Jas and Sheila had returned to the room and were staring at me curiously. "Okay, um...girls, it was so amazing to hear your voices—"

"Are you trying to hang up on us?" asked Mandy.

"Sorry, guys, I should go now."

"Ohhh!" cried Carrie.

"Esha, take care of yourself," Reet said with a hint of caution.

"You too, Reet. Bye, Carrie!"

"Esha, think about what I said."

"No, Mandy!" yelled Carrie.

"Stop it, Carrie! Esha, just—"

"Think about it? Yes, Mandy, I said I would, and I will. Now all of you take care, and hopefully I'll see you all very soon. Love you! Bye!"

"Love you, Esha! Bye, Esha!"

"Bye," I said sadly, putting down the receiver. I really did miss those girls.

"Esha? Breakfast is ready," Jas said, sitting down at the dining table, but I was in no mood to eat any more. Hearing my friends' voices had brought back all the gloominess. I was homesick now, more than ever.

"Sorry, Jas, but I've lost my appetite," I said softly as I passed the table and headed back up the stairs. I crawled into bed and hid under the sheets, hoping with all my heart that when I opened my eyes again, I would be back home where I belonged.

EIGhT

"What does it matter to me if she's not eating?"

"*Ekant*! What does it matter? She is your sister! You must care for her!"

"Dhadhi, stop it!" Ekant's voice roared through the halls of the house.

I rubbed my eyes and looked around in my room. The sun was still up, and the streets were bustling with noisy cabs and people. I had slept into the afternoon, something I had been doing a lot of in the past week. Dhadhi and Ekant seemed to be going at it again, but unlike before, Dhadhi was shouting too. I got out of bed and slowly walked towards the hallway. I poked my head through the door, trying hard not to make a noise. The voices sounded as if they were very near.

"The poor girl has not said a word for two days. She has been shut up in her room. She has barely eaten anything. I cannot take her sadness, Ekant. Please see reason!"

"It's too dangerous, Dhadhi!" Ekant yelled back.

They were next door in Dhadhi's room. I quietly stepped out into the hallway and tiptoed to her bedroom door. With my back to the wall, I craned my neck to the left, trying to catch a glimpse of what was going on inside. From what I could see, Dhadhi was sitting up against the headboard on her bed, and Ekant was once again pacing around the room.

"There are protests and fights constantly in this country,"

Dhadhi continued, "but that does not stop the millions from travelling, Ekant! I quietly agreed with you in the beginning, but now your stubborn behaviour has dragged on too long. We both know that if you and Chotu travel with Esha and the ashes, then no harm will come to you. It is only a matter of a few hours. My son, why do you stall?"

Dhadhi sounded exhausted. I didn't blame her. Ekant's stubborn behaviour was nothing but exhausting.

"You do not know, Dhadhi. I do!"

"Oh, stop it! Stop lying to me! You have never feared anything. Why behave as if you fear now? I admit there has been unrest in that region. Jageero's son was badly beaten, so I know firsthand what has gone on. But you have a reason, and proof for travel. Plus, with Esha, no one will mistake you for a terrorist. Tell me, what is the reason for your behaviour?" Dhadhi demanded.

"There is no other reason—"

"Stop lying to me!"

"Fine! I admit it! I am not afraid to travel. I just do not like having to do anything for that…that girl!" He had stopped pacing and was facing her. "I doubt anything would seriously happen if we were to travel," he confessed in a hushed voice.

The son of a bitch was afraid I might overhear him!

"Then why are you forcing Esha to stay and wait in this house any longer?"

"Because I want her to see…"

"See what?"

"What it is like to stay here, while everyone else is back in Canada enjoying a luxurious and carefree life! Let her burn here for a few more days, maybe then some of that attitude will disappear."

So he was doing it on purpose!

"Ekant, what is this that I'm hearing?" Dhadhi asked, her tone revealing her surprise over his confession. "That child has no attitude. You are jealous? This is unlike you, son."

"I have had to survive here and make a life for us, have I not? All the while, she and her family enjoy their lives in Canada. I see the way she looks at us, as if we are inferior."

"Ekant, you are punishing her? Your anger has nothing to do with her, my son. Stop being angry—"

"Stop being angry? Dhadhi, you of all people know what I have lived through. Now, I beg you to stop bringing up this topic with me. We will not travel to Kiratpur; she will not complete this journey until I say so. For once, I am asking you to listen to me. Let the princess rot a while longer. Maybe she will learn something." Ekant turned around and headed towards the door. I ran quickly back to my room and hid behind my door just as he stormed out and disappeared down the hallway.

"So this is why he's been stalling. What a jerk! I can't believe it. I can't believe it!" I gasped as I stomped around the room. All this time I had thought there was some real danger in travelling; instead this idiot was just having fun keeping me caged up in this damn house! I kept pacing, I didn't know what to do. I was livid. "How could he? He's made a fool of me." I stormed over to the chest beside the washroom door and yanked it open. There lay the emerald green sack. I lifted it out of the chest and removed the sack, revealing the rich wooden urn.

"Daddy, what the hell is going on? For sure this isn't what you wanted," I said, hugging the urn with one arm. I walked over to the window and looked out onto the street below.

A little boy was herding three cows down the street. I watched as he guided the cows with a long, skinny stick. The animals would moan each time the boy whipped them from behind.

As they passed by, one cow stopped right below my window. It wagged its tail for a while as the boy screamed at it to continue moving. The cow just moaned and didn't budge. Then suddenly it relieved itself. It came shooting out from behind, releasing the most grotesque smell I have ever experienced.

"Eeeewwww!" I covered my nose as I leapt away from the window. "Did you see that, Dad? See, I don't belong here! Shit! Literally shit, shit, shit!"

I placed the urn on top of the closed chest.

"What do I do now? I have to get out of here. The political climate being dangerous was one thing, but now I know it was all b.s.—Ekant was talking crap. He wants to teach me a lesson. *Me? A lesson?* I'll show him," I said angrily, turning to look at the urn directly. Just then I realized I had placed it directly beneath that Sikh Guru's photo which still hung from the wall. Looking at it now, I felt as if his large dark eyes were piercing right through me. I hadn't really noticed it since that first night, when I'd arrived in the country.

"These Indians are driving me insane," I said, looking in the direction of the urn and the portrait. I wasn't sure which one my comments and anger were directed at, but it made no difference now. "These are your people, not mine. You hear that? *Your* people! I don't belong here! I told you that over and over, and still you sent me here. I wonder what Mom would say now, after I tell her what Ekant's really been up to." I turned on my heels, determined to go call her and repeat every little detail that I had overheard. As I approached the door, my eyes fell on the photo of the girls, and specifically Mandy's beaming face.

"Finish what you went there to do," her voice rang through my head, "…three things are needed: you, your dad's ashes and Kiratpur."

"Mandy was right. I don't need Ekant. I can do this on my own." I looked at my father's urn once more, but this time with determination burning in my eyes. "Dad, I'm going to take you to Kiratpur by myself. Let's see who tries to stop me now."

I began to smile as I walked back and gently placed the urn back into the emerald suede sack.

*   *   *

The rest of the day felt like torture. My mind was racing with ideas, primarily about how I was going to convince Sumi to help me. I had Sheila bring my dinner up to my room. I was still furious with Ekant and didn't want to raise any suspicion that I had overheard him that morning. I needed to play it safe for as long as I could and ensure that no one spoiled my plans. My mind was fully alert, pushing away any thoughts of sleep. There was a strange excitement about travelling on my own and defying Ekant. I giggled, just imagining the look on his face when he realized I had taken off without him.

Giving up on sleep, I jumped out of bed and got dressed before dawn. My excitement wasn't going to dissipate until I spoke with Sumi, so I walked up to the rooftop balcony to watch the sun rise in the east.

The air was fresh in the morning. The sounds of prayers echoed in all corners of the neighbourhood. A few moments later, there it was. The sun cast a bright orange glow across the sea of houses as it slowly rose into a clear blue sky.

For the first time since my arrival, I witnessed something stunning and magical. It was impossible to believe that any danger could exist under such a beautiful sky, absolutely impossible. Watching the sunrise had placed me in an oddly soothing and trance-like state, but that too was soon destroyed as the streets became increasingly noisy. Trilokpuri came alive, as did the entire city. I had come to realize that Trilokpuri was a small resettlement colony, consisting largely of Sikh families. Most of the alleyways were long and narrow. The majority of the families were low income earners, but you could find some well-to-do families spread around the neighbourhood. I was never told why my grandparents had chosen this house after they left Punjab, and I didn't ask either. Our upper middle class family seemed almost out of place here, and I now understood why Dhadhi and Ekant commanded such respect in the neighbourhood.

I stayed on the roof until I felt it was safe to go downstairs without raising any suspicion. When I did venture down, I eagerly awaited Sumi's arrival. I was more than pleased to find out that my wait wasn't long. She showed up early with her little brother who went to school with Bhagat.

"Esha!" Dhadhi called out from the courtyard.

"Yes, Dhadhi?" I answered, joining her.

"Sumedha is here, and she will be dropping her brother and Bhagat at school today. Since you are already dressed, you should join her and get some air."

The perfect opportunity! Now was my chance to work on Sumi. "Yes, Dhadhi!" I exclaimed. "I mean…sure…if you want me too."

"Now be careful and watch the cars, children!" Dhadhi called out as Sumi and I led the boys out of the house.

"This is so much fun, Esha Puah! I am so happy you are dropping me today!" Bhagat exclaimed, skipping along as I held on tightly to his hand.

"Okay, Bhagat. Stop doing that, the street is busy."

The street was in fact very busy. The four of us had to manoeuvre around cars, bicycles, vendors pushing their carts, scores of people, and to make matters worse, cows and dogs that were roaming around at their own leisure. I hadn't expected such a commotion. During the few times that I had ventured out of the house, I had been safely in a car with Chotu and Jas. This was the first time I had walked the streets. In less than a minute, my sneakers were covered in dirt. This was a far cry from the neatly-paved roads and sidewalks back home.

"Um, Sumi, how far is the school?" I asked, jumping over a pile of cow manure. Bhagat laughed hysterically.

"What are you laughing at?" I snapped.

"You! Your face is so funny!" he chuckled.

"Sumi!" I called out, "How far?"

"Oh! Sorry, Esha! Yes, just right around this corner. Not too far."

As we rounded the corner and stepped into a quiet alley, I was relieved to discover that she wasn't exaggerating. We were quickly approaching a tall yellow building where children swarmed the courtyard and mothers yelled and chased after their kids, reminding them to eat their lunch and to be on their best behaviour.

"Thank you, Esha Puah. We can go from here," Bhagat said as he gave me a quick hug then bolted towards the school's gates. Sumi's brother hurried behind.

The walk had barely been ten minutes, which didn't leave me much time to convince her. I would have to work quickly.

"Esha? Shall we return?" she asked in her usual soft voice.

"Sure, let's go." I had to swing into gear now. "Sooo...how is the wedding planning coming along, Sumi? You must be so excited?"

"Huh? What? I mean why?" she stammered.

"Your wedding? What? Did I say something wrong?" I asked as she began to giggle.

"No, Esha, it's just that you have never asked me anything before. You always seem so so…"

"So what?"

"Not…interested…" she said hesitantly.

"Oh! Oh, please, that's not it," I lied. "I've just been really preoccupied. I'm so worried about my father. It hurts me that his soul is not at peace yet, because his ashes have not reached Kiratpur."

"What is the delay?" she asked, sounding worried. "I mean, Ekant is to travel with you, right?"

"Ekant is too busy with work. It's already been over two months. Who knows how much longer he will delay. It's a sad situation," I said, stopping at the end of the alley. I wanted to speak to Sumi where it was quiet.

"Don't be sad, Esha. I am sure it will work out soon."

"No, I don't think so, Sumi. I heard Ekant say yesterday that he thinks I'm a burden and that his work is too important."

"No."

"Yes. And…" I paused for a few seconds for a dramatic effect before continuing. "He also said that if I care so much about my father, then I should just…go on my own."

"On your own? But how?" she asked.

"I don't know. I mean, I'd have to find some means of transportation. I don't mind, but there's another problem."

"What?"

"Dhadhi doesn't want me going alone. She doesn't understand how we Canadian girls can be so independent and responsible. I mean, going to Kiratpur wouldn't be such a big deal for me. It's just a few hours. I've done loads of longer and more complex road trips back home," I said with a wave of my hand for added effect.

"Really?" Sumi asked, her eyes wide with curiosity.

"Yeah, of course! One time, my friends and I got lost in the mountains for two whole days. I was the one who led us back out. But Dhadhi is old, you know, and I don't want to stress her out."

"Yes, but I am sure she is just worrying about you, Esha, because she loves you."

"Oh, yeah, definitely. It's just so heartbreaking, you know. This delay isn't my father's fault. I feel terrible and don't know what to do," I said, biting my lower lip. My eyes welled up with tears from the pain of the bite.

"Please do not cry, Esha. I am truly sorry about what you are going through, and I wish I could help you."

"Yeah, me too... Hey! Wait a minute! Maybe you *can* help me," I exclaimed, grabbing her hands.

"Really? How?" she asked.

"Actually, forget it. I shouldn't get you involved."

"No, Esha, please. I want to help you," Sumi pleaded.

"Well, Ekant already said I can go on my own, and Dhadhi gets worried. But what if I took care of the details myself? That way I can prove to Dhadhi that I am responsible enough to do this."

"Will she agree to let you go?"

"Oh yeah, I'll convince her. Don't worry about that," I said, lying again.

"But how do I help?"

"You can help me find out about a bus or train that travels to Kiratpur and book a ticket for me. Can you do that, Sumi?

Can you help me get the information I need?"

"I do not know, I—"

"Oh, please, Sumi!" I begged, "For my father. Won't you help a girl out? Help a daughter carry out her father's last wish?"

"Oh, Esha when you say it like that...I...how can I refuse you?"

"Oh, thank you, thank you!" I threw my arms around her and squeezed her tight.

"You are very welcome!" she replied happily.

"Now, get me all the travel info and meet me back at the house, cool?"

"Cool, as you say it," she said, smiling. Sumi was clearly excited to be helping me. For a moment I almost felt bad for misleading her. Well, I wasn't *entirely* misleading her. Plus, it was for a good cause; the cause of getting me the hell out of there.

I didn't see Sumi again until after sunset. I sat in the courtyard all day long, afraid that Dhadhi might catch her before I did. When she did finally arrive, she wore a wide grin, which quickly disappeared when Dhadhi called out to her.

"Sumedha, dear! What brings you by and after sunset?"

"Oh nothing Dhadhi, I...umm...I just..."

"I told Sumi to come back later in the day, Dhadhi," I said coming to her rescue. "She was, uh, interested in...seeing some of my books!! So, uh, I told her to come back later in the day, so that we could...well...look...at them." I said with a weak smile. I could feel my cheeks burning.

"Hmm, okay, but not too late, okay. I do not want her walking home late at night."

"Yes, Dhadhi. Come on, Sumi." I grabbed her hand and dragged her to my room.

"Esha, slow down!" she cried as she struggled along.

"Sorry, sorry! I'm anxious to know what you found," I said closing the door behind us. "Come have a seat on the bed. Sooo…what'd you find out?" I asked impatiently.

"You have to take a bus from the ISBT, which is the Inter-State Bus Terminal. There is a bus that leaves in the morning at seven. That will take you to Chandigarh, and from there you will take another bus into Kiratpur. You should be able to reach there by the late afternoon. You can most likely get an evening bus to come back to Delhi, but you may have to wait until the next morning. I am sorry, but I could not get any specific times for the return trip. It all depends on when you reach Kiratpur and how much time you spend there."

"That's all right. I'm sure I can figure it out when I get to the station. So, in the morning at seven o'clock?"

"Yes."

"Where's the station?"

"You will have to go into New Delhi, which is on the other side of the Yamuna River. You cannot walk there, Esha."

"Shoot, now what?" I asked, disappointed.

"Can Chotu—"

"No! Too risky…err…I mean, he's needed by Ekant," I stammered.

"Esha, you said you were going to tell Dhadhi before you leave," Sumi reminded me.

"I will, don't worry," I said, trying to sound convincing. "That doesn't mean she'll be okay with it."

"Well, there is one other way," she offered.

"What is it?" I said jumping to my feet.

"Maybe it is not a very good idea, I mean—"

"Oh, come on, Sumi! Remember that this is for my father."

"Well…I suppose I can ask Daya to help us."

"Daya?" I asked, thinking back to all the people I had met since I'd arrived, but the name didn't ring a bell.

"My fiancée, Esha!"

"Oh yeah, sorry, I totally forgot his name," I said sheepishly.

"I can ask Daya to drive you to the station in the morning."

"Perfect! Wait, so that means you two are pretty close, eh? What happened to the whole being shy before the wedding thing that usually goes on with your people? I mean, Indian families here freak if the guy and girl hang out beforehand, no?"

"Oh, stop it. Daya and I have known each other our whole lives. Is it so surprising that two Indians could find true love?" she asked, her cheeks turning a bright shade of pink.

"True love, eh?"

"Yes. If I ask, Daya will not refuse," Sumi said confidently.

"Okay, Miss True Love, perfect! Tell Daya to meet me at the end of the street with his car. I'll wait on the bench in front of the chemist's shop. Ask him to be there by six?"

"Yes. I will also give him the details about the station. Are you sure this is what you must do? Think about it one more time."

"This is it, Sumi. I can't bear to think that my father's soul is not at peace yet. I mean, all of this delay for no apparent reason. You have no idea how much you have helped. You're amazing. Thank you so much," I said, hugging her, and I did mean it. With her help, I was much closer to achieving my goal.

"You *are* going to tell Dhadhi before you leave?" Sumi reminded me again, only this time she stared at me as if she were trying hard to read my face.

"Of course," I said with a smile. "I'll tell her in the morning before I go to meet Daya. That way it'll be too late for her to refuse. Now, what about the ticket?"

"You get it at the station. Daya will help you."

"Great! You know what, I'm beginning to really like this Daya," I said, laughing.

"He is wonderful," Sumi added.

"Oh, true love," I teased. "Okay, you should get going. It's late, and I don't want anyone getting curious," I said, ushering her out of the room.

"Promise me, Esha," Sumi said, stopping at the doorway, "you will be careful. Delhi can be a dangerous place for a girl alone. Remember, Daya will be in a silver car."

"Yes, yes thank you," I said impatiently.

"Promise me you will be extra careful," she demanded again.

"Okay, yes! Yes! Now, come on, let's get you home," I pleaded.

She smiled and walked happily through the doorway. I walked her to the front gate, watching her until she turned the corner. Her house was just a few steps away from that very corner. Satisfied that she had probably already reached home safely, I turned back and headed to my room. As I made my way to the stairs, Jas announced that dinner was ready. Not wanting to face the family members before my "big escape", I told Sheila to serve me in my room once again.

I waited impatiently as she laid out my dinner. Before walking away, she gave me a suspicious look.

"Sheila, what are you looking at?" I asked, annoyed.

"Esha Ma'am, are you all right? I mean, why you are again not eating with the family?" she asked.

"I'm just not up for company, okay, Sheila? No more questions, please," I answered.

"Sorry, ma'am. I was just—"

"It's okay. You can leave now, I can manage," I said, trying to get rid of her.

"Yes, ma'am," she said, appearing somewhat saddened by my response.

"Oh, and Sheila, one more thing before you go," I called.

"Yes, ma'am?" she asked, stopping by the door.

"Please don't disturb me in the morning for tea. I wish to sleep in. I'll come down on my own, okay?"

"Okay, ma'am."

"Thanks. See you later," I said cheerfully. I pretended that I didn't notice as she hesitated and gave me another suspicious look before closing the door behind her.

Just a few more hours remained before I would be on my way. I couldn't decide what excited me more: being out on my own finally, or the look on Ekant's face when he found out that I had done it without his help. Just the thought of it was electrifying. I could hardly wait.

NINE

Ileft my dirty dishes on the nightstand. Sheila could grab them later. I then opted to shower and get dressed. I covered my jeans and t-shirt with my robe, just in case Dhadhi or Jas decided to check up on me. I packed up all of my items and closed my suitcases so they would be ready for my departure once I returned from Kiratpur. After everything was packed and sorted, I sat on my bed and listened carefully as the house fell silent. It was midnight, but I didn't dare sleep, fearing that I might not wake up in time.

Lady Luck seemed to be siding with me, since Ekant wasn't coming home until the following evening from his business trip, around the same time I would be headed back. Chotu being with Ekant meant there was no one downstairs in the courtyard to catch me sneaking out of the house. It was almost too easy. So while I waited out the night, I indulged in another book, checking the time every so often. I would have to leave a bit earlier, as Dhadhi often woke up at the crack of dawn for her first set of prayers.

At precisely five thirty a.m., I grabbed my backpack and carefully placed my father's urn inside. I swung the backpack over my right shoulder, rubbing my increasingly heavy eyes as I tried to fight off the ensuing drowsiness. This was not the time to get sleepy. I opened my door as quietly as I possibly could and was overjoyed when I heard Dhadhi snoring next door. The house was still dark, with the only glimmer of light coming in from the east, where the sun was preparing to rise. I didn't have much time; Dhadhi would be getting up very soon. I pulled out my Canadian house keys, which I was now grateful I had brought along with me. Contained in the bundle of key chains was a tiny flashlight, a necessity for small-towners. I quickly flicked it on and tiptoed downstairs and out into the courtyard. Upon reaching the front gate, I glanced around me. There was no one in sight. I thanked my lucky stars again when I saw that the family cow, tied beside the gate, was also flat on its stomach without a care in the world.

"Perfect," I whispered.

The gate was way too creaky to risk opening, so the only option remaining was to climb the wall. I secured my backpack around both shoulders and climbed onto the barrels against the front wall.

"This shouldn't be too difficult, Esha. You're an athlete. Just climb up and jump over…and…well…land on your feet," I said, scratching my head. "Okay, get it together, here goes nothing."

I jumped up and grabbed hold of the top edge of the wall. Quickly planting one foot firmly against the wall, I pulled myself up and leaped over without hesitation. Fast and quick, just like a professional climber. My gym teacher would have been very proud.

I checked my watch. Five forty a.m. I still had twenty minutes before Daya was scheduled to arrive. I casually walked to the end of the street and sat down on the bench outside the chemist shop, as I had told Sumi I would. I hoped Daya would show up before anyone realized that I wasn't in the house. There were a few men straggling along the street, but no one paid me any attention. Just as I had assumed, Ekant was worried for nothing.

Looking at my watch, I saw that another ten minutes had gone by, and my patience began to grow thin. The sky was becoming lighter. Dhadhi definitely would be getting up by now. My leg began shaking fiercely. Daya *had* to show up before it was too late.

I breathed a sigh of relief when the headlights of a car finally appeared and slowly approached the bench where I sat. There was a lone driver who rolled down his window as he stopped the car in front of me. It was a silver car. Daya had arrived!

"Thanks, Sumi," I whispered as I walked towards the car.

He looked a decent fellow, with large, defined eyebrows, a mushroom cut, and he was clean-shaven. Despite the hair cut, he wasn't so bad looking.

"Daya, right?" I asked with a smile. He returned my smile but remained silent. Perhaps he was shy. I was a foreigner, after all. "I've been waiting for you for a while. Shall we get going?" I asked eagerly as the rays of the sun grew stronger by the minute.

"Sure, of course, jump in," he said. His eyes seemed to widen as I smiled back.

I ran around to the passenger side and got into the car, grateful that I had successfully escaped the house unnoticed. "So how long will it take to get there?" I asked buckling up.

"There?" he asked.

"The bus station? New Delhi? Didn't Sumi tell you where you're taking me? I need to catch the bus to Kiratpur."

"Oh, yes! The bus station! New Delhi, of course! Sorry, really early, you know," he said with a sheepish laugh. "Don't worry, I will take you anywhere."

"Anywhere can wait. The bus station is fine for now. So, how long?" I asked again.

"Not too long, dear," he replied as we turned onto the main road.

Dear? My muscles immediately tensed, hearing him use such a sexist tone with me. However, right now I was just thankful he was helping me out. I took a deep breath and looked out the window as we drove onto the bridge taking us over the Yamuna River and into New Delhi. The city looked beautiful and almost innocent as a new day began.

"So, dear, how long can you be out?" he asked, once again with that *dear*.

"Listen, I appreciate you giving me a lift and all, but you can save the endearments for Sumi, okay?" I said annoyed.

"Sumi?" he asked.

"Uh, yeah, Sumi, Sumedha, your fiancée..." I said, surprised that he failed to acknowledge her name.

"Hmm...yes, of course," he said after a long pause and in a slightly more serious tone.

Something about his reply unnerved me. Who was this guy? *No, shut up, Esha. What are you thinking?* Sumi had said that Daya would come to the meeting place in a silver car. It would be too big of a coincidence for a guy to show up in a silver car at the same time and place. Impossible...or was it?

As I battled my growing suspicions and discomfort, Daya, or hopefully Daya, continued to speed through the streets of New Delhi. Signs directing the way to the airport, Parliament, and various monuments and parks were showing up. The roads were slowly getting crowded as vendors prepared for another busy day in the markets. Businessmen, students and labourers were also appearing sporadically as we zipped through the streets. Unfortunately, these roads were unfamiliar to me. When I had arrived with Chotu, it was in the thick of the night. Right now, the sun was casting its rays over the city, and I didn't recognize a single thing.

Passing by another traffic light, I saw a sign indicating that the ISBT was just ahead. Good, at least we were going in the right direction. I was being silly for no reason. This had to be Daya. As we approached the entrance to the station, he didn't stop; instead he drove right through and headed towards the parking lot.

"Um, Daya, it's okay. You can drop me at the front. I can manage from there," I said.

"No, no, it's okay. I will take care of you," he said in a soft tone. He continued to drive the car slowly towards the back of the still-deserted lot. He constantly moved his head around as if he was looking out for something. This time my gut told me that something was definitely not right, and it was time I made sure.

I picked up my backpack with one hand and unbuckled my seat belt with the other. "So Daya, Sumi never told me how it was when you two first met. I mean, were you really okay with your parents arranging your wedding to a girl that you'd never met before?"

"Well...strangers are not so bad, especially female strangers," he said as he stopped the car and killed the engine. "Besides," he said turning to face me, "there is time for me to get to know her." He then proceeded to lick his lips and smirk. Oh, shit! Sumi had said she and Daya knew each other and had been in love since they were kids. *This is not Daya!*

I froze as the realization of my predicament registered. I struggled to get my head together and suppress the trembling that was increasing at an exponential rate as this stranger just sat there staring at me. His eyes were tracing my body, locking onto every part, every angle, as if he were trying to…to… mentally undress me! *Esha get out of the car, NOW!*

"Um," I said, clearing my throat, "so thanks for the ride, but I should go." I turned to open the door, but he reached over and grabbed my wrist.

"What is the hurry, dear?" he said playfully. "We are just getting to know each other."

"I think I know you pretty well," I retorted, trying to free my wrist, but his grip was too tight. I tried to think back to my high school self-defence classes. Was it twist then pull back, or pull back then twist? What was the point of all those classes if a girl couldn't remember when she needed it the most? I only had one choice left: the old street way of handling things. "Oh, yeah and, uh, just one more thing," I said through clenched teeth, "I'm not your dear!" I swung my right arm and made contact with his left eye. He immediately lost his grip on my wrist. I pushed open the door and jumped out of the car as he held his face and howled behind me.

"You stupid bitch!" he yelled as he kicked open his door and stumbled out after me.

I slipped both arms through the straps of my backpack and raced towards the station building. There had to be someone inside. As I continued to run, my assailant continued to gain momentum and was now at my heels.

"Get the hell away from me, you pervert!" I screamed, hoping that I had damaged his eye enough that he'd trip over himself as he chased me.

"You whore! Wait, you just wait and watch what I do when I catch you!" he barked.

"Ha! Just try. I'm not some helpless Indian chick! You pervert!"

"Stop it!"

"Pervert! Pervert!" I screamed, running as fast as I could.

"Shut up!"

"*Perrrverrrrt!*" I yelled, taunting him. It probably wasn't a good idea, but whether it was adrenaline or stupidity, at this point I couldn't control myself.

I jumped over the curb and made a hard left, racing head on towards the front doors. *Please be open! Please be open!* I was overjoyed to find the doors unlocked as I burst through them. I ran into the lobby, desperately seeking someone, anyone! I quickly scanned the room for a security guard or police officer, but couldn't find any. There were a few families in the waiting area, a clerk behind the ticket window and a few lone men wandering about. I ran to a middle-aged man in a grey business suit who looked somewhat civilized. He looked up from his newspaper as I approached.

"Sir, I need your help!" I cried.

"I'm quite busy, young lady. Why don't you go speak to a guard or someone," he said, sounding annoyed. He quickly turned his attention back to his paper.

"No, I don't think you get it. I'm in trouble!" I yelled. A few people turned my way as I raised my voice.

"Whatever your trouble is, I'm not getting involved. Ask anyone, and they'll tell you that it's better to stay far away from other people's troubles. These days the police place blame on anyone and everyone."

Before I could say anything further, my assailant came up behind me and clasped his hand around my mouth. He wrapped his other arm around me, locking me in.

"I'm so sorry, sir," he said to the businessman. "My wife has these fits every so often. I always tell her not to forget her medicine, but still she forgets!" He sounded so calm, like a real concerned husband. Damn him! For sure these people wouldn't fall for such a ridiculous story.

"That's all right. I could tell something was wrong with her," the businessman responded without taking his eyes off the paper. *Was he joking?*

My assailant dragged me towards the nearest door, and I tried to wrestle with his every move, but he was just too strong. My eyes pleaded with people that we passed, but they either quickly diverted their attention or walked away. *What was wrong with them? Why wouldn't anyone help me?* He dragged me through a plain wooden door that led into an empty hallway. Here he stopped and switched his hold to my neck with one hand while he struggled to take my backpack off with the other hand. I threw my hands in every direction, trying to free myself or hit him in the process. I kicked as high and as hard as I could, but he was too fast, and he was too angry. Eventually he tore the backpack off me and tossed it to the side.

"Hey! That's...fra...gile," I said choking.

"Shut up! Now I am going to show you!" he sneered.

"Show...me...wh...at...you...sssoon...of...a...itch...et... ur...ands off...ee..." I spat out as his grip around my neck tightened.

He offered no reply and just stared at me with a terrifying determination in his eyes. He pulled me into a tighter embrace and began dragging me away again. I struggled and fought him with every ounce of strength I had left, but it was useless. My breathing was slowing down. I was starting to lose consciousness as his grip around my neck remained steady. This was it. I was going to become headline news back home. I could already picture the headlines.

My face was going to be plastered on *60 Minutes* and *Time* magazine with testimonials from my precious girls, Dhadhi, and perhaps Ekant. "I told her it was dangerous." I could just hear him say it. Damn it! Now what? I was being dragged away! I had to look for an opportunity. Something, anything that would help me escape.

He burst through another door and threw me down. I stumbled to my feet, but my ribs hurt from his suffocating grip and my back from being tossed to the tiled floor like a piece of garbage. I bit my lip, trying to conceal my pain. I didn't want him to feel that he had the advantage. The four urinals beside me indicated that we were in the men's washroom. He closed the door and locked it.

"Now where are you going to run, my dear?" he asked in an evil tone. He made the Wicked Witch of the West sound like an angel. *Oh, God! If there is a God, my mom prays to you all the time, how about you help me out here?*

"Stay the hell away from me!" I cried out as he advanced towards me. "You have no idea who you're messing with. I'm a Canadian citizen. You mess me up, and everyone will be after you. Everyone! So just stay away!" I yelled in a last-ditch effort to scare him away.

"Say whatever pleases your heart, because no one can help you now," he hissed.

"My brother will kill you, damn it! He's a big Sikh dude with a dagger and all, and he's not afraid to use it." I didn't quite know or care what I was saying, but every second I spent stalling was another second that I was alive. "Touch me

116

again, and he'll cut you into pieces, you shit!" I was definitely grasping at straws now.

"A Sikh brother?" he laughed. "Ha! Just my luck. Well, that would make you a Sikh now, wouldn't it? Well, well, well, I'm going to enjoy this even more. You bloody people complain so much. First you cry over your crops and now your temple. It is a block of gold, put it—"

"Hey! Watch your mouth!" I snapped. He stopped his advance and gawked at me. I used this opportunity to look for something that I could use as a weapon, but suddenly he lunged at me. I leapt to the side, but he caught my arm and pulled me down, smacking my head against the dirty tiled floor. As I groaned in pain, he pinned my arms. I tried to pry them free, but pain seared through my head. I was quickly losing consciousness again.

"Like I said," he hissed, his hot, disgusting breath now in my face, "I'm going to enjoy this, as no one, no one, can help you now. Do you hear? *No one.*"

"Well, my friend, that depends on your definition of 'no one'," came a voice followed by the sound of a flush. Someone else was in the washroom with us!

My assailant jumped to his feet, releasing me from his hold. I held my head as the pain increased. A stall door swung open, and I looked up in the direction of the voice, even though my vision was becoming increasingly blurred. The light was hurting my eyes. I could only see the silhouette of a tall man. Light emanated from all around him. He appeared like an angel.

"Who the hell are you?" my assailant demanded in disgust and disappointment. I strained my ears to hear. It was as if the two men were speaking from the other side of a tunnel.

"Well, I am one person, but I carry the strength of my

Gurus. Would you like to see?" he asked. I could hear the sound of water. Was he washing his hands? What kind of rescue was this?

"Just get out of here and leave us to our business! This has nothing—" demanded my would-be rapist.

"Now just shut up, will you? I've already listened to enough of your nonsense when you dragged that poor girl in here and began taunting her. I now understand your intentions clearly, and well, you see, I cannot leave you, but do not worry. I promise I will not disrupt your enjoyment. We are going to have lots of fun!" the stranger replied with what I hoped was sarcasm.

I heard a nasty snarl and what sounded like a scuffle, then there was a loud bang against a stall door. I tried to see what was happening, but my head was becoming heavier, and my vision darkened.

"Ma'am, excuse us as I take our friend for a little walk. I will send help," came the angelic voice. I tried to reply, but my mouth was dry, and I couldn't manage any words. He must have noticed my helpless state, because he moved closer to me and peered over. I could see his silhouette once again, but this time it was in the shape of a turban. He shifted slightly, and I saw that it was white. There was a beard, but I couldn't see any more. "Have no fear," he reassured. "When we need Him most, He gives us strength." He turned around and disappeared with my attacker.

After what seemed like hours but was probably only minutes, I finally managed to sit up and remove my hand from my head. Just as I had feared, my head was covered in blood, explaining the nausea and dizziness.

"My backpack," I gasped, remembering that it had been left outside the washroom, along with my father's urn. Mustering every bit of strength, I stood up and stumbled out of the washroom.

In the hallway I thankfully found the backpack still in one piece. I surveyed the area around me. The mysterious angel and the would-be rapist were nowhere to be seen, so I went out into the lobby. A uniformed man was making his way through the lobby, pushing a cart. When he saw me staggering, he started towards me curiously. Kneeling down, I unzipped the backpack to ensure that my father's urn was still intact. Fortunately, it was.

"I'm so sorry, Daddy," I finally cried. Relief and regret began to set in as I realized what had almost happened. "Look at what I've gotten us into. I'm so sorry." Tears streamed down my face as I carefully placed him back into the backpack.

I wiped my face and took a breath as deep as my injured ribs would allow. This was no time to cry. I still had to decide what to do next. As I stood up, sharp pains pierced my body. My vision blurred once again as I was blinded by pain. Then everything went black as I fell.

TEN

There was a light, a soft yet illuminating light. It was like the eastern sunrise as it swam all around me. I was floating, but where? Someone was with me, moving beside me and holding my hand. I turned my head and there he was, the white-turbaned angel. His touch was soft, his smile warm, and his eyes peaceful, but I still could not fully make out his face. Then, suddenly with a POP! it was all gone.

I opened my eyes and found directly above me, not the light of heaven or even a sunrise, but a light bulb. *Where am I?* I looked around the room. Dhadhi was slumped uncomfortably in a chair in the far corner of the room. On the other side I saw Jas reading a newspaper. She hadn't noticed that I was conscious yet. A machine beeped somewhere nearby. I looked down at my arm and found an IV. I was in a hospital. I cleared my throat, and Jas immediately threw down her paper and rushed over.

"Esha! Dhadhi, Esha is awake!" she cried.

"Jas, get the doctor," Dhadhi instructed.

"Yes, Dhadhi!" Jas exclaimed as she raced out the door calling for a doctor.

"Esha? Esha dear," Dhadhi called, walking over. She bent down and placed a loving hand on my cheek. "Do not worry, child, you are safe," she whispered softly into my ear.

Remembering the attack and the blood, I slowly brought

my hand up to my head. A thick gauze bandage was wrapped around it. And my hair…*oh my god, my hair!*

"Dhadhi…" I croaked. "My…hair…"

"Oh dear, they had to shorten it a little while they attended to the wounds to your head. Not to worry, you look beautiful as always, and it will grow back. It is not like you had a long Punjabi braid anyhow!" she chuckled. She was actually finding humour in my dilemma. "Now, your hair is only a little shorter," she said.

I ran my hand over my head. A *little* shorter? They had given me a buzz cut! A buzz cut! I looked at Dhadhi in alarm. She gently patted my hand.

"It was needed," she reassured, but her smile quickly faded away. "I was so worried about you, Esha. If something happened to you…what face would I show my son when I meet him in the afterlife? What answer would I give him and God? And now, to your mother, what do I say to her?"

"I'm…I'm sorry, Dhadhi. I just—"

"Esha, Dhadhi, the doctor is here," Jas announced as she entered the room with a man in a white lab coat and glasses. Three nurses, each holding a chart, followed closely behind.

"Miss Esha, I must say it is a pleasure to see you awake," the doctor said. He was a middle-aged man with grey hair. The dark circles under his eyes and the lines on his face spoke of years of experience and many sleepless nights. "Your vitals are stable. The wounds have been treated, and in a few weeks, the stitches can be removed. If you feel well enough to get on your own two feet, then I do not see any reason why you cannot go home today."

"Great," I said with a sigh of relief. "Thank you."

"Nurse, prepare the release papers. She can leave, but she'll have to come back in a week to have the stitches removed," he said and left the room. One nurse hurried out behind him, while the other two pounced on me. They paid me no attention as they worked quickly on removing the IV and disconnecting the monitors.

"I feel much better now," I remarked as the nurses closed the door behind them. "But they shaved my head! All of it!"

"Esha, why did you run off on your own? We were so worried about you!" Jas said.

"Yeah, about that...I'm sorry, Jas. It wasn't to hurt you, really. I just thought I could handle it," I replied. I truly was sorry about what I had done. My great escape had landed me in the hospital instead of Kiratpur. I felt like a total idiot.

"But why would you even try. Ekant said—"

"Ekant says a lot, Jas," I snapped, and she immediately fell silent. "Look, I'm sorry you were worried. I shouldn't have gone. Look at the mess I got into. If that...that...and if he... he didn't save me—"

"He? Who, Esha? Who saved you?" Jas asked.

"I...I'm not sure. I couldn't see clearly. All I remember is that I was being attacked, and I hit my head hard, and then there was someone else, and everything just went black. How did I get here?"

"Sumi informed us of your plan," Jas answered. The disappointment was clear in her tone. "Apparently Daya was late in meeting you. After you failed to show, he notified Sumi, who in turn came looking for you at the house. That was when we realized you were missing. When we contacted the police, we were told that a young Canadian girl was found unconscious and taken to the hospital. Esha, what were you thinking? Getting poor Sumi and Daya involved? We did not even notice you leave the house. Sheila refused to go to your room, saying that you had forbidden her from waking you. Lies, Esha, *lies*? Do you not trust us?"

"That's not it, Jas," I said soberly.

"Ekant said it was dangerous. He was talking about the danger that faces us because we are Sikh, and you are Sikh, Esha. But for a girl, any girl, to be out and alone in the streets at dark is dangerous. Why would you take such a stupid risk?"

I opened my mouth to speak, but no words came out. Just thinking about how close my assailant had come to raping and perhaps even killing me was terrifying. My plan had backfired colossally.

"Jas, stop it," Dhadhi said, sounding exhausted. "Esha has been through enough. She needs rest. Come on, let us prepare for her return home." She had been very quiet while Jas lectured me, and her silence was discomforting. My father used to behave in a similar manner whenever he was furious over something I had done. Watching Dhadhi now felt like I was watching him.

"Dhadhi," I said, more subdued.

"Yes, child," she replied.

"Where's Ekant?" I asked.

"He is still at the police station. He will make sure that the man who attacked you will never get the opportunity to do it again to another girl."

"Can Ekant do that? I mean, I thought he was afraid of the cops. Can he get the guy charged?"

"Do not worry yourself with the details," she said with a loud sigh as she began pulling the sheets off me. I decided not to ask anything further. Instead, I busied myself getting out of bed and dressing.

As Dhadhi helped me, I tried to imagine what Ekant was

doing right now at the station, how he might react to seeing my attacker. There was something oddly comforting about Ekant intervening to ensure my attacker was punished. I mean, I was confident he would have been here otherwise, mocking me and telling me I had gotten what I deserved. Yet he was securing punishment for the man who had dared to touch me. Perhaps Ekant did care a little.

"Esha, Dhadhi ji," Jas said poking her head through the door. "You two ready? I have the release papers, and Chotu is bringing the car to the front."

"Oh yes, Jas dear. Esha and I are ready. Come, child, time to go home," Dhadhi said. I quietly followed her out. Home sounded like a good idea.

*   *   *

My room was exactly as I had left it. The suitcases were still packed and lined up against the wall. The bed was still unmade, and my dirty dishes still sat on the night stand. No one had touched anything. After much effort, I finally convinced Dhadhi and Jas to stop fussing over me and to leave me alone to rest. When the door closed behind them, I walked over to the mirror and examined my hair. The medical team had done a pretty decent job of shaving the hair off. It wasn't as uneven as I had feared it would be. Thankfully, my hair usually grew pretty quickly, so it was sure to grow back to its regular shoulder length in no time. In the meantime, however, it was going to give the neighbours another reason to gawk at me. After I removed the gauze wrapping from my head and examined my bruises and the stitches in front of the mirror, Sheila arrived with my medication. She quietly walked in and set down the painkillers, along with a hot cup of tea.

"Thanks, Sheila. My head is pounding," I said, popping the pills into my mouth.

"Esha Ma'am, are…are you okay?" she asked nervously.

"I'll survive," I replied.

When she finally looked up at me, she gasped and pointed at my head. "Ma'am, your hair!" she screamed. "Your hair, it is—"

"Short? Yeah, so you noticed, eh?"

"But why, Esha Ma'am? It is like a boy's hair!"

"I think the doc felt I needed to go shorter. What do you think?" I asked, amused at her sudden reaction.

"I am so sorry for what you experienced, ma'am. It must have been so very horrible."

"Sheila, I'm fine. Stop worrying now and let me get some rest," I said. My initial amusement was rapidly disappearing. The last thing I wanted to do was get into another discussion about what I had gone through and how I had failed.

I ushered her out of the room and quickly shut the door. As I walked back towards the bed, something green caught my eye. There it was, the emerald sack carrying my father's urn. It was resting on the iron chest. Dhadhi must have had it placed there after they found the backpack.

"Oh, Daddy," I sighed as I kneeled down before it. "I can't believe I almost *lost* your ashes. If that guy had his way with me…if he had succeeded…then who knows what would have happened to you. I mean, I *dropped* you. I…I hope you know I was just trying to get to Kiratpur. I was only trying to fulfill my promise of pouring your ashes there. I didn't plan on all of this other stuff! If that…or he…if he hadn't saved me…I failed you…"

It was the truth. I *had* failed my father. How could I have been so stupid? I could feel my cheeks burn as I tried to suppress my anger. I had allowed my father's ashes to be treated so disrespectfully and had almost been the victim of a moronic and clearly depraved man. Just the thought of it made me want to pound my head against the wall.

Get a hold of yourself, Esha! I had to calm down. I had to push it behind me. I was still here, and thankfully the ashes were still safe. Unfortunately, I was back to where I had started. Now, more than ever, I would be at the mercy of Ekant. Realizing there wasn't any other choice, I wiped my tears and gently placed the urn inside the chest, where I knew it would be safe.

I found my way back into bed as the drowsiness from the painkillers began to set in. I didn't open my eyes again until Dhadhi came in with tea the following morning.

"How are you?" she asked. She was sitting beside me on the bed. Her expression was soft, but the tired eyes could not mask her worry.

"I'm fine, Dhadhi, thanks for the tea," I said, taking the cup from her hands. My ribs were still very sore, and the bandages were itchy. The sweltering heat wasn't helping either, but I wouldn't dare complain any further in front of Dhadhi. Surprisingly, she was still being very calm about the whole ordeal. "You've been awfully quiet," I said, trying to bridge the distance between us. It was inevitable that we would discuss what had happened. Better to just get it over with.

"I am sad, Esha," she said. "I am sad that you felt you had no other choice. I understand that Ekant left you in a very difficult position, but—"

"He has been nothing short of rude and impossible, Dhadhi," I said, quickly pleading my defence.

126

"One thing you should understand about Ekant, child, is that he has had a very difficult life. He is a wonderful person who loves his family, his work, and he is a man of God, but there are demons that he also fights."

"Mom told me about what happened with Jeet uncle," I said. She nodded slowly and didn't look too surprised that I knew the family secret.

"We moved to Delhi, thinking we could escape the past and start anew," she began. "All was fine until one day Ekant found out from his mother that he was conceived from a heinous act."

"Why on earth would his mother tell him *that*?" I asked.

"She did not intend to, but she could no longer ignore his growing curiosity regarding his father. When he was twelve years old, the truth came out, and his small, fragile world fell apart. As long as he struggled to make sense of it, he could not meet anyone's gaze. He would hardly speak to anyone, even at home. He looked broken and ashamed, until one day he found God."

"Found God?"

"He has never revealed how it happened or what he saw, but he came to his mother and me and said that he knew."

"Knew what?"

"That he should show courage, because there was a purpose for him. He said there was still beauty left in this world. That knowledge has allowed him to continue on and love his family, his work and his life. News of your arrival, however, has ignited old, buried feelings of shame and anger. As difficult as it is to imagine, I believe when he saw you, he became jealous."

"Jealous? What about all that stuff about finding God?"

"Child, God may offer grace to a man, and he may receive God's message. That man, however, is still a man. He does not become God. And so, that man still carries with him all the inhibitions that plague any human being." She stood up and walked over to the painting of the Sikh Guru. "We all grow up with different experiences, but those experiences should not give us reasons to be at odds with each other. Esha, I cannot imagine what sort of life you have in Canada, but I am confident it is very enjoyable. My son knew how to take care of his family, and your mother is a kind woman.

"When Ekant thinks of you, I believe he thinks of the life that he missed out on. A life where there is a respectable father and a happy mother. He feels inferior. Of course, that does not excuse how he treated you upon your arrival in Delhi," she said, turning to face me again. "I am not upset with you. You tried to give my son peace. However, you took the wrong path." She sat down beside me and folded her hands over mine. "We could have lost your father's ashes," she said firmly, as if I hadn't already realized that possibility.

"I know, but I just want to get this over with, Dhadhi!"

"Are you so determined to leave and return home that you would venture off into the dark in a country that is not known to you? Is there nothing else that you wish to do while you are here with us?"

"Like what?" I demanded.

"Get to know your people. Give this country a chance. Your father loved India."

"But isn't it dangerous to wander about?" I asked.

"I mean the people around here, Esha. There is life in every corner of this city. Every neighbour has a story and a lesson. Oh child, stop resisting it so. Learn about this other part of yourself, and never lose sight of who you are and where you come from. I am sure your father would have wanted this for you, and he—"

"He did," I said solemnly.

"Did what, dear?"

"He said…before he… Well, he said he wanted me to explore this other part. Sikhism, India… He wanted me to see what he saw, to feel what he felt," I confessed.

"Now that sounds like my son," Dhadhi said, smiling.

"Yeah, but it's impossible," I said pointedly. "I don't know what he saw or felt, and I can never know. It's not like he described it to me."

"How can you say it is impossible?"

"Because it is!"

"Have you tried?"

"Well, I'm here."

"Have you *really* tried, Esha?" Dhadhi repeated.

I fell silent as I mentally revisited my journey in Delhi. Minutes passed by uninterrupted, and still I had no answer. I reluctantly shrugged in defeat.

"Then perhaps you should, hmm?" she suggested. It was difficult to argue with her loving face, so I remained silent. "Get washed up, dear, and come down. You must call your mother and inform her of what has happened. No need to worry her with all the details, of course, but she deserves to know what her daughter has been up to." I nodded, and like an obedient child, I made my way into the washroom as Dhadhi closed the door on her way out.

I stood still as I let the warm water in the shower soothe my body. I was careful not to get the stitches wet, which wasn't too difficult, since I really didn't have any hair that needed washing. Instead I let the water flow over my sore muscles.

My attacker had left his marks on my body. Traces of his hand could still be seen on my neck and arms. I could hear his voice in my head and feel his hands on me. I felt dirty and disgusting. He was suffocating me, and I couldn't get away until…there…it was the white light, and there rose the silhouette of a man in a turban; my white-turbaned angel. The air flowed back into my lungs. I was okay.

"Give it a try, Esha," Dhadhi's voice rang in my ears.

"I want you to realize what it is to be Sikh." My father's voice took over. His words kept repeating, getting louder and louder in my mind.

"Daddy?" I gasped, opening my eyes. I was still in the shower. The water was running cold now. How long had I been in here? Now shivering, I shut off the water.

"Esha, are you here?" a soft and familiar voice called out. "It's me, Sumi."

"Hey! Yeah, one sec! I'm just getting out!" I called back. I threw on my clothes and stepped out. Sumi was sitting on the edge of the bed, waiting patiently for me. She looked up as I walked out of the washroom and immediately stood up.

"Oh, no! Esha, your hair!" she cried. I really hoped this wasn't going to be a constant reaction.

"Yeah, let's not talk about that."

"Are you okay? Oh, I was so worried! Daya told me that you never showed up, and then you were not home. I was so scared, I did not know what to do!"

"It's okay, Sumi."

"No, Esha," she said in an unusually firm tone. "You promised you would tell Dhadhi about the plan, and you did not do that. You lied to me, Esha, you *lied*. And now Daya is not talking to me, my parents are very disappointed, and I am not allowed to leave the house!" Sumi sat back down on the bed in tears. Unsure about how to comfort her, I hesitated momentarily before sitting next to her.

"Why are you in trouble? It wasn't your plan," I said. "But wait, if you're not allowed out, then how did you get here now?"

"How do you think? I lied also," Sumi said, looking away as if she was too ashamed to admit she was capable of such a thing. "I begged my mother to allow me to visit the Gurdwara, but instead I came here to see if you are okay. Jas told me about the attack."

"Yeah, I got into the wrong car, apparently. I thought he was Daya. Obviously, I was wrong, very wrong." I looked away from her. I felt foolish in admitting that I could make such a stupid mistake.

"Did he not say his name? How could this happen?"

"He showed up in a silver car around the time that Daya was supposed to meet me. He didn't correct me when I called him Daya. How was I supposed to know it wasn't him? That damn idiot was smart. He just played along."

"Daya said he was running a few minutes late, and now it makes sense why you were not there when he arrived."

"So why isn't Daya talking to you?" I asked, shifting the focus back to her.

"He is angry that I brought him into this mess, but he is a good man. I am sure he is upset because he was worried about you and because I have gotten into so much trouble at home."

"So just go to him and make things right," I suggested.

"How so?"

"Just tell him you're sorry and that you love him. There! Then you two can kiss and make up!"

"Kiss and make up? Make up what? Oh, I do not understand, Esha," Sumi replied, looking confused.

"Like make things right between you, but kiss. You do that, don't you? I mean, you're about to marry the guy."

"No, no, no, no, no!" Sumi cried, jumping off the bed.

"What? What did I say?" Now I was confused by her sudden reaction. She continued to shake her head and pace around the room. "Sumi! You're acting weird. Sit down," I said grabbing her. "What's the big deal about a kiss?"

"Esha, you say it so easily," she said, lowering her voice. "I simply cannot *kiss* Daya. Have you gone mad?"

"What? Why not? He's your fiancé. You told me you two have been in love since you were kids."

"Yes, but if I kiss him, then I will…" she trailed off, and so too did her gaze, as if she was at a loss for words.

"You will what, Sumi? You're not making any sense!"

"Pregnant," she gasped.

"*Pregnant?*" I almost choked on the word before bursting into hysterical laughter.

"Yes! Esha, please quiet down. Someone might hear!" she pleaded.

"Oh, Sumi," I laughed. "Dude, you can't be serious! Sorry, but you do *not* get pregnant by simply kissing someone."

"You do not?"

"No! Trust me, doesn't happen."

"So, if I kiss Daya, I will not—"

"You won't get pregnant," I repeated, trying hard to maintain a straight face. "I promise you."

"Oh." She blushed. "I am so embarrassed. That is what my mother always says. Anyway, it does not matter. Before marriage, all this is a sin."

"Really? So I take it there's no health class in school, is there?" I couldn't help but giggle, which only added further to Sumi's confusion.

"What?" she asked, still sounding alarmed.

"Oh, never mind. Just forget I said that." I had always

132

taken Sumi to be one of those innocent and obedient Indian girls, but until now I had never fully realized the extent of her innocence. For some reason, I didn't want to spoil it. It was somewhat comforting to see her like this.

"No, tell me please," she insisted.

"You'll find out after marriage, Sumi, but basically, it takes a whole lot more than just a kiss to get knocked up, okay?"

"Knocked up?" she repeated.

"Okay, now I've said too much. Just leave it, cool? I gotta get downstairs and call my mother. You better get home before Rano realizes where you really are."

"Oh, yes, yes, I better go!"

"And hey, listen, I am sorry that I got you involved. You've been pretty cool to me since I got here, and I ended up getting you into trouble."

"It's okay, Esha. It was my choice to help you and to ask Daya. This trouble is no big deal. The family will get over it. But I am sorry you got hurt. You know, you are a good person. I like being around you," she said warmly.

"Well, in that case, friends?" I said, offering my hand.

"Friends!" she exclaimed, pushing my hand aside as she pulled me into a tight embrace.

"All right then, now get out of here!"

"Bye, Esha!" she called as she ran out of my room.

I followed slowly behind. Jas and Dhadhi were both in the living room when I walked in. There was no sign of Ekant yet. I was burning to know what had happened to my attacker, but no one was telling me.

"Esha Puah!" Bhagat called as he ran and jumped onto the sofa beside me. "Wow! Your hair is like a boy's hair! Can I touch it, Esha Puah?" he asked curiously.

"Bhagat, leave Esha alone!" Jas ordered.

"Nah, it's okay Jas," I said. "Go ahead, buddy, but be careful of the stitches, cool?"

"Okay," he said as he ran his fingers over my scalp. "You look like my friend Harry. He has the same haircut," he giggled.

"Very funny," I replied.

"Bhagat! Where are you, Bhagat? Come on, it's time to go!" Ekant called out as he descended the main stairs.

I looked at Ekant nervously. I wasn't sure exactly what his reaction was going to be. But I did expect him to make some sort of snide remark. Perhaps an "I told you so". But it never came. I sat waiting for his reaction, but he paid me no attention. Ekant simply picked up Bhagat's school bag and led him out into the courtyard and into the waiting car. He uttered not a single word to me.

I turned to Dhadhi, seeking an explanation, but she had already started a conversation with Jas about the weather. They both pretended that Ekant hadn't just blatantly ignored me and my injuries. Dhadhi and Jas only looked up when they were interrupted by the telephone.

"I will see who it is," Jas said as she walked over to answer the phone. "Hello? Yes, you too. Uh-huh, sure. She was just about to call you. One moment, I will give it to her." Jas set the receiver down and turned to me, "Esha, it is your mother."

"Oh, perfect timing," I said as I carefully climbed off the couch and made my way to the phone. "Mom?" I said softly into the receiver.

"My sweet, sweet child! How are you?"

"Okay, Mom. How are you and sis holding up?"

"We are good, just missing you. It is lonely without you."

"Yeah, I think I know what you mean," I said solemnly.

"Esha, is everything okay? I had a very bad dream last night, and all day I have carried a very bad feeling. A mother's heart never lies. Something is not right."

"I'm fine, Mom. I just…" I took a deep breath, knowing full well that she wasn't going to be very happy with what I had to say next. "It's weird that you called me right on cue. I was just about to call you to tell you about yesterday."

"Yesterday? What is it, Esha?" She already sounded alarmed. I closed my eyes, as if that would provide a shield to her shouting that I knew was soon to follow.

"I kinda…well… I sorta tried to get to Kiratpur on my own and—"

"What? Alone? *Esha, have you lost your mind?*" I pulled the phone away from my ear as she shouted at me.

"Mom, calm down! Look, I thought I could do it. Ekant admitted he was making me wait on purpose, and that I had attitude about staying here, like that mattered at all. I had no choice!" I said. I spoke quickly, trying to get as many words in as I could before she contined shouting.

"Of course you had a choice!" she snapped. "And what do you mean, you tried? Did you not reach Kiratpur? Oh, Waheguru, Esha, are you in trouble, are you okay? What on earth is going on over there? I worry so much about you, when are you going to become responsible—"

"Look, Mom, I'm sorry. I tried to go out on my own, and it didn't work, and I…well, I realized that it wasn't a good choice, and then I came back to the house. Okay?" I said, sidestepping the story about the attack. Details didn't seem like a very good idea right now. Besides, she was so far away, so why worry her?

"Well, as long as you are safe," she said, sounding calmer.

"And stuck here longer," I added remorsefully.

"You need to start paying attention to the signs, Esha. Your father sent you there for a reason other than to simply dispose of his ashes. There must be a reason for the delay. Remember, God has a plan for us all," she said, sending a shiver up my spine. I looked around to see where the breeze had come from, but everything was still. I hated that she brought her spiritual explanations into everything.

"Okay, enough of the 'God has a plan' stuff. You know I don't like it when you start talking like that. It freaks me out. Just tell the girls I say 'hi' and have them call me when they can." I wanted to tell Mandy about the result of her master plan.

"Tell them yourself," she replied.

"What?"

"They are here at the house. Girls, pick up the phone!"

"Hi, Esha!" Mandy, Carrie and Reet yelled together.

"Oh, hey! Wow, you're all there!" I said.

"Yeah, we all wanted to speak to you," Carrie answered. "Mandy and I are in the kitchen, and Reet picked up from the living room. So tell us, how've you been?"

"Um, okay. Hey Mom, are you still there?"

"Yes, sweetie."

"Let me talk to the girls alone for a bit."

"Sure, sure, I understand. I can find something else to do while you girls talk. Esha, I love you and remember—no more trouble."

"Yes, Mom, bye," I said impatiently.

"Trouble? What kind of trouble, Esha?" Mandy asked after my mom had hung up.

"Oh, where do I begin?" I sighed.

"What happened?" Reet urged.

"Yeah, you're worrying us," Carrie added.

"I got myself into a bit of a mess the other day—"

"So, did you try out my idea?" The excitement in Mandy's voice was unmasked. It was an almost too-perfect of a setup for me to reveal the disastrous result of her advice.

"Yeah, I tried it," I replied.

"No shit! And?"

"And, I got my ass kicked! Royally! So thanks for putting the idea in my head, Mands."

"I knew it was a bad idea!" Carrie cried.

"Mandy's ideas always have trouble written all over them," Reet added.

"Quiet, you two. Esha! What do you mean you got your ass kicked?" Mandy demanded.

"Long story short, the plan got screwed, and I ended up in some stranger's car who, surprise, surprise, turned out to be a total pervert!"

"Oh my god!" cried Carrie. "Then what happened?"

"What do you think happened? He tried to...well...to rape me," I answered as all three girls gasped in horror. Judging by their silence, I assumed they were at a loss for words. I understood their silence. I had said it in what sounded like no more than a faint whisper, but the term *rape* still terrified me out of my wits. Realizing that they were waiting for me to finish, I continued my account. "I fought him as much as I could. I ran away, he chased me and then...he grabbed me... and...threw me down...he pinned my arms down, and I thought..." I didn't realize how difficult it would be to recount my experience. I took a deep breath as I fought back the images of my ruthless assailant and the feel of his hands on my body.

"Oh, Esha," Reet whispered.

"It's okay. I got a concussion and some broken ribs, but other than that, I'm cool."

"So what happened to him? I mean, how'd you get away?" Carrie asked.

"Well, I'm not really sure what happened to him. Before he could…well you know, someone showed up and stopped him. It's a bit fuzzy, but it looked almost like…"

"Like what?" Carrie asked.

"Like…I dunno it sounds stupid, but like an angel. There was a light, and he was wearing all white—"

"Wow, that's so cool!" Carrie's reaction didn't surprise me. She always was the dreamer in the group.

"But, then again, I had just banged my head, so I could have imagined it. Besides he couldn't be one anyway."

"Why not?" Carrie asked, sounding disappointed.

"Because he was wearing a turban."

"An angel with a turban? Hmmm…well, you *are* in India. I guess anything is possible," laughed Mandy.

"Oh, shut up, Mandy. Anyways, I think the perv is in police custody, because Dhadhi said Ekant was at the station sorting it out."

"I thought Ekant was afraid of the cops?" Mandy asked.

"Only ones outside of Delhi, apparently," I replied.

"So you never made it to Kiratpur, and Ekant is sorting out your mess? How's he taking it?" Mandy asked.

"Very quietly. He hasn't said a word to me about it."

"Really? I thought this guy savoured any and every opportunity to insult you. What's gotten into him now?"

"Honestly, I don't know—" I started.

"Maybe he really cares, and he was worried about you, so much so that he's too angry to talk to you," Carrie suggested.

"I seriously doubt that, Carrie, but regardless, I'm back at square one. Only now Dhadhi is on my case to listen to my father's wish."

"Which is what? He wanted you to go to Kiratpur," Carrie said.

"Yeah, and he wanted me to discover the things that made him so happy and proud, like his country, the culture, the people and above all else, Sikhism."

"Excellent! So now begins another quest!" Carrie said, overjoyed.

"Oh stop it, Carrie," Mandy snapped. "Esha just escaped from a crazy ordeal. Let her relax. Esha, don't worry, girl, I'm sure it'll all go down all right. Soon your bro will take you to Kiratpur and then you can come home. I'm sorry that our idea, well my idea, didn't work out." Her voice became more sombre now. "I mean, if anything had happened. I mean it already *did*, but…if…I'm just really sorry that I got you into such a mess. I guess I really should learn to keep my brilliant ideas to myself, eh?"

"Mandy, it's okay. I mean, it was my choice in the end, and I chose to follow through on it," I reassured her.

"Hey, girls, Esha's mom is in front of me, making some very weird gestures with her arms. Call me crazy, but I think she wants us to hang up," Carrie said, bringing our conversation to an end.

"She's probably worried about the phone bill you're racking up," I laughed.

"Okay, Esha, we're gonna go. Take it easy, cool?"

"Yeah, you too."

"Hey Esha, can we talk for a second longer?" Reet asked in a lower voice after Mandy and Carrie had hung up.

"I was wondering what happened to you. What's up?"

"I think we should talk," Reet said.

"Sure."

"I just got to thinking," she began, "that perhaps what your Dhadhi is saying is right."

"You do?"

"I mean, come on, Esha, both you and I come from Indian families. That's where our parents are from. There's a whole world there that has shaped and made them who they are. Hours before he passed away, during your last meeting with him, your father went out of his way to talk about his character, his beliefs and his religion. I mean, of all the things he could have discussed, he chose *that*. Why would he spend his time confessing to you and persuading you to analyze his life? Why choose *you* and not someone else?"

"What's your point, Reet?" I demanded, growing impatient with her impromptu lecture.

"Aren't you the least bit curious?" she asked.

"Curious?"

"Yes, curious! There could be a whole other part of you that you haven't discovered yet, because you've been working so hard against it."

"Reet, where's this coming from?"

"I dunno, I guess hearing about what's been going on with you there in India, I've just been doing a lot of reflecting, and I've started paying attention to my own family, specifically my parents, and all the things they've been saying all these years. Things that sounded annoying and forced before, but now appear to be quite interesting, and some translate into some pretty useful lessons."

"Why didn't you say anything before?" I asked.

"Because it's so not us, Esha. We've always worked against our parents, trying hard not to conform. But today, hearing about what happened to you, I think enough is enough. Look, all I'm saying is that while you're there, you've got an opportunity. Honestly, what have you got to lose? Just go for it. At least in the end, you'll know that your father would be proud that you tried."

"Tried? Reet, I *am* trying. I'm here, aren't I?"

"That's not it, Esha. It's not about physically being there. That's not all of it—"

"Then what is?" I demanded.

"Discovery! Understanding! Accepting! Out of everyone you know, I'm the only one that can understand what you're going through. Besides, aren't you curious to know if there's more to you, or if you're capable of being much more than you thought possible?"

"I get what you're saying, Reet, but—"

"Listen, I gotta hang up before your mom comes back, but before I go, just know that I love you and I'm just trying to help you. The rest is up to you, but honestly, you're a smart person, Esha, so just stop being so stubborn and stop fussing around like a kid."

"Reet—"

"Gotta go! Bye!"

"Reet! Wait!"

Click. The line went dead.

Stop fussing around like a kid? How could Reet, of all people, say that to me? I wasn't being stubborn, and I wasn't being a kid...was I? I mean, I was trying, was I not?

"What is going on here?" I wondered aloud as I walked up to the roof. First it was my father's words about trying and

141

discovering, followed by Dhadhi's so-called words of wisdom about knowing who I was, and now, to top it all off, Reet had joined their group! "Argh!" I screamed. "They just don't see it from my point of view!"

I walked over to the edge of the balcony, trying desperately to shrug it all off. I looked out over the neighbourhood. As usual, it was a beautiful day. Right now, the deep blue sky and bright warm sun were my only source of comfort. I lifted my face to the sun and closed my eyes as the warm rays hit me.

Perhaps Reet was right. What was there to lose? I couldn't try going on my own again, not after... I was pretty much stuck until Ekant agreed to take me. What was I supposed to do in the meantime? Keep reading, drive myself crazy, remain holed up in this house and roast in this heat? I might as well just... I mean, it couldn't be *that* bad to try to see if... Maybe I'd have fun seeing this place, meeting its people. Sumi was pretty cool. I could just hang with her...maybe... Unable to answer my own questions, I sulked back into my room and allowed the rest of the day to pass by.

The next day, Sumi's parents showed up at the house with a bright red card and a box of sweets. Sumi's wedding to Daya had been planned. Both sets of parents had come together and decided that September 29th would make the ideal wedding day, even though it only left a month for preparations. Rano was rambling uncontrollably to Dhadhi about the wedding plans, the outfits and the money being spent. Her enthusiasm was so great that she even greeted me with a smile and a hug when I reluctantly joined them.

"And how are you, Esha?" she asked cheerfully, pretending that she didn't notice the state of my hair.

"Uh...oh...okay," I stammered. Her cheerful advance towards

me had caught me off-guard.

"Wonderful!" she exclaimed. "You know my Sumi is getting married! September 29th is the date. It is going to be a wedding to remember. The whole town will not forget it! Daya's family is leaving no room for complaints, and neither are we, of course. Oh, but dear, what will you wear? I do not imagine you brought any Indian outfits with you? But you must come to the wedding," she said, almost sounding worried, as if she cared about the details of my wardrobe.

I was taken aback by her sudden generosity towards me. Coming into the living room, I had expected her to lash out at me for the incident at the station and for getting Sumi involved. I was wrong. Rano was carrying on as if nothing had happened, and as if she actually *liked* me.

"We will have something made for Esha, of course," Dhadhi intervened. As she spoke, I remained speechless, still trying to figure out Rano's sudden shift in attitude. "And I am sure dear Sumi would love Esha's company until the wedding," she added with a comforting smile.

"Oh, of course, I agree!" Rano said, as if she had any choice in the matter. From what I had witnessed during my stay, no one in this neighbourhood had the guts to refuse Dhadhi.

I sat quietly and listened as they discussed the upcoming wedding. The large man, who I assumed was Sumi's father, sat quietly beside Rano and paid me very little attention. It was as though the whole ordeal hadn't happened at all. He just sat there sipping his tea and indulging in the plateful of sweets laid out before him. His long black beard was carefully trimmed into a sharp rectangular shape. His moustache was also carefully styled, both ends pointing sharply upwards. Every now and then, he nodded in agreement when prompted

143

by his wife. Finally, after an hour of bragging, Rano jumped to her feet and announced it was time to go.

After they'd left, I asked Dhadhi what had just transpired. "Dhadhi, why was Rano so...so..."

"Nice to you?"

"Yeah."

"Oh, Esha, dear," she said, laughing and shaking her head, "her daughter is getting married into a wealthy and well-respected family. These types of prospects do not come often, and not to everyone. There is no way she will let anything spoil that, not even your antics. To admit that Sumi had anything to do with your scheme would be a public humiliation for a woman like Rano. Daya has not said anything to his parents, probably for Sumi's sake. Therefore, Rano is acting quickly. Get the two kids married as soon as possible and just pretend like nothing happened."

"Is that so?"

"It would not be the first time that someone has turned a blind eye in order to achieve their goal," she explained.

"Well, it doesn't matter anyway. At least now maybe she'll lighten up on Sumi."

"We can never be sure what Rano says behind closed doors. She is not an entirely trustworthy woman, as she prides herself in competing with others all the time. Our dear Sumedha, on the other hand, is the exact opposite. She is a sweet and innocent child. Her loyalty is what persuaded her to help you, Esha. No other reason. The fault was yours, not hers."

"I know, Dhadhi, I'm—"

"Everyone is allowed one mistake, child. I have already forgiven you. I am not here to scold you. I am finally seeing you for the first time. You are my granddaughter, and I am so overjoyed that you have come. I just want to ensure that you remain safe. Now, while we wait patiently for Ekant to come around, you busy yourself with Sumi's wedding preparations," she ordered.

"Me?"

"Yes, you! It will be a good experience for you. Help out that poor girl. Give her some company and meet some new people. Get out of this house, but be careful, of course," she instructed.

"Sure, but it's like a month away. Ekant won't take that long, will he?"

"I cannot answer that," she shrugged. "In the meantime, try to enjoy it here."

I nodded as Dhadhi left me alone to contemplate the new situation. A wedding! Sumi's wedding, meeting new people, and shopping! Such fun, because that's *exactly* the reason why I came all this way!

Eventually I faced my defeat head on. "I've got nothing better to do, so why the hell not?" I let out a long sigh and held my face in my hands. "Besides, I'm dying of boredom!" I kept my face hidden as I slumped back onto the sofa. Something told me that with Rano heading up the wedding preparations, the coming weeks were going to be anything but boring.

Part Three

Acceptance

ELEVEN

I was right about things not being boring. Rano had the entire neighbourhood on its feet all through September. Every household was in action mode. Some were preparing decorations, some were preparing food, while others were at the beck and call of Rano and her million and one demands.

Each day, when I ventured into Sumi's home, it was crawling with people. Men were repainting the house and making repairs, while women crowded around jewellers and merchants who showcased the latest styles. And if that wasn't enough, cases upon cases of pure gold jewellery sets were stacked high on the tables. They were complete with earrings and heavy neck pieces. Rano sat proudly in the midst of this circus, and with a smile stretching from ear to ear, she showed off the pricey outfits and jewels to anyone that would listen.

Whoever said India was poor definitely hadn't seen a proper Indian wedding planned by the likes of Rano. Looking at the money being spent and the jewels being collected, you'd think it was a royal wedding. Preparations fit for a queen were definitely not what I'd expected for the simple, shy and innocent Sumi. So while Rano ranted and raved, Sumi and I quietly kept to ourselves and counted down to her big day.

Two days before the wedding, I walked over to their house to pick up the outfit I had reluctantly agreed to wear. As I wandered in through the main gate, Rano was once again yelling at the top of her lungs. The unlucky recipient this time was a poor fellow who stood motionless with his head down. I carefully snuck past them, doing my best not to attract her attention.

"I cannot believe this! All ruined!" she howled. "You idiot! What am I paying you for?"

"Ma'am—"

"Not one word! I do not want to hear your voice! Look at what you have done! Now I have to buy the milk all over again! What were you thinking?"

"I did—"

"Just go do your work! Leave me! Jyoti! Oye, Jyoti! Tell Jora to go buy more milk, fast! Argh! I cannot believe these servants!" she barked as she stormed back into the kitchen. Thankfully she hadn't seen me, and I reached Sumi's room unnoticed.

She was sitting quietly on her bed, fully absorbed in a book.

"How can you be so calm while your mother is freaking out downstairs?"

"Esha!" she said with a huge smile. "What has my mother done now?"

"Ha! Not *your* mother, I'm afraid, but some poor helpless man. Something about milk. I dunno, but she was laying it on him pretty thick. I feel sorry for anyone who gets in her way. She's getting worse with each passing day!"

"She is very stressed about the wedding. I am sure it will be fine," replied Sumi.

"Speaking about fine, look at you! You look pretty fine yourself!" I teased, but it was true. Sumi's skin was smooth and glowing. Her nails had been painted a rich red shade and the unibrow had finally been tweezed.

"Stop it," she said, blushing.

"What? It's true! Look at you. Oh, the blushing bride with the perfect skin, the perfect smile and the long flowing hair."

"Your hair is not so bad either. You said that your hair grew quickly, but I seriously did not think that in one month it would already reach below your chin!"

"Yes, well, I've tried to maintain it as best I can without a proper hairstylist," I replied as I ran a few fingers through my hair. "Anyway, forget me, this week is about you. I'm happy to see that someone is in good spirits in this house. No offence, but your mother is scary."

"I will not argue with you on that," Sumi said, laughing.

"Seriously though, you seem pretty calm for a girl who's getting married in two days. Aren't you the least bit nervous?"

"What is there to be nervous about? I am getting married to a man I have loved my entire life," she replied. "As children, we played together. In school, we were inseparable. You know, he always sat next to me in class and at lunch. He always remembered things when no one else did, like my favourite book or my birthday. He has always been my best friend."

"So when did it turn into love?"

"One day in our college English class, we began studying Shakespeare. As we read *Romeo and Juliet*, I began to understand love. Shakespeare puts it so eloquently and with such passion. And so the moment I first learned the meaning of the word 'love', I knew that it was forever attached to Daya's name. So how can I be nervous when just saying his name soothes my heart and my soul?"

"Soul? Love? Oh, be still my heart," I sighed, falling back on the bed.

"Esha, stop laughing! I am serious. Why do you insist on mocking me? Have you never loved?"

"Love?" I asked, almost choking on the word. "I'm not sure I even know what that feels like, really. I mean yeah, there have been crushes and stuff, but love? That's a bit serious, like serious bondage."

"Bondage? Oh Esha, you make it sound so negative!"

"I say it like it is, dude."

"Well, I suppose that in one aspect, we can call love a sort of bondage; to belong to someone, attraction, submission, all of these things. And yes, it is as if your soul is being pulled towards another. Your waking thought is your love, all day you are mesmerized by that love, and at night your last thought is again that love. So yes, we can attach the term 'bondage' to this class of emotions."

"See, you get it! Although you didn't have to make it sound so literary or complicated. It's plain and simple, bondage."

"But Esha, there is another meaningful term that must be attached equally, just as we have done for bondage."

"And that would be..."

"Freedom," Sumi replied cheerfully.

"Freedom? Now isn't that a contradiction to our first definition?"

"Well, yes," she replied.

"So how can we have bondage and freedom together? That doesn't make sense."

"Esha, even though you may be stricken by neverending thoughts of your loved one, to be in love instills in you an extraordinary level of confidence and strength. No matter how unrelenting your attachment may be, you develop this powerful sense of survival, and your fears begin to disappear, because you have an incredible person that supports you and loves you and...and you feel like...like..."

"Like you can do anything?" I offered.

"Yes! You do know what I am talking about!" Sumi cried out joyfully.

"Noooo... I've just heard it thousands of times in every sappy chick flick or television show. All that 'love conquers all stuff' is nonsense."

"Oh, my dear friend, it is not nonsense. One day you will know. One day your soul will feel a pull towards another. One day your heart will beat for someone just as my heart beats for Daya. One day it will—"

"Okay, okay, okay! Sumi, I get it! I'm happy to see you so in love. All this time I've known you, this is the first time I've seen you so excited about something—"

"I told you, it is love!"

"Ha! Okay, okay, enough already! Now, where's that outfit you're supposed to give me? I want to get back in time to nap before dinner."

"Nap?"

"Yeah, I'm tired."

"Not sleeping well?" she asked as she slipped off the bed to fetch my outfit.

"Nah, not really. I'm still...it's just since that night... I'm..."

"Still having nightmares?"

"Not nightmares really, more like flashbacks. The attacker I'll gladly forget, but it's that other thing."

"What other thing?"

"I just have a couple of blurred images from that morning that keep coming back. I can't even be sure what I saw or heard, but I'm almost certain I heard a guy's voice and saw in the light...a..."

"What? Esha what did you see?"

"A...turban..." I said quietly. I felt foolish just mentioning it again.

"A turban? Oh, you mean you saw a man with a turban! Did he help you?"

"Well, I kind of only remember seeing a turban. It was like a silhouette in the light. I think it was white, and he had a short beard, I think... Oh, I don't know. I was practically unconscious at that point! Regardless, another guy in the washroom would make sense, otherwise how would I have survived? I could not have imagined all that I heard and saw. Just because I didn't get a good look at the guy's face doesn't mean I imagined him, right? I'm not crazy, because he was real; a real human being saved my life," I concluded.

"Yes, of course."

"But I still don't get it. Why wouldn't he see me afterwards?"

"After what?"

"After everything that happened? I mean at the station or at the hospital?"

"Perhaps he was unable to see you. I mean, you were hospitalized. Maybe he could not visit. It could be for numerous reasons, Esha. You fell unconscious, and sadly none of us was there, so only he knows what really happened, whoever he was."

"You got a point. Anyways! Where's that outfit?" I changed the subject, but as much as I tried, I couldn't stop picturing the silhouette I had seen in the washroom that morning. I desperately wanted the blurred image in my mind to clear. I yearned to see his face.

"Here it is!" Sumi exclaimed as she carried over the pink outfit that I had sadly agreed to wear for her wedding. "The tailor brought it by this morning. Isn't it just beautiful?"

The bottom half was designed almost as tights. They

hugged my legs all the way down, highlighting my lean and tall figure. The top was like a dress. It had a round neck and was fitted to the waist, after which it flowed outwards just like a knee-high dress. I had wanted it to be sleeveless, but Dhadhi flat out refused, claiming that it would not be "appropriate" for me to "show so much skin to strangers." After much debate, we settled on short sleeves that cut off just above my elbows. The silk fabric was soft and the embroidery had turned out quite nicely. The outfit was completed by a long scarf referred to as a *dupatta*, which I was to wrap around and wear over my head during the morning ceremony.

"Do you like it?" Sumi asked nervously.

"Yeah, yeah, I do. Thanks for getting it stitched. It turned out great," I reassured her.

"Are you sure? You don't look so happy."

"No, I am, I mean, I really like the outfit, and I'm happy for you," I said, and this time I really meant it, but that didn't cure the anguish I felt inside. "It's just, your wedding is here. We're nearing October, Sumi, and I'm still here," I sighed. Looking at the outfit, I realized another month had gone by, and Ekant still hadn't said a word to me.

"Well, I am happy that you will be with me on my wedding day," she said apologetically.

"Oh, it's not that. It's just been so long, and I haven't fulfilled what I came here to do. It's frustrating. Have you ever heard of anyone being stuck like this for this long? Talk about bad luck, eh? Since that night when I went off on my own, Ekant hasn't said one word to me."

"Why does that bother you?" she asked.

"What do you mean?"

"Well, you never really spoke well of Ekant before. I

thought you would be happy that he is leaving you alone, so why does it matter now if he speaks to you or not?"

"Because...he's...he's done so much since," I admitted. "I mean, like how he made sure that psycho got what he deserved. Ekant really went out of his way, and now the least he could do is let me say 'thank you', you know? Instead, he's ignoring me. It's like I don't exist!"

"I do not think I will ever figure you out," Sumi replied, shaking her head. "You are upset when he speaks to you, and you are upset when he does not speak to you. I will never understand you."

"Anyways, I can't go on my own again, and my mom won't let me leave India, so my fate is in the hands of a guy who refuses to even look at me, and that's the bottom line. So what can I really do?" I threw my hands up in the air.

"You can enjoy my wedding. You know you will meet Daya; the *real* Daya!" she laughed.

"Very funny!" I said, throwing a pillow at her.

"I am sorry, but I could not resist! His friends will also be attending. Some of them are quite nice. Oh! I have an idea! Maybe you can meet some of them, Esha! You may find a liking to one of them. What say you?"

"Oh, please! I really doubt that, Sumi! Can we just focus on you, the bride-to-be?"

"Come on, be a good sport," she pleaded. She was actually being serious! "If you like one, then you might stay here in Delhi with me!"

"Sumi, no offence, but the moment I fall for an Indian guy, cows will have wings. Again, no offence, but marrying and staying here with an Indian guy would be even worse."

"You are impossible, Esha!"

"Come on, forget all this and rest up. Your big day is almost here."

"Oh, I cannot rest any more. I have rested enough."

"Well, in that case, let's go spy on your mother. I'm sure she's found someone else to yell at. What do you think?"

"Oh, yes," Sumi giggled. "I am right behind you." We went cautiously downstairs together, confident that Rano would not disappoint.

*　　*　　*

On Saturday morning, everyone fussed about in the house, getting ready. Bhagat ran around the courtyard in nothing but his underwear, screaming uncontrollably. Jas chased after him with a shirt, but he was too fast for her.

"Bhagat! Stop right now and put this on!" she demanded.

"No! It's too hot for clothes!" he yelled. At least someone else noticed the heat besides me. It wasn't until Ekant scolded him that Bhagat finally surrendered.

Jas lent me jewellery and make-up to complement my outfit. I stood before the mirror and took in my new look. I had to admit, the Indian look suited me quite well. I was the first to get dressed and waited impatiently as Ekant took his sweet time getting ready. I pleaded with Dhadhi to let me go on ahead, seeing as the ceremony was taking place at Sumi's house, but she insisted that we arrive as a family. Guests had already started to arrive by the time we finally got to the house.

"Esha! I was beginning to worry!" cried Sumi as soon as I stepped into her room. I was at a loss for words the moment I set eyes on her. Seated carefully before the dressing mirror in a blood-red Indian bridal *lengha*, she looked absolutely stunning. Her fitted short-sleeve blouse was cut off at the waistline, meeting with the long baggy skirt-like length which reached down to the floor. Her *dupatta* carefully covered her head then was neatly wrapped over her arm. Looking at her was like looking at a portrait. I don't think I had ever imagined Sumi could look as beautiful as she did at that moment. "Esha?"

"Oh, yeah...err...sorry..." I mumbled, trying to gather my thoughts.

"Did you hear what I said? What took you so long?" she asked, looking slightly worried.

"Dude, I'm really sorry. I know you wanted me here earlier, but Ekant held me up."

"Ekant? Is he finally talking to you again? Oh, how wonderful, you must be—"

"Not so fast, Sumi. He's still not talking to me, but let's not ruin the day talking about him. Why aren't you downstairs yet? The guests are already arriving."

"Oh, we are right on schedule. I cannot be downstairs yet, silly. No one should see me before it begins."

"So what can I do in the meantime?" I asked, standing next to her in front of the mirror.

"Hmmm...well, you can stand by the window and watch as Daya and his family walk in. Tell me what is going on. I want to know everything!" she exclaimed, her excitement growing with each passing moment.

"You want me to spy? Anxious, are we?" I teased.

"Oh, Esha, please!"

"Okay, okay," I said, walking over to the window overlooking the main entrance. By now there was a steady stream of people. Sumi's parents were stationed at the front gate, greeting the guests as they arrived. Whenever her husband's gaze would wander off, Rano would nudge him firmly with her elbow, bringing his attention back to the task at hand.

"Sumi, your dad looks as if he's going to doze off."

"I can imagine. He was very drunk last night. He spent much of the night dancing and singing. My mother had a tough time getting him into bed."

"No shit!" I laughed.

"Esha, must you swear?" she protested.

"Oh yeah, sorry," I said, remembering that she was overly sensitive to foul language. According to her, there was no logical reason why a person should feel the need to speak with a foul tongue, especially when there were so many "sweet" alternatives.

"Is he wearing his sunglasses?" she asked.

"He sure is."

"He is disguising his eyes. Fathers..." Sumi said with a long sigh.

"Yeah, fathers," I repeated.

The night before a wedding, the family of the bride and groom each hold a gathering at their respective homes. Certain rituals are performed to "ready" the bride or groom for the wedding ceremony.

Watching Sumi's father the night before and now this morning brought back memories of my sister's wedding. My father, who normally would go nowhere near alcohol, had let loose the night before.

"Oh, stop it, Kuli," my father had pleaded when my mother tried to talk him out of drinking. Kuli was his nickname for Mom when he was trying to charm her. "Today I am very happy! I am as happy as a father can be for his daughter.

Tonight I will drink, I will dance, and you will not stop me! Not tonight!"

The next morning, the headache, the bloodshot eyes and the nausea had convinced him that he would be happier without the alcohol. "This time I celebrated with drinking, but for your wedding, Esha, I promise I will not drink, and I will celebrate double! After all, you are my little princess, right? I will be the proud father telling everyone, 'that is my little girl!'" he had proclaimed, topping it off with his signature smile. *Oh, what I would give to see that smile once more.*

"Esha? Are you okay?" Sumi said as she made her way towards me. "You went quiet all of a sudden. Is something wrong?"

"Nothing, I just... I was thinking how sometimes we don't recognize how important some moments are until much later, when we long for them but find that it's already too late."

"I am not following," she said.

"Don't worry, it's nothing. I was just—hey! Get down!" I ducked below the windowsill, pulling Sumi down with me.

"What? What is it?" she cried.

"Sssshhhhh, keep your voice down!" I hissed. "Daya is here!"

"Oh no, did he see me? Did he see me?"

"Sssshhhhh, I said keep your voice down!"

"You also yelled."

"No, I didn't, *you* yelled! I'm whispering...a little loudly, but I'm still whispering! No, I don't think he saw you, he was just coming in. Go back over there!"

Sumi crawled away from the window and ran back to her seat in front of the dresser mirror. Realizing that I had no reason to hide, I stood up again and looked out over the courtyard.

The two families had gathered in a large circle. Men were taking turns placing garlands around one another's necks. I recalled this ritual from my sister's wedding. It signified the two families welcoming and accepting the union. Daya was in the middle and stood completely still, as if he was too scared or too nervous to move. He looked quite tall in his cream-coloured traditional Indian pantsuit, which consisted of a long-sleeved top reaching just below his knees and finished with gold embroidery. A bright red turban and a magnificent sword completed the outfit. He looked very princely and nothing at all like the crazy man who had attacked me at the station.

"Nice job, Sumi," I commented.

"Really? Does he look good?" she asked.

"Good? He looks amazing!"

I watched as Sumi's father greeted the groom's family and guests. Usually very quiet and without expression, he completely transformed when Daya made his grand entrance. Her father was now wide awake and overjoyed, and his bright smile could be seen clearly from where I stood. He bounced around from one person to the next, demonstrating his overflowing excitement.

An unusual emptiness seeped through me as I continued to watch her father. I began to realize what my own father's absence truly meant. If I ever decided to get married, he wouldn't be there to race between guests just as Sumi's father was doing right now. He wouldn't be flashing his famous smile; nor would he be there to support me or perform his duties as the father of the bride. *I'll be the fatherless bride...*

Just thinking about it put my stomach into knots. As I continued to watch Sumi's father, the emptiness grew. She had something I didn't. To this point, I had just mourned my father's passing and his absence at home. Until now, I hadn't even begun to consider his absence from my future life experiences. I hadn't thought about what it would feel like to get married without him there, or when I started my career or when I had kids, or even on my birthdays, Christmas, Father's Day. It was unimaginable!

"ESHA!" I jumped as Sumi's voice startled me. "What is the matter? I have been calling you for so long? You are so lost today. Is everything all right?"

"Oh...no, no, I'm sorry. Everything's cool, what's up?"

"They are calling me downstairs. It is time," she said joyfully.

"Already? Wow, okay, well let's jam," I said, taking a deep breath and forcing a smile.

"Yes. Now I begin the most wonderful day of my life," she said as she wrapped her arms around me. I quietly hugged her back, trying to push the images of my father out of my mind. Sumi's wonderful day had quickly turned sour for me.

The ceremony began as soon as Sumi made her entrance. The priest was seated behind the Guru Granth Sahib, the Holy Scriptures for Sikhs, which was perched on a beautifully decorated podium with four pillars on each corner, each one draped in flowers. The guests were seated on the floor facing the Guru Granth Sahib, women to the left and men to the right. Three men were seated on a smaller podium to the right, playing instruments and singing hymns. Sumi and Daya were sitting at the front, directly in the centre and facing the Guru Granth Sahib.

As the happy bride and groom took the required four laps around the Guru Granth Sahib, Sumi's brother, Yuvraj, and a selection of her cousin brothers escorted her. It was another custom that I had never quite understood. The laps represented an oath, from what I had been told by my parents. It was an oath that the bride and groom were making to each other and to God, but I had never understood why the brothers accompanied the bride. Usually six or seven would line up, one brother passing her on to the next as the groom led the way around. Therefore, there was always a third person included in the oath or the "sacred lap".

I looked around to see if anyone else objected to the tradition, but everyone looked pleased. Rano cried throughout the ceremony and was comforted by the many women who sat around her. As usual, she stole the spotlight.

When the ceremony was complete, the priest and the Guru Granth Sahib were carefully and respectfully escorted back to the Gurdwara by five men. Rano's trusted workers then turned the tent into a reception room while the guests indulged in an extravagant lunch. There was a constant stream of waiters with trays of food and drinks. A band and singer came out and began entertaining the crowd, and Sumi and Daya made another grand entrance, but this time as newlyweds.

Daya smiled enthusiastically while Sumi looked down at her feet, enacting perfectly the role of a shy new Indian bride. They sat down on two large red chairs that were of course fit for a king and queen. After they settled in, money began to flow as a huge line formed, and guest after guest congratulated the happy couple by placing bills in their laps.

I sat beside Jas in total boredom. Dhadhi was off chatting with a group of old friends. Bhagat was out on the dance floor with Yuvraj, thoroughly enjoying the live music. The other boys their age had joined in, and now each was trying to show off to the others. Ekant stood at the back, chatting with some men. I tried to smile when I caught his glance, but he just looked right through me as if I were invisible and went back to talking with his friends. Giving up, I slumped back in my chair and wished the night would end soon. Sumi noticed my sad state and waved me over to join her. She had a waiter pull up a chair beside her and Daya.

"Daya, this is Esha," she said as I took my seat.

"Well, it is a pleasure to finally meet you, Esha," he said warmly. "Sumi is always talking about you. I feel like I already know you!"

"Hi, Daya, it's nice to meet you as well. You both look great, and the wedding was amazing and a lot of fun," I said, thinking that's what people usually said to a bride and groom.

"Thanks, and you look very beautiful. Sumi, I am going to have to set her up with one of my friends, or they will never forgive me!"

"I was just telling—"

"No! Wait, hold up, you two," I said, cutting them off. "That's okay. I'm good."

"They are not all bad, you know," Daya insisted.

"I'm sure they're not, but I'm good."

"If you insist, but do not blame me if you get a lot of stares today. These boys see a lot of foreigners living in Delhi, but for some reason they always find beautiful foreign girls exotic."

"Oh, Daya, tell your friends Esha is off limits!" Sumi scolded.

"My wife, I have already told them. Everyone in town has been talking about Esha. You know this."

"Excuse me?" I interrupted.

"Daya's right, you have been here awhile," Sumi answered. "Everyone knows who you are, and Dhadhi and Ekant command a lot of respect. Do not be alarmed if any of the ladies here today

162

try to set you up with their sons, or if their sons try to—"

"Oh, please!" I said, laughing.

"It is true, Esha. Sumi is right to warn you. These ladies are like a lioness, preying on beautiful girls, especially foreign ones that they can entrap for their sons. I stopped my mother long ago by telling her that my heart already belonged to a special someone."

"And she was cool with that?"

"Well of course, why not?" he said casually.

"Remember that he is a male, Esha," Sumi pointed out. "It is only we girls who cannot express so freely our desire to marry the one we love or even admit to our parents that we have found such love. I was fortunate that my parents were smitten with Daya and his family." She turned to him and smiled. He returned her admiration with an intense look. These two were inescapably in love, and watching them now, I suddenly felt like a third wheel.

"Hey, I'm gonna go get something to drink. You two enjoy!" Neither of them responded as I quickly walked away.

I made my way to the bar to grab a soda. There was no hope of getting a shot of whisky, or a shot of anything for that matter. I was confined to behaving like a good little Indian girl, so I opted for an orange soda.

My walking up to the bar had caused a stir among the men, who were well on their way to becoming insanely drunk. None of them said anything to me; they just stared as if I were in a showcase. They didn't even flinch when I glared back, so I grabbed my soda and stepped out of the tent. The sun was starting to set, and the temperature had finally cooled a bit. It felt good to escape the commotion in the crowded tent. I had come to adore Sumi, but truth be told, this was one boring party.

My sister's reception, on the other hand, had been a blast. The DJ had played music until one a.m., since almost everyone had refused to leave the dance floor. Johnny and the boys had hooked us girls up with an endless stream of drinks, after which the rest of the night had become somewhat of a blur. It all seemed so long ago. The type of parties I use to go to all seemed like they were a part of a whole other lifetime.

"You look lonely. Why not join us?" came a male voice. He spoke in Punjabi. I spun around to find four guys standing at the side of the house. Each was holding a drink. None was dressed for a wedding. Three were wearing pants with polo shirts, while the fourth wore just blue jeans and a black t-shirt. They looked like definite crashers.

I looked away and began walking back towards the party. Before I could reach the tent, however, the one in jeans ran over. He stood with both arms stretched out, blocking my path.

"What do you think you're doing?" I demanded, crossing my arms over my chest.

"I said why not join us? You did not reply. I just want an answer," he said. He was standing close enough that I could smell his cheap cologne, see the stubble on his face, and the horrendous amount of gel that he had smeared onto his hair. He would make the perfect thug in any film.

"Get lost!" I snapped.

"Wow. You're a fiery one," he snickered, taking a step closer. His advance towards me triggered images of my first attacker. I quickly stepped back. It was disconcerting to think how close that pervert had come that morning at the station, and now I had to deal with this creep who belonged on the set of *Grease* instead of in a houseful of Indian people. Speaking of people, where the hell were all those annoying and strict Punjabi parents? Couldn't anyone see this creep was bothering me?

"Listen, I need to get back to my family. So just let me go," I said in a more pleasant manner, hoping he'd get the message.

"Hmmm...I don't like that option," he replied.

"Fine then, you stay here!" I retorted as I turned in the opposite direction and made straight for the house. I could hear him laughing with his buddies behind me, but I concentrated only on the wide open door of the house. I walked as fast as my feet would take me.

The creepy voice of my first assailant kept playing over and over in my head. Weeks had passed, and I had virtually pushed that night out of my mind, but one moment had brought it all back. A stupid, greasy thug had brought it all back; the chase, his hot breath, his sweaty hands, that hopeless feeling...

I ran into the house and took refuge behind the door. I held my breath and listened carefully. The music and chatter from inside the tent was still very loud, but there was no sign of the guys and no sound of footsteps coming in my direction. I let out a sigh of relief. No one had followed me.

I closed my eyes and focused on my breathing. "Just breathe, Esha. Just breathe," I repeated over and over until my heart stopped racing.

"Excuse me, are you okay?" came another male voice, only this time in English.

"I'm fine. Leave me alone, will you!" I growled.

"Are you sure? You are hiding behind a door," the voice said, still sounding very calm. I opened my eyes and saw that I indeed was still hiding behind the door. Feeling silly, especially now that someone had caught me, I slowly pushed the door away.

Standing before me was a tall man of medium build. He was wearing a grey suit and tie with a small red turban. His beard was very short, hugging his face and not extending further like those of most turbaned men I had seen so far. His large grey eyes, well-defined eyebrows and creamy complexion were very attractive. Whoever he was, he definitely was well-to-do. His demeanour was so incredibly pleasant that I just simply stood there and sized him up. He appeared to be somewhere in my age range, maybe a tad older; mid-twenties, not any older than that.

"Miss, you okay?" he asked, snapping me out of my daze, which only made me feel even more foolish.

"Yeah, I'm...fine. I'm fine," I said, clearing my throat.

"Sure? You *were* hiding behind that door," he said, almost sounding amused.

"I...wasn't...hiding," I stammered.

"I believe you were. I found you—"

"I said I wasn't, so I wasn't," I said sharply. My face was starting to feel hot. *Esha, you're letting a guy in a turban embarrass you. Get a hold of yourself and do it quick!* "I was just taking a break from the party. It's been a long day."

"Yes, it has," he said, with a smile that showcased his perfect teeth.

"Anyway, I should get back to the tent. Sumi must be wondering where I am."

"Well, I was headed there myself. I can walk with you," he said, heading out the door. I wasn't too keen on walking anywhere with a complete stranger, but I also didn't want to risk running into those creeps again. I hesitated as I weighed my options and eventually decided that going with this guy felt safer.

"Are you coming?" he called.

"Yeah, right behind you," I said, rushing to catch up. I followed him back into the tent and sat down beside Sumi again.

"Esha, where were you for so long? I do not know what to say to any of these people. There are so many of them!"

"I was just getting some air, and some creeps got in my way."

"Oh no! How? Why? Who was it?"

"Sumi! Calm down, people are looking," I hissed. Sumi quickly dropped her eyes, afraid she might have briefly tarnished her shy-bride reputation. "I'm fine, and it was nothing. I think they were just fooling around, but still it's crazy that this keeps happening with me. Then I met this guy who walked me back here."

"You met a guy? Who did you meet?" she asked, looking up again.

"He was right..." I looked around and saw no trace of him. "He was right with me. I followed him in and then... I don't know. He's gone."

"Well, I must see him. The look on your face tells me he must be really something special."

"What?" I said, choking on the sip of water I had just taken.

"Well, look at you! Your face is flushed, Esha. He must have made quite an impression, because all the time you have been here in Delhi, I have not seen you like this. There is a sparkle in your eyes. I *must* know who has done this to you!"

"Honestly, Sumi, I think the heat is getting to you."

"Esha Puah! Esha Puah!" Bhagat cried as he ran up to me.

"Yes, Bhagat?"

"Dhadhi wants to leave. She said I should tell you thaaat... oh, I remember! She said I should tell you that you should go with her!" he exclaimed, overjoyed that he had successfully relayed the message. It was times like these that I questioned whether it was possible for Ekant to have such a jubilant and adorable son.

"Where's your mom?" I asked.

"Momma and I will come after papa eats. You have to go now," he ordered.

"All right, tell her I'm coming," I replied. Bhagat obliged by nodding and running back out of the tent. "Sorry Sumi, seems like I gotta go."

"I wish you could stay longer, at least until I leave with Daya and his family."

"It's gonna be tough not having you around here," I lamented.

"I am still so close, Esha. It is only a few more minutes. Promise me you will visit."

"Call me any time, and I'll be there."

"Okay then, take care," she said, wrapping her arms around me. "Stay strong and keep faith. Waheguru will take you to your goal when the time is right."

"Well, *He* seems to be taking his sweet time," I quipped.

"Have faith, Esha," she said more firmly.

"Bye, girl. You enjoy Daya, and you also stay strong. Later, Daya!"

"Bye, Esha. Come over soon. I still have to introduce you to my friends!" he laughed.

"For sure," I said sarcastically. I left Sumi and Daya to contend with their now drunken male guests and ventured outside once again, this time to find Dhadhi.

I found her waiting by the front gate chatting with Rano. I hung back while the two ladies bid farewell. I still had no desire to cross paths with Rano. Now that her daughter's wedding was over, her ego would be sky high, and she had nothing to lose by attacking me. After a few moments, Rano left Dhadhi and quickly chased down another family that was trying to make a swift exit.

168

"Dhadhi, you want to head home?" I asked, approaching her.

"Yes, child. I have had too much, more than this body can handle."

"Shall I walk you, Dhadhi ji? It is quite dark." Immediately recognizing that deep yet soothing voice, I turned around. It was the same guy in the red turban. He had mysteriously reappeared.

"Oh, son, you are right, but it is not a long walk. You need not bother," she replied kindly.

"Oh, no bother, Dhadhi ji. It would give me pleasure to see you home safely," he insisted.

"Well, how can I refuse such a kind gesture?" Dhadhi replied.

"But Dhadhi—" I started in an attempt to warn her of the potential danger, as he was still a stranger.

"Come along!" she called, walking out the gate. Did Dhadhi know this guy? Was he following me?

I watched him carefully from behind as he walked with Dhadhi down the street. They made small talk as they strolled side by side. Rapidly, however, I lost all interest in their words and became absorbed in watching him. He carried himself in such a graceful manner, that it was almost...almost...*dreamy*.

"Oh, Esha, snap out of it!" I said to myself.

"Child, are you okay?" Dhadhi said, stopping to look at me.

"Oh, sorry...umm...nothing..." I stammered. Shit, I had said it out loud! Once again I had behaved foolishly in front of this mystery guy. Yet he just smiled and carried on with his conversation. Still embarrassed, I slowly tagged along. A few moments later, we were finally in front of our gate.

"Thank you, son, we are home. Take care," Dhadhi said, opening the door and walking in.

"No problem, Dhadhi ji, and goodnight!" he said, waving behind her. "And to you too, Esha," he said softly.

"You know my name?" I asked in shock.

"Why, of course," he replied.

"How? And you never mentioned *your* name."

"Well, you never mentioned yours either, but I still managed to know it," he said as he dragged a stick along the dirt road.

"Really? Well if you want me to know your name, I'm sure you can easily tell me," I said, somewhat snobbishly. I didn't want him to think I cared.

"Hmmm... Yes, I suppose I could," he replied as he tossed his stick away. With a smile, he waved and retreated towards Sumi's house.

"Wait!" I called out, but he didn't turn back. Instead he disappeared around the corner. How rude! He hadn't even said his name. How dare he brush me off like that!

I turned to walk into the house, but something in the road caught my eye. There was something written in the sand where he had stood talking to me. I crouched down and read it carefully: ANGAD

"Now, that wasn't so difficult, was it?" A smile crept onto my lips as I repeated his name. "Angad." It had a nice ring to it. Soothing, just like him. I closed the gate behind me and headed to my bed, ending what had become quite an extraordinary day.

TWELVE

During one semester in university, I had taken a course on International Human Rights Law. Throughout the course, one topic had stood out the most and caused me great discomfort. That topic was infanticide.

Our professor had explained in great detail about some of the cases in South Asia, where the practice was most commonly reported. In some remote villages, a few families still practiced it, but people were largely starting to shift away from committing this monstrous act. As the international community began to discuss it and condemn it, many people did not want to be associated with the term "infanticide". Too disturbed to dig into it any further, I had shrugged it off as just a barbaric practice that had nothing to do with my life. Then on one sunny October afternoon in Delhi, every lecture the professor had given on the subject came flashing back.

I was in the courtyard, reading as usual, while Dhadhi sat doing her prayers, when a crowd of women came crashing through the front gate.

"A grave sin has been committed!" screamed the first of the ladies to break through.

"It is the end of the world!" cried another. There were a lot of them, at least fifteen, and they all looked alike. All were dressed in traditional Indian outfits; some had their heads covered with scarves, and others didn't. Most looked familiar, since I had seen

171

them in town, while a few were complete strangers to me.

"Waheguru save us! Bless this child!" yelled the lady, holding the baby, which had been wrapped in a red cloth and was crying non-stop.

"What in Waheguru's name has happened?" Dhadhi asked, rising to her feet. "What is all this commotion, and who *is* that child?"

"Oh, Dhadhi," sobbed one of the younger ones as she stepped forward. "A grave sin has been committed. Someone has tried to kill this baby girl. Someone has tried to kill her!"

"Waheguru! What are you saying? Who has done this?"

"Dhadhi, my husband recently started working in the fields. He travels to the neighbouring villages, and this morning, while he was walking, he thought he heard something. After a while, he realized it was a baby's cry. Dhadhi, he found this poor baby girl wrapped and buried!"

"Buried? Alive?" I gasped in horror.

"Yes, alive."

"But how...how did he hear her?" I asked as if it mattered. If she were buried beneath the ground, it seemed unlikely that any passerby would hear a small baby's cry. I knew it wasn't exactly the right time to get technical, but I couldn't contain my curiosity.

"Whoever those demons were, they did not dig deep enough. Her face was covered in a cloth. I guess, God willing, she still had air to breathe."

"Oh, Waheguru, how can this happen? Will these people never learn?" cried Dhadhi.

"Dhadhi, we do not know who she belongs to, and what if they try to kill her again? We brought her to you for help. Please, tell us what to do!"

"Oh, I am unsure. By committing such an act, her parents have lost all right to her, but she is still theirs—"

"Dhadhi!" I yelled. "You can't possibly send her back! Those people are animals. Backward Indians is what they are!"

"Esha, do not say such things," she snapped.

"Why not? I used to hear about this, but never thought... Now I'm *witnessing* it. What's wrong with this country?" I yelled angrily. The group of women gathered around us just stared blankly as I ranted.

"Esha, one family's actions do not speak for all families. Right now we need to decide what to do with this poor innocent child."

"Simple. Call the police," I suggested, wondering why someone hadn't done that already.

"They will not come," said one of the women. "These cases are messy, and she is just a baby girl. The police will not care unless we throw money at them. There is no way to find out whose daughter she is. Even if we do find out, they will just pay the police to leave them alone. It is hopeless."

"But who will care for her then?" Dhadhi asked. The question wasn't directed at anyone in particular. She was already clutching her prayer book and pleading with God. "Waheguru, she needs a home. Who will help this child?" She took the baby in her arms and held it close to her chest as if it were her own.

"I will help her, Dhadhi," said a voice from behind us. All eyes immediately turned in the direction of the voice. It was Ekant. He walked up to Dhadhi with a determined look and gently took the baby girl into his arms. He smiled as the baby settled in comfortably and finally stopped crying. "Every child born into this world has a home," he continued. "Perhaps hers

173

is not with the people who gave birth to her, and that does not mean that her home does not exist. She is God's child, and she has been saved, perhaps because someone is in need of her love. Do not worry, I will help her. I have an idea," he said confidently. "Dhadhi, I may be late. Please do not worry about me."

"Oh, my child, you warm my heart," Dhadhi, said crying softly. "Go now, and may God be with you."

I stared at Ekant, shocked at his surprising display of humanity. I couldn't believe that this was the same man who had insulted me repeatedly and was holding me hostage in this city.

"Wait! Take me with you!" I blurted as he turned to leave.

"Esha, this is no simple task. It may be very dangerous," Dhadhi warned.

"It doesn't matter, I want to go with Ekant," I insisted. I don't know why I even cared, but after his little show of human feeling, something inside me just wanted to be a part of whatever it was he was planning to do. "I want to help. Please, Ekant? Who knows, maybe my foreigner skills will come in handy."

Ekant turned around, and for the first time in a month, he looked me in the eye. After studying me carefully for what seemed like forever, he finally nodded. I tossed my book on the chair and ran behind him.

"Wait," he said, stopping at the gate.

"What?"

"Please put on something more appropriate if you are to accompany me out of this house."

"Appropriate?" I looked down. I realized I was still wearing a tank with shorts. "Oh gosh! Fine, I'll go change!" I ran into the house and threw on the first pair of jeans and t-shirt I could find. By the time I came back down, Chotu had the car ready, and Ekant was comforting a clearly distraught Jas.

"Oh, Esha, be careful, okay? Stay close to Ekant and stay out of trouble," she pleaded.

"I'll be fine," I said, trying to reassure her. I didn't under-stand why everyone was so worried; I mean, we were just going to go find this baby a home. It couldn't be that big of a problem.

"Okay, let us leave now," Ekant announced. "Esha, you can hold the baby." He handed me the tiny wrapped bundle. The baby was quiet; the women had cleaned her up and fed her some milk. I sat down in the car and held her somewhat awkwardly. I didn't exactly have much experience with babies.

"She is a baby, not a bomb!" Ekant snapped, noticing my discomfort.

"Sorry, I'm a bit new at this."

"Then why did you insist on accompanying us?" His curiosity almost sounded genuine.

"I'm not sure," I admitted. "Something just told me I should."

"I see," he said, turning to face the front again. Call me crazy, but I could swear I saw a smile on his face.

"So where are we headed?" I asked eagerly.

"We are going to the villages that border the area where the baby girl was discovered."

"Why? I mean it's pretty clear they don't want her!"

"We need to speak to the parents. Everyone deserves a chance to atone for their sins, Esha. Besides, we cannot be certain that this was their choice until we speak to them face to face."

"Do you hope they'll take her back?"

"We have to try. After, that we will see," Ekant replied.

We drove east for what seemed like an hour. Chotu had spoken with the man who'd found the baby, and according to him, the girl had been found near some villages bordering the

Delhi and Uttar Pradesh divisions. The plan was to first find out which village had given birth to a baby girl either the night before or earlier that morning. I was made to sit in the car holding the tiny girl while the two men made their enquiries. I was sceptical of their plan, but Chotu explained that every village contained at least one lady who knew everything about everyone and loved to share it, kind of like a "Gossip Queen". The trick was to find her without drawing any unwanted attention. I thought the plan was pretty ridiculous, not to mention a waste of time, but my protests fell on deaf ears.

We came up empty in the first two villages. There had been no births reported in the past twenty-four hours. The third closest village to the division was actually quite far out and particularly small. As we drove through it, we attracted several unpleasant stares from the men. This time around, Ekant ordered Chotu to remain in the car with me. Half an hour later, he reappeared.

"So what's the verdict?" I asked as he approached the car.

"I think this is the village," he said. "There is a woman who gave birth to a daughter in the early hours of the morning. The family has told the town folks that they sent the child to the city to live with an aunt who is barren."

"So what makes you think they're lying?" I asked.

"According to the village people, this is the third female baby they have sent into the city. The woman I spoke with revealed that there are past cases of female babies mysteriously disappearing in this village. Something tells me this is our village."

"What do we do, sir?" Chotu asked.

"I am not too sure," Ekant replied. He let out a loud sigh as he looked down at the baby in my arms.

"How about we surprise them?" I suggested. "Just confront

them with the baby. Their reaction will tell us the truth."

"It could be dangerous," Ekant warned.

"We have no other choice. The police are out of the question, right?"

"They will not care to do anything, at least not any time soon," Ekant answered. After a few moments, he gave in. "Perhaps your idea will work. Chotu, get the pistol out of the car and follow us. Come, Esha, but be very careful and stay beside me."

"Okay!" I said, getting out of the car. Excitement was rising within me. I felt protective of the baby held tightly in my arms, but I was experiencing a unique and exhilarating feeling. Hearing Ekant say that it might be dangerous didn't scare me; instead it made me feel stronger. He was finally doing something I had suggested. I couldn't believe it.

I followed him through a series of small dirt roads. People peeked out of their homes and stopped in the streets as we passed by. Chotu walked close behind us, fully alert, with his pistol tucked beneath his shirt. Ekant had no need for extra protection. As usual, his religious Sikh dagger, a kirpan, was proudly displayed over his shirt and trousers, and with his size, anyone would think twice before offending him. We stopped before a white gate, the colour of mourning for Indians. How fitting...

"Is this it?" I asked, looking up at the gate.

"From what I was told, this is the house. Now, be on your guard. Esha, remain silent."

"But—"

"Not a single word," Ekant said firmly. Realizing this wasn't the time to argue, I nodded.

While Ekant knocked and asked the servant if we could see the man of the house, I stood to the side with the baby, praying that she would remain silent, at least until the time was right. We were finally ushered in. The servant looked confused when I appeared, but before he could say anything, I strode ahead defiantly and joined Ekant and Chotu. Before the servant introduced his master, Ekant stepped in front of me, shielding me and the baby from view.

"What can I do for you, sir?" the man asked. His voice was deep and his words slightly slurred.

"There really is no easy way of explaining why I am here. I mean no offence to you, sir, but this morning I was faced with a gruesome reality. Something very terrible has happened," Ekant replied. There was not the slightest hint of fear in his voice. He spoke firmly and with complete confidence.

"And how does that concern me?" the man asked, sounding annoyed.

"Upon my enquiry, I have been led here, sir, to your doorstep."

"Here? Speak clearly," the man demanded.

"I understand you had a baby girl born here this past night," Ekant said calmly.

"Well, yes. The whole town knows this. I do not see how this concerns you," the man said carefully.

"I wish to give her my blessing if possible."

"She is not here. I...I have a sister, in the city. She cannot have children, so...I have given her my daughter," the man replied. I could hear the guilt in his voice now.

"Are you sure?" Ekant persisted.

"Excuse me? Who are you to ask this? I do not even know you!"

"How about you tell me if you recognize this baby?" Ekant stepped out of the way, revealing me and the baby girl. The man gasped as I displayed his living and breathing child to him.

He was huge and his eyes were bloodshot, probably the result of heavy drinking trying to forget his sins. He stared at the baby in shock and terror. His guilt was now obvious for all to see.

"What is...she...where did..." He struggled with his words and took a huge leap back, as if he didn't have the courage to be in such close proximity to the child he believed to have already been successfully disposed of.

"We found her exactly where you buried her." Ekant's tone was now ice cold.

"That is...that is not my child! Get out of here!"

"You deny her even now?" roared Ekant. "You barbaric man! You are an insult to all fathers!"

"She is not mine! I have no filthy daughter! Get out of here! Ramu, throw these people out!"

"You have committed a grave sin! How dare you try to kill your own daughter? She is your own flesh and blood!" Ekant's voice was growing louder and louder with each word. His anger was rising. I was speechless.

"Get out of here now, or I will tear you into pieces!" the man warned.

"Not until you accept your daughter," Ekant demanded.

"Never! Now, you leave me no choice!" the man barked as he pulled a rifle off the wall and pointed it directly at Ekant. Chotu was quick to react and pulled out his pistol, aiming it at the man. The servant, Ramu, and I stared at the three men in disbelief without a clue as to what to do next.

"Nobody has to die here today," Ekant said, sounding calm again. "But if one decides to shoot, then all die together. No one will walk away alive."

"Please, that's my brother!" I blurted out. "We'll leave. Just put the damn gun down," I pleaded.

"Brother?" The man nudged Ekant in the chest with the gun.

"Yes, my *only* brother! You don't want her, that's fine, we'll leave." I was trembling, but I couldn't refrain from speaking. Ekant gave me a stern look. He had warned me not to speak, and I had once again disobeyed.

"I said, that is not my daughter," the man said. "*Now leave!*"

"Okay, we're leaving," Ekant replied. "Chotu, lower your pistol. Esha, follow me."

We all stepped back slowly and carefully. The man stood perfectly still, holding his rifle firmly in both hands, his gaze fixed steadily on our movements. On my way out I caught a glimpse of a woman looking through a window. I turned to get a better look. She had tears streaming down her face. Her eyes were locked on the baby. No one, not even I, could ignore the look in those eyes. It was a mother yearning for her child.

"Esha!" Ekant called.

I took one last look at the distraught mother before joining Ekant and Chotu outside. Finally, away from the house, we all stopped to catch our breath.

"Well, that was a bust," I said, disappointed by our failure. "That man is crazy!"

"It is a shame, the mentality of people. A real shame," Chotu said casually, as if what had just happened was an everyday occurrence.

"Never fear, they will answer one day. We all do at some point," Ekant said.

"I hope they get theirs soon enough," I said bitterly. "He almost killed us!"

"Esha, thank you," Ekant said, looking at me.

"Thank you? For what?" For the very first time, he actually sounded sincere.

"Pleading for my life, even though I had told you not to speak," he answered as we began walking back to the car. "I have never been called...a brother before."

"Yeah, well, neither have I. I mean, I've never called anyone that before...you know...a brother," I said sheepishly.

"Sir, where do we go now?" Chotu asked, interrupting our warm yet totally unexpected sibling moment.

"Hmmm...well, I guess it is on to our second plan, Chotu."

"There's a second plan?" I asked.

"I have a friend, Rohan. His sister lost her husband and daughter in a tragic accident a few months ago. She has been quite distraught. She now lives with Rohan, and I have already spoken with him today about our situation. He agrees that it will be a good idea if his sister adopts the baby girl."

"You sure it'll work?" I asked.

"I have faith that it will, Esha. You worry too much," Ekant said, smiling. He was definitely sounding lighter. Could he possibly be letting up on me?

We drove back towards Trilokpuri and ended up at a house in the neighbouring town of Kalyanpuri. Chotu beeped the horn twice, and the blue gates swung open. We pulled into a courtyard where two women were sitting on straw beds sorting through vegetables. I assumed they were preparing dinner, since that's all women did around here. They woke up and prepared the morning meal, then busied themselves with the afternoon meal and dinner. That was their day.

Chotu opened my door and let me out with the baby in my arms as Ekant walked over and shook hands with a tall and handsome, clean-shaven man. His hair was short and combed back carefully. He was tall like Ekant and well-built. Watching him, I was reminded of my friendly encounter with

Angad at Sumi's wedding. I had managed to see two good-looking guys in two weeks. Not bad, not bad at all. I waited for Ekant's cue before walking over and joining them.

"Rohan, this is Esha and the baby girl we discussed," Ekant said.

"Hello, Esha," Rohan said, smiling.

"Hi," I replied as I looked up and met his gaze. His hazel eyes were soft and comforting.

"Esha, Rohan's sister has agreed. She is to take the girl," Ekant informed.

"Oh, wow, that's really amazing. Where is she?" I asked, looking at the two women on the straw bed.

"She is inside. Please follow me," Rohan replied.

We were led into a living room, where we all waited anxiously while Rohan went to get his sister. Moments later, she appeared. She was a frail-looking young woman. Her face was sunken and her eyes had dark circles around them. The grief over her recent loss had taken a severe toll on her. When she saw the baby in my arms, however, her eyes lit up, and she instantly came alive. She ran over and held out her arms.

"Can I?" she asked, already weeping.

"Oh, yeah, I mean, yes, of course," I answered, placing the child in her arms. She held the baby close and wept quietly, thanking us and God for making her a mother once more.

I hadn't imagined how profound this moment would be. On the drive over, I had still been affected by what had transpired in that crazy man's house. Until this very moment, it was just about finding this baby a home. I didn't realize how we would be affecting others. This woman, who was so visibly scarred by the loss of her husband and child, seemed almost whole again. Watching her now, it seemed like she had just found a new reason to live. When I handed her the baby, I helped give her hope and purpose, even though this child had no blood relation to her whatsoever.

"We should take our leave," Ekant announced.

"Please, brother, stay a bit longer," Rohan appealed.

"No, Rohan. It has been a long day. We must return, as Dhadhi ji will be worried. Come, Esha." I followed Ekant and Rohan to the car, where Chotu stood waiting for us.

"Thank you for this gift," Rohan said.

"We should thank you for your help," Ekant replied.

"It was nice to finally meet you," Rohan said turning to me. "I hope you will visit. I am curious to know what Canada is like, and I am sure my sister will need help." He smiled, and my heart skipped a beat. His eyes glistened in the twilight.

"Um..." I couldn't seem to catch my breath.

"Sure, Rohan," Ekant said, stepping in. "Chotu will bring Esha around, and you too, brother, come visit. It has been too long since you have come around."

"Of course. Have a safe drive home. Bye, Esha."

"Bye, Rohan," I said weakly. I quickly hopped back into the car and exhaled.

"He is a nice guy, do you agree?" Ekant asked.

"Uh-huh," I murmured. "Nice."

*   *   *

The women were still gathered at the house when we returned. Jas said that they had refused to leave until they heard news of our quest. As expected, everyone was outraged to hear of the father's reaction. We made sure to leave out the part where we were threatened by a rifle, especially since Jas and

Dhadhi were already so terrified that we had confronted the family. Nevertheless, they were overjoyed when we revealed that Rohan's sister had taken the baby in. Comforted by the conclusion, the women finally left.

Jas prepared an exceptionally delicious dinner that night, and we all sat around and enjoyed each other's company. For the first time since my arrival, I felt as though I belonged. I was unusually cheerful and couldn't stop smiling at Dhadhi's stories. I laughed as Bhagat pranced around the dining table, refusing to finish his food while Jas chased him. They were a good, whole family. They were *my* family.

Shortly after midnight, I decided to call it a night. Making my way to the staircase, I thought about how the girls would react when I told them about the day's events. My thoughts were suddenly interrupted by Ekant.

"Esha, may I speak with you?" he asked. I turned around and saw that he had followed me to the stairs.

"Sure, what's up?"

"Let us go to the roof and speak," he said, leading the way. I hurried behind, curious about what he wanted to say.

We stepped out onto the rooftop. Since it was October, the nights were becoming cooler. The full moon was bright and illuminated the vast, clear sky. As always, it was a beautiful night. Ekant stopped at the edge of the roof overlooking the western part of the town. In the distance I could just barely make out the city lights.

"Esha, I wanted to commend you on the way you handled yourself today. You did well," he said without looking at me. His gaze was fixed on the moon, as though he were entranced by its beauty.

"I, uh, I didn't really do anything," I replied, slightly taken aback by his compliment. "I'm not sure I even understood what was happening. I mean, it was so fast, you know."

"Still, it is not an easy thing to see; a father denying his newborn even after he has been confronted with his sin of trying to bury her alive. I would imagine that you do not see things like that in Canada."

"No, I guess not. I just can't believe someone would deny their own child like that. I mean, he tried to *kill* her, and he very well could have succeeded if that lady's husband hadn't found her when he did. That's so...messed up! How can people get away with stuff like that here? Does the law mean nothing?" I was bewildered that such a thing could just happen, and there was no real recourse through the police. Rohan could pay someone off and get cooperation to legalize the adoption for his sister, but no one even bothered to push the police to punish the father who tried to kill his newborn baby. It was insane.

"Society here is very complicated, Esha. Right now, money talks. A person of authority may be tempted to do justice, but then someone comes along and offers a bribe, and the temptations to do good subside. That is not to say there is no good in this country. If you look carefully, you will find heart, passion and devotion. At the same time, however, there is a lot of injustice. Many people still follow some very old and inhumane practices, and the corruption allows them to get away with it. Perhaps in the future, as younger and more educated generations begin to command the social and political institutions of this country, things will change for the better. For now, sadly, we must deal with the current reality."

"Until now I have only read about female infanticide in school," I said, drawing a long breath. "But today, it became reality. When I was holding that baby...I mean, if a few more hours had passed before that man found her, she would have... she would just be another statistic...but I held her. She was alive and breathing, and thanks to you, she'll have a life. Ekant, you surprised me today. I thought so badly of you before."

"Well, I did not give you much choice," he said apologetically. "Esha, this is why I wanted to speak with you tonight, and I could not wait until morning. You have been here for quite some time, and you have been very patient."

"Ekant, I just want to know why you've been so angry with me," I demanded, cutting him off. "At first, whenever you saw me, you always had some rude comment or insult ready for me. Then for the past, like, month, it's like you just look right through me!"

"I am sorry. I just...I could not stop myself. My emotions took control. When Dhadhi told me that you were coming, I do not know what happened, but it was like something snapped inside of me. Feelings of anger and resentment surged within me."

"But why? What did I do?" I asked.

"Not you, Esha. It is my past, my reality, who I will never be and who you are," he answered.

"Sorry, but you're not making any sense. Indian people always speak in such philosophical riddles," I said, annoyed.

"I am hardly philosophical," Ekant laughed. Hearing him laugh was uncanny. I didn't think he had it in him!

"Great, now you're laughing."

"Look, I am just speaking from the heart."

"Fine, so what's the 411?" I asked.

"411?"

"The deal?"

"411? Deal? Ah, you American people and your English."

"Canadian."

186

"Same thing," he said casually.

"Actually—"

"Just allow me to speak!"

"Sorry, you were saying?" I bit my lip.

"I believe you are aware of what transpired shortly after your parents were married?" he asked. "I mean...how I was..."

"Yeah, um, Mom told me after Dad...well, yeah, I mean, I know," I stammered.

"Yes, well, as you can see, it is difficult to just say it, so imagine how it feels to experience it; to be a product of it." I shied away from his gaze. I didn't know how to react, because the truth was that I didn't want to think about how it would feel to experience it or to be a product of rape. I had been tormented just listening to my mother as she had recounted the story. I had no interest in hearing it again, but I didn't want to tell Ekant that, so I remained silent.

"When I was younger," he continued, "I always wondered why I did not have a father like my friends did. My mother never had the ability to lie. So she simply said that he could not be with us. Dhadhi said the same, and no one else would even entertain my curiosity, so I learned not to question his whereabouts, until one day when I forced my mother to reveal the truth."

"Your *mother* told you what happened?" I stared on in disbelief as he nodded.

"I was twelve years old, and some of the boys at school started to hassle me. They said I was a bastard. I screamed at them that they were wrong, and that I had a father just like them. They said if that were true, then why had he been absent my whole life, and why had no one else seen him. When I could not find the answers to their questions, they beat me.

"That day, I was so angry and hurt. I went straight to my

187

mother and demanded to speak to my father. I demanded that she take me to him if he could not come himself, but of course she could not. No one knows where he is, or if he is even alive," she said. Ekant dropped his shoulders and shook his head repeatedly as though he were still trying to make sense of the situation.

"Did she tell you the truth then?" I asked.

"Not right away. I pushed and pushed. I called her names and accused her of...well, I just said some very nasty things, most of which I had heard from the other boys. My anger knew no bounds that day. Then suddenly she snapped and said three words that forever changed my life: 'He raped me.' She quickly tried to take it back, but it was too late. I knew the truth. I could see it in her eyes; the pain and the humiliation. She was ashamed; ashamed of something that she had no control over.

"Later, Dhadhi explained what had happened, how my real father had abandoned us and how Dilawar uncle, your father, had saved my mother and me. It took me a very long time to come to terms with the truth. For years I shut down. At school I would keep to myself and avoid the other kids, and at home I would hide away in my room. At night I was plagued by nightmares. I would wake up screaming for my mother."

"But you look like you've sorted everything out now. I mean, you have a beautiful family, and a business," I said, trying to offer some positive reassurance.

"You are right, I do have a beautiful family and a strong business. I thank Waheguru every day for my good fortune," he replied.

"So when did that happen? I mean, when did you bring yourself back into the light, so to speak?"

"When I was eighteen, I saw something, or experienced it

really, and that was it," he answered.

"Dhadhi said you found God. What did she mean by that?" I asked.

"Hmm, well..." he trailed off. His eyes seemed to light up, but he remained silent for quite some time before looking at me again. I followed him carefully, waiting to hear what miraculous experience had finally forced him out of his depression. I half-expected it to sound like something right out of a movie. "Perhaps I will tell you another day."

"*Another day*? Oh come on, Ekant!"

"Another time, Esha. Be patient. Know this; I am very happy that you have come here to carry out your father's wish. But of course, I was disappointed that you tried to do it all on your own and got into all that trouble—"

"Well, you *were* being difficult," I pointed out.

"Perhaps," he said, giving me a stern look, "but still, it was the wrong decision. I apologize if I have made things difficult, as you say, but I did care about your safety. After learning of your big plan and the subsequent attack, I was very troubled about the role I had played. I understand now I should not have been so harsh, regardless of what I was experiencing."

"Well, thanks, bro. I appreciate you admitting that now," I said.

"Seeing as things appear to be calming down, I think soon we can travel to Kiratpur—"

"FINALLY!" I shrieked. "How soon?" I asked, jumping up and down.

"Soon. Now calm down, Esha, before you leap over this railing," he said, grabbing me by the shoulders and forcing me to remain still. "I have to stay in town to complete a few projects for work. They require my personal attention. After that we can all travel. How does November first sound?" That was two and a half weeks away. I'd waited all this time, so another couple of weeks wouldn't make much difference at this point.

"Sure. This is final, right? I mean, you can't back out of it," I said, waving my finger at him.

"Now look, it has been a long day, and we should get some rest. I will walk you down," he said, turning to leave.

"No, it's okay. I'm going to hang around a bit longer."

"Esha, it is late," he objected.

"I'll be down soon, I promise."

"There is no purpose in fighting with you, that much I know by now," he said with a sigh. "Good night, sister."

"Night," I said, smiling as I watched him leave. I looked back up at the moonlit sky and soaked up the energy the moon and the stars offered. As tragic as the day had begun, it had ended even more remarkably. I had helped an innocent baby girl find a home, Ekant had finally come around, and in a few weeks I was going to see Kiratpur and lay my father to rest. Suddenly being in this country didn't feel so terrible.

THIRTEEN

"Chotu, I'm ready, let's go!" I yelled, running out into the courtyard.

"Drive carefully, and Esha, do not be too long. Be home before dark," Dhadhi instructed, following me to the car.

"Yes, Dhadhi," I replied.

"And give my love to Sumi and Daya. Be respectful to his family, okay?"

"Of course, Dhadhi!" I answered. I kissed her on the cheek and got into the waiting car. I was seeing Sumi for the first time since her wedding. I could hardly wait to tell her about the baby girl and about my discussion with Ekant the previous night.

Sumi was only a few minutes away, but Dhadhi had insisted that I wait at least a week before seeing her. According to her, I needed to allow Sumi time to settle in with her new family. As if my presence would hinder her adjustment. It had been two weeks now, so after minimal pleading, Dhadhi had agreed to let me visit.

Not long after we backed out of the driveway, Chotu pulled up in front of a large red gate. Two servants quickly pulled it open after he honked three times successively.

"Chotu, calm down!" I snapped.

"You do not know, madame. These servants are very lazy," he replied.

Sumi was already eagerly waiting for me when we drove

191

in. I jumped out of the car and ran to her.

"You look good!" I said as we hugged.

"Thank you, Esha! I am so happy you have come. I missed you. How is everyone?"

"Good, they're all good, and they send their love. So where's the family?" I asked, looking around the vast courtyard.

"They have gone to a wedding in Gurgaon. They will be gone all day, but Daya is home. He is inside with a friend."

"So how they treating you? Well, I hope?" I asked.

"Yes, very well," she said smiling. "Daya's parents have welcomed me lovingly, and his younger sister, Sony, is like my own. She loves me dearly."

"That's great to hear," I said.

"Oh come sit, Esha, let us be comfortable. Raja! Please bring some cold drinks!" Sumi called out as she led me to some chairs in the shade.

The house was quite extraordinary. Looking up at the carefully designed complex, I now understood why Rano had been so impatient to get Sumi married to Daya. Every square inch of the enormous house screamed money. The doorways had beautiful mouldings around them and contained exquisite handmade designs. The creamy white walls and the gorgeous auburn window sills and pillars gave it an air of elegance. The floors were all marbled, even where we stood in the courtyard; not one speck of dirt.

"Sumi, the house is amazing!"

"Yes, Daya's parents designed it themselves. It took some time to get it made, as it usually does here in any case, but it is a beautiful place. There is a garden in the back. You must see it. It is a sight to behold. Shall I show you?" Sumi offered.

"Nah, maybe later," I said, sitting down. "First, I need to fill you in on what's happened."

"Happened? Oh no, Esha what has happened?" Sumi looked worried. Indians were always so quick to worry. Her reaction reminded me of my mother.

"Nothing bad has happened! Don't worry so much," I said, trying to reassure her. "Well, actually something bad, but then it was good still and...oh you're confusing me, just listen!"

"Okay, okay, please tell," she said, beaming with curiosity.

"Well, I don't know if you heard about that baby girl that was found buried alive but—"

"Buried alive?" gasped Sumi. Apparently she hadn't heard about it yet.

"Yeah, some father didn't want her, so he tried to kill her."

"Oh, Waheguru."

"Anyways, we took her back, and the father like freaked out, like, totally freaked out. He pulled a rifle out and everything!"

"Are you okay?"

"Oh yeah, totally, we got away safely. Ekant had a friend, a very good-looking friend, mind you, and well, in the end we found the baby a brand new loving home, and we made a lot of people very happy," I said. I couldn't help but feel satisfied about the role that I had played. "And at the end of it all, Ekant is talking to me."

"He is? Oh, that is wonderful! I hope you are not still angry with him?" Sumi asked warily.

"Well, I still don't particularly like the way he treated me in the beginning. Then there was all that crap about forcing me to stay for so many months. I mean, look at what happened at the station!"

"I know it is a lot to forgive," Sumi said softly.

"Yeah, but you know what, after listening to Ekant talk

about his childhood and how he's suffered, it just... I dunno, I guess you could say I saw another side of him; a side that seemed more honest and genuine."

"What do you mean by *suffered*?" Sumi asked. I had forgotten that she had no clue about the family secret.

"Oh, nothing, just some family stuff," I said, shrugging it off. "All that matters is that on November first, I will be in Kiratpur."

"I am so happy for you, Esha."

"Yup, November first, the whole family is going. I can finally give my father the peace that he deserves, then after that head home and get on with my life. I mean, I have sooo much to do when I get back. Before coming here, school had just finished, and now I have to go back and figure out what I want to do next. I also have to get back to training for soccer before next season and—"

"You will leave us," Sumi said solemnly. I stopped mid-sentence and looked at her as she dropped her head.

"I have to go back, Sumi, you know that. It's not for another two weeks though," I said.

"I have gotten so used to having you in my life, Esha. Before you, I never really had a close friend."

"Oh, come on, don't be so melodramatic. You have friends!" I said.

"They are not the same. Besides Daya, I never had a close friend. At least, I have never had a close girlfriend who understood me and was genuinely happy for me. Then you came, and it has been fun. I have been able to speak so openly, and you have taught me so much!"

"Taught you so much?" I repeated. "I'm almost afraid to ask what you could possibly have learned from me."

"Esha, stop it. Just know it has been a pleasure to be your

194

friend," Sumi said as she reached out to hold my hand.

"Oh, stop being so sad now. There's still two more weeks," I said, patting her on the head.

"Esha!" Daya called as he walked outside. "Well, ladies, shall we enjoy this wonderful day, or do you two prefer to stay bored in this stuffy old house?" he asked, sitting down across from us.

"Stuffy old house? Daya, I'd hardly call it that. Your house is so huge and gorgeous."

"Yes, well, I suppose we have to spend our money some-where," he said casually.

"An outing sounds like fun, Daya. Esha has not seen the city," Sumi said.

"Is that right?" he asked, looking surprised. "You have been here for so long. How is that possible?"

"Just never got around to it," I answered, not wanting to reveal that in the past months I had cared very little for anything outside the walls of my own room. Besides, I didn't want to rehash family issues in front of Daya and Sumi.

"Let us take you, then. We can have lunch by the Red Fort," Daya suggested.

"Red Fort?" I asked.

"Oh, it is beautiful," Sumi said.

"Okay, it is done then. You ladies collect your things. Esha, I will tell Chotu to notify your family that you are with us. We will drop you home later," Daya said as he stood up.

"Sure, sounds good," I replied.

"Great. Meet me by the car. I am just going to get Angad," he added, running back inside the house. I stopped in my tracks.

"Wait, did he just say Angad?" I asked, remembering the breathtaking guy I had met on the night of the wedding.

195

"Yes, Daya's friend, Angad. Why? Do you know him?" Sumi asked.

"Um, no, I don't. I just asked what name he mentioned, that's all," I said, trying to act cool. How could I admit to Sumi that upon hearing Angad's name, butterflies began fluttering about inside my stomach? There was no way I could possibly admit that to her, when I couldn't even understand why I was feeling that way to begin with.

"The look on your face!" Sumi cried out.

"Oh stop it, Sumi," I retorted.

"But Esha—"

"Come on, where's the car?" I asked, changing the subject.

While Sumi led the way to the car, I quickly straightened my clothes and ran my fingers through my hair, which thankfully now reached my neck, and I was able to make it look somewhat decent. *Why do I care so much?* I pinched myself, trying to snap out of it.

"Ouch!"

"Esha, did you just pinch yourself?" Sumi asked in amazement. Damn it, she had seen me.

"Nooo..." I lied, rubbing my arm, "um...mosquito bites..." She studied me for a moment before looking away.

A few moments later, Daya stepped outside, with Angad following close behind. He was wearing khakis with a white t-shirt and a small, neatly-wrapped black turban. It wasn't like the traditionally tied pointy turbans that I was used to seeing. His was more circular, with only enough fabric to cover his head comfortably and respectfully. His golden complexion was glowing in the bright sunshine.

"Ouch!" I looked around, grabbing my arm. Sumi had poked me. "What was that for?"

"Stop staring!" she whispered.

"I'm not staring!" I hissed back.

"Esha, this is my friend, Angad," Daya said, stopping before me. "Angad, this is—"

"Esha, how are you?" Angad asked, stepping forward and interrupting the now-confused Daya.

"I'm fine," I replied. My throat felt dry, and suddenly the sun felt hotter than before.

"You two already know each other?" Daya asked.

"We met at your wedding," Angad replied, flashing his perfect smile.

Sumi had a puzzled look on her face. It wasn't until Daya and Angad got into the car that she poked me again and mouthed, "He was the one you met!" I looked away, trying to conceal my joy at seeing Angad again. Granted, he wasn't really my type; actually, no Indian had ever been my type, but he seemed different. As much as I tried, I couldn't escape the attraction I felt to him. Even Johnny couldn't play it that smooth. Angad was tall and manly. He made Johnny seem like nothing more than a silly little schoolboy.

Travelling with Sumi, I realized, made New Delhi finally begin to seem safe again. As we passed through those familiar streets, I tried to block out images from that treacherous morning that now seemed so long ago. Sensing my agitation, Sumi reached out and held my hand. I thanked her by giving her hand a quick squeeze.

It was nearing the noon hour, so the roads were crowded with commuters. I tried not to look as Daya darted in and out of traffic, but he nonetheless got us safely to the Red Fort.

It was located in the northern part of Delhi, most commonly referred to as Old Delhi. A massive fort, more like

197

a palace, entirely built out of red sandstone, stretched out before us. The grass and trees surrounding the fort combined with the clear blue sky made it look exquisite. I wished I had a camera to capture the moment.

"This is the Red Fort," announced Daya, in case I hadn't figured it out yet. "Have you ever heard about it? Your parents must have mentioned it, or you may have read about it."

"Actually, no, I don't know anything about it," I admitted, feeling foolish. "What's it for?"

"Well, it does not serve any real purpose now. The military still uses parts of it, and on Independence Day there is a parade here, which the president and prime minister attend with a bunch of other dignitaries, along with carefully selected members of the public."

"Can we go inside?" I asked.

"We can walk around wherever the military does not restrict entry. Hey, shall we all have lunch somewhere in Chandni Chowk?" Daya asked.

"Is that a restaurant?" I asked.

"It is an area of Delhi, silly," Sumi laughed. "It is right across from the Red Fort. There are some wonderful restaurants on that street, and some very good shopping. It is an area that is worth seeing."

"Cool, but back to the fort, why was it built?" I asked, following Daya, who had begun walking towards the fort.

"The Mughal Emperor, Shah Jahan, built this and the city surrounding it in 1639 A.D. The city is called Shahjahanabad," Daya answered. Sumi and Angad trailed as we made our way around the fort. Military personnel could be seen here and there, but the area looked very calm and welcoming.

"Wait, Shah Jahan? The dude who built the Taj Mahal?"

"You do know your history!" Daya exclaimed.

"No, not really, but everyone knows about the Taj Mahal."

"Esha is right," Angad said. His voice startled me, and I quickly looked to Sumi. As feared, she had caught my reaction. I turned away and tried to compose myself as we continued walking.

"Shah Jahan is famous for his labours of love," Angad continued without looking at me. "This Red Fort is another testament to his creativity. His successors added to the structure and completed it, but Shah Jahan laid the foundations of the fort, and it still speaks volumes about his architectural brilliance. The artwork in the palace combines many styles: Indian, of course, but also European and Persian. The brilliant designs, the rich choice of colours, everything is an expression of the Shahjahani style. From the imperial apartments, the main gates, the audience halls, women's quarters to the Pearl Mosque; it is all magnificent."

"It is," I agreed. "And it's massive."

"Yes, it is. It spans about 1.5 miles. The walls on this side facing the streets are roughly 110 feet high, and on the river side they are about 60 feet. I suppose you could say that the Mughals never spared any cost, extravagance, or safety measure in their palaces. "

"So I think we should get some lunch in Chandni Chowk. That way Esha can see Delhi's most famous market. What say all of you?" Daya asked, already leading the way.

"Yes, come, Esha," Sumi said grabbing my hand. I was disappointed when Angad walked on ahead and joined Daya instead of walking beside me.

He wasn't being as forthcoming as he had been the night of the wedding, but he had no reason to be. We had only met that one night, so why should he care enough to spend time chatting to me? More importantly, why did I care so much if he did or didn't?

"Esha, there again you have gone off somewhere, and I have lost you," Sumi complained.

"Huh? What? I'm right here."

"What are you thinking, my friend?" she asked.

"Just trying to figure out your friend Angad, that's all," I said frankly.

At that moment Daya turned around. "Try to catch up. You two are so behind." Sumi and I just nodded as the two guys turned around and continued walking.

Sumi lowered her voice. "I just remembered Angad was the one you met at the wedding. You have told me nothing."

"It's nothing, really. We met briefly at your wedding. He was nice, and he walked me and Dhadhi home. That's all," I replied.

"He walked you home?" Sumi asked, amazed.

"Well, yeah, and stop looking at me like that, Sumi. He walked us home, so what? He knew my name, and I asked for his, but he wouldn't say it. Instead he sort of wrote it on the ground and walked away."

"He *wrote* it on the *ground*?" she asked carefully, making sure to emphasize her words.

"Yeah, that's what I said."

"But that is not like him! Oh, Esha, perhaps he likes you! Angad is a very private person. This is not like him!"

"Sssshh! Keep your voice down, Sumi. You're wrong. I think he was just being friendly," I said, shrugging off her suspicions. "I mean, look at him now. He's totally keeping his distance. Anyway, what difference does it make? Just forget it, *please*."

"If that is what you desire, but do not forget what I said. Angad is a very private person, and if he approached you

200

the way you say he did, then he must like you very much. Now, until we find out more about him, let us concentrate on showing you the rest of Delhi," she said, quickening her pace to catch up with Daya and Angad.

Sumi did have a point. Until Angad gave me a further hint as to what he was thinking, why should I concern myself with it any longer? He wasn't even my type! Feeling much better, I ran forward and joined the three of them, taking in the colourful sights of Chandni Chowk.

* * *

Sumi was right; Chandni Chowk was truly an experience. It was heavily congested, but it had a unique character of its own. It was a long road lined with shops, restaurants and residential quarters. Daya pointed out that it had once been one of the grandest markets in all of India. I was amazed that some of the temples and buildings in the area dated as far back as the 1600s. I had never seen anything so *ancient*. The history was clearly evident in every stone, every pillar, and every grain of sand. For the first time I didn't care about the pollution or the hordes of people. None of it affected me. Instead I was drawn into the historical background of the city.

We ate lunch at a small restaurant that offered South Indian food. Daya insisted that I try it, and in the end I was pleased with his choice, since it turned out to be delicious. We then walked through the streets visiting various shops. As we approached a shop carrying shawls, Daya insisted that we go in so he could buy one for his new wife. When Sumi refused, claiming she already had too many things, he grabbed her hand and dragged her inside.

"Oh, come on, Sumi! I would like to buy one for my beautiful wife. Please just pick one!" Daya pleaded to his surprisingly stubborn wife. It was a quaint place where shawls of every colour and design hung from the walls and were stacked carefully in neat piles.

"No, Daya, stop it. I have so many! I do not need any more," Sumi protested.

"Daya, just pick one for her," I intervened. "You know she'll never agree."

"Oh, Esha—"

"Esha, you are so right!" Daya cried, cutting her off. He ran over to the shopkeeper and asked to see the best of his collection. "I shall get one for you also."

"Oh no, Daya, I'm fine," I said.

"You must take something back to Canada," he insisted as he settled into a chair. The shopkeeper presented shawls of every colour, pattern and design. Much to Sumi's horror, Daya turned the entire store upside down in his attempt to find the perfect shawl for her.

As I rummaged through the mess Daya was making, a soft pink shawl caught my attention. It was gorgeous with its intricate stitching. It was soft and simple yet so perfectly elegant. I wrapped it around me and instantly fell in love. Then I saw the price tag. I wasn't too good on my currency calculations, but I knew that it cost way more than I'd like Daya to spend on me, and I didn't have any money on me. I never carried money with me when I ventured out of the house. Dhadhi insisted that I let Jas and Chotu pay instead, and she would reimburse them later. She claimed that it was safer, since I was a foreigner and a target for thieves. I argued that it made me more vulnerable, but Dhadhi was firm as usual with her decisions. With a deep sigh, I unravelled the shawl from around me and sadly tossed it aside. If Daya saw me gushing over it, he would insist on buying it.

After what seemed like forever, Daya walked out of the shop satisfied. He had picked a beautiful red shawl for Sumi and a cream cashmere shawl for me.

Once our tour of Chandni Chowk was complete, Daya drove us around the city, stopping briefly at Quitib Minar, followed by a quick tour around Indira Gandhi's brainchild, New Delhi, and India Gate. Our final stop was Connaught Place, where we wandered through the shops.

Throughout the day, I was careful not to mention Gandhi's name or Operation Bluestar. I didn't want another repeat of my first encounter with Ekant. Of course, this time it would be with Daya and Angad; two guys whom I liked enough that I didn't want to disappoint them. I soon found out, however, that I had no cause for worry. Daya, Angad and Sumi mentioned Gandhi's name in simple conversation, not once bringing up what had happened in Amritsar. I found it strange, especially since up until now, any time someone said her name, the neighbourhood had erupted in heated debate over Operation Bluestar and her role in the attack. After hearing them mention her name numerous times, I quietly tapped Sumi's shoulder and decided to ask her.

"Hey, how come you guys are so cool talking about the P.M.? I mean, everyone I've heard to this point is pretty pissed with her."

"She is our prime minister, Esha. It is only natural that we would mention her," Sumi replied.

"Yeah, but what about all that's happened?"

"Well, as infuriating as it is, it is still too soon to jump to conclusions about what happened," she said. I could tell she was picking her words carefully. "We have anger about the role she has played in the conflict and the role that she ought to have played as prime minister. That is a separate issue from discussing her work on other matters. She has been and remains an integral part of Delhi, and that work is enjoyed by all citizens. Just look around you. She has put in a lot of effort to develop New Delhi by making it modern and clean. It is a dream of hers. She has said that when she is done with it, New Delhi will be like Paris."

"Paris? She's reaching a bit far, isn't she?"

"No dream is too big if you have the will, and in her case she has the will and the resources!"

Sumi did have a point. Compared to Old Delhi, where things were congested and polluted, New Delhi was very westernized, clean and spacious. Just driving through it, one could see that it had been carefully planned and constructed.

"So let me get this right. You three aren't upset about her role in Operation Bluestar?" I asked, hoping for clarification. We were now sitting in a small cafe by Connaught Place. As I persisted with the subject, Daya and Angad both moved closer to where Sumi and I were sitting.

"Of course we are upset," Daya said. "She did her best to divide Sikhs. Angad here just barely escaped from Amritsar!"

"What?" I cried out.

"Please, let us not discuss that," Angad said impatiently.

"Are you okay, though?" I asked, restraining myself from asking any further questions. I was desperately curious to know what had happened, what he'd seen, and how he had escaped.

"I am fine. Thank you for asking, but Daya is right. We are upset, of course we are. Amritsar is very important. True to its name, it is the 'Abode of God', literally. Whatever the issue, no religious symbol should be attacked in any political conflict. Whether she gave the order or not, as prime minister, she has a responsibility to protect all Indians, and Sikhs are Indian. They reside in this country, they have fought to protect this country, and they have sacrificed for this country. It is a shame that this country should then turn on them. However, we must remember that events are never the sole responsibility of one person. If we are to place blame, then we have to consider all factors. For example, why did Gandhi send her forces into Punjab and Amritsar? Why did she declare an Emergency State? Who else was involved?"

"I thought it had to do with that man, Sant Bhindrawale. At least, that's what I heard on the news in the summer."

"Yes, well, Esha, you are right to bring up Sant Bhindrawale, but now we have to ask ourselves, why did he take such a strong stance against the central government? More importantly, what was he doing exactly?"

"Angad, honestly, I have no clue when it comes to Indian politics, religion or whatever. All I know are the bits and pieces I picked up from news broadcasts when I was waiting to travel to Kiratpur over the summer. So why don't you just enlighten me?"

"Okay, well, it's quite simple. He was preaching equality, which lead to Sikhs uniting, that's all," Angad said. "One day, the leader of the Nirankaris—a new sect among Sikhs that the PM supported, some would say in order to divide Sikhs—marched with his people, declaring that he was going to establish seven beloved men of God. In Sikhism, our last living Guru, Guru Gobind Singh Ji, had established five beloved followers. This man now claimed that as a living Guru and leader, which was all nonsense, by the way, he had the knowledge and authority to defy Guru Gobind Singh Ji's decree and establish seven beloved followers. Seeing it as sacrilegious, a man by the name of Bhai Fauja Singh and a few followers interrupted the march with a peaceful protest. The Nirankaris and police opened fire on Bhai Fauja Singh and Sant Bhindrawale's devotees. Thirteen Sikhs were killed, including Bhai Fauja Singh. The police helped the Nirankaris escape by using government cars. That was in 1978, and since then, Sant Bhindrawale concluded that the Central Government is on a mission to divide Sikhs.

"He was also of the conviction that Sikhs needed to be reminded of their history and their religious and spiritual teachings. Eventually people flocked from all corners of the country to hear him speak. Many had fallen in love with his wisdom. I once heard a man claim that when he heard the Sant speak, his heart, mind and soul instantly obtained peace. Unprecedented numbers of people became baptized Sikhs. There was nothing dangerous about it. In the Seventies and Eighties, Sikhs have increasingly stepped away from their identities. Wearing a turban and keeping the hair uncut, this is not easy. Giving up alcohol, meat and eggs, pride and lust, and devoting yourself to God and your community, this wasn't a lifestyle that tempted the youngsters any more. Sikhism was dying out, and Sant Bhindrawale saved it by uniting them."

"Sorry to interrupt, but something has to be made clear here," Daya interjected. "We all have to agree that who and what Sant Bhindrawale was is still up for debate. Not all Sikhs agree with his espousing a theocratic state of Khalistan, and there were many different stories and rumours about his political connections and what exactly his goal was."

"Daya, what matters is that he saved Sikhism," Angad retorted.

"Did he? Or did Sikhs save it themselves? He merely ignited a debate," Daya countered.

"What difference does it make? He got the discussion going, didn't he? He got people to pay attention to what was happening with Sikhi and its future survival. It's not like he attacked anyone or created an army or revolted."

"Of course he did!" Daya retorted. "He took refuge in the Golden Temple, for crying out loud!"

"What choice did he have?" Angad shot back.

"There is always a choice my friend, always!" Daya said, shaking his head.

"Okay, both of you stop it!" I cried. "I get it. There are different opinions. It's okay, I'm an educated person, and I don't just blindly accept one view. Now, can we get back to Angad's story?"

"Okay, but just remember, keep an open mind. History is trickier than people think," Daya warned.

"Fine. Now, Angad, you said he was uniting people, and they loved him. So what went wrong?"

"Politics, of course," Angad answered. "The Punjab government, led by the Akali Dal party, saw an opportunity to make demands of the central government. The past few years have been rampant with tension between the Punjab State and the central government. There has been severe inequality, and it has existed for a long time. Punjab has five rivers that run through it, and this is a large resource, so it is heavily directed by the central government. Then there are the bountiful fields and the grain production in Punjab, which plays a critical role in feeding India. Thus, the central government keeps a tight control on the state. There have been scores of protestors, mostly Sikh, arrested. The government has gone to all extremes to suppress our demands, and finally in June, they attacked our spirit.

"On May 31st, the Akalis threatened to stop Punjab's resources from being transported out of the state. This was not a threat to be taken lightly, especially since grain from Punjab accounts for sixty per cent of the total production of grain in India. So the army was sent in to stop any type of protest or act of defiance.

"Things, however, went wrong. Once in Punjab, the army established curfews, they restricted communications and electricity, and then the focus shifted to capturing Sant Bhindrawale and his men, who, as Daya has already pointed out, had taken refuge inside the Golden Temple complex for over two years. As pilgrims sat peacefully inside the complex to commemorate the martyrdom of Guru Arjan Dev, the fifth Sikh Guru, the army began acting out. It is still debatable whether they were following orders or acting of their own free will. Shoot-at-sight claims were made, forcing the pilgrims to remain inside the complex, wait it out and seek safety there. No one could have ever imagined that any violence could take place in such a holy shrine. But the army eventually did attack.

"The prime minister says she never ordered the attack, but she is their leader. How could such a big thing happen over several days? It wasn't a spontaneous attack; rather it was carefully planned and executed. Regardless, the point remains the same: a major incident and an historical event is never the sole responsibility or to the credit of just one person. Take Mahatma Gandhi, for example."

"What do you mean? How does he even compare?" I asked, slightly confused.

"What have you been told regarding India's independence?"

"Well, Gandhi and the whole non-violence campaign. Wasn't that it?" I answered.

"Are you sure that's it?"

"Angad, what are you getting at? What else is there?" I was annoyed with his slow-paced explanations.

"Ever heard the names Shaheed Udham Singh or Shaheed Bhagat Singh?"

"Can't say I have," I replied impatiently.

"Shaheed Udham Singh travelled the globe getting people to discuss the need for India's independence by highlighting the atrocities of British rule in India. Take, for example, the massacre inside the Jallianwalla Bhag in Amritsar, just a few steps away from the Golden Temple. He was there serving water with his friends to the thousands of innocents who had gathered in the court when they were locked inside by the army and gunned down, all of them, men, women and children. He survived and later assassinated the man responsible for that massacre, Michael O'Dwyer. O'Dwyer was the Governor of Punjab in 1919 when the shooting was ordered. As per order of command, only he could have instructed or stopped General Dyer from carrying out the massacre.

"Shaheed Udham Singh was among the many who believed India could only achieve its independence if the British were forcibly removed. Force required violence at times, which was in stark contrast to Gandhi's non-violent stance. This was the path Shaheed Bhagat Singh took as well. They rallied people, assassinated the British officials that they deemed accountable, disrupted parliament and basically drove the British mad, causing undoubted financial damage.

"All of this went on while Gandhi promoted his campaign;

two very distinct approaches, but both striving for the same goal, independence. Both Udham Singh and Bhagat Singh were hanged, making them martyrs in the eyes of many revolutionaries. Eventually, Britain could no longer afford India following World War II, so it was granted independence. However, Gandhi was credited worldwide for achieving it through his non-violent and philosophical campaign. Of course, post World War Two, it made the English look better internationally to succumb to such a peaceful philosophy."

"Wait, you can't rag on Gandhi. He did do a lot!" I protested.

"Yes, he did, and I fully believe that too. Do not get me wrong, I am a fan of Mahatma Gandhi. He reinvigorated belief in diplomacy. He left behind a great example and ideology for people to aspire to, but it wasn't all him. We have to consider what other factors may have played a role. As I have said, a major historical event never occurs because of one person. Only God has such power," Angad said, smiling.

What he said went against everything I had absorbed from textbooks and discussions in school. Yet something in his voice and his words convinced me that he spoke from a place of knowledge and experience. It was clear that he was an analytical person. He wasn't insulting Gandhi, one of the greatest minds ever to have existed; rather he was considering all the variables.

Angad struck me as a person who had experienced a lot more of life than I could ever imagine. Suddenly I was more inspired than ever to discover just who he was. So what if he had a beard and turban? He seemed so intelligent and fit and...with a perfect smile, and to top it all off, he had a great fashion sense. I stood there and watched him carefully, soaking in every quality that made him seem so attractive. It was Daya's voice that brought me back to reality.

"Now that we've brought this day to a screeching halt with all this talk about history and politics, shall we head back?" he asked with what looked like a fake yawn to illustrate his boredom.

"We have been gone a long time," Sumi added, looking at her watch.

"Yeah, actually, you're right," I agreed as I looked out in the direction of the sunset. "It's getting late. If I don't make it for dinner, Dhadhi will worry."

"Dhadhi is aware you are with us. She will not worry," Daya reassured.

"No, Daya, I shouldn't be out too late. I don't want to piss off Ekant again either. I'm finally making headway with him, and I don't want to ruin that now."

"Okay, but there is just one place remaining. I promise I will drop you after we go there," Daya insisted.

"Where?" I asked.

"Well, seeing as you cannot travel to Punjab yet, and most of the wonderful Sikh spiritual sites are there, we still wanted to give you an experience."

"And where would that be?"

"Bangla Sahib Gurdwara. It is just here—"

"Oh, I don't...I mean, it's cool. I don't need to see a Gurdwara," I said, cutting him off. "We do have those in Canada, I'm sure it's not any different."

"Oh, Esha, you must see it!" Sumi pleaded. "It is a wonderful place to visit."

"Yes, please, you must come along," Angad added.

"Well...oh...how can I refuse you," I sighed and headed to the car. Sumi poked me again before jumping in beside me. This time I quietly let it go as I felt my cheeks flush.

"Let's go!" Daya yelled as everyone quickly climbed in after me.

*   *   *

There were many people at the Gurdwara when we walked through the main gates. I used the shawl that Daya had bought me to cover my head. As we entered, I looked up at the majestic structure ahead. It was nothing like I had imagined it would be. I had expected any old building similar to the ones that Canadians use to set up Gurdwaras back home, but this was something else. It was like a beautiful palace. The main building reached high into the sky in solid white, topped off with a golden cupola. The Gurdwara was lighting up as night approached, further adding to its heavenly appeal.

We first made our way around the vast sacred pool of water where people dipped their feet and washed their hands and faces. A few people had immersed themselves completely. Sumi bent down and took a sip of the water, and after noticing my confusion, she explained the reason behind it.

"Esha, this water is sacred. It is said that the well in this complex contains powers of healing. Holy water is always okay to drink," she said.

"I see..." I said hesitantly. I carefully stepped into the water and splashed the water on my hands and arms. "I think I'm good with just this much. Why don't you take a sip for both of us?"

"Oh, be a good sport. Try it!"

"No, I'm good, Sumi," I said, climbing out. "Besides, I'm a hundred per cent healthy, so I'll leave my portion for someone who needs it more than me."

"You are impossible!" Daya said, laughing. "Come on, let us show you inside."

We made our way up the marble steps leading into the main hall. Walking through the simple but spacious hall, I carefully observed the details of the floors, the soft walls and pillars and the high ceilings, which led us towards the open central shrine where the Guru Granth Sahib was respectfully displayed in a golden dome. The evening prayers were being read and were carried out over the loudspeakers. The atmosphere was peaceful and welcoming. It was like walking into God's court.

Each of us paid our respects to the Guru Granth Sahib, and I followed Sumi to the left side, where the women were seated, while Angad and Daya took a seat to the right with the men. Sumi closed her eyes and became absorbed in the prayers while I people-watched.

Most of the people were locals, but there were a few tourists. It wasn't difficult to spot the difference between the two groups. The locals looked more comfortable, as if they were in their own home, while the tourists turned their heads from side to side, taking in every aspect of the Gurdwara. The non-Indians struggled to sit cross-legged on the carpeted floor like everyone else, desperately trying to hide their discomfort.

Everyone gathered in the hall was so quiet. Adults, children, locals and tourists, they all seemed to be at peace, listening to the melodious voice of the priest seated behind the Guru Granth Sahib. I just didn't get it. How could they be so absorbed in a language they didn't even fully understand? I assumed some of the more orthodox-looking people understood parts of it, but it wasn't in modern language; it was ancient terminology and very complicated at that. I looked over to Angad and found him sitting at the very front with his eyes closed. I was surprised to see his lips move in unison with the prayers.

After another ten minutes, and to ease my sore back, I decided to step outside. The priest showed no sign of concluding his prayers any time soon, and Sumi, Daya and Angad were still fully engrossed, so much so that they didn't even notice me leave the room.

While I waited outside, I watched as the moonlight cascaded across the sacred pool. The silhouette of a turbaned man bathing in the pond caught my eye as he emerged from the water. His sacred dagger was respectfully draped around him on a black belt. It was the perfect pose in a perfect setting for any artist. I almost regretted that I wasn't that artist.

"Beautiful night, is it not?" Angad asked, walking towards me. He stood beside me and looked up at the clear moonlit sky.

"Oh, hey. Yeah, I guess that remains a constant here. A beautiful night followed by a beautiful morning, followed again by a beautiful night. I mean, it's nothing like in BC, with the breathtaking mountains and the clean air, but still this place definitely has an appeal of its own."

"Yes, I suppose every place does," Angad agreed. "Every morning in Punjab, I would wake up to the smell of the fields, to the birds singing and hear the crisp noise of the trees swaying in the wind. It is very moving to hear Mother Nature before you hear the rest of the world."

"I agree."

"So you left early," Angad said. "Sumi was looking for you. I told her I would find you, as Daya wanted to show her something. You did not wait for the completion of the prayer?"

"Well, it's a bit tough to do if you can't understand what

the guy is saying," I answered, feeling a little pressured.

"I would not assume that this is the first time you are hearing a Sikh prayer." Angad sounded confused.

"Of course it's not, Angad! But it's still a foreign language basically. I mean, how can I connect with something that I don't understand? How can any of those people inside? No one speaks like that any more."

"So you are not religious?" he asked with what sounded like disappointment.

"I just don't get it, that's all. Come to think of it, I've never really cared to pay much attention. My parents took me to the Gurdwara when I was a kid. As I grew older, I was required to attend family stuff, but I've never had any formal teachings regarding Sikhism. Simple attendance doesn't really mean that you are actually learning what it all means. So I suppose you could say I've grown up *around* it. Mom is always going on and on about Waheguru this and Waheguru that, and Dhadhi is no different, but—"

"But you have never discussed what it is or what it means with anyone," Angad said, completing my thought.

"Yeah...until now," I said, admiring the fact that he understood me so well. "You just got me to go and on about something that I never care to talk about, and you get it—you get me."

"I take Sikhi very seriously," he replied.

Great, Esha, he takes Sikhi seriously, not you.

"So tell me, do you understand a word that priest was saying?" I asked.

"Not completely. It is very complex," he answered.

"Then how do you get into it?"

"Through feeling, of course."

"Huh?"

"Look at it this way, Esha. What that priest was reading, those are teachings or lessons, if you will, compiled by the Gurus and placed in the sacred Guru Granth Sahib, thus making it the embodiment of all Ten Gurus, and now the only remaining living Guru for Sikhs. We can connect to God through understanding those lessons. There is also another step, which involves feeling. Guru Nanak Dev Ji, the first Guru of—"

"I know who he is!" I snapped.

"Just checking!" Angad said, laughing. "Well, Guru Nanak Ji said that before thought is sound...music. The ancients have declared that there are seven energy points in any given human body. As such, there are seven notes on a musical scale, and each note hits an energy point. We are connected through energy. We are connected to God through our energy, which we turn into spiritual energy in our meditations.

"Sikhi is very simple: God is within reach, because God is within us. Not just in Sikhism, but you will find that many religions state this fact, if not all. However, we must strengthen our own spiritual energy in order to attain God. The prayers and the hymns are melodies. Music and sound reverberates in our bodies and in our soul as we listen and absorb them. So while I may not understand word for word what that priest is reading, I could still absorb the sound and the energy, and therefore focus on God."

"Wow."

"Wow?" Angad repeated.

"Yeah, you're so...that was...I've never..." I stammered.

"Esha, you are not making any sense," he said, laughing. There I was looking foolish in front of him again. I cleared my throat and took a deep breath.

"I've just never heard anyone speak like that," I explained.

"Your devotion is audible in your words and visible in your eyes." At my last remark, Angad's eyes locked with mine, and my heart skipped a beat.

"Do not take my word for it," he began. "There is a lot to Sikhism, but as a Sikh you are encouraged to always look beyond what you see." His words were so soft, I could stand there all day and just listen to him speak. "There is never an end," he continued. "Life is a pursuit to attain spiritual bliss, to build a community and to fight for justice. If something happens, we are meant to ask how it happened, what it means and what course of action we must take next. We must realize what lesson we are to take away from it and from life as a whole. We must accept God's will, and we must carry on with courage and spirit, never forgetting Waheguru. This is who we are."

"We?"

"Sikhs, humans, anyone and everyone."

"You're so confident, so sure about who you are and what you want."

"I would not say that, Esha. You appear quite confident yourself," Angad replied.

"I thought I was a few months ago, and then everything just...fell apart."

"So tell me then, who are you, Miss Esha, and what do you want?" he asked in a whisper.

"Good question," I replied, trying to formulate an answer. As hard as I tried, I couldn't think of anything. My thoughts flashed back to my life in B.C. with my friends, and I could easily use it to answer, but a part of me wanted to hide that from him. A part of me wanted to say that I could find a peaceful life and a clear devotion as Angad had. *But that wasn't who I was...was it?*

"Esha! Finally, let us leave now!" Sumi rushed towards me. I was relieved to see her and to escape Angad's curious eyes. "Sorry we got so late. Daya is impossible sometimes!"

"Where were you?" I asked.

"He wanted to introduce me to some old priest. He says the man taught him when he was younger. When Daya gets an idea, it is next to impossible to dissuade him. He dragged me all over, asking for the whereabouts of the old man. When we finally found the priest, we found out that he wasn't the one who had taught Daya, instead it was his son who has adopted his father's name. The one we were looking for has retired and has moved back to Punjab, where he is living out the rest of his days."

"Daya never ceases to surprise!" Angad laughed, and I joined in, imagining Daya dragging poor Sumi around the Gurdwara.

"All right, let's head out then," I said, walking away. "Dhadhi's probably standing in the street by now waiting for me."

"Oh no, you think so?" Sumi asked worried. "Daya, come on!" she called out. Daya was just making his way out of the Gurdwara. His shoulders were slumped, and he was dragging his feet, clearly disappointed with the outcome of his search.

"Hey, you all have a safe trip home. I will get a taxi and head home from here, since I am already halfway there," Angad said.

"Oh, stop it Angad, I will drop you," Daya insisted.

"No, you will be too late. You should take Esha and Sumi home before it gets too dark. The streets are not so safe at night," Angad replied, glancing in my direction. I remained still and pretended that his remark didn't affect me, but memories of early morning at the station flashed through my mind when I heard him say that. "I will catch up with you later this week, Daya."

"Okay, if you insist," Daya replied. By now we had reached the car, and he jumped in to start the engine.

"Bye, Angad!" Sumi said, waving as she climbed into the passenger side. Angad smiled as he closed the door after her.

"Bye, Angad," I said, stopping beside him. "I really enjoyed hanging out with you today."

"As did I," he answered with a warm smile.

"So...um...will I see you again?" I asked, sounding undoubtedly like a total loser. My tongue might as well have been hanging out.

"I hope so," he said, maintaining his smile. "And remember this, Esha: sometimes tapping into our feelings, we can discover something that does not make sense to us or is not so familiar in the beginning. Nevertheless, do not forget the strength of your emotions, and do not ignore the energy that you carry within. You may just surprise yourself."

I nodded as I watched him slowly back away, and I didn't move until he disappeared around the corner, as he had on the very first night we'd met.

On the ride home, I listened to Sumi and Daya bicker about his failed attempt to find his teacher and his refusal to attend another upcoming family wedding. Sumi tried to persuade him to follow his parents' wishes to attend, but he complained that it was too long of a drive, and he'd rather enjoy quiet time with his wife instead of being surrounded by extended family. It wasn't until we rounded the corner onto my street that Sumi brought up the topic of Angad.

"Esha, you and Angad seemed to get along well," she said. "Perhaps there is hope yet of you settling here with me."

"Oh, stop it Sumi," Daya retorted before I could reply. "Esha has already made it clear, Indian guys are not her type.

We have already bothered her enough. Leave her alone."

"But, did you *see* them today? They get along very well, and they look—"

"That is not for you to decide. Indians are not Esha's type, and Angad is Indian, therefore, Angad is not Esha's type. Plain and simple, right, Esha?" Daya asked, looking back at me in the rearview mirror. By now we had reached the house, and he brought the car to an abrupt stop in front of the gate. "You did not answer. Tell Sumi, because she will not listen to me. I believe that is the habit of any wife."

"Daya, that is not true!" snapped Sumi.

"Look you two, stop fighting over me!" I said, finally finding the words to interject into their silly little battle.

"Okay, sorry. Look, Sumi, we must respect Esha's preference, and Esha, Angad is a nice guy. I can vouch for him, but I understand you have already stated that this is not your type. So that is that, right?"

They both turned around in their seats to look at me. They were incredibly relentless. Sumi still had a look of hope in her eyes, and Daya almost looked like he was hoping I'd prove him wrong and say that Angad was my type. I just had the urge to run out of the car.

"Goodnight, you two," I said as I pushed open the door.

I could have simply answered their question and agreed with Daya. Indians were not my type; therefore, Angad was not my type. I could have said that and easily put an end to their curiosity and bickering, but I didn't. Now, as I made my way into the house, I tried to figure out why this day had left me so tongue-tied.

FOURTEEN

I could feel Rohan's eyes on me. One full hour had gone by, yet his gaze remained steady as Jas and I played with the baby and made small talk with his sister, Riya.

After much insistence from Ekant, Rohan had finally made time for a visit. Since his arrival, he had sat quietly on the sofa across from me with a newspaper held wide open in his hands. When he didn't flip a page after the first ten minutes, I realized something was up. Another ten minutes went by, and still I heard no ruffling of the newspaper. I glanced in his direction only to catch him staring at me then quickly ducking his head into the paper as soon as he realized he'd been caught. I let out a loud sigh and made sure to avoid looking at him.

I didn't mind having a gorgeous guy stare at me, but it just wasn't what I needed at that moment. Ekant was taking me to Kiratpur in a week, after which I'd be on a plane back home. Besides, things were already complicated enough with Angad. I didn't need another distraction.

Sumi had called me every day that week asking whether I had seen Angad again or if I had changed my mind about "choosing" him, as she so casually termed it, as if it were all up to me. I told her that if he really wanted to see me, then he could easily contact me first. Why should it only be up to me? However, she only explained that this was India, not Canada, and guys could not just show up at a girl's house or simply call her. I didn't see why not. Ekant and Dhadhi seemed perfectly cool. In any case, I was down to a few days now, so it didn't really matter any more what happened or didn't happen.

"Rohan, I see the ladies have not driven you to boredom!" Ekant said, walking in through the screen door.

"Not at all, brother. How are you? Jas said you were away on business," Rohan replied as they shook hands.

"Yes, business is keeping me very busy lately, but I cannot complain. It is a blessing."

"The economy seems to be growing well now. I really believe India is finally on a path towards great development," Rohan said, tossing the newspaper back onto the table, as if he'd even read a word of it.

"It is no secret that the government has focused on expanding the public sector, but the private sector is growing also and is more liberated," Ekant said. "Businessmen like you and I are in a position to gain from recent growths in the market. In this month alone, I have been able to take on the right projects and make the deals that will ensure my business and family's financial security for the future. It is my hope that this time next year, I will shift the family into New Delhi. It is better for work and for Bhagat to be closer to some good schools, and it is a better atmosphere for us all. Trilokpuri has become quite congested in recent years."

"That is excellent news, brother," Rohan replied.

"Yes, but I still wonder if it will happen," Ekant said soberly.

"Why do you say that?" I asked as both men turned and almost looked surprised to see me intervening in their discussion.

"With communal violence breaking out every now and then in India, there is never any guarantee of security. In this

222

past year, look at what has gone on between Delhi and Punjab. What if one day there is such violence and it directly affects my business, then what will we do? How will we recover?"

"Ekant, I am surprised to hear you speak like this!" Rohan cried. "This is unlike you. Speak positively, brother. The violence this summer was most unfortunate, but the situation seems to be calming down, and your business is thriving. Look at all of the trucks, employees and contracts that you have under you. You are safe. Take joy in that."

"Yes, you are right!" Ekant agreed as he took a deep breath and offered a bright smile. "I just got caught up in the moment, I suppose. You know, I have put everything into this business. There is no one else here to look after the family. Sometimes the pressure builds, but never fear, I am happily looking forward to the future and am most humble to be blessed with so much."

"Wonderful! Esha, you are lucky to have such a brother," Rohan said.

"I know," I said. Ekant cheerfully returned my smile.

"Now, we must take our leave," Rohan said, pulling out his car keys.

"Oh, must you leave so soon!" Ekant protested.

"We must, brother," Rohan answered apologetically. "I have much work to do before this day is done. Plus, Riya and Mother need to prepare for their spiritual pilgrimage to Haridwar. There she wants to pay her respects and visit the old Ma Kali temple. After her husband and child perished, she asked Ma Kali to show her the way. Now that she has this new gift, she wants to return to the temple to offer her prayers and gratitude that such a beautiful baby girl was saved. Come, Riya, gather your things."

"But I have not even held the baby girl yet!" Ekant lamented.

"Why don't you carry her to the car?" Riya suggested sweetly.

"Excellent! Here, place her in my arms," Ekant said, holding out his arms. As Riya gently placed the baby there, Ekant's eyes grew tender. "She is absolutely incredible. You are a wonderful mother, Riya."

"All thanks to you, Ekant brother. I will forever be grateful for the day that you brought her into my life, and I will spend my days ensuring that she is happy," Riya replied as she wiped away her tears.

I hung back as the family walked out with Rohan and Riya. As they got in the car, I could see Rohan looking over everyone. Eventually his eyes found me, and he bid me farewell with a nod and smile. I gave him an awkward wave and ran back into the house. As hot as Rohan was, there was something seriously discomforting about the thought of Ekant's best friend crushing on me.

That evening, Ekant announced that his new business partner would be joining us for dinner, which sent Jas scurrying to the kitchen to prepare a wonderfully delicious meal in honour of the guest. Ekant explained that since Jas had convinced him to take time off work, he now had to entrust a lot of the responsibilities to his new partner.

"Do not be mistaken," he said when I quizzed him about why he was sharing his business with a stranger. "I am still the controlling partner, but I believe that it is time to expand. He is an individual that I can trust completely. His uncle is a retired colonel and was a dear friend of our grandfather. I have faith that together we will achieve great things. Besides, little sister, this makes taking a vacation easier. However, first we have much work to complete before we leave. It is already Sunday, and we leave Thursday! That does not leave much time."

"Well, all the preparations for our trip are basically done, and I called the agency yesterday. They were able to book me on a return for November fifth, which gives us enough time to go to Kiratpur, and then travel to Amritsar, where I can see the Golden Temple and return just in time to make my flight," I said cheerfully.

"Have you notified your mother of your plans?" Ekant asked.

"Uhh....oh shoot, I didn't—"

"You did not inform her?"

"It totally slipped my mind! I promise, I'll call her tomorrow," I answered. "Oh, she's totally going to be psyched. I can't believe I'm going to see her again so soon! And all of my friends and my room, my bed, my shower, my TV—"

"Yes, yes, I get it, Esha. Perfect. Now go and please change into something more appropriate, we have guests coming tonight."

"It is not wise for a girl to show so much skin, and I say that to you because I am your big brother."

"Oh please, you say it to annoy me, Ekant, admit it."

"I do not!" he countered.

"I guess some things never change, eh?" I teased as I jumped off the couch and made for the stairs.

"Now where are you going?"

"To change, of course! Isn't that what you wanted? Unless you agree that this is fine."

"No, no, carry on. Make it quick. They will be here soon!" he called out as I ran up the stairs.

After four different shirts, three pairs of jeans, tights, followed by a dress, I finally settled back into a pair of dark blue jeans and a loose-fitting long-sleeved white cotton top. It was comfortable and "appropriate", as Ekant would say. In any case, the evenings were becoming chilly now, and the long sleeves would keep me warm.

I judged my appearance in the mirror and decided that my skin was still quite flawless. The intense heat surprisingly hadn't damaged it. Instead I had a gorgeous golden tan. The girls were going to freak when they saw me. I could already hear their jealous screams. Now, I couldn't really blame Rohan for staring at me earlier today. It wasn't his fault I was so hot, now was it? "Oh, Rohan, if I were you, I wouldn't be able to stop myself either," I said, still gazing into the mirror.

As I continued to freshen up, Sheila began knocking frantically at my door. "Sheila, what's wrong?" I demanded as I pulled the door open.

"Sorry, ma'am, but everyone is waiting," she said, trying to catch her breath.

"Waiting?" I repeated. I looked at the wall clock and realized I had been in my room for an hour already! "Wow, it's been that long? I didn't even notice. Okay, I'm coming." I ran my hand through my hair and followed Sheila downstairs.

As I descended the stairs, I could hear light chatter coming from the living room. The aroma of Jas's cooking was now ripe in the air. My mouth watered as I breathed it in. A man's voice roared through the room as I entered. He was an elderly man with a turban. He had to be at more than sixty, but he still looked fit. This must be my grandfather's friend, the army dude that Ekant had mentioned.

"Esha! Come here and let me introduce you to one of the most decorated colonels in our country!" Ekant said, clearly overjoyed at the elderly man's presence.

"Young man, you are too kind," the Colonel said with a wave of a hand.

"And Uncle Ji, you are too modest. Now meet my young sister, Esha. She is only with us a few more days, but I am very pleased that you two have the chance to meet." Ekant stood up, placed an arm around my shoulder and led me to where the Colonel was sitting. "Esha, this is Colonel Singh, a dear friend of your grandfather's."

I looked up as the colonel rose to his feet. He turned out to be even taller than Ekant. His white beard was tied up carefully and very neatly. I couldn't help but notice the shiny leather shoes, perfectly creased pants and the gold watch on the wrist. Something told me he wasn't just decorated, as Ekant had put it, but he was definitely wealthy also. I could just smell the money on him. Apart from all this, however, the colonel's most profound feature were his cheeks; they looked so...so... so *jolly*. How did this fit? One of the India's most decorated soldiers with jolly cheeks? It was like looking into the face of Santa, only a more toned version.

"Well, hello, my dear, how are you?" he asked. His words were clearly pronounced, as I would imagine any army officer's would be.

"I'm very well, Colonel—"

"Oh, not Colonel. To you, I am only Uncle, okay?"

"Er, sure, I mean okay," I answered nervously. Before now, I'd never been face to face with a colonel, and a decorated one at that. I mean, if he was decorated, that meant he was important. People probably kissed up to him royally, and here I was stammering away. Should I stand tall and add "sir" at the end of every sentence?

As I thought about it, I straightened my back and tried to keep my head high, not too high, of course, but enough to make me look "army-like". What are you thinking, Esha? You're being

227

crazy again. I slowly brought my head back down and just took enough care to keep my chin level with the ground. That's what Mandy's modelling instructor always told her: "Keep your chin level with the floor, no matter what happens!"

"My child, are you okay?" the Colonel asked, snapping me out of my thoughts.

"Oh, yes! Yes, I am okay, perfectly okay. Thanks," I replied sheepishly.

"Ekant, dinner is ready," Jas announced just in time to save me from humiliation.

"Excellent! Uncle Ji, please come," Ekant said as he ushered the Colonel into the dining room. Dhadhi and I joined the men at the table as they laughed and reminisced about our grandfather. "Your nephew still has not returned, what can be keeping him so long?" Ekant inquired after a few moments.

"Yes, it has been long," the colonel said glancing at his oh-so-expensive watch. "We will have to find him, otherwise he will miss dinner! Um...Esha? Esha, child,"

"Yes, Uncle," I answered.

"Could you kindly step outside and send my sometimes ridiculously lost, but most of the time very intelligent, nephew back inside here? He stepped out to get something from the car but somehow has not yet returned. Please have a look," the Colonel said. *My first order*! I nodded and quickly retreated out to the courtyard. Maybe I should have given him a "yes, sir" or a "right away, sir" before I jetted out the door.

It was dark outside now, and the courtyard was pitch black. There were no lights, which was odd, since Chotu always left at least one light on for safety. How was I to find the nephew? "Um, hello?" I called out into the darkness, but as far as I could see, there was no one there.

First things first, I'm not going to find him in the dark. I need the light, I thought as I traced my way over to the fuse box at the far corner, where I had seen Chotu switch on the lights in the courtyard several times before.

I opened the fuse box, but of course without any light, I couldn't really make sense of what was before me. "Great, no light, no nephew, and now I have to go back in there and tell the Colonel I've failed," I complained as I felt around for a switch, but it was pointless. "What the hell am I looking for anyway?"

"This, perhaps?" came a strong voice from behind. Before I could turn around, he put something in my hand. My body immediately tensed as I realized just how near he was to me. My first instinct was to push him back and run, but there was something oddly familiar about him, something that was comforting. Placing his hand over mine, he directed it into the fuse box and helped me plug something in.

"What the...who—" I began, but before I could finish my sentence, the lights flickered on, revealing the man before me. "Angad!" I gasped.

His hand was still over mine, and we were standing just a few inches away from each other. Had he snuck in to see me? Was this planned? My heart was pounding fiercely, and suddenly my legs felt weak and wobbly. I didn't know how much longer I could stand there, but I couldn't escape, nor did I want to escape his gaze. There was an intensity in his eyes tonight that I hadn't seen before. If we were anywhere but here, I might even have mistaken it for passion. However, that couldn't be right, could it? That was not what I expected, but I had to admit, it was something I had thought a lot about in the past week. But this was weird...it was...uncharacteristic of me...this was...this was...hot...this was really hot; something was really hot right now. I looked at my hand, which was still pushed up against the fuse, and realized that the situation wasn't hot, my hand was, and the fuse was heating up!

"Ouch!" I cried, yanking my hand back. Angad jumped back.

"Esha! Are you okay?"

"The damn...thing...burned it!" I yelled, flapping my hand around in the air.

"Here, let me," he said, grabbing my wrist. "Come over here. Sit down." He led me to a chair and sat down next to me. "It is just a little red, you will be fine."

"Easy for you to say, your hand's not on fire!" I snapped.

"You are worse than a baby," he teased. He pulled my hand towards him and gently blew on it. "Does that help?"

"Um...hmm," I stammered as I felt a tingle go up my spine. He looked up as I fumbled with my words and flashed one of his oh-so-perfect smiles.

"Esha! What happened?" Jas asked as she stormed through the screen door. I quickly pulled my hand back as Angad jumped out of his seat. "I heard you scream. Are you all right?"

"Hey, yeah, I'm fine. Stupid fuse thing, it kinda burned me," I answered.

"Burned you? How did that happen?" she shrieked, grabbing my wrist and examining my hand.

"Jas, it's nothing. The lights weren't working out here, so I went to check it out...and Angad here helped me...anyways, it's all good. My hand is already feeling better."

"Yes, very well then," Jas answered, flashing us a suspicious look. "So you two have met by now. Perfect. Come along then, everyone is wondering where you are!"

Angad hurried inside, while I followed behind Jas, since

she still hadn't released her hold on my wrist. As expected, she dragged me into the kitchen, where she examined and re-examined my hand and fussed about what remedy she should choose to help cool it off. After much bickering, I finally managed to reassure her that my hand was not burned and that I didn't require any remedies.

Back in the dining room, as I sat across from Angad and listened to the Colonel narrate his war adventures, I found out that Angad not only was the Colonel's nephew, but also Ekant's new partner. Apparently he had inherited some parts of the family business after his father had passed away. The Colonel explained that it was now time for Angad to make decisions on his own and to follow his business sense. Personally I thought it was a risk for Ekant to take him on so soon, but Ekant and the Colonel seemed more than pleased to accept Angad's offer to become involved.

"Uncle Ji, I have made a decision that I am hoping both you and Angad will agree to," Ekant announced as everyone settled back into the living room after dinner.

"Oh, and what would that be, my son?" asked the Colonel.

"Angad and I still have plenty of work to complete before I leave Thursday with the family. By that time, he has to make a smooth transition into a leadership role. If my men are to take orders from Angad in my absence, then they need to have confidence in him, which requires further familiarity. There is much for him to learn before Thursday."

"I agree. However, you will be back in a week's time, no?"

"Yes, Uncle Ji, we will return from Punjab early next week. However, I do plan to take a much longer holiday from work. Bhagat is getting so big, and I have spent most of his childhood busying myself with work. I wish to spend some quality time with him, maybe take him on another trip," Ekant said, much to Jas and Bhagat's delight.

"You are a dedicated father, Ekant. I like that in a man," said the Colonel. "So what do you propose?"

"I propose that Angad stay here with us this week. That way he will be in close proximity to me. We can easily head to the office in the morning and continue our business in the evening undisturbed."

My jaw dropped as Ekant revealed his plan. *Angad in the same house as me?* I glanced at him, only to find him with his head down. Strangely, his eyes were fixed on the ground. Was he being shy?

"Stay here?" the Colonel repeated. "Well, I see the logic in your suggestion, but I do not wish for my nephew to burden you or your family."

"I assure you it will not be a burden; instead it will resolve many issues and benefit us all in the end. It will enable us to be much more productive in the coming week," Ekant answered.

"Angad?" the Colonel asked.

"Yes, Uncle Ji," Angad replied, slowly looking up at the Colonel. "I agree with Ekant."

"Well, it is settled then!" the Colonel announced. "Angad will stay with you, Ekant, until you see fit. I will have the driver bring some of your things."

"Thank you, Uncle Ji," Angad replied.

"You have nothing to worry about, I will ensure that he eats and sleeps well. I will take care of him better than Ekant!" Dhadhi said with a big smile.

"Then I have no worries!" the Colonel laughed. "Now, I shall take my leave."

After saying goodbye to the Colonel in the courtyard,

everyone decided to call it a night. Dhadhi, of course, was the first, seeing as anything past nine p.m. was extremely late for her, and it was almost midnight.

"Angad," Ekant said, placing a hand on his shoulder, "the guest room has been made ready for you. Please make yourself comfortable. Treat this as your home."

"Yes, brother Ekant. Thank you for your hospitality. I am looking forward to working alongside you and learning all that I can." Angad sounded like the perfect apprentice.

"Oh, do not mention it! Now, it is late, and we have much to do in the morning. I shall retire for the night, and I suggest you do the same. Esha, show Angad the guest room."

"Me?" I blurted out.

"Yes, you ought to know by now where it is. Now hurry along, it is getting very late. Good night to you both. Come on, Jas." Jas hesitated for a moment and watched both me and Angad, almost as if she were contemplating something. After a few seconds, she followed.

"Hmm...alone again in the same place. Shall we carry on from where we were interrupted earlier?" he said, clearly amused.

"Well, someone is happy. I wouldn't be, if I were you," I said, walking away.

"Hey! Where are you going?" He followed me into the house.

"I have things to do," I answered, doing my best to sound indifferent.

"What about my room?"

"What about it?"

"Did you not hear Ekant just now? You have to show me my new room."

"Find it yourself. I'm sure you're very capable of doing that.

Besides, I'm not a servant," I said as I made my way to the stairs.

"Oh, come on Esha. How am I to find it on my own?" he complained, following closely behind. "And where are you going?"

"Nowhere," I snapped.

"Nowhere? Then why are you walking?"

"It's none of your business. Go find your room," I said, adding a flare of annoyance to my tone. I didn't know why, but I wanted to create some distance between us, to let him know that my guard was back up.

"None of my business?" he repeated. "Very well then, I will follow you."

"You can't do that!" I hissed, stopping abruptly at the top landing. Angad crashed right into me, and we clung together for a moment, trying to regain our balance. He wrapped his arms around me as he caught me, while my arms naturally found their way around his neck. Once again my heart was beating uncontrollably.

"Of course I can," he whispered. His face was so close that his breath felt like a light breeze upon my face. The sensation was hypnotic. "And watch your voice. Dhadhi is asleep. It's just you and me. What if someone were to catch us like this? Unless you show me my room, I will stick right behind you."

"Do what you want," I said, unravelling myself from him and stepping back. No matter what I was feeling, it would be a disaster if someone caught us clinging to one another in the dead of night. I walked defiantly away and mounted the steps leading to the roof.

"I should have known," he said as he followed me.

"Known what?" I asked.

"I should have known that *this* was where you were headed.

I remember you saying that you enjoyed the beautiful night sky." *He remembered, he actually remembered.*

"Yes, well, there aren't any surprises hidden in a moonlit sky, I suppose." I walked to the edge of the roof and drew a long, deep breath as I looked up. "You can expect to see the moon and the stars. Even its timing isn't a secret; when to expect it, when it disappears in the morning. No surprises. Sometimes if I look long and deep enough, I can almost fool myself that I'm back home."

"You miss it?" Angad asked.

"Of course."

"But this is also your family, is it not? Dhadhi, Ekant, Jas, they all seem to show you a lot of love."

"Don't remind me. I'm even starting to regret that now."

"Regret?"

"Well, yeah, I mean, I don't deserve it," I answered. "Angad, I came to Delhi with the worst intentions. I didn't care for any of these people. The truth is that I was forced to come here and forced to stay. When I first got here, I planned to do the least possible, just perform the last rites for my dad then jet off to Canada again, never to return or even look back. But—"

"But what?" He sounded hopeful.

"Everything's changed," I confessed, taking another deep breath and looking at him directly now. "They all love me, Dhadhi, Jas, Bhagat, Sumi, even Ekant. They treat me like a family should treat one another. All this time, I've been upset that I was forced to be here. I even tried to escape and got Sumi involved in a plan that got royally screwed up. In these past months, I've gotten to know them. It makes me feel horrible that I was ever that ignorant towards them. To top it all off, I've treated my father and his ashes...I almost lost them. What kind of daughter does that? I'm just horrible. I am a horrible and undeserving daughter," I said with misty eyes. I was beginning to tremble again.

"Esha, you are not horrible," Angad said softly. He brushed a lock of hair away from my forehead, and my heart skipped a few beats. I couldn't believe that a simple touch from him had such an impact on me. What was it about this guy in particular? I was almost perplexed at the influence he had on me. "What you are feeling is nothing terrible," he continued. "You have been through a lot."

"No, I am, I am a horrible daughter," I persisted. "You don't know what I've done; what I've continued to do. How I've disrespected him!"

The tears were now flowing freely down my cheeks. I couldn't hold back any more. Angad's sudden touch had given me strength. It had ignited a confidence within me and an urge to clear my conscience. All these weeks, regret had been building up inside me. With each passing day, I was learning to love and appreciate the family that my father had cared for all these years. It disgusted me to think that I had tortured and ridiculed him so terribly and that I'd made him think his own daughter hated him.

"Esha, listen to me," he said firmly. "You are a good person. You have stuck it out for many weeks when you had every right and opportunity to give it up and return home, but you did not. You stayed, and you are determined to carry out your father's wish. That not only makes you a good daughter, but it makes you a daughter that any father can be proud of."

"I *deserted* my father on his deathbed!" I sobbed. "I deserted him! I didn't have the courage to face it. I didn't want to see him like that any more. I didn't want to believe how bad it was, that he would never come home again. When he needed me most, I was foolish and weak! I left him...I was weak. Angad, I was weak."

I continued to sob as he wrapped his arms around me and pulled me into a tight embrace. I welcomed the comfort he offered and was hit by an unusual feeling: I wished he would hold me forever and never let go.

"Esha, you are *not* weak. I know what you are feeling," he said.

"You don't know, Angad. No one around me does. I should have been there to help my father through it, but I couldn't watch him, and now I wonder. I wonder what it would have felt like...to see him...I mean, I still can't imagine what it would feel like to watch your own father die..."

"I know." Angad's reply was sombre. He pulled away and walked to the opposite side of the balcony. I couldn't feel his presence any more. It was as if he had travelled somewhere else.

"Angad?"

"You stand there, and you feel helpless," he began, still staring off into space, perfectly still. "All of your love and wishes cannot do *anything* to save him, but your heart aches as you fight this end. You pray that God instills within you the power to save him; to put life back into the man who held your hand and supported you always. You pray that your hand that is placed on his chest and is now feeling his slowing heartbeat can be given some force through God that can heal him.

"At that moment you are no longer bound to just one religion or race. You are everything and everyone, and you wish that all spiritual and biblical stories of healing and miracles that you heard as a kid are true; that miracles do happen. You pray to Waheguru, you pray to Jesus, to Allah and to Shiv to save your father and give you more time. Soon, he becomes colder, but right before that, there is a sudden surge of energy within the body. For a moment you almost believe that God is granting you a miracle. However, the energy quickly lifts upwards and out of his body, and it is *then* that you realize that his soul is leaving the body behind. You look into his eyes, and you see nothing. You feel for his heartbeat, and you feel nothing. He is cold, he is still, and he is gone."

There was a long silence between us as Angad stared off into the night sky, and I gaped in shock at his unexpected response. Finally, I realized that he was done speaking, and that I should say something to acknowledge the pain he was clearly still experiencing.

"Angad, I didn't realize...I'm so sorry. I mean, I—"

"It's okay. There was no way for you to know."

"But how did it happen? When—"

"Recently, in Amritsar," he answered.

"Amritsar? You mean Operation Bluestar?" I said shakily. I dreaded asking the question. I feared hearing a haunting tale about what had gone on inside the Golden Temple during the attack.

"Yes, in Operation Bluestar. My family and I were there to celebrate the anniversary of Guru Arjan Dev when all hell broke loose. There were thousands of people there the night before. Mother expressed worries about the army's presence, so we resolved to go home. Unfortunately, that was not possible."

"Why not?"

"As we attempted to leave, we were informed that the army was arresting anyone leaving the premises. There were also rumours of people being shot. So we couldn't take that risk. We decided to wait until morning. However, when morning finally arrived, so too did bloodshed. Tanks, gunfire, destruction, all of it consumed the Golden Temple. People were being tied up and shot at point blank range. The sacred pool was tainted with blood and the Golden Gurdwara chipped by bullets. The library, the archives, hundreds of years of history went up in flames. Dismembered bodies, women and children screaming...Esha, it was too much..." Angad dropped his face into his hands.

"Your parents...they..."

"I was able to get my mother to safety. I promised my father I would protect her, but when I came back to find him, it was already too late. I found him clutching a copy of the Guru Granth Sahib. A bullet had pierced his throat. His eyes were wide, and he just stared at me as I held on to him and prayed that God would save him. After that day, Amritsar became even more dangerous for male Sikhs. Everyone was being labelled as a militant or a terrorist. My mother sent me here to live with my uncle and to make a living. When I am settled, I will call her here to live with me again. But that day, those moments that I spent with my father as he lay there clutching to his faith, to his life, I will never forget it.

"For the rest of your life, you do not forget how helpless you felt at that moment. It shakes you up, and life is now something completely different. It may have been an hour, or a few minutes or a second, but when you walk away from that experience, it is as if you are walking away after spending a lifetime in God's sanctuary. And now after that moment, you have been made to venture out alone and make sense of it and apply the lesson."

"What lesson?" I asked.

He turned around now to face me again. His lips curled

into a warm smile. "That life is more than just having a body. Life is in the soul that journeys."

I considered his answer for a minute before letting out a long sigh. "Well, it's obvious *that* lesson's not meant for me, at least not in this lifetime."

His expression grew serious again, and his eyebrows gathered in the middle. "Why do you say that?" he asked.

"Because *I* didn't even have the courage to be there with him, and because of everything else I've told you. It's just not in me."

He came closer now, and his eyes probed mine. "Then why are you here?" he asked firmly.

"What do you mean?"

"Is *this* not a journey?"

"This?" I repeated. "*This* exists because I was forced to come and stick it out."

"Forced? I think not, Esha. No one handcuffed you, and no one put a gun to your head, unless you're not telling me something," he chuckled. He was amused by my answer! "Listen, *you* got on that plane, *you* carried your father's ashes, and *you* stayed when you could have left. You were not handicapped in any matter. You chose to stay out of your own free will." He grabbed me by the shoulders. "This is your journey, and this journey is your lesson."

I looked at Angad fiercely, wanting his words to be true. What he said made sense as usual and gave me strength. If what he said was true, then my guilt could be resolved. But could it be so simple?

"In any case," he said when I didn't speak up, "I must take my leave now before someone finds us huddled out here on the roof alone and at night. Something tells me that would not be a good thing, especially now that I am Ekant's new business partner." I snapped out of my half-daze and realized just how close he was to me again. He slowly removed his hands from my shoulders and flashed that perfect smile. His teeth gleamed in the darkness of the night. "As for the room, I will find it on my own."

"It's past the study, first room on the left," I said, giving in.

"Thank you. Farewell and goodnight, Esha. I hope to see your beautiful face in the morning. Oh! And before I forget, here this is for you," he said, reaching into a bag that I hadn't noticed before. It was lying on the chair. He whipped something out, and as he brought it closer, I saw that it was a shawl.

"Where did you get that? Did you have it with you all this time?" I asked.

"I snuck it up here after dinner," he answered as he swung the shawl over and draped it around me. "Absolutely beautiful," he marvelled.

I looked at it closely and recognized it at once. It was the pink shawl I had fallen in love with during our trip to the Red Fort. "How did you know?" I asked, completely in awe of his gesture.

"I was watching you, even then," he said. He placed a hand on my cheek and held it there, sending another set of currents through my body. My heartbeat quickened, and I worried it would combust right then and there, if hearts are capable of combusting. As I wrestled with my feelings, he gently removed his hand and walked away.

"Are you part of it?" I asked. My voice cracked, since I still wasn't fully composed. He stopped at the top of the stairs and turned his head in my direction.

"A part of what?" he asked.

"My journey. Are you a part of it?" I asked, turning away. I was too shy to face him now. My heart pounded uncontrollably as I awaited his answer. *What am I doing?*

After what seemed like an agonizing eternity, he answered. "If you allow me, then yes, I am. However, it is your decision. In my heart, you already are a part of mine."

With that he quietly left, leaving me to ponder his words under the dazzling night sky.

FIFTEEN

The next morning when I woke, it was as if I had been transported into heaven. I had slept in perfect tranquility. No frustrations, no nightmares and surprisingly, no feelings of regret. My confession last night to Angad about this past year had taken a load off my shoulders. I felt lighter and more relaxed. My room was bright and peaceful when I opened my eyes. The noise from the outside traffic sounded almost melodious. As I made my way downstairs for breakfast, I felt as if I were floating. My mouth was set in a permanent smile. Each breath was fresh and energizing. Everyone around me looked beautiful and happy. Most important, Angad looked like an angel.

"Esha, there is a glow about you this morning," he whispered as he sat next to me at the table, sipping his tea.

"A glow?"

"Yes, but I imagine you are this beautiful each and every morning." I turned to face him and couldn't help but offer a seductive gaze. It was difficult to refrain from reaching out to his free hand that he had so carefully placed on the edge of the table between us. "There it is," he continued in a whisper, "the smile, the sparkle in the eyes. I watched you when you came down. I have never seen anyone move with such grace. Be careful Esha, or someone may think you have fallen in love."

I dropped my spoon when I heard him use the word "love".

"Is everything okay?" Ekant asked, looking up from the newspaper he was reading at the far end of the table.

"Yeah, everything's fine. Sorry, still sleepy, I suppose," I stuttered.

"Stay up late last night?" Angad asked loudly for everyone to hear.

"Our Esha has a habit of watching the night sky before bed," Ekant answered.

"Is that so?" Angad replied, seeming thoroughly amused. "Well, I must try that also sometime!" I stomped on his foot to shut him up. "Well...okay then, Ekant, we should head to the office. I can't wait to get started." Angad got to his feet while I smiled between spoonfuls of my cereal.

"Ambitious! I like that in a man," Ekant said proudly. "We can all learn a lot from you. You agree, Esha?"

"Absolutely," I said. Angad smirked at me as he followed Ekant outside, but I stuck out my tongue to get the last laugh.

After they finally left, I called my mother to inform her of my plans, just as I had promised Ekant I would. It was night in B.C., but she was ecstatic nonetheless to hear from me, and even more overjoyed to hear that I would be returning so soon.

"Everything finally seems to be coming together," I said.

"Oh my sweet, sweet daughter! You see, I told you that you must keep faith. In a few days, you will have fulfilled your task, and you will return to me. Oh, how I have missed you, Esha. This house is so empty without you." I could hear her crying softly.

"Mom, I've missed you too, you know that. But listen, you've got nothing to worry about. We're leaving Thursday morning, and Ekant is taking care of the details. Things are cool, Mom."

"Well, I am happy to finally hear that!"

"Okay, I just wanted to fill you in on what's going on. I should let you get some sleep now. I want to call Mandy before it gets too late over there."

"Oh, those girls! One of them calls every day, asking if you called and when you are coming home. They bug me so much!"

I laughed as she complained. "Chill out, Mom. Look I'll call you when I get back and before I get on the plane. Love you and can't wait to see you!"

"Oh, my sweet child, this will be a tough journey with your father's ashes. Remember that my heart and strength are always with you. Never forget how much I love you."

"I won't, and Mom?"

"Yes?"

"Thanks," I said warmly, and this time I really meant it.

"For what?" she asked.

"For sending me here and convincing me to stay."

"I may have pushed you, but you did it of your own accord. Your father would be very proud of you, sweetheart."

"Thanks, Mom."

"I am so happy. It appears your father's wish is coming true. See you soon," she said softly before hanging up. I hung up too and wiped at my tears.

Speaking to my mom had reinforced what Angad had said the night before. This was my journey, and I was controlling it. I took a deep breath and composed myself while I dialled Mandy's number.

"This better be important," a groggy voice answered on the other end.

"Now, Amanda, is that any way to answer your phone?" I teased.

"Wait...Esha? Is that you?" she shrieked. "Is that really you?"

"Yes, stupid! Quit screaming. You're going to wake up your parents."

"Oh, don't worry, they're not here," she answered. "I had a house party, so I told them to leave for the weekend. I can't believe I still live with them! As soon as I save enough money, that's it, I'm outta here!"

"Wait, slow down, babe. What house party?" I asked.

"For commencement, duh! We had it last week, so I got the gang together at my house for the weekend and we—"

"Commencement? Meaning you all...without me..." I felt a stab of pain in my heart. I had missed commencement. I couldn't believe it. I had totally forgotten.

"Oh, Esha, we missed you. This whole weekend, everyone kept asking about you. Parties aren't the same without you, you know. Even Johnny won't look at another girl. This is getting beyond insane now, babe. We need you back here, fast!"

"I'll be back soon—"

"How soon?"

"Next week. That's why I called. I wanted to let you know," I answered, trying to push away her mention of commencement and Johnny.

"Ah! That's amazing! I can't wait to tell everyone. Oh my, it's going to be crazy! I'll have to organize another party for sure!" she screamed.

"Yeah, we'll see about that when I get there," I replied, trying to calm her. For some reason, I was finding it difficult to match her level of enthusiasm.

"Esha, you don't sound happy. What's wrong?" she asked more seriously.

"Nothing. It's just that talking about all of this makes me think about everything and everyone I'll be leaving behind here. I mean I'm *really* leaving. It's finally come to that. I'm just getting it now..."

"Yeah, you're leaving," she said sternly. "After everything that's happened, aren't you hell bent on getting out of there? And now that you are, you should be totally psyched. But you sound almost...*depressed*."

"I *am* happy, Mands. But things have kind of changed around here—"

"Changed how? What's happening there?" she snapped. My hasty reply had aroused her curiosity.

"First, things are cool now between Ekant and me," I began.

"Really?"

"Yeah, we sorted it out, and it's good. Also I've sort of... kind of..."

"You sort of, kind of what?" she demanded.

"Met someone," I whispered. I wasn't sure if I was afraid of someone overhearing me or of admitting my feelings to my friend.

"Met someone?" cried Mandy. "Who? Where? *There*?" Her reaction said it all. Why did I have to start this now? Now that it was out, Mandy wouldn't give up until she knew everything.

"Yes, here," I answered. "Actually, as of yesterday, he's in the same house as me, but that's a long story. I met him a few times before, and now, surprisingly, he's Ekant's new business partner."

"How is he? What does he look like?" she asked, still with a hint of disbelief in her voice.

"He's young, and he's cool. He's got the perfect smile. You'd be so jealous. But when I'm with him, it feels good. We always

247

have such deep conversations, which is so damn rare for me. But I love it...and...umm...well, I think I—"

"Don't say it!" yelled Mandy. "You can't be...you know. A few chance meetings can't determine *that*! And *there*, of all places? Come on, Esha!"

"What?" I snapped, insulted by her abrupt conclusions on a topic she knew nothing about.

"What do you mean *what*? You know what I'm talking about," she said matter-of-factly.

"Is it so unimaginable that I could fall for an Indian guy?" I demanded.

"You've *fallen* for him?" Now she was patronizing me, and I suddenly felt I couldn't breathe properly. The disbelief and judgement in her tone made me feel bullied.

"Yes!" I cried out. "I mean...I don't know...maybe. Oh, Mands, we can discuss the degree of attraction later, but tell me, is it so impossible? I mean, it didn't exactly happen overnight. I've considered my feelings for a while now. In my head, I've constantly battled the fact that he's not exactly my type. But really, so what if he has a turban, he's an amazing person."

"A *turban*?" Mandy asked again in that patronizing tone. "Honestly, a turban? Esha, now you've gone off the deep end. What are you doing there, babe, what?"

"I don't get you, Mandy," I sighed.

"Esha, do you remember Grade Twelve, when that new kid came from India? The first time you thought he was hitting on you, you smacked him and warned him against ever trying it again. Since then you've never given a second look at any Indian guy. I thought that's what you wanted."

"That was before..." I replied, trying to get the image of that poor kid out of my mind. I really had hit him hard. The rest of the year, he had gone out of his way to avoid me.

"So what's changed?" she persisted.

"I don't know. Everything, I guess. I mean, come on Mands, this past year hasn't exactly been like every other. Some serious shit has gone down. I don't know if I can go back to..."

"Back to what? Us? Your life here?" she demanded. She sounded offended now.

"No, that's not it. You know I love you all. I'm desperate to see you again, to be home. But that doesn't mean what I'm feeling is wrong. Why can't I have both?"

"Can you? Look, Esha, I always want what's best for you. You're my girl, and you know that. If you say you like this dude, then fine, I'm happy if you're happy. What happens, though, when you get back to your old life, to your *real* life?" Mandy's words caught me off-guard. I knew what she was getting at, and she had hit a nerve. Realizing I wasn't going to answer, she continued, "You say he's got a turban?"

"Yeah," I answered.

"Meaning he's religious to some degree, but definitely more than you've ever been your whole life. Esha, it's not rocket science. We've been friends our whole life, and I've been around your family long enough. Something tells me he wouldn't be too happy with your partying and drinking, which I don't think you're ready to give up yet. We just graduated university, we're starting a new phase, and we're young."

"That's all true, Mandy, but—"

"Have you mentioned to him, even once, about the kind of life you have here?" she cut me off mid-sentence. My mind quickly flashed back to all the conversations I had shared with Angad. After a long pause, I realized I had said nothing.

"It never came up," I replied in a docile tone.

"Never came up, or you didn't want to scare him away?" she retorted, as if she were already expecting my answer.

"Mandy, don't you think you're over-reacting just a little?"

"Maybe, or maybe I'm giving you the dose of reality that you so obviously need right now. He doesn't fit into your life, and you don't fit into his. I get it, you've been away from here for a long time. You're surrounded by people like him, and you're cut off from the rest of us. It's like you don't have a choice but to like it there for the sake of your own sanity." I wasn't sure if I agreed with or even appreciated her view of my situation, but I kept quiet. "It's easy to get caught up in that, but face reality. You're not ready to give up your life, *our* life; the fun, the parties, the carefree world, and Johnny. This isn't you."

"Mands, I don't want to talk about this any more," I said with a sigh. I didn't care if I sounded defeated, but I couldn't listen to her any longer.

"Okay, but just come back to us, Esha. In the meantime, I'll plan your coming home party. Just watch, it'll be amazing! You'll be surrounded by your friends, then you'll see I'm right. So until next week?"

"Next week," I said and hung up.

Mandy had proved to be as relentless as ever. She had always been a self-appointed protector of us girls, never afraid to voice her opinions. Disagreements were nothing new, but a part of me still wished she would approve of my choice. As much as I hated to admit it, she had made a valid point. Angad was so mature. Since I'd met him, I hadn't been myself. Talking about religion, life, analyzing my conscience, this wasn't me. How would Angad fit into the life I led back in B.C.? I could hardly imagine him basking in the sun at one of our beachside parties or even jamming at a club. I got through all these weeks, but I'd always known I'd go back one day. It was never permanent, so how could I be sure that what I was feeling now was permanent or just a manifestation of the random and isolated time I had spent here in Delhi?

I stood in perfect silence struggling with what I knew was the eventual conclusion: It wasn't possible. No matter how much I wanted it to be, it wasn't possible. Angad wasn't a part of this journey.

"Esha, is everything all right?" Jas asked from behind me.

"Oh, hey, Jas. Yeah, everything's fine. I just called my mom and my friend to let them know the plan. That's all." I tried to sound cheerful, masking the despair I felt.

"They must be so happy. Soon you will get back to your life. We have kept you too long," she said, smiling as she hugged me.

"Yeah, back to my life," I said solemnly.

"Well, we need to start preparing, so why don't we go sort your things. There is much work to be done."

"Sure," I replied, following her upstairs.

As we worked, I tried to forget my frustration at Mandy's words and my feelings for Angad, but as the day dragged on, I became increasingly agitated. A battle waged in my mind between Mandy and Angad, and I couldn't put it to rest. I zoned out while Jas and Dhadhi fussed about housework, preparations for the trip and my eventual departure from India.

As evening approached, I became nervous about having to see Angad. When the men finally pulled up in front of the gate, I felt feverish and edgy. My breathing became shorter, my heart pounded rapidly and my palms became increasingly sweaty. I ran to my room, claiming I wasn't feeling well and needed rest. Sheila was sent after me to bring water and later, dinner.

"Esha Ma'am, Angad Sir wanted me to ask you if you are feeling okay?" she asked hesitantly.

"I'm fine, Sheila. I just need sleep. See you in the morning, and don't let anyone disturb me," I replied.

"Okay, ma'am." She closed the door quietly behind her.

True to her word, Sheila didn't allow anyone to disturb me that night, and I slept in late enough to miss Ekant and Angad as they left for work the next day. When I eventually ventured downstairs, Dhadhi sat alone in the living room knitting.

"How are you feeling today, my child?" she asked, placing a frail hand on my forehead.

"I'm fine, Dhadhi, just tired. I'm going to just chill out upstairs for the day."

"Very well, you need to rest up. The drive to Kiratpur will be long and gruelling. Rest as much as you can now. I'll make sure no one disturbs you."

"Thanks, Dhadhi," I said, relieved, and kissed her on the cheek.

After lunch I hid in my room once again and buried myself in another book. When Sheila brought dinner, she again informed me that Angad was inquiring about my health. I tried to ignore her suspicious stare as she explained his growing curiosity.

"Sheila, I'm fine. I just want to be left alone," I said firmly.

"Okay, ma'am, but tomorrow you cannot sleep in too late."

"Why is that?" I asked, looking up from my food.

"Did Dhadhi Ji not inform you? Sumedha Ma'am is coming to visit for the day. She called this afternoon. Her family has gone away for another wedding function, and Daya wishes that she not be alone while he works. So she is coming here to spend time with you."

"Okay, tell Dhadhi I'll see her in the morning."

"Okay, ma'am."

I left my dirty dishes by the door for Sheila to collect later and walked over to the window. It had been two full nights since I'd visited the rooftop balcony. I felt more trapped now than on any other day since the start of my time in Delhi. I missed the starry moonlit sky. I missed how peaceful it made me feel. But I couldn't risk running into Angad. I couldn't handle any more questions or be frustrated any longer over how I felt about him. The truth was that this time next week, I would be on a plane headed back home, and this chapter of my life would be closed forever.

I got back into bed and picked up another book, determined to absorb myself in the story. I needed to distract myself from the sound of Angad's voice, which now reverberated through the halls of the house, or the memories of his touch, his scent and his presence. All of it had to be forgotten. I just wished the next few days would pass by quickly and painlessly.

Part Four

Courage

SIXTEEN

October 31st, 1984

When I opened my eyes, I knew it was way too early to be awake. I had grown accustomed to sleeping in, another indication of just how long I had been in this country. Holding another cup of tea in her hands, Sheila pleaded for me to get up and get dressed.

"Oh, please, Esha Ma'am. This is the second time Dhadhi has sent me upstairs. Sumedha Ma'am will be here shortly. Please get dressed!"

I wasn't worried about Sumi walking in while I was still in bed. It wouldn't be the first time. Besides, we had nothing planned for the day, meaning we would spend it like any other, sitting around gossiping and telling stories. I let out a long, tired sigh just thinking how much I was going to miss that after I left.

"Ma'am pleeease...please get up, ma'am, please—"

"Okay, okay, okay Sheila!" I called, ripping the comforter off. "Cut it out, I'm getting up!" I stumbled reluctantly out of bed. The mornings were much colder now, making it almost unbearable to depart from the nice warm comforter.

Sumi was already enjoying a warm cup of tea and dishing about married life to a delighted Jas and Dhadhi when I joined them in the living room. I stood at the door listening. She looked very much the beautiful bride still, with her perfectly composed posture, glowing complexion and a bright red Indian suit. The customary wedding bangles on her arms, which she was required to wear for a month and half, still clanged at the slightest movement of her arms.

"Honestly, Dhadhi, as soon as my mother-in-law walks into the room, mother just goes silent and is perfectly still. It is like she is terrified to speak!" Sumi explained.

"I find that hard to believe, Sumi dear. It is not an easy task to silence your mother," Dhadhi laughed.

"Well, my mother-in-law has done the trick! Mother was horrified when she learned that Daya's parents wanted to travel in the same car as her and Papa today for the wedding in Chandigarh. Mother worked quickly, though, and made up an excuse, saying that she and Papa can't leave until tomorrow. So now they will drive separately. Daya's family has already left today, and Mother and Papa will drive tomorrow. It is so strange to see her like this."

"Well, I guess Rano Aunty finally met her match, eh?" I laughed, walking into the room.

"Esha, you are awake!" Sumi said, standing up and holding her arms out for me. I raced to give her a warm hug. "I am so happy to see you. How are you, though? Dhadhi tells me you have not been well?"

"I'm much better, don't worry. I'm just glad you're here. Now we can hang out before I leave," I said. "So what do you feel like doing first?"

"First, you need to do something for Ekant," Dhadhi interrupted. "He is with a client and needs something done urgently, Esha. So he has asked that you carry it out for him right away."

"Ekant is finally asking for my help, eh? That's a first. Please tell, tell Dhadhi! What do I get to do?" I was intrigued to know what wonderful task Ekant needed me to perform for him.

"You need to go drop these papers off in Sultanpuri—"

"Sultanpuri? That's quite a drive," Sumi interjected.

"How far?" I asked Sumi.

"It is eight o'clock. At this time, it will take much more than an hour. It is in the far northwest corner of Delhi. Basically, you will have to cross the city to the other side. It will take some time."

"Yes, that is why I am sending you girls together with Chotu," Dhadhi announced. "Angad has gone up to see his uncle, the Colonel, in Sultanpuri on some urgent business. However, he left behind some important papers that Ekant says must reach him right away. That is why you must go at once."

"We have to see Angad?" I blurted out.

Dhadhi hesitated for a moment, and I looked everywhere but at her probing eyes before she answered. "Yes, you must meet with Angad. Now, you will be fine, and this way your day will pass by. Otherwise what would you have done all day? Just laze around and gossip? Now, shall I tell Ekant you will take care of this?" It was more of a statement than a question, so I simply nodded.

Seeing Angad was something I had been avoiding for the past two days, and now I had to face him directly. I dreaded his expression when he saw me standing at his doorstep or the questions that I was sure he would ask me. Perhaps I could make Sumi run in and drop the papers. I could deal better with her curiosity rather than *his* questions.

Sumi and I climbed into the back seat, Angad's papers secure in my hands, while Chotu started the engine. Soon, we found ourselves victims of Delhi's traffic. Chotu joined the hundreds, perhaps thousands of drivers honking their horns relentlessly. I had learned long ago that it was pointless to complain about the honking to Chotu. Regardless of the fact that his hand remained on the horn, he refused to admit that he was like any of the other drivers. Instead, he maintained that all others were crazy and didn't belong on the road.

"So Dhadhi mentioned that Angad has been staying at the house since Sunday?" Sumi said quietly. I quickly glanced at Chotu to make sure he wasn't eavesdropping. I wasn't sure if he could understand us. In any case, he seemed too absorbed in the difficult task of manoeuvring through the traffic.

"Yeah, Ekant made him," I answered.

"I am surprised he was so close by for so many days, but he did not contact Daya."

"I'm sure Ekant kept him busy," I said casually and looked out the window as if something interesting had caught my attention.

"Yes, or perhaps he was too distracted with something or *someone* else," Sumi said, sounding hopeful. This is just what I had dreaded talking about.

"I've barely seen him," I retorted, glancing at Chotu again, but he showed no interest in our conversation.

"How is that possible? You are in the same house. I don't see...or wait a minute. Esha, are you avoiding him?" Sumi's eyes grew wide as she stared at me.

"I am not. Now stop it!" I hissed.

"No, it makes perfect sense. Why else would you hide away in your room, as Dhadhi said you have been doing for the past two nights. You fear being around him...hmmm...but you do not appear repulsed by the mere mention of his name, so I rule out hatred. What does that leave? Love? Oh, Esha you *do* like him."

"Sumi, please *shut up*," I demanded, pointing at Chotu.

He still seemed highly uninterested in our discussion, but I couldn't risk him taking a phrase or even a word back to Ekant. That would definitely do major damage to all the progress I'd made with him. I glowered at Sumi until she finally clued in. "It's not what you think," I explained in a whisper. "I'm flying back home next week. My friends, my family, they're all waiting for me. Angad isn't a part of that, okay? I get that now, and so should you. Now drop it."

For a while Sumi just stared at me. She looked like a little girl who has just learned that her dog had been run over by a car. Choosing not to respond to her disappointment, I casually turned away from her and watched Delhi pass by. It was shaping up to be a clear day. The hustle and bustle of the busy capital was the same as every other day. I enjoyed the drive; it felt good to be out of the house. Eventually, however, we reached our destination and my stomach twisted into knots.

The Colonel's house was larger than I had imagined it to be. It was a mansion, set in white sandstone and three storeys tall. The vast property was boarded off with what looked like a ten-foot wall and a black iron gate at the main entrance. As we drove in, I saw that Angad was already waiting for us at the foot of the front stairs leading into the house. My stomach lurched as I finally set my eyes upon him after two whole painful days. He looked flawless in his black business suit. No surprise there. Instinctively I sat up in my seat and ran my hand through my hair. Sumi flashed me an "I know what you're thinking" smile, and I glared at her. She only giggled in response, making me even more uncomfortable.

To make matters worse, Chotu decided to stop the car so that Angad was now standing directly outside my door. I took a deep breath as he opened it and offered a hand to help me out of the car. Before stepping out, I glanced once more in Sumi's direction, and as expected, she sat wide-eyed with a big smile waiting for me to respond. I rolled my eyes at her and stepped out of the car without taking his hand.

"Esha, how are you?" he asked with a smile.

I quickly stepped to the side, far enough that there was a comfortable distance between us.

"I'm fine, thanks," I said, ignoring the baffled look on his face.

"Hello, Angad!" came Sumi's voice from the other side of the car. I breathed a sigh of relief as she stepped out and distracted him.

"Sumi! A nice surprise. How are you?"

"Good, Angad, thank you." Sumi walked to the front of the car but stopped short of coming anywhere near us.

"And...Daya...how is Daya?" he asked. Even though the question was directed at Sumi, I could still feel his attention on me.

"Good, he is good." The conversation was quickly becoming strained, and I could hear it in Sumi's voice. "It is a nice day today, isn't it? I mean, the nights are still chilly, but the days remain beautiful."

Great, not the weather!

"Yes...it is a nice—"

"So, uh, here are the papers you needed," I interrupted and thrust the file at him. He hesitated a moment before reaching for it, not once releasing me from his puzzled gaze. Meanwhile, I looked everywhere except at him. I figured I looked like an idiot, and I could feel Sumi glaring at me, but I didn't dare risk making eye contact. But as he reached for the folder, his fingers brushed mine ever so softly, and it was too late; the damage was done. The touch caught me off-guard, and my eyes jolted in his direction. The intensity in his eyes proved that he had felt it too. We both let go of the file and stood in perfect silence amid the scattered papers.

"Clumsy today, are we?" he said. My cheeks burned as I attempted to look away, but he held my gaze intently.

"Here, let me help you with that!" Sumi offered, running over to where we stood.

"Thank you, Sumi," he answered, picking up a few sheets. She was out of breath as she stood up, clutching a stash of papers in both hands. "Why don't you two come in? You can bring the papers with you. I'll make some tea."

"Um, actually—"

"Sure!" Sumi said, cutting me off. "We're right behind you."

"Sumi, what are you doing?" I hissed as we followed him inside.

"You are being rude enough, Esha! The poor guy is being so kind. Get it together and stop acting like this."

"I need to get out of here," I whispered back.

"Why? You were fine before. What happened all of a sudden?" she asked, this time sounding more worried than disappointed.

I could have given Sumi an answer, but I feared saying out loud what my heart and mind knew all too well. I was falling; I was falling hard, and I needed to get out. It wasn't right, but how could I explain that to Sumi without sounding rude and hurting her feelings? After all, she had been in love her whole life with a guy who was so similar to Angad.

I avoided her question and stared straight ahead as we followed Angad into the living room. The house was spacious and had an open concept design. The right side was mainly sitting areas, with two separate sofa sets. The left side had a dining room and a library. Towards the back was a doorway that I assumed must lead either to more sitting areas or to the kitchen. Stairs in the centre swirled upwards to the top two levels.

To escape Sumi's curiosity, I picked up one of the magazines stacked on the coffee table. The words made no sense to me, nor did the images or titles, but I looked through them all. My only focus was avoiding Sumi's questions and Angad entirely. As we waited for our tea, a phone rang in the distance. I could hear the murmur of voices, and as they continued, my eyes wandered over the many photos that the Colonel displayed on the mantelpiece.

He stood tall in every picture, wearing his decorated uniform, beside famous dignitaries. Some I recognized from past television newscasts and school history books. There was a single portrait of Prime Minister Nehru, which the Colonel seemed to have framed out of respect for the man. There was one of him standing in a large group photo where even the current prime minister was included. There were two shots with famous actors whom I recognized from some of the Indian movies my mom was so keen on watching over and over again at home. It appeared our Colonel got around.

Angad reappeared. His expression this time was unexpected. He looked grim. "I am afraid I have some...well, some very shocking news," he began. This time *he* was avoiding direct eye contact.

"Angad, what has happened?" Sumi asked nervously.

"Um, that was..." he paused and took a deep breath. Whatever he had to reveal, it was already making me nervous.

"Please, what is it?" I urged.

"That was my uncle, and he has informed me that a

shooting has taken place at the prime minister's residence."

"What?" Sumi and I gasped in unison.

"Yes. The reports are not very clear at this point. She has been rushed to the All India Institute of Medical Sciences…"

"The All India what?"

"The AIIMS is a hospital, Esha," Sumi answered.

"They will be able to save her, right?" I asked.

"It is…uncertain. We will have to wait and see what happens," Angad replied, sounding dejected.

"Oh, may Waheguru watch over her," Sumi said.

"There is more, I am afraid," Angad announced wearily.

"What more could there be?" Sumi cried.

"Uncle has some good friends in the force, and he was able to get some further information about what happened. It appears that two bodyguards have been taken into custody."

"Bodyguards?" gasped Sumi. Her eyes were wide with worry again.

"Yes, her bodyguards. Right now there is no time to discuss this any further. If what uncle is saying is true, then you have to get home immediately. There is no telling what is going to happen when the news breaks to the public. Chotu will take you straight home. Do not stop anywhere, do not speak to anyone. Once home, lock your doors and close the windows until things seem calm."

"Go home? Lock the doors? Angad, you're not making any sense," I said. "I get that what's happened is terrible, but what's to fear?"

"The bodyguards that have been taken in are Sikh," Angad answered.

"Sikh?"

"Yes, that is the word at the moment. You have to understand, politicians are loved here, especially the prime minister. People worship them. The public will take this very personally, and amid the sadness, there can very well be anger and, God forbid, violent outbreaks."

"Against whom, though? I mean, they caught the shooters, right?"

"Esha, just please listen to me! The prime minister has been shot!" I jumped as Angad shouted. I never imagined him to be capable of such anger. "Everything is uncertain at this point," he continued. "Who did it, why they did it, what the fallout will be, we do not know! This is India, anything can happen. Sumi, take her to the car and have Chotu take you straight home. I am sure all will be calm, but..." Angad trailed off as he paced around the room. I became increasingly uneasy at his disconsolate state.

I looked to Sumi, expecting a response, but instead she grabbed my hand and headed out the door, dragging me along with her. I followed her to the car and got in after her. Something told me I should follow her lead and ask questions later. Sumi didn't have to say anything to Chotu. He had the radio on, and the shooting was already being broadcasted on the airwaves. As soon as I shut the door, Chotu revved the engine and shot the car forward, driving fast in the direction of Trilokpuri. The broadcaster was talking at warp speed, trying to sum up the tragic shooting, and at times he would begin sobbing as he struggled to continue speaking. People on the road seemed to be in a perfect standstill. Shock and disbelief was settling in rapidly on Delhi.

"Chotu, drive us by that All India Institute, where the prime minister is," I ordered.

"Esha, no!" Sumi protested.

"I want to see what's going on. Come on, Sumi, nothing

will happen to us. We're in a car, Chotu is with us. You and Angad are freaking for no reason. The prime minister is in the hospital. There are no reports about her condition yet. I'm sure it's pretty calm still. Come on, Chotu, step on it."

"Esha Ma'am, I think—"

"You think nothing, Chotu. Just drive, or I'll jump out at the next stop and take a cab." I demanded, grabbing a door handle.

"Well, there certainly is no arguing with you. I will drive us through there, but I will not stop. I must admit I am curious myself," Chotu replied.

"That's good enough, thanks!" I said, sitting back in my seat. I ignored Sumi's now familiar expression of alarm and concentrated on watching the street.

Within a few moments, Chotu slowed the car as we met with a huge crowd gathering at the gates of the AIIMS. The streets were blocked as streams of people crossed over. Some were crying hysterically, and others were either shell-shocked or outraged. Reporters were already on the scene, and they raced between the crowds gathering public reaction to the attack. An eerie feeling settled on me, and I shuddered as a chill made its way down my spine. I wasn't prepared to see such a tragic sight. The wails emanating from the crowds ignited memories of my father's funeral. Everyone was so sad and angry. Coming here didn't seem like such a good idea after all.

"Chotu, let's get the hell out of here, quick," I said firmly. Chotu quickly turned away from the crowds and once again raced towards home. Sumi gave a sigh of relief, and as I turned to look at her, I saw that she too had tears streaming down her face.

"Sumi, you okay?" I asked, holding her hand. She didn't reply and placed her head on my shoulder, sobbing quietly. I assumed the scene at the hospital must be the cause of her sorrow, but I didn't question her any further and just tried to soothe her as we sped home.

The streets were quiet as we approached our neighbourhood, something that wasn't very common in the late afternoon. Everyone seemed to have retreated into their homes. Dhadhi and Jas were glued to the radio and television in the living room when we walked in. Every servant in the house, including Sheila, was also in the room, eagerly waiting for some positive sign or report.

"Oh my girls, come here to me. I am so happy you are back safe and sound!" Dhadhi cried as we walked in. She threw her arms around both of us and pulled us into a tight embrace.

"Dhadhi...Dhadhi...we're fine!" I croaked, trying to release her suffocating hold.

"What is going on out there? Did you hear about Indira Ji? I cannot believe it. Even after all that has happened, now this? It is unbelievable."

"I know, it's pretty crazy. We heard it at Angad's, and we actually drove by the hospital. The crowd was—"

"Esha, you went there?" Jas screamed.

"Chotu, why would you take the girls there?" Dhadhi yelled, glaring at poor Chotu, who was now regretting that he had followed us into the living room.

"Guys, come on, it's not his fault. I made him drive by. Besides, we didn't stop. The crowd was a tad scary."

"People must be so outraged. I mean, this will hit the country hard. She is loved by so many. I still cannot believe it!" Jas sat back down on the sofa and drew a long breath.

"I'm sure it'll blow over soon. They've had her there all morning, and no one has reported anything serious yet. She will pull through, and this country will pick up the pieces, right?" I said, doing my best to sound reassuring and lighten the mood. The sadness hovering over everyone was overwhelming.

When no one responded, I continued speaking. "Look, people get hurt all the time, it doesn't mean immediate death, right? And the dude on the radio said that she was...or...the shooting took place at around nine a.m. or so this morning, and look it's afternoon now, and nothing has been reported yet. So she's probably still hanging in. Like Angad said, we should all just hang together and wait for everything to calm down. I mean, of course, people will be pissed, we saw it at the hospital, but look at what happened in June and what's been going on in Punjab, but people didn't start lashing out. Things stayed calm here, right? So that's it, we just chill out and wait for the report that she's fine and healthy. Cool?"

"You are right, Esha," Jas replied soberly.

"Thanks. Now why doesn't everyone just have some tea and eat something? We haven't had lunch."

"Jas, have something prepared for Sumi and Esha," Dhadhi ordered. "I am sorry, dear, we have been so caught up in the news that I forgot to ask if you have eaten!"

Jas and Sheila made their way to the kitchen, and the rest of the servants dispersed as well. Sumi seemed calmer now as she took a seat beside Dhadhi on the couch. Not knowing what to do, I ran upstairs and grabbed two of the novels I had purchased on a recent trip into New Delhi. I figured diving into the world of American literature would help Sumi and me cope while everyone waited for more news. I cuddled up beside her and we both dove into the book. Soon after, Jas and Sheila brought us two platefuls of lunch, and we ate with one hand while we read with the other.

The afternoon passed by quietly. Everyone sat around

drinking tea and doing their best to ignore the angry crowds chanting for revenge that were constantly being shown on television, as reporters stuck with the crowd outside the AIIMS. As the crowd waited for news on the prime minister's condition, they grew increasingly angry. Their anger and the chants of "Blood for blood" could be heard on Doordarshan, the nation-wide TV channel that Jas had turned on. I tried to ignore it as much as possible and continued to immerse myself in my book. Sumi's parents eventually came over, as did a couple of other neighbours. Jas called Ekant several times at the office, begging him to close up for the day and return home. He refused, saying he had to wrap things up and that there was nothing to worry about. He said we were safe because we were in our own neighbourhood, and we knew the people around us. What was there to fear?

It wasn't until evening that the mood suddenly shifted, and what everyone feared became reality. At precisely six p.m., All India Radio announced that Prime Minister Indira Gandhi had passed away as a result of her injuries. The discussion now wasn't about an attack, it was about an assassination.

When the radio host made the announcement, everyone in the room gasped, and many broke out into tears. Suddenly I became very conscious of my body. I wasn't sure what to do, where to sit, stand, or what to say. The servants were hysterical, and Sumi was just about reaching their level of sorrow. Rano wailed about what a tragic year this had been for everyone, besides her daughter's wedding to Daya, of course. Dhadhi sobbed as well, which surprised me the most. Looking back on our discussion of Operation Bluestar, I honestly didn't believe that anyone here would be capable of feeling this grief-stricken over the prime minister's passing. However, they were now behaving as if she had been their mother and that this was one of the most tragic losses of their time. An hour after the announcement, Ekant burst through the door, and without looking at anyone walked straight to where Bhagat was playing with Sumi's younger brother and took him in his arms.

"Ekant is everything all right, my son?" Dhadhi asked.

"President Zail Singh's car was stoned as he approached the AIIMS. The crowd there is very angry. Some angry people are pulling Sikhs out of buses and taxis and beating them."

"Waheguru!" cried Dhadhi.

"Rajiv Gandhi has been sworn in as prime minister. Do not fear, Dhadhi, by morning everything will be calm. There have not been any serious incidents, just some fights here and there. Tonight, however, everyone should stay in their homes and just wait until morning before going into the city if need be. This is just an abrupt reaction to the news of her death."

"Ekant, are you sure it'll be all right?" I asked.

"Yes," he said, offering a reassuring smile. "If it was going to be any worse, I am sure by now there would have been reports of killings. However, nothing of that sort has happened. Like I said, just a few fights here and there, and some very angry and hurt people, that's all. Everything will be fine by morning."

"Okay, I trust you. What about our trip to Kiratpur? I mean, do you think we can still carry that out tomorrow? Please, don't put that off!" I pleaded. I dreaded the idea of having to wait any longer.

"I am sure we can still travel. It might be a good idea to leave the city for a while. Be ready in the morning, we will leave after breakfast. Everyone should retire to their homes and for the night," he said.

"Yes, we should leave now. We have to travel in the morning

for the wedding," Rano said, getting up from the sofa. Sumi's father followed suit without uttering a word, of course. "Sumi, is Daya coming here, or should we drop you home?"

"Ma, Daya will be here shortly. I'm fine," Sumi replied as she hugged both parents goodbye and turned to her brother. "You, my sweet little brother, come see me soon. I love you." Yuvraj nodded and kissed her on the cheek before chasing after his parents.

Shortly after, the other neighbours also retreated to their homes, and the servants went back to their respective chores. By the time Daya arrived to collect Sumi, she was feeling much better, and the gloomy look on her face had passed. We said goodbye, and she wished me luck on my journey to Kiratpur. I promised her I would get in touch with her before I left for Canada, and she hugged me again at the mention of my leaving for good.

Daya seemed completely unfazed by the day's events. He was certain everything would be calm by morning. A new prime minister had been sworn in, and despite sporadic acts of violence around the city, the neighbourhoods on the outskirts of New Delhi appeared calm. According to both him and Ekant, we had nothing to worry about. I was relieved to hear them say that, because it meant by this time tomorrow, I would have already completed my purpose for coming here in the first place. I would have given my father his final rest in Kiratpur, then I could finally go back home.

After dinner, I went up to the roof as usual. It was still calm. Nothing was out of the ordinary, as some had feared it would be. Ekant had been right. Whatever violent acts had broken out had been centred in the main city areas. The east was relatively quiet. I stood outside for quite some time, thinking about what tomorrow would bring. I was getting excited again about travelling to Kiratpur and fulfilling my duty as a proud daughter. I was finally going to make things right by my father.

I took a deep breath and smiled one last time as I took a mental picture of the beautiful moonlit sky and turned around to head back inside. As I turned on my heels, however, I was distracted by a loud shuffling, followed by several male voices from the street below. I walked back to the edge of the roof and peeked over. There must have been at least fifteen men huddled together in the street, and they were moving along the road. They were looking through sheets of paper that several men were holding. What caught my attention was the manner in which the men would look at papers then walk to a house and point it out to the rest of them. What were they doing? I was looking on in confusion when suddenly one man looked up and met my gaze directly. He didn't motion to the others that he had caught me spying on them; instead he just glared at me then casually walked away. A chill flew down my spine, and I quickly turned away and ran back inside the house. I went to bed trying to disregard what I had seen. If it was anything dangerous, I was sure he would have said or done something right then and there, but he hadn't. The men weren't harming anyone. I was sure it was nothing.

Stop worrying, Esha, and go to sleep. Tomorrow is going to be a big day.

SEVENTEEN

November 1st, 1984

The phrase, "The calm before the storm" has been repeated countless times in books, movies and shows. It's nothing surprising to hear. I mean, it's used so commonly. Who knew, however, that experiencing it could be so traumatic?

Before I heard the screams, before I saw the fires, and before I saw the glimmer of the blade, everything stopped. All was quiet and still, as if someone had pushed the pause button on a remote. I stood still on the balcony, where I had raced to get a clearer picture of what was transpiring around us. In that instant, everything flashed before me. The bright sunny morning of November first, the laughter, the warmth of the family inside the house, the excitement over our plans for the day, then chaos, total, heart-wrenching chaos erupted, and none of it mattered any more. All that mattered now was finding safety.

"Esha! Eesshaaa! Where are you?" I could hear Jas calling me, but I was unable to respond. I ran from one point on the balcony to the other, desperately trying to figure out what was going on. The neighbourhoods around us were going up in flames. Trilokpuri, maybe all of Delhi, was going up in flames! Women were screaming, men roared with anger, and I could hear the clanging of swords and iron rods. From where I stood all I could see was people racing through the streets. Twenty men chasing after one Sikh, sometimes more, the numbers kept increasing. More and more men were joining the mobs.

"Esha! What are you doing here? Come on, we have to go!" Jas had reached the balcony. She grabbed my hand and pulled me downstairs with her. As soon as I saw Dhadhi weeping and desperately clutching Bhagat, I finally snapped out of it. I ran over to Dhadhi and embraced her. Ekant was racing through the house, and I chased after him, finally catching up to him in the courtyard.

"Ekant, what's happening?" I cried. "People are going insane. I saw it from the balcony. There are mobs...and...fire...they're attacking people... Sardars are being chased...women screaming... tires, Ekant, they have *tires*. What are they doing with tires?"

Ekant only stared at me. He appeared tense, but there was an unfamiliar expression on his face, and I couldn't read him. I just didn't understand. So I stared back, my eyes pleading for some explanation of what we were facing.

"Chotu, get in the car! Dhadhi, Jas, let's go! Esha, in the car now!" he ordered, picking up an array of daggers and swords and carrying them to the car. "Chotu, make sure there are enough bullets in that pistol."

"Ekant, what's happening? Where are we going?"

"Esha, I have to get all of you to safety now. I don't know what's happening, but this much I do know, and that is that it is very dangerous for us to be here."

"Us?"

"Sikhs, Esha, Sikhs! Damn it! They're torching all the Sikhs!" he cried out. I gasped in horror and shook my head in disbelief. "Just get in the car. I already spoke to my friend in Ghaziapur. He is a Muslim, and his wife is a Hindu. They live on their own, and no one pays any attention to them. They will hide you there until it is safe. This is the best we can do at

273

the moment. Jas, Dhadhi, hurry! Leave everything!"

"We're here, we're here!" Jas carried Bhagat in her arms and held Dhadhi's hand as they made their way into the car. I climbed in after them as Ekant jumped into the passenger side.

"Jas, take the turban off Bhagat and tuck his hair into this hat," Ekant ordered, tossing a baseball cap into Jas's lap.

"Ekant, why—"

"Just do it! I will not take any risks with Bhagat."

"I don't want to take my turban off!" Bhagat cried.

"Do as I say now!" Ekant yelled, and a terrified Bhagat quietly nodded in defeat, allowing Jas to remove his turban and place a cap over his head.

Chotu sped out of the house and drove as fast as he could, swerving to avoid the people running in the streets. The attacks were starting up on our block now. Chants of "Blood for blood" could be heard in the distance. Chotu made a sharp left turn and instantly brought the car to a shrieking halt. I flew forward, banging my head into the back of his seat.

"Chotu, what the f—"

"Quiet, Esha!" Ekant hissed.

Holding my throbbing head, I looked over Chotu's shoulder. Blocking our path about thirty yards ahead was a large bus. Hordes of men carrying sticks, swords, tires and kerosene were quickly getting off the bus. As they gathered in front of it, they all looked ecstatic. They had seen us. One man stepped forward, raised his iron rod in the air and began the chanting. "Blood for blood! Blood for blood! Kill the Sardars!" A loud roar erupted from the mob.

"Shit, that's like a hundred guys right there!" I said, looking at Ekant.

"Chotu, get us out of here now! Reverse!" Ekant ordered as

he drew his own dagger in one hand and clutched the pistol in the other.

Chotu geared the car in reverse and slammed his foot on the gas pedal. He swung the car around and raced in the opposite direction. The mob chased after us, their chants growing louder and louder, but Chotu was fast and smooth, and he very quickly increased the distance between our car and the mob.

"Esha, have you ever used any weapons in your life?" Ekant asked, turning around.

"What?"

"Weapons, have you ever used any?" he repeated like it was a common thing to ask.

"No, of course not! Why would I have the need? This sort of shit doesn't happen in Canada!"

"There's a first time for everything," he said, bending over in his seat. "Here, take this." He handed me what appeared to be a small dagger. "It's a kirpan, baptized Sikhs carry it. It is not meant for battle, but we have no choice right now. I have longer ones too, but I think this size is best suited for you. Now tuck it into your belt on the side. It will be secure there, and if you find yourself in a situation where you need it, then do not hesitate. Do you understand?" he asked firmly.

I took the kirpan from him and nervously tucked it into my belt as instructed. "I understand."

"Sir, which path should we take? These men are coming from all over," Chotu said, sounding surprisingly calm considering the circumstances. Something told me that he was doing it for the sake of Bhagat, who at this point was starting to hyperventilate. Jas held Bhagat's dead down in her lap, and I placed a hand over his face, trying to shield him from the horrific scenes outside. People were still bustling through the streets, and Sikh men were struggling to fight off the mobs while the women screamed from the top floors of their houses. Chotu made sure not to slow down, and he swerved in and out, trying to avoid collisions.

"Just get us onto Ghazipur Road," Ekant answered. "After the bypass, turn into the first alley, and we should be safe. There are hardly any Sikh populations there. We should be able to reach Azfar's house safely. Until then, just keep driving no matter what."

"Yes, sir," Chotu said like a loyal soldier.

"Ekant, why don't we just go to Rohan's house? I mean, he's not Sikh, and he's much closer," I suggested.

"Rohan is in Kalyanpuri, and that is *too* close to here, Esha. For all we know, these mobs could be raging through there as we speak."

Chotu eventually found Ghaziapur Road, and the coast seemed clear. I heaved a big sigh of relief and looked down at Bhagat. He still had his eyes shut tight, but thankfully his breathing had slowed. Dhadhi was still busy reciting her prayers. Her eyes too were shut tightly. Jas sobbed quietly and was shaking her head in disbelief. She refused to loosen her hold on Bhagat.

I drew out the kirpan that Ekant had given me and examined it closely. I now noticed its beauty. The handle was gold, and it felt heavy enough to be real gold. There were diamonds extending down the length of the handle on either side. My finger trailed over the six small diamonds set in a perfect line. The blade had to be silver or made of iron, I couldn't tell. It wasn't like I dealt with this sort of stuff everyday, but whatever it was made of, it looked expensive.

"That belonged to your father," I heard Ekant say. I looked up and found him peering into the back seat, watching me.

"My father?" I repeated.

"Yes, Esha, your father. It was a gift from Dhadha ji, our grandfather. Dhadhi tells me that the day your parents got married, your father enjoyed the kirpan he was required to carry throughout the ceremony so much that he was saddened to give it up. So Dhadha ji had this smaller version made, especially for him. When he left India, it was left behind. He always said that he would come back for it, but..." Ekant trailed off, and I could see tears in his eyes as he quietly turned back to the road. "He never came."

I looked down at the kirpan again. It had belonged to my father. I couldn't believe it. Stuck in Delhi, fighting to save ourselves, and my father's kirpan had found its way to me. I wiped my own tears and tucked it back securely in my belt. I felt oddly comforted now having it with me, but I got the feeling that something was missing. I couldn't imagine what that could be, but I could not shake the feeling that I was forgetting something. My thoughts were interrupted as Chotu pulled into the courtyard of a house. It was an average house like any other, but most importantly, it looked welcoming. A young couple ran out as soon as our car pulled up.

"Ekant, thank Allah you are all right!" the man cried. I assumed he was Ekant's friend Azfar. He was dressed in a pair of khaki pants and a red plaid shirt. His wife, wearing a green and white Indian suit, ran to Dhadhi and helped her out of the car.

"We were fortunate to escape quickly," Ekant replied. He was talking fast, barely masking his anxiety. "Things are getting worse by the minute. Thank you for taking in my family, Azfar. I cannot express what this means to me. If anything should happen to them..." Ekant folded his hands before Azfar and began sobbing.

I was shocked as I watched him cry before his friend. For a man like Ekant to *sob*, that was terrifying in itself. I understood then that the calm demeanour that Ekant had been displaying during our escape had been a façade. He really was terrified like the rest of us.

"Ekant, brother, please do not insult me with your gratitude. We are friends, and we will always be friends. This is an honour for me to help you," Azfar replied as he grabbed Ekant's hands.

"You do not know what they are doing...they are attacking everyone, but they are chanting to eliminate the Sikh men, *all* of them...even boys...I mean...Bhagat..."

"Stop, Ekant, do not say any more. You are his father. In this time of tragedy, he will look to you for guidance and comfort. So please get a hold of yourself, because there is much to do still. We have to be on our guard."

"You are right," Ekant replied, wiping his face and taking a deep breath. "They depend on me. Bhagat will be safe, and he can count on his father."

Father...father...father... The word kept repeating in my head. *Father...* Why did that hit me so hard? Again I felt like something was missing...like I was forgetting something...

"I cannot believe what this day has turned into," continued Ekant. "By this time, we should have been well on our way to Kiratpur, and instead..." His eyes drew wide, and he turned to me. My jaw dropped at the same instant. We both were thinking the same thing.

"Daddy!" I gasped. "I...I left Dad behind...his ashes..." My mind raced back, thinking about where I had placed the urn. I ran back to the car and checked the seats. I must have brought it along, but I couldn't remember. Then it hit me. The urn was still inside the iron chest. I hadn't taken it out. "Ekant, we have to go back! I have to get him! It's still there...he's still there in the house, in my room! We have to go back!" I cried.

"Esha, calm yourself!" Ekant demanded. "We cannot go back there, you saw what is happening. By now things will have gotten much more dangerous!"

"I can't leave him there! He's supposed to rest in Kiratpur, that's why I'm here, dammit!"

"Esha, it is not safe. I cannot let anything happen to you," Dhadhi cried.

"I know, but Daddy, he's *there*. What if something happens?"

"Oh, child, I know, but we cannot go back!"

"Dhadhi, I have to! I have to go!"

"I will go," Ekant announced firmly. We all turned to look at him. His announcement had caught us all off guard. Jas put Bhagat down and ran to Ekant, throwing her hands against his chest.

"You cannot go! It is too dangerous! I will not lose you!" she wailed.

"Jas, stop it! I can take care of myself," he said, holding her hands. "Azfar, get them inside and keep them safe. I'll be back soon. Come on, Chotu!" Ignoring Jas and Dhadhi's pleas, Ekant got back into the car. Without hesitating, I jumped in the back.

"Esha, get out!" he demanded.

"Ekant, Jas is right. You can't go back, especially on my account. This is something I have to do. I left him, I should go back," I said.

"You are a girl, you cannot go. Get out of the car, Esha!"

"No! I have to go!" I protested.

"No!" he said, getting out and opening my door. He grabbed me by the arm and yanked me out of the car.

"Ekant, stop it!" I cried.

"Listen to me," he said sternly as he held me by both arms. "You are strong, I know that. I need you here with Dhadhi, Jas, and especially with Bhagat. They need you. I will be back soon. Please, promise me you will stay."

I opened my mouth to speak, but I couldn't make the promise. Ekant was making a mistake. Every bit of instinct screamed out that it should be *me* going back and not him, but he left me standing there and drove off with Chotu. We all stood speechless for what seemed like forever. I stared at the gate, hoping he would change his mind and return. It should be me, not him. Eventually, I slipped into the house as Jas and Dhadhi began sobbing again.

We were all camped out in the small living room, eagerly waiting Ekant and Chotu's return when Azfar made the mistake of turning on the television. The reporters were gathered outside Teen Murti, where crowds of people were paying their last respects to the late prime minister. Instead of a display of sorrow and loss, the crowd was vengeful. Chants of "Blood for Blood" were drowning out the reporter's words. Not one mention was made of the horror that was taking control of the neighbourhoods. I prayed that everyone I knew was safe and out of danger; that Sumi, Daya and Angad had been spared the horror that I had seen in the streets.

"Why the hell are they even airing this?" I asked as the chants on the news continued. Fed up, I stormed out of the room.

Two hours passed, and still there was no sign of Ekant. He shouldn't even be out there! This was my responsibility, not his. I paced around the courtyard, trying to figure out what to do next. What if Ekant was in trouble or worse? No, that couldn't be. Ekant was a strong man, and he would be able to handle things. I tried over and over to convince myself, but when another hour went by with no news, I began to realize what I had to do. I had to go after him.

*   *   *

I left a brief note on the kitchen counter informing Dhadhi and Jas of my decision to go after Ekant. I didn't want anyone thinking I had been abducted. At least now they would know it was my decision, not that it would make it any easier for them to understand. While everyone was still in the living room, I ducked out of the back door and rounded back onto the main street. From what I could remember, it hadn't taken us very long to reach Ghaziapur Road, meaning I could race back on foot. I was an athlete, and I wasn't worried about the distance. I could cover two miles in fifteen minutes. It was the mobs that made me nervous. Without hesitating, I clutched my dagger and ran back the way we had originally come. I couldn't entertain any sort of doubt at this point. I was on a mission, and I had to follow through.

I tried as much as possible to stay off the main roads and instead raced through the fields, cutting through parks and alleys. All I knew was that I had to go southwest, which wasn't too helpful at first, but once I saw the local hospital, I realized I was back in familiar territory. I was surprised to find the hospitals relatively empty. How was that possible? I had imagined hundreds would be seeking help. Where were the victims? However, I didn't have time to entertain my confusion. I needed to keep running. I could see the smoke of the fires now, and even smell the kerosene and what I hoped was just burning rubber and nothing more. But as I got closer, I soon realized that it wasn't just rubber that was burning, it was bodies.

Where were the fire trucks and the cops?

A car was making its way out of Trilokpuri and driving towards a group of men who stood blocking the entrance into the neighbourhood. I stayed low, ran up behind some abandoned cars and tried to sneak by undetected. The car stopped beside the men. I was close enough to hear their voices and decided to hide until they moved on.

"The damn Sardars are putting up a fight!" one man complained. His tone was rough. "Sir, what do we do?"

"Go to the police station and bring the constable here," said a second voice. This one sounded more calm. He wasn't slurring his words like the first man. "Tell him to bring reinforcements so they can disarm the bastards. Hurry! We only have thirty-six hours left, do you understand? Thirty-six hours left to burn each and every one."

"Yes, sir."

"And listen, tell your men not to give up. They need not worry about punishment. My colleagues and I will take care of them."

"Blood for blood!" shouted the men in unison.

"Now hurry!" the second voice demanded. The car drove off and disappeared out of sight.

"What do you think, sir?" asked another man.

"Everything is going as directed. Just make sure the lists are followed. We don't want any mistakes. If they do not find them at first, tell them to go back. They have to be quick but thorough. We can only avoid media coverage while the funeral is taking place."

Going as directed? Avoid media coverage? The police? Colleagues? What colleagues is he talking about? The government, maybe... Oh shit, they're all in on it. The police, the government, all of them! No, that couldn't be right. That just couldn't be right. I didn't believe what I was hearing. I was mistaken, I had to be. I covered my mouth with my hand to suppress my cry of shock. If the police weren't going to help us, then who would we call?

A woman's scream interrupted my thoughts. I carefully peeked over the edge of the car to get a better look. Two men were dragging a fully stripped woman by the hair. They were bringing her directly towards the two men I had overheard talking.

"Sir, this one is for you!" announced one man joyfully. He threw the woman down in front of the man wearing the white Indian pantsuit and black vest. The man turned slightly to the side so I could now make out his side profile. He had black hair and a closely trimmed goatee. The smirk on his face sent a chill through my body.

The poor woman was hysterical and was desperately trying to shield her nakedness. "Stand up, you whore!" the first man shouted as he held her by the hair. "Show respect. Don't you know who this is? You elect them, and then you forget?"

"Calm down, Pandey. Now leave us here, we will take good care of her. You go back and finish your work," said the evil man who I now deemed to be Satan's brother.

As much as I yearned to help her, to save her, I knew that I couldn't. I felt helpless as he began to circle around her like a wild animal zeroing in on his prey. I fell back to the ground and vomited. This poor woman needed an angel. Why couldn't she be saved just as I had been that night at the bus station? The anguish was too much to bear. I wanted to run back to Ghaziapur and be with the family, but I was here for a reason. I had to get to my father's ashes, and I had to find Ekant. The question now was how to get into the block without ending up like this unfortunate woman. Oh God, help me!

Wait...the Gurdwara!

I could cross in through the Gurdwara. It was large, and it had several entry points. Or I could simply climb over some connecting rooftops. The mobs were attacking people in the streets and in their homes. This could work. It *had* to work. I had to cut through Block 32. It was the only route I knew from this point on to reach the house. The Gurdwara was my only option. Oh, how I wished my grandparents had chosen a more affluent neighbourhood to live in!

I quickly cut through the back alleys that I had learned to follow with Jas during the few times I had allowed her to drag me here. I made my way by hiding in bushes and behind abandoned vehicles to avoid being seen by passing assailants. Finally, I made it to the scaleable wall boarding off the Gurdwara from the back. I took a few steps back then ran hard at the wall. I leaped up and caught hold of the top edge. I heaved myself over with every bit of strength that I could muster and landed perfectly on my feet.

"Well done, Esha," I said, brushing my hands, but my excitement was cut short. I looked up to find Sardars scurrying around the Gurdwara in panic. Women and children were racing to the upper floors. Shouts and cries of war could be heard from the front entrance. I quickly ran to the front, not expecting what I saw next.

There were at least one hundred Sikhs, mostly Sardars, gathered at the front entrance of the Gurdwara, daggers and swords drawn as they fought off a mob that doubled their size, if not more. Everything seemed so utterly medieval. What had happened to the guns? The enraged mob was chanting again, thirsting for the blood of Sikhs, but the Sardars were too quick for them. They fought fiercely. Now I understood what the man in the car had been saying to the others. The mob was getting frustrated that they were being fought off by this crowd of Sikhs.

I took a deep breath and swallowed my fear. I instinctively drew out my dagger and gripped it firmly. It didn't matter that I had no formal training, because something told me that adrenaline was about to take over from here on in. I watched the Sardars move, trying to pick up as many pointers as I could. My observation didn't last long, however, as two assailants broke through the crowd by climbing the walls. They made directly for the women and children who were trying to escape to the top levels of the Gurdwara.

Without thinking, I chased after them. My heart raced as my legs picked up speed. The two men grabbed ahold of a mother trying to shield her two toddlers. The innocent boy and girl cried out in terror. My eyes caught sight of the sharp blade as one man raised his arm, preparing to make the first cut. I let out a loud cry as I jabbed my dagger into his back. He fell forward, dropping his blade. As he howled in pain, the other man threw the woman aside and turned his attention to me. I waved my dagger at him, but he easily ducked. I attacked again, but again he escaped. He grabbed my wrist and twisted it as he gripped my throat with the other. I shrieked in pain and tried to wrestle free from him, but he was beginning to overpower me. I took one step back with my right leg, causing him to lean in and separate his legs. I kicked forward straight into the groin. He wailed as I freed myself from his disgusting hold.

"You Sikh whore!" he cried out, clutching his groin.

Without responding, I began kicking him again. Over and over, I aimed for his groin. I thought about the doomed woman I had seen on the dirt road. I thought about all the innocent women that these bastards were dishonouring. I kicked and I kicked. He finally fell to the ground, but I only kicked harder. Then with my best soccer leg back I kicked forward, giving a hard blow to his head. It snapped in the other direction, and his body went still. When he didn't move again, I stopped, slowly realizing what I had done. I trembled as I looked up from my crime. The mother and her two toddlers were still there. They were crying and trembling with fear, but as the mother's eyes met mine, she offered a weak smile and nodded in what looked like appreciation. I only shook my head in disbelief.

I had *killed* someone.

The adrenaline suddenly vanished, and my legs became weak. I felt sick to my stomach. Everything around me began to spin. I stumbled away, arms stretched out as I desperately tried to find something to hold on to. The screaming, the chants, the fighting all became blurred. All I could think was that I, Esha, was now a killer. I was a *killer*. My legs gave way, and I fell back. But instead of hitting the ground, I was in someone's arms.

"Esha! Esha, snap out of it!" said a voice. I knew it. I knew *him*. "Esha! This is no time to faint! Get up!" the voice demanded.

I opened my eyes to find Ekant staring at me, terrified. "Ekant? Ekant, you're here!" I felt the energy flow back into my body. There was hope yet.

"What in the world are you doing here, Esha? I told you to stay with the rest of the family!"

"I'm sorry, I had to come back. I had to make sure you were okay!" I explained, getting to my feet.

"What if something—"

"I killed that man, Ekant..." I said sombrely. Ekant stopped talking and looked down at the two men lying before us. "I killed *both* of them! I'm a murderer...I'm—"

"You are a survivor," he said firmly. "You hear me? A

survivor! Besides, we don't know if they're really dead, and we don't have the time to find out. Now snap out of it! We still have to get out of here. I do not think we can hold off the mob much longer."

"The house, did you make it to the house?" I asked eagerly.

"I tried. This is much worse than I imagined. Chotu and I had to make a run here and now for...I am not even sure how long we have been here. All we can do is keep fighting, but this mob is getting more agitated and growing in size."

"I know, and they've gone to get the cops to help them," I revealed. "Ekant, we have to get to the house."

"Damn, Esha, what are you doing here? I cannot even send you back alone. Just promise me you will remain by my side. Do not do anything rash."

"I promise! Right behind you, that's where I'll be."

"Beside me, Esha, *not* behind me. I will not risk having someone grab you when I am not looking!" I nodded and grabbed his free hand. That's when I noticed his long blade was also stained with blood. The capital of India had officially become a medieval battlefield.

We found Chotu escorting a group of kids on the second floor. He was shocked to see me but refrained from saying anything in Ekant's presence. We looked out from the balcony as police sirens neared the Gurdwara. I almost cried out in relief, forgetting for a second that the police weren't on our side. I had been raised to trust police officers and view them as protectors. These officers, on the other hand got out of their cars and started announcing on their loudspeakers that Sikhs had poisoned the water supply.

"Unbelievable!" yelled Ekant. The police further instigated the mob by saying that Punjabi Sikhs were now sending trainloads of dead Hindus into Delhi. And to top it off, they announced that Sikhs had celebrated the assassination of their "mother" by dancing and distributing sweets.

"What the hell are they doing?" I demanded. "They're the police, for crying out loud!"

"This is absurd, absolutely absurd. Oh, Waheguru, have mercy!" Ekant prayed. After a brief moment of silence, he snapped back into action. "Right, listen to me now, since they are focused here, this is a chance to try making it to the house. We need to leave *now*!"

The three of us made it down to the back of the Gurdwara. We moved carefully as Ekant led the way and Chotu brought up the rear. I was still holding Ekant's hand firmly. His grip made me feel safe. Now if only we could get to the house, and back to Azfar's house undetected. We made it back over the wall with little effort. Ekant couldn't help but look on in surprise as he watched me leap over the way he and Chotu had.

"Get that look off your face, Ekant. I am an athlete, you know; a very *good* athlete. Give me some credit, will ya?"

He shook his head and grabbed my hand again, keeping me close on his right. Ekant was left-handed, so that worked out well for us. My dagger was firmly in my right hand, and he held his sword in his left hand.

"Ekant, look at us, we're like a double-edged tag team. Okay, you be Superman, and I'll be Superwoman. No wait! You're He-man and I'm She-ra! I think they were brother and sister..." He gave me a stern look, and I bit my lip. "Sorry, I talk a lot of nonsense when I'm...well I don't know what I am right now...but I guess, crisis mode?"

"Just keep walking," he ordered.

As we rounded the corner, we heard a roar, followed by

gunshots, and breaking glass, then we saw it. A cloud of smoke emerged from where we had just been. The Gurdwara had been set on fire. I looked down at my watch: three thirty p.m. The Sardars had fought off the mob for several hours, but it now seemed that they had lost the fight. My heart sank as the worst possible thoughts crashed through my mind. There were still so many innocents trapped inside. Cheers could be heard from the crowd, and I knew it was the mob celebrating its victory.

"We don't have much time," Ekant said through clenched teeth. "Try not to listen."

His grip on my wrist became painful, but I didn't dare complain. Now we began running. He had been right. The mob was fully concentrated on the Gurdwara. That gave us ample opportunity to race through the alleys and back into our deserted house. I tried not to look at the charred remains littered on the streets. My focus was just on my father now. I desperately hoped that the ashes were still where I had left them. Chotu stood on guard as Ekant made a quick sweep through the house. I ran straight for my room. Surprisingly, everything was still intact. Finding the house empty, the mob must have moved on, or perhaps they hadn't come here yet...

I grabbed my backpack and placed my father's urn inside. I also threw in my wallet, passport and plane ticket. I didn't want to leave any important documents behind. I also threw on a hat. I was already in jeans and a t-shirt. With my hair still quite short, perhaps I could disguise myself with the hat. I shuddered again, thinking about the woman in the street... *Get a grip, Esha!* After taking a deep breath and one last look at the room, I ran back downstairs. Ekant was ready and waiting for me.

"Let's get the hell out of here," I said, swinging the backpack over both shoulders.

"Great. There's a car waiting in the back. Chotu found one with a key still in the ignition."

"Aw, sweet!" I said, following Ekant through the back door.

Chotu was already in the car, ready for the big escape. It wasn't going to be easy. By now the men had probably moved on from the Gurdwara, and with a car there was only one way to get out of the neighbourhood. We needed a road, and the attackers were sure to be blocking them as I had seen when I had returned.

"How are we going to manage this?" I asked as we drove off.

"We just keep driving, ma'am," answered Chotu. "If we hit something...someone...then we hit, but we do not stop."

"Wait!" I shouted, thrusting my door open.

"Esha, what are you doing?" Ekant yelled, but I didn't listen.

"Oh, ma'am, you are making this very difficult. The plan was to keep driving!"

"Chotu, just stop!" As soon as Chotu stopped the car, I jumped out and ran. My heart was racing again, and the now familiar nausea was coming back. I stared in horror at Sumi's parents' house, or what was left of it. It was engulfed in flames. Everything was destroyed.

"Esha, stop!" Ekant demanded, grabbing me by the arm.

"Ekant, Sumi's family!" I cried out.

"There's nothing we can do! It's too late. Please, get in the car!" He dragged me back into the car as I wept. What if Rano was still in there, and Sumi's dad, and her brother? What about Sumi? Was she safe? Oh, God! I tried to breathe and collect my thoughts. I couldn't break down, not now. There was no reason for Sumi to be at her parents' house. Daya had taken her home last night with him. She was safe. My friend was safe...she had to be.

I looked on as we drove away. I wasn't sure where Chotu was going, but he was driving fast, and that was all that mattered. Once we hit the main road, we were in plain view of the mob. They threw stones and chased after our car, but true to his word, Chotu never stopped. He raced through the growing crowds with a determined look on his face. I threw my head down on the seat and shielded my head in case any of the stones or bricks the attackers were throwing made it through the windows.

"Please, Dad, get us through. Please Dad, please Dad, please Dad, please Dad..." I pleaded over and over again.

"Chotu, watch out!" Ekant yelled. I looked up terrified out of my wits. A few men were trying to shift a large concrete pipe across the road leading out of the neighbourhood. "We *have* to get through that, Chotu, hurry! Hurry, before they block us in!"

Chotu stepped on the gas harder, still swerving from side to side to avoid the bodies and debris on the roads. "Uhh...just make sure we don't tip over either, Chotu..." I said nervously as I held on for dear life.

"Do not worry, Esha Ma'am. I am aware of what I am doing," he calmly replied. It was a wonder he could be so cool and collected.

He planted both hands on the steering wheel in a perfect 10-2 position. It was odd how desperate the men were to prevent our escape. They basically had the entire neighbourhood; most of them were already at the Gurdwara when they overpowered it. Why were they so damn determined?

The gap was becoming smaller and smaller. Ekant hid his head as Chotu raced the car forward. Ekant did his best to hide his turban, but I doubt it mattered much at this point.

The mob wanted us. Only a few short metres remained in the closing gap, and I closed my eyes as we neared it. I felt the car veer left, but we never stopped. We were still moving. I opened my eyes and looked around. We had made it! We had gotten through! All three of us cheered loudly. Luck was still with us. Thank the lord, luck was still with us!

When we got back to Azfar's house, everyone was overjoyed at our safe return. Dhadhi and Jas scolded me in between hugs, kisses and tears of joy. Bhagat had a million and one questions about where we had gone, what we had done, what we had seen. His questions kept coming until Ekant finally silenced him.

The euphoria didn't last long, as Ekant quickly shifted into action mode, telling Azfar that we had to prepare for the worst. Both men went into the kitchen, and I looked on nervously, knowing full well what they were discussing. When they returned, Azfar's pallid face said it all. Ekant hadn't left out any details regarding the situation outside.

"My child, you made it to the house?" Dhadhi asked weakly.

"Yes, Dhadhi," Ekant answered.

"And is it..."

"It's still there, Dhadhi," I replied, trying to sound hopeful. "The house still stands, and I got Daddy. He's right here," I said, pointing to my backpack. "He's safe." She nodded and offered a smile. Tears were still rolling down her cheeks. I couldn't even begin to imagine what it felt like for her, especially at her age. I wanted to soothe her fears, but I had no idea how. I just hoped this nightmare would end soon.

"Jas, put this towel around Bhagat and sit him up," Ekant ordered, tossing a towel at Jas.

"Why?" she asked.

"We have to protect him," Ekant answered firmly. "Bhagat, sit up!"

"What are you doing, Papa?" he asked nervously. His eyes went wild with fear when Ekant pulled out a pair of scissors. "Papa, what are you doing with that? Papa!"

"Bhagat, stay quiet, please! Just sit still." Ekant loosened Bhagat's long hair that had been so perfectly tied up. He grabbed a huge lock of it in his hand and prepared to snip it off.

"Papa, no!" Bhagat shrieked as he began wrestling in the chair. Ekant dropped the scissors and tried to maintain his control.

"Bhagat, stop it!" he yelled.

"No, Papa, no! Not my hair, Papa. Please don't cut my hair!" Bhagat was hysterical now. He ran to his mother, and she threw her arms around him. He buried his head in her stomach, still pleading with his father not to dishonour him.

"Ekant, is this necessary?" Jas asked.

"They are killing Sikhs, Jas. You heard the slogans earlier, but things are worse now. They will not spare any Sikh child. If they cannot identify him as a Sikh, then how will they determine that he is one? I have to cut his hair. The turban has to go, at least for now!"

"No, Papa! I will not cut my hair!" Bhagat cried. "I *am* a Sikh. Always be proud, you told me that. I will *not* give up!"

"You do not know what is happening, Bhagat. I am your father!"

"Then why are you doing this?" he cried. "I am not afraid. Let them come, I will die a Sikh—"

"NO!" Ekant roared. "I can die for my faith, for my family, but I will NOT sacrifice my son! No harm will come to you while I am breathing, do you understand?" Bhagat was too frightened now to respond. He nodded silently. "Your hair will grow back, Bhagat. You will not be punished for doing this. Think of it as an act of bravery to save your mother. How will she survive if something happens to you? Live to fight back another day, son. Now please, we don't have much time."

Ekant went and stood behind the chair again. Very slowly, and utterly dejected, Bhagat walked back and took his seat again. He sobbed as Ekant grabbed another lock of his hair and snipped it off. Jas, Dhadhi, even Azfar and his wife watched in horror as the heart of a little seven-year-old boy broke repeatedly with each snip.

Biting my lip, I walked away. I couldn't stand to watch Bhagat in such terrible pain. He had been incredibly proud of his identity as a Sikh. He beamed with satisfaction every morning after Jas had tied his turban. It was he who had explained the significance of the second portrait containing the two young boys which hung in my room. He'd related how they were the sons of Guru Gobind Singh Ji, the tenth Sikh Guru, and how they had been encased, while still alive, in a brick wall because they refused to deny their faith and their identity. It was obvious to me at the time how inspired he was by their story, and now the poor child sat weeping downstairs as he was stripped of his sacred hair. It just wasn't fair.

In my desperation to flee the sad scene, I had found my way to the rooftop balcony. The sun was starting to set, and I badly needed to see and feel something familiar. I prayed that the night sky I had come to depend on would not disappoint. However, I regretted my decision as soon as I stepped out. Clouds of smoke rose from every part of the city. The once soothing and breathtaking sky was now polluted by dark smoke clouds. My heart sank as I thought about how my father's ashes could have been lost in the fires and the destruction. I tightened the straps of my backpack, which I now refused to take off. Nothing was going to separate us now. He would stay with me until I reached Kiratpur, and now more than ever I resolved to make it there and fulfill my promise.

My solitude didn't last very long. In the distance I saw something shifting. It was kicking up a lot of dirt, and there were things sticking up into the air. Poles? Sticks? Iron rods! I gasped. The shape was a mob of angry men. They were running together, and they were running fast in our direction.

I ran downstairs in a panic, leaping over stairs. I stumbled into the living room, making everyone jump to their feet. "They're coming! Get out! Get out now!" I screamed.

"Esha, what are you saying? Who is coming?" Jas cried, but Ekant already understood. Terror struck his face as he glanced at his family. He knew *exactly* what was coming.

"Outside, now!" Ekant ordered. "Azfar, you also may not be safe. You have sheltered us. We must all leave at once!" Grabbing Bhagat, Ekant raced to the door. Chotu was quick to follow, already taking out his pistol. I drew out my dagger again and grabbed Dhadhi's hand. When we stepped outside, it was already too late. The mob's chants could be heard. They were zeroing in on us.

"Azfar, get in the car and get them out of here! Chotu and I will hold them off!" Ekant yelled.

"Noooo!" Jas cried, but Ekant was already out on the street, charging at the mob with the loyal Chotu in tow.

"Get the bastards!" shouted one man. "The Muslim and his wife too! Kill them all! How dare they protect these roaches!"

I threw Dhadhi into the car and shut the door. I ran over to the other side and pushed Jas in with Bhagat. Azfar's wife got into the passenger side. Ekant and Chotu were still holding off the mob. Chotu didn't hesitate to shoot, and the gunshots deterred the mob long enough for me to pull Azfar to the car again.

"Azfar, get into the car! Get us out of here!" I yelled at him.

"That was my neighbour. My neighbour! That dog told the mob about us. He…"

"Azfar, forget it! Just get in the car *now*!" I said, pushing him into the driver side. He snapped out of it and revved the engine.

"Esha, get in!" cried Dhadhi. I ran and slid in beside her. Azfar reversed and spun the car away from the mob. Before he could shift into drive, the car was pummelled by bricks and stones. The women shrieked uncontrollably. My door was yanked open, and I could feel four different hands pulling me out. I realized then and there that we weren't going to make it.

"Azfar, just drive! No matter what, don't stop. Get them to safety now!" I yelled, and I jumped out of the car, taking my assailants down with me just as Azfar pushed down on the gas.

I reacted quickly and lunged at my first attacker, jabbing my dagger hard into his throat. Another hand pulled me back by my shoulder, and I swung my arm around again, catching him just below his chest with the kirpan, then I ran. I didn't look behind me, I just kicked up my feet, and I ran as fast as my legs would take me. It wasn't me any more, it was the adrenaline, and it flew me across the fields and away from the mob. The chants grew loud behind me. The men howled after me, and I could hear them chasing me. I could *sense* them, but I didn't dare look back. I knew Azfar had listened to me. I heard no female screams. He had gotten them away, but I didn't know where Ekant was.

"Ekant's tough, he'll be fine," I told myself breathlessly

as I continued to race through the streets, still clutching the dagger. *Where am I?* Fires burned everywhere. Charred remains of once-proud Sikhs littered the streets. I leaped over them as I struggled to remain ahead of my assailants. I made sharp turns into random alleys, fell over limbs and burned-out tires, and avoided looking at the naked flesh of innocent women. "Don't look, Esha, don't look. Just keep running!"

As much as I tried to convince myself that everything was going to be okay, the fear kept rising within. My legs were getting heavier, and hope was slipping away rapidly. How is it possible to reach such a hopeless moment? *Please God, do something!* But before I could think any further, I heard the voice of safety. It was a whisper, but comforting enough to stop me in my tracks.

"Esha! Esha! In here, quick!" It was Sumi! She was standing behind a blue house gate with her head slightly arched out towards me. I took her hand and followed her into a house that looked all too familiar when I stepped inside. I embraced her in relief that I had found my friend safe and sound, and relief to be off the road and out of the clutches of the mob.

"Esha, are you okay?" I looked up to see Ekant's friend Rohan walking towards me. It was his house.

He was dressed in a long black traditional kurta, which consisted of cotton pants and a loose long-sleeve top extending to his knees. The kurta highlighted his large build, but also gave him an air of intimidation. Instinctively, I stepped back as he approached.

"Esha, do not be afraid. I am still your friend," he reassured, noticing my hesitation. I felt foolish, but there was no time for me to apologize, as the shouts of the mob now cornered the house.

"Esha, Sumi, in the house now. I shall handle them if the need arises."

We raced into a back room and shut the door behind us. I tried to slow my breathing as my heart raced and Sumi grabbed my hand for support. We both sensed it was going to be a long night.

"I'm worried for Rohan," I whispered.

"Do not be worried, Esha," Sumi replied. "He did the same for me and Daya earlier. He tells the truth when he says that he can handle the mob. They do not have anything against him. Do not worry, they will not find us here. The only reason I stepped out was because I saw you running from the roof. I snuck up there to see what was going on. I guess we can agree that I was meant to see you. Now that you are here, we can wait out the night in safety. Rohan says that there are rumours that this will end tomorrow."

"Really?"

"Yes, but why do you sound so surprised, Esha?"

"It's just weird. I heard some politician guy saying to the mob that they had only thirty-six hours left. I can't believe what's happening. All of this bloodshed for no reason at all. Innocents are being butchered. It's a massacre out there, Sumi, and no one is stopping it."

"Daya and I barely escaped, but thankfully Rohan saved us."

"Where is Daya?" I asked, looking around the room.

"In the other room, sleeping. He spent hours watching the news for any reports. So far no one is even talking about what has happened. I was so scared, Esha."

"I'm so happy you're okay," I said, hugging her again. "Did they attack your house?"

"Yes, but we escaped from the back and just ran for our

lives. Daya literally carried me away. He was very quick, and he came here directly. Daya and Rohan know each other well through Ekant and Angad. We did not know where else to turn." Sumi began sobbing quietly, and I walked her over to the bed. "What about your family, Esha. Are they okay?"

"I hope so. But I'm worried about Ekant. We were attacked in Ghaziapur, and I lost Ekant and Chotu. The mob was so big...so angry...what if they..."

"You must stay positive. Ekant is strong. I am sure he is okay."

"Sumi, have you heard anything from Angad?" My voice trembled, since I dreaded any more bad news, but Sumi just shook her head and continued crying. "Okay, just get some rest, babe. We can talk in the morning," I said softly.

Sleep seemed like a good idea. The chants had subsided, meaning the mobs had passed us by. We were safe for the time being. I comforted Sumi by talking about all the crazy things we would do when this nightmare ended. About how I would *entertain* the idea of marrying one of Daya's friends, just so that she and I wouldn't be separated. I talked about how I would take her to visit Canada and even teach her how to play soccer.

"I doubt I would be much of a soccer player," she giggled.

"Well, we won't know until you try," I replied.

"Oh, I do love you, Esha. You are my sister," she whispered sleepily.

"I love you too, sis."

As Sumi slowly dozed off, I noticed a small smile curl her lips. How I would give anything just to be surrounded by my family. I was thankful to be with Sumi, though. Her friendship had come to mean a lot since my arrival. She was a good person, and it suddenly dawned on me that I couldn't imagine a life without her friendship.

I sat next to her and thought more about what she had said. What if Rohan was right, and tomorrow was it? That would mean this *was* organized? The chanting, the rumours…the way the mobs knew exactly which houses belonged to Sikhs, where to find them and how many were in each house…the lists… What did this mean? This couldn't be an outcry over the assassination. There hadn't been enough time since yesterday morning and today to organize thousands of men, hand out kerosene, lists, tires, rods, get the transportation and food ready. It smelled of something more than just a mere act of rage. Hitler didn't plan his Holocaust in a matter of hours.

I pushed my head back against the bed frame and decided the questions could be asked later. Right now, I might as well try to sleep. Much to my dismay, I soon realized that closing my eyes triggered haunting images. The heartwrenching screams of innocent people; children torn from their parents; sons, fathers, husbands, all beaten and lit on fire in front of their families. Women ripped apart by men hungry for a taste of their flesh. Helpless women, young and old pitted against a mob of twenty, maybe fifty or hundreds were dishonoured, humiliated and left for dead…it was too much!

I opened my eyes, sobbing. Beads of cold sweat trickled down my forehead. My hands were pressing down hard over my ears, a fruitless attempt to block out the screams that were already embedded into my memory. I looked to Sumi to see if she had heard me, but she was fast asleep.

EIGhTEEN

November 2nd, 1984

The sun rose just like any other day, but unlike other mornings, this one was quiet. No merchants on the streets, no prayers on the loudspeakers. There was an eerie silence in the early hours of the morning. I opened my eyes to find the bed empty. Sumi had already risen. I expected Sheila to come running through the door with a cup of warm tea, complaining about how I had slept in again. Of course, nothing of the sort happened. When I entered the dining room, I found Daya, Sumi and Rohan quietly eating breakfast. They all looked up as I walked in and did their very best to offer reassuring smiles. I imagined my own smile was just as unconvincing as theirs were right now.

"I am so glad you are okay, Esha," Daya said, embracing me.

"I'm happy you two are okay. Yesterday was..." I trailed off, not able to find the words so early in the morning.

"It's okay. Now, just refuel and enjoy breakfast. You must be starving!"

"Daya, you don't even know the half of it!" I replied, dropping into a seat next to Sumi as she prepared a plate for me. "Have they mentioned anything in the news yet?"

"Nothing," Daya answered. "They broadcasted some emergency relief numbers both on TV and on the radio."

301

"Oh, that's excellent. Did you call?"

"None of the numbers work," Rohan answered gravely.

"What?"

"They don't work. No one wants to help us!" Daya shouted. "The new prime minister came on TV saying it was normal that people would react to the assassination—"

"This hardly seems like a reaction," I said, interrupting. "Look at how they've organized this. This isn't a riot; it's a massacre, a well-planned massacre. Who even knows who was behind the assassination?"

"Everyone please, lower your voices," Rohan hissed. "We still cannot trust our neighbours."

"Oh right, right," Daya said, biting his lip. "Sorry."

"What I'm curious about is, who are these people?" I whispered.

"What people?" Sumi asked.

"In the mob, the ones attacking everyone, who are they?" I asked.

"Neighbours and people that have turned on the Sikhs," Daya answered.

"Yeah, but not all of them, Daya. I've seen the mobs. Most of them look like criminals, and some are like villagers, not like the people I've seen roaming around in the neighbourhoods here."

"The buses are bringing them in from neighbouring states," Rohan answered. We all turned to him, baffled by his response. "I have seen them, heard them talk, and this I will swear to you, many of them are not from around here. They came to me yesterday morning, trying to get me to join them. I told them I had to look after my family but that I would report if I saw any Sikhs wandering about."

"I can't believe it," I said. "They've *recruited* them. This is absurd. I saw a politician yesterday, he was...and then later I saw another...the police too...they're helping the mobs, making it easier for them...clearing the way..."

"I am worried about the families. I know our parents should be safely in Chandigarh, but I have not spoken to my parents yet," Sumi revealed. I looked away as she went on discussing her parents. I didn't have the heart to tell her what I had seen. I couldn't tell her that her parents' house had been reduced to nothing but a pile of ruins. "Esha, did you see anything when you escaped? Were my parents still home?"

"I...I don't know, Sumi. I mean, everything happened too fast..." I shook my head and looked away again.

"Sumi, I am sure your family is safe," Daya said reassuringly as he held her hand. "We will be with them soon. Have faith."

"I do, Daya, I do," she replied. "I feel safe with you. I am so happy you are here with me."

"I will never leave your side, Sumi," he said, leaning over to take her hand. Their love and support was so moving that I felt calm just watching them. How could anyone want to harm such incredibly lovable human beings? Their relationship was one for the books. It was a bond that deserved a lifetime and much more. Every love poem, every cheesy chick-flick moment, every famous love quote, it was all for them. They were that poem, that moment, that quote.

I left them alone and found my way to the washroom to freshen up. My jeans still felt comfortable, but my grey t-shirt felt disgusting, especially after yesterday's exertion. I looked and smelled like death. I untangled my hair and tied it back again. I splashed some cold water on my face and washed as best I could. The few minutes I spent in the washroom made me feel a little fresher and a little rested.

A loud bang at the front gate got us back on our feet. Sumi, Daya and I hid in the back storage room as Rohan went to investigate. It wasn't long until we heard the voices of a fresh and energetic new mob. We heard their footsteps and shouts as they stormed into the house.

"Brother, I have already told you, there is no one here! Who are you looking for? I will help you," Rohan said, trying to appease the mob.

"We were told you are hiding Sikhs!" howled an angry man.

"That is absurd!" cried Rohan. "Why on earth would I do such a thing?"

"That is for us to find out! We are looking for a Daya and Sumedha Singh. I have been told they are friends of yours." Sumi and I both gasped as we heard the man say their names. My heart raced faster with every second that passed. This wasn't going well.

"I...I...used t-to know them, buhh...but times have changed, you know that," Rohan stuttered.

"We have already checked their home many times, and they are not there. No one has seen them, and no one has crossed them off the list, meaning they are still alive!" the man roared.

"Look! There are four cups of tea here. He is not alone!" shouted another man. I slipped my second arm into the backpack and held the straps firmly. I had been right to keep it with me. It now appeared we would be making another rapid escape.

"Sumi, do not let go of my hand until we are out of here. Then run with Esha, and don't look back," Daya whispered.

"Daya—"

"Sssshhhhh...I love you, Sumi."

"I love you too," Sumi said, trying to suppress her tears. I remained quiet and inhaled deeply as the men began to tear through the house. I carefully drew my dagger again. I wasn't going down without a fight. I had gotten through one day, and I could definitely get through another. I finally exhaled and prepared myself.

It didn't take them very long to find us. The storage door swung open, and staring me dead in the eye was one dirty hoodlum with bloodshot eyes. We all froze for an instant, sizing each other up. No one really knew what to do next, then both Daya and I reacted simultaneously. We pushed through, knocking him down, and raced through the house. But they were already waiting for us in the courtyard. Twenty, maybe thirty strong, I lost count as they narrowed in. Daya stepped in front of us, and I held onto Sumi's hand as tight as I could, still clutching my dagger behind my back.

"You lied!" a tall burly man yelled at Rohan.

"They are not all Sikh!" Rohan replied. "The girls are my family. The one in front is my sister and the girl in the jeans, she is…she is my fiancée! She is visiting from Canada. She isn't even Indian!"

"You lie!" the man repeated.

"They are Hindu!" Rohan insisted.

"He is right!" Daya shouted. "I came here seeking shelter, and he was just about to throw me out when you arrived."

"Shut up! You lie!" said another man, stepping forward. He was younger-looking and was dressed in pants and a dress shirt, unlike the rest of them. "This is Daya, and that one behind him is Sumi, his wife."

"How the hell does he know that?" I whispered in Sumi's ear.

"He went to school with us," Sumi said solemnly.

A classmate? They were being ratted out by a former classmate?

"So the truth comes out," the man sneered, waving his machete at Daya. "You bastards are the progeny of Bhindrawale. How dare you celebrate our mother's death and distribute sweets!"

"That is a lie!" Daya objected. "We have done nothing of the sort!"

"Blood for blood! Blood for blood!" the mob began chanting. Their voices grew louder each time. "Blood for blood! Blood for blood! *Blood for blood!*"

"Nooo! Nooo!" Rohan shouted, but two men held him back. The rest of them charged at us. Daya began swinging his fists around, and he managed to knock the first few down, but very quickly the mob seized him and carried him out to the road. I dragged Sumi around me as I swung my dagger around. Blood sprayed all around us as my blade made contact with numerous assailants. Eventually they too succeeded in disabling us. We were dragged to the road behind Daya and held down as the mob cheered the leader, who now circled around him.

Daya, who had been tossed to the ground, stumbled to his feet, only to be kicked down again. Their leader swung his machete back and thrust it forward into Daya's leg with such strength that Daya's cries of pain drowned out Sumi's. I shut my eyes, refusing to watch any further, but I couldn't shut out the sounds of his limbs snapping. His cries grew louder, and eventually he stopped screaming. Instead, he began chanting something. I opened my eyes slowly. Both hands and both feet had been broken. His face was wet with tears and sweat. They forced him to kneel down in his blood-soaked pants. But Daya wasn't screaming any more. Now only Sumi's sobs could be heard, and the laughter of the crowd. Daya was reciting something. I strained my ears to pick up his words. It sounded like a prayer; Daya was *praying*.

"Asking for your Guru to save you?" the leader said mockingly. "Well, let's see if he'll save your wife. Bring her to me!"

"No! No, *not Sumi! Leave her! Leave her!*" I screamed as I struggled to escape my captors' grip, but they were too strong for me. They kicked me hard behind the knee, forcing me down. Sumi was hysterical as they dragged her to the leader. Daya sobbed in horror.

"Hmmm...very pretty. How is it that a bastardly Sardar like yourself can get such a beautiful wife?" the leader sneered as he caressed Sumi's face.

"Leave her!" I demanded, but no one paid any attention to me. How could I make them listen to me? They could take me instead, but not Sumi! Daya continued to pray, never stopping for a second. *Oh, Sumi, just deny it, deny you are a Sikh.* Why wasn't she saying anything?

The leader wrapped his hand around her neck, and with the other hand tore the sleeve off her right arm. Both Sumi and I shrieked as he began to slap her around and tear at her clothes. Sumi bounced from one man to the next, with each one tearing at her.

"How do you like this, Daya?" the leader teased. "You still want to pray, or do you want to save your darling wife?"

Daya still remained committed to his prayer. His concentration was unwavering at this point. I looked on in horror as they continued to toss Sumi around like she was a football. They tore at her like animals fighting over a piece of meat. I began shaking hysterically, and I couldn't even scream. I couldn't call out to her. I just shook uncontrollably, knowing full well where this was leading. My heart stopped when they lifted her and took her back into the house. Everything went dark, and the voices disappeared. I felt like I was drowning, and I couldn't breathe. I gasped for air, I tried to open my eyes, but everything was black. This was the end. It had to be.

It was Rohan's pleas for mercy that eventually brought me back. He pleaded relentlessly, and I could hear his voice grow louder, but he wasn't pleading for Daya or Sumi. No, he was saying something different. He was pleading for *me.*

"Please, she is my fiancée. She isn't a Sikh! Please spare her. Her family is too affluent in Canada to let this go quietly if anything should happen to her. Please!" Rohan cried.

"We will deal with it later!" the leader said, waving his hand so as to shrug him off. "Right now we must finish with this terrorist. You there, bring me the tire!"

A tall, skinny man in ragged clothing came running with a big tire. The leader took it and threw it around Daya's neck. He ripped the turban off and told two men to hold Daya steady. Then with his blade, he chopped off Daya's hair and tossed it around in amusement. The men howled with laughter as the leader stomped on the hair and the turban, which was now nothing more than a few yards of a bright orange fabric strewn across the ground. But Daya didn't respond. With closed eyes, he continued to recite his prayers. Even when they poured kerosene over him, he remained focused. It amazed me that such deep faith could replace one's fear of torture and ultimately death.

"I need a match!" the leader shouted. There was a scramble amongst the men, but no one could produce one. "Have we run out already? Go find me one now!" he demanded.

"Here," came a voice from behind the crowd. Everyone turned around and quickly stepped to the side to let him through. He was tall and well-kempt. He wore a white kurta and a black vest, similar to the politician I had seen yesterday. He had a beard greying at the tips like the rest of the hair on his head. He walked over casually, and without even one glance at Daya, handed the match to the leader.

"How much longer are you going to be here?" he asked calmly.

"Not too long. Why do you ask, sir?"

Sir?

"We need to start cleaning up. Trucks are being brought in. Finish here quickly and return to Block 32, understood?"

"Yes, sir, but we have to deal with these two," he replied, pointing at both Rohan and me.

"Who are they?"

"That man is a Hindu, and he says this is his fiancée from Canada."

"We do not want mistakes, remember, but do whatever you like," the man in the vest replied then calmly walked away in the direction he had come from.

"You two take the man and girl and leave," the leader said, gesturing in our direction. "Raju, bring the other girl out!"

Two men began dragging Rohan and me away from the crowd and down the street. We struggled and tried to break away. I didn't want to leave Daya and Sumi to their fates, not like this. There could still be hope for Sumi.

"Let go of me, you pervert!" I screamed. "Rohan, do something, we can't leave them!"

"I told you, we are *not* Sikh. Why don't you leave us?" Rohan shouted.

We all stopped as the street flooded with Sumi's screams again. I forced my captor to shift with me as I turned around to look back. There was a big ball of fire in the middle of the road, exactly where...where Daya had been. The crowd was holding Sumi over their heads, and with a sickening battle cry, they heaved Sumi into the air, and she fell into the fire.

"*Suuummmiii!*" I cried, tears streaming down my face. I jumped up and down. I did everything I could to free myself from my captor, but he fought back with equal strength. "You killed her! You killed her! You idiots! She was innocent! You killed her! You killed her!" I pummelled him, and I kicked and kicked. I didn't know where my dagger was, but I didn't care. I used my arms and my legs. My body was my weapon now. He cried in pain as my foot made contact with his shin, and I bit hard into his hand until I drew blood.

"You whore!" he yelled. The man holding Rohan left him and came after me. Rohan jumped him from behind, and they both fell to the ground in a struggle. I looked back to where Sumi and Daya had been. Satisfied with their work, the mob had disappeared. I ran back towards the fire, desperately hoping that perhaps there was still something left to save. I looked around frantically for something to douse the flames, but there was nothing. There was nothing left. Nothing but the remnants of Sumi's broken bangles scattered about in the dirt road. It was too late. The fire had devoured them both. My sweet, innocent and loving friends were gone.

"Esha, run!" Rohan's shouts diverted my attention. I couldn't abandon him either. A few feet away, something gold shone in the sunlight. It was my dagger! I ran and picked it up while Rohan continued to struggle with the two attackers who had managed to pin him down. I charged at them and demanded that they release him.

"Prove you are not a Sikh!" they yelled at me. "Say it!"

"What difference does it make? I'm his fiancée!" I yelled back.

"Say you are not Sikh!" the taller one who had been holding me demanded as he stood up. He had an iron rod, and he was twirling it playfully in his hands as he came menacingly towards me.

Just say it, Esha, just say it! But I couldn't. I opened my mouth, but no words came out. I steadied the kirpan and got ready for his attack. He swung the rod down hard, and I tried to intercept with my kirpan as I had seen it done in action flicks, but it didn't go as planned. The rod collided painfully with my wrist, and I dropped my kirpan. His next blow was quick. The rod came crashing down on my head. I fell to the ground but still remained somewhat conscious.

I could hear Rohan's voice. It seemed like it was far away, but I could still hear it. Soon there were more cries of pain. I could hear the banging of the rods. I tried to move, but I couldn't, it hurt too much. I forced my eyes open, but everything was blurry. And then the tearing began. The men were on top of me. I tried to struggle, but I couldn't. I could feel their hands all over me. I tried to push their hands off as they tore at my shirt and tugged at my jeans.

Oh, God, please, please not this way, please not like this! And then it stopped just as quickly as it had begun.

There was shouting and more battle cries. I heard a clanging noise then a loud thud beside me, rapidly followed by another loud thud. Something or someone had dropped. My head continued to spin, but I desperately tried to refocus my vision. I looked up, but the sun's glare blinded me. Then suddenly the bright glare disappeared and was replaced with the silhouette of a man. I gasped as I looked at the familiar

311

silhouette of the turbaned man. I looked carefully and saw that the turban was white. It was *him*. It was the angel from the bus station. It was my white turbaned angel. He had come back to rescue me! But wait, did that mean I was dead now? Was this it? But instead of disappearing like last time, the angel bent over me. As his face neared, my vision became clearer, revealing the identity of my angel.

"Angad?"

"I'm here, Esha." His voice was soft as always, and once again I felt safe as he lifted me in his arms and carried me away. My eyes slowly closed as I allowed the darkness to engulf me.

*   *   *

"Esha! Esha, wake up!"

My face felt wet, as if I were lying in the rain. There was an awful smell surrounding me. I coughed as I took in a huge whiff of the polluted air. When I opened my eyes, I found Angad hovering over me with a glass of water.

"Look, you probably have a concussion, so you must not sleep, okay? Please, Esha, stay awake."

I just looked at him with a blank stare. I wanted to reach out to him, to touch him, talk to him, but I couldn't. Sumi's cries still rang in my ears. The images remained in focus. My body began to feel the weight of the loss I had just experienced. It hadn't been a nightmare, it was reality. She was gone. The gash on my head didn't matter any more, nor did the throbbing headache. I just wanted Sumi back. I wanted both Daya and Sumi back with me, with Angad. I wanted the four of us to be together as we had been on our trip through New Delhi. I wanted it all back, and I wanted none of this. I slowly sat up, looked around me and realized we were in some kind of large hall.

"It's a Gurdwara," Angad said, noticing my curiosity. "We are still east of the Yamuna River. It's not safe to cross over yet. We cannot risk exposure. This Gurdwara was already ravaged by the mobs. It seems part of it was set on fire, but the flames have been extinguished since, and by some miracle this portion survived."

When I didn't respond, Angad continued. "There is nothing to fear, Esha. I believe we are safe. We can hide out here until morning. Things should be calm tomorrow. The prime minister will be cremated tomorrow, so a lot of international dignitaries will be coming in. From what I know through my uncle, that means the military will be here to provide security. Listen, I am not sure how to say this, but Rohan did not make it. I think he held off those guys as long as he could. By the time I got there, it was too late. But do not worry, this cannot continue any longer. We will be safe soon. Everything will be all right now, Esha, I promise."

Angad kept talking, but I couldn't hear him any more. I felt numb and alone, even in his soothing presence. He followed me then as I walked through the Gurdwara that had been so terribly ravaged. I walked into the main hall, unprepared for the scene that awaited us.

It had been completely destroyed. The podium where the Guru Granth Sahib ought to have been respectfully placed was in pieces. All symbols of faith had been painted over or torn down. I noticed that the donations box that was usually situated right before the podium was missing. The floor was dirty and littered with papers, but most shocking of all was that the main hall reeked of urine and human feces.

"Bastards!" Angad roared as he examined the damage.

I bent down beside a pile of torn papers, which I realized weren't just papers of any sort; they were pages from the Guru Granth Sahib. I began to shake as I picked up some of the torn pieces and cradled them in my arms. My face was wet again, but this time with my own tears. I held the pages tight against me as my insides burned with rage, and I finally let it out. I cried and I wailed and I screamed. Angad ran to my side and tried to comfort me, but it wasn't enough. I couldn't take it any more. Holding the shredded and tainted pages of the Guru Granth Sahib in my arms, I felt defeated and violated. I refused to let them go as Angad dragged me out of the main hall and back to the large dining hall where I had first woken up.

"Esha, you must calm yourself," I could hear him whisper in my ear, but his voice didn't help eliminate the chants of the mob, Sumi's cries, or Daya's pain. I could hear them again as if they were right there in front of me, demanding that I say it; say that I was not a Sikh.

"Angad?" I finally said through sobs.

"Yes, Esha," he said, sounding relieved to hear me speak.

"Why couldn't I say it?"

"Say what?"

"That I'm Hindu, Muslim, Christian, or anything else besides a Sikh. Why couldn't I just say it like they wanted me to?"

"I cannot answer that for you," he said carefully. "Perhaps something inside of you did not want to lie. But you should have said it. They would have killed you if I had not arrived when I did, Esha. They would have torn you to pieces! You should have said it," he said, sounding unusually angry now. "You should have denied it, denied that you are a Sikh!"

"No," I said, shaking my head.

314

"Yes, Esha! You cannot die! You should have said it! Why didn't you? What difference does it make to you now? You should have said you are not—"

"BUT I AM! I AM A SIKH! I AM! I AM!" I cried out. "I am Angad. I am. There, I've said it! That is the truth, and I've said it!" I sobbed again as I finally gave in. I gave in to my father, to my mother, to all those who wished I would. I gave in to that voice inside of me that had nagged for weeks on end since my arrival in Delhi. I gave in.

As easy as it would have been for the Esha travelling fresh from B.C. to deny being a Sikh, it was that much more difficult for the Esha who had spent so many weeks with a loving family, and who had seen so much love and hatred in the past twenty-four hours. When push came to shove, I couldn't deny it any more. I couldn't deny it if it was going to be the last thing I said, and now I understood. I understood why Daya hadn't denied it, and why Sumi hadn't denied it. They had accepted their fate. They looked beyond this life. I wasn't going to sell myself short by denying a part of me that had meant so much to my father. If this was how it was going to be, then so be it. If I was meant to see all of this, then I accepted, but I wasn't giving up. My father was still with me. Despite the carnage that was taking place all around me, I still had his urn strapped to my back, and that strengthened my resolve.

"Now I wish someone would tell me how being a Sikh qualifies me for being brutally raped or slaughtered or both!" I said, continuing my rant. "I am a Sikh, but I have no relationship to Gandhi or to the men who killed her. So why am I in danger? Why are we in danger? I don't know *them*, neither did Sumi, or Daya. Oh, my poor Sumi," I said, crying harder this time. "My sweet, sweet Sumi..."

"Sumi? Daya?" Angad asked confused.

"Angad...they...they took Sumi, then they...and Daya... with a tire and...and a match...and then poor Sumi, they... they threw her in. They threw her in, Angad!"

"No! No...Waheguru, no, not them!" Angad dropped his face into his hands as he wept over his friends. "Not them, Waheguru, not them!"

"What is this, Angad?" I asked. "What's happening? Two men shoot the prime minister, and before any investigation or court hearing, all hell is unleashed. What right do these people have to attack me, my family? That they can kill *children*? You've seen what's going on, Angad. Every Sikh home has been turned into a slaughterhouse, and these mobs, they're enjoying every second of it. Is this how they mourn the loss of their so-called leader? By dancing over dead bodies?

"I've seen the buses that they're being shuttled around in. The kerosene and the weapons they're being supplied, along with the lists that are being handed out, I've seen it all. The police, the politicians, they're all in on it. I keep asking myself where I am. This isn't the India my parents used to speak of. They talked about beauty and warmth. This is hell, Angad. They've desecrated our Gurdwaras, our Guru Granth Sahib! Wasn't the Golden Temple enough for them? What is this? What is it going to take to stop the violence? I just...I just want to be with my family. I want to be home."

"Things are not any different in the other parts of Delhi, Esha," Angad said, wiping his face as he stood up. He turned away from me as he continued speaking. "I was still at my uncle's yesterday in Sultanpuri when it began early in the morning. Everyone there knows who my uncle is and knows that he has very high ties, but the mob attacked persistently.

They threw stones and petrol bombs demanding that we surrender and come outside. By three p.m., DTC buses were showing up, bringing more and more men. By four p.m., we faced a mob that I swear was three to four thousand strong."

"DTC?"

"Delhi Transportation Company. They are government-owned buses. The mob eventually broke through the gates with iron rods and some sort of flammable powder that they were carrying with them. Uncle finally shot his gun, but into the air. The police showed up, telling him to surrender or they would charge *him* with disrupting the peace, or even murder if he harmed anyone with his gun. Against my wishes, my uncle forced me to leave. My aunt and cousin needed me. I got them in a car, and the driver took them north. I told him not to stop until he reached Chandigarh. They'll be safe there."

"Why did you come back?" I asked, walking over to him. He turned around and faced me directly.

"To find you, of course," he said. He looked at me with such intensity, and it was the look that I had missed in all the days I had avoided him. A very familiar feeling was beginning to reappear within me. My legs felt weak again, and something told me it wasn't because of my injuries this time. "I had to find you," he repeated.

"Me?" I asked foolishly.

"I had to make sure you were all right. The deeper I ventured into the city, the more I realized how large-scale the attacks were. It is a massacre. All entry and exits points to Trilokpuri have been completely blocked by concrete pipes."

"Yeah, we saw that yesterday," I said, sitting back down.

"I decided to come through Kalyanpuri then. I know Ekant has many friends in the area. I prayed that you all had found a safe haven to wait out this...this..."

"We did in Ghaziapur, but that didn't last too long," I replied. "The mob eventually found us. Azfar and his wife drove off with Jas, Dhadhi and Bhagat. Ekant and Chotu distracted the mob, and I somehow wound up separated from them all. We all got separated... I...I don't know what happened to them..."

"Esha, I found some areas where Sikhs have gathered together and set up refugee camps. I am sure some may have been set up here in the east side. Do not worry, we will find your family. Waheguru is still looking after them."

"Do you think they made it to a camp?" I asked with a hint of hope.

"We will look in the morning. Now we have to stay here and try to be comfortable. Are you hungry?"

"Angad, food is the last thing I crave right now," I said.

"Then what do you crave?" he asked.

"Sleep!"

"No, no sleep for you, at least not until tomorrow. I know it's a terrible time to follow the rules, but we cannot risk having you sleep while suffering from a concussion."

"Fine, then talk to me," I demanded. I dragged him back to the comforters he had placed me on. I brought him down beside me and curled up on his shoulder. "Okay, go ahead, talk. I'm listening."

"Well, what would you like me to talk about?" he asked.

"Were you the one who saved me at the bus station all those months ago?" I asked, remembering the familiar silhouette that I had seen and now realized to be Angad.

"I was not sure when you would bring that up," he said reluctantly.

"Just tell me, Angad, was it you who saved me?"

"I found you in the washroom, yes, and I handled your attacker."

"Why didn't you say anything? I mean, we've known each other all this time, and not once did you think to bring it up."

"How was I supposed to tell you that? Besides, it's in the past. I hardly thought you would want to rehash that night, so I remained quiet."

"Okay, I believe you. So basically you're like my knight in shining armour. Now that that's settled, talk about something else," I said with a sigh.

"Like what?"

"Umm...tell me all the wonderful things we're going to do once this nightmare passes," I said solemnly. "All the things that Daya and Sumi will miss now, the things that so many others have lost forever..."

"Oh, Esha, there are plenty of wonderful days ahead of you; ahead of *us*. Together we will keep Sumi and Daya's memory alive. I will never leave your side," Angad said, placing an arm around me and pulling me in tighter.

"Never?" I asked.

"Never. Not even God can separate us now. My soul is forever connected with yours, my love. I have never been so terrified my entire life as I was these past two days when I searched for you endlessly. I feared what might have already come to pass. For once my life seemed valuable to me."

"Your life *is* valuable, Angad."

"But I never cared for life as I do now. I want to be with you, beside you, forever. And if forever is not in the cards for us, then at least I needed to see you one last time. To tell you how much you mattered. Life and tragedy can teach a man many things, Esha. You know, I always wondered why Sikhs made such wonderful warriors. Why they were so great and effective in the times of the Gurus and what continues to make them so strong, so resilient."

"What do you think it is?" I asked.

"Love. Pure, genuine, unconditional love. When they fight, they do so with their mind, body and soul, and they do it with love. It gives them confidence and wisdom. When you do it for love, then you fear nothing, least of all death, because you know it does not end there. When I set out to find you, I knew I would succeed. I didn't fear running into mobs of angry men who would want nothing more than to tear me apart. All that mattered was finding you and protecting you. But of course, I should have known better."

"What is that supposed to mean?" I demanded.

"I found a kirpan beside you. I imagine you put up a good fight."

"You found it!" I said, sitting up in relief. "That belonged to my dad. It's what got me through yesterday and..." I stopped short of saying that I had also *killed* in my defence. That was something I wasn't ready to admit to Angad yet.

"If you used it, you did so in self-defence, and I am proud of you," he said, as if he knew what I was going to say.

"Yeah, well, it's a far cry from what I'm used to. I feel like I'm on some movie set, and any minute the director is going to yell 'cut', and then we'll all just turn around and joke about how intense it was. The bodies will come to life again, and the backdrop will shift, revealing the *real* sky, which is still very clear and beautiful."

"So I take it that yielding a dagger and hiding out in Gurd-waras isn't exactly what you are accustomed to back home?"

"Of course not!" I said. He chuckled as I scowled at his

sarcasm. "Truth is, Angad, that I grew up very different from what you might think. To this point, I never gave any thought to Sikhism, nor did I ever see myself as a Sikh. That label was reserved entirely for my parents. I was always more interested in my friends and looking out for the next great party. I mean, I went to the Gurdwara, but I did so very passively, and basically because I was forced by my family. But I never connected, never felt like I belonged. I shut it out.

"And then today, today when out of all days, it may have been a defining matter in my ultimate survival, I went numb. I couldn't answer it, I couldn't deny it. That wasn't me. I mean, the old Esha would have said it in a heartbeat. Why didn't I? Heck, I would have said it to escape anything treacherous, even some boring class. This was more dangerous and had ultimately had the capacity to tip the balance between life and death, so why couldn't I lie about it now?"

"Perhaps your experience here has taught you something new. Perhaps you are realizing your journey, Esha."

"I definitely have learned something new," I replied.

"And what might that be?"

"That it doesn't matter how I define myself. The world has its own conclusions, and it always will."

"Is that all?"

"Well, I learned how to open my heart. I learned how to understand my father. I learned the love of a brother, a grandmother, a sister-in-law, and my sweet nephew. Most important, I learned how to love back."

"Then am I part of your journey?" he asked carefully.

"You always were, Angad. You know that," I said with a smile.

"I suppose I just needed to hear you say it," he whispered

softly. His breath brushed my hair, sending one last electrifying chill through my body as I closed my eyes. I couldn't fight the sleep any more, and neither could he. We quietly but lovingly fell asleep in each other's arms.

NINETEEN

November 3rd, 1984

Their hands were on me again. I desperately tried to push them off with my free hand as I clutched the Guru Granth Sahib with the other. I tried to crawl away, but they would only drag me back towards them. I cried out, but my screams were inaudible. I couldn't get away, I couldn't escape. I tried to struggle, to kick them, but nothing happened, nothing worked. I was helpless.

"Esha! Esha! Wake up! Esha!"

I gasped as my eyes flew open. Above me was a blackened ceiling. Light poured in from all sides of the hall. I was still in the Gurdwara. I was safe.

"Esha, are you okay? " Angad asked frantically.

"Oh...uh...nothing...just a nightmare. I'm fine," I mumbled, rubbing my eyes. It was lighter now than it had been when I had first woken up in the Gurdwara. Was it morning already? "How long was I asleep?"

"You were very exhausted yesterday. I am not sure when, but we both seemed to doze off around the same time. This morning, when I awoke, I realized you were breathing normally, so I opted to let you rest some more." He placed a plate of bread with jam and another plate stacked with cookies before me. "It's amazing what you can find in a

Gurdwara. Sorry, no toaster to heat the bread, but at least you have something to spread on it."

"Thanks, Angad, for everything. You've done so much, I—"

"Stop right there," he interjected. "Do not thank me, ever."

I nodded as I took a big bite out of the bread. I didn't care how it tasted. Right now my body needed energy, so whatever I consumed was for the purpose of refuelling. There was no telling what today would bring. I devoured the bread in record speed and washed it down with the water Angad had found for us.

"Is the water okay?" I asked, remembering the announcements that the drinking supply had been poisoned by Sikhs.

"Of course it is. The rumours are false. The whole of Delhi would have dropped dead by now if it was poisoned."

"So what's the plan for today?" I asked.

"I think we should wait a little longer and then venture out. It might be safer to be in New Delhi, especially with press being here for the cremation. There's a relief camp set up at Nanaksar Gurdwara. We can head there, and then when things calm down, we will look for Ekant and the family. Does that sound okay with you?"

"Yeah, it sounds like a plan. I'm going to go to the washroom. I doubt it's working properly, but I need to freshen up and assess the state of my injuries."

"Esha, you look wonderful, and you will be fine," he said.

"Let me be the judge of that," I retorted as I limped away towards a sign that read Restrooms. The damage was just as I had feared. Even after Angad's efforts, both my head and neck still had bloodstains on them. My t-shirt had been ripped at the sleeve and abdomen. I was thankful for Angad's shirt. I smiled, thinking about how he was roaming around in his undershirt, revealing his muscular torso. I really wished I had picked up another t-shirt when we had gone back to the house. I tried to ignore the bruises on my body and neck as I washed up. I wanted to busy myself with thoughts other than what I had experienced in the past twenty-four hours. I feared what would happen if I let the distress take me over. So instead I tried to focus on Angad and on our goal to find safety. We would make it, I just knew we would. One way or another, we would be safe together. When I headed back out to the hall, Angad was speaking to another man who surprisingly wasn't Indian, but a Caucasian.

"Esha, this is David, he's with an American news channel. David, this is Esha. She is also from your region, Canada, actually," Angad said.

"Hi, Esha," David said with an encouraging smile. "It's amazing to meet a Canadian in the midst of all this." He was dressed in khakis and a polo shirt and carried a camera around his neck. His blonde hair was a mess, and his face was covered in dirt, as were his clothes.

"Hi, David, it's really nice to meet you. Judging by the camera, I take it you're with a newspaper?"

"TV, actually, but my cameraman lost all his equipment. We were chased away as we tried to film what was happening in Trilokpuri. I got separated from my crew and found my way here. I was asking Angad if he'd show me the way back into New Delhi."

"We are heading over there, actually," Angad replied.

"Excellent! Look, just a quick question. I know this Gurdwara has been attacked, but should I take my shoes off? I mean, I know it's customary, but I just didn't know what to do. But here, I'll take them off now."

"Oh, David!" I said, throwing my arms around him and hugging him tightly. Angad and David looked on in utter surprise as I cried on his shoulder. I didn't know what else to do. Hearing him speak of showing respect to the Gurdwara brought tears to my eyes. It was incredible that someone still cared.

"Okay, I think what Esha means to say is that we'll leave soon anyhow," Angad said, pulling me away. "We were going to wait, but with you I think we will be okay. We'll head out now, so no need to take them off."

"I'm sorry, David, I didn't mean to jump on you like that," I said, feeling rather foolish now. "It's just really moving to hear someone show respect after what has happened to this place."

"Esha, there are many people around this world who still care. You have to trust that. We won't stay silent."

"Thanks," I replied. "Somebody has to do something about this."

"Yes, but for now we have to get to safety. Come on," Angad said as he led the way out.

Smoke still swirled in the air outside. I covered my face with my sleeve in an attempt to filter the air, but that didn't stop me from coughing. Aside from the smoke, however, the streets appeared calm. There was not a soul in sight. I still didn't know where we were. Angad hadn't explained which Gurdwara we were in. All I knew was that we were still in the east, and nothing here looked familiar. I tried to hide behind Angad and not look directly at the bodies that littered the streets or hung out of gates leading to what I presumed were Sikh homes. No chants were heard, only some distant noises of cars and trucks. It was virtually a ghost town.

"We have to get out of this area quickly, before we get sick from smoke inhalation," David explained, coughing.

"I agree, but we still must move with caution," Angad replied. "We take this street to the main road, but we will stay low and out of sight. We will have to cross the bridge, but I do not think anyone will attack us in plain sight of foreign media. There is too much going on in New Delhi today. We just need to ensure that we do not get cornered in an alley by a mob. As long as we stick to the main roads, we should be okay. Once in New Delhi we will cross below Connaught Place and take the road that cuts through the forest, taking us to the Gurdwara. Is that clear?"

"Got it," David replied. I nodded and held onto Angad's hand. He had placed the dagger back in my belt. He said he didn't believe I'd need to use it again, but just in case, it was safely in my possession again.

As we passed through another alley, we saw a truck idling. The engine was still running. A small trailer was attached, and the back door was left open. Angad covered my mouth and pulled me to him as we realized what was in the truck. It was bodies.

"Oh my god, oh my god, oh my god..." I cried into his chest in shock as the image of the pile of bodies flashed before me.

"Esha, please get it together," Angad pleaded, holding me tight. "David, where are you going?"

"I'm just going to get a picture. This is evidence, I can't ignore it."

"Okay, just be careful and hurry, *please*!"

"Oh, Lord in heaven!" David cried out. I pulled away from Angad and looked in David's direction.

"What is it?" Angad asked.

"They're not all dead!" David said in shock as he ran back to us. "They're not all dead! Oh, Jesus! They're not all dead! What do we do?"

We all looked at each other in horror as we tried to think of what to do next, but we were speechless. We understood the hopeless situation we were all in. There was no one to help us. There wasn't even a soul in sight, and if there were, who would we ask? Before we could decide on a plan, the truck sped off down the alley. My heart sank as it disappeared out of sight taking with it the evidence of our nightmare and the victims still breathing.

"Just when I think things can't get any worse... Angad, get me out of here," I pleaded. He nodded and took me back into his arms, and we continued walking in silence.

We passed piles of burning corpses and were passed by numerous trucks carrying away even more of the evidence and the bodies. I stopped counting the trucks after I reached thirty. Once in a while we would cross paths with a weeping widow. We would encourage them to come with us to the relief camp, but they refused to leave the remains of their husbands and children. These women were completely shattered.

David continued taking pictures, trying to capture as much as he could of the carnage. We eventually made it to the Vikas Marg, the bridge leading into New Delhi. Angad found a scooter on the side of the road, which someone had abandoned in haste with the key still in the ignition. Angad drove, as I sat holding on tight from behind. David opted to sit at the end, and Angad didn't object, thinking I was safer wedged between the two men.

Driving into New Delhi, I understood what Angad had meant by what a large-scale attack this had been. Gurdwaras were still ablaze in some areas, while others were reduced to nothing but ruins, and clouds of black smoke still hovered over the city. A large contingent of military personnel looked on in shock as we drove by. I suppose they were surprised to see Angad, a turbaned Sikh, driving around unharmed. Some men chanted angry slogans in the streets but were quickly silenced by the soldiers. There were more foreign reporters on the roads now. They quickly took their shots then moved on, never lingering for too long in one place. Angad paid no attention to the people around us. He drove with determination, and soon after, we reached the gates of Gurdwara Nanaksar.

We dismounted from the scooter only after we'd reached the front of the gates. Thousands of people were scattered about. Many were racing through the crowds trying to locate loved ones. Others were trying to provide relief to their fellow victims. Food, water, clothing and sheets were being distributed amongst the survivors. David reacted quickly and started snapping pictures immediately. As he made his way through the crowds, Angad got me some water.

"Where do you want to sit?" he asked cautiously.

"Angad, I'm fine, you don't need to act like I'm about to break down at any minute. We got here in one piece, meaning things are coming under control. I'm okay, I promise."

"I know you are strong, but that does not stop me from worrying. Listen, how about we go inside for a minute. After that, we can come out here and help out."

"Sounds good," I said, following him inside the Gurdwara. The main hall was packed with people. Hymns were being played through the speakers. Almost everyone in the main hall was either in a state of shock or sobbing. It wasn't the calm and peaceful environment I had hoped for. Instead it seemed everyone was just holding on by a thread. I couldn't blame them. The ordeal that they had experienced was unlike anything any of them had ever seen or experienced before.

Most importantly, it didn't make any sense. It had swept through unexpectedly, and those who were in a position of authority and should have protected them had done the exact opposite. Now these poor souls who'd worked and contributed their lives to this country were *refugees*. Sikhs had been forced to become refugees in their own country.

After paying my respects to the Guru Granth Sahib, I walked back outside with Angad. I wanted to do what I could to help the victims. We had been lucky, and now it was our turn to help the others. We walked around and offered clean sheets and water to the survivors. I tried to engage in friendly conversations with some of the younger kids, but they were worse than the adults. They looked like empty shells. They sat still and didn't utter a word. It was only through their eyes that they related the horror that they had witnessed at such a tender age.

"Esha, Angad! I need your help," David said, running up to us.

"What is it?" I asked curiously.

"I want to jot down some firsthand accounts from the survivors. People around the world should know their plight, but I don't think they're too comfortable talking to me alone, especially the women, and look around, practically all the survivors are women." David was right. There were hardly any men in the thousands that had gathered in the camp, a tragic reflection of how successful the mobs had been in the past two days. "Do you think you two could help me out?"

"The world needs to know," I agreed. Angad nodded reluctantly and followed me as I led both him and David to a large group of survivors who were just finishing their meal. The women avoided making any eye contact with David and Angad but seemed warm towards me. I opted to speak with the lone elderly man first. His turban was messy but still intact. He looked tired and defeated. I addressed him in Punjabi.

"Uncle Ji, my name is Esha, this is Angad and this is our friend David. He is an American journalist. Uncle Ji, we need to tell the world what has happened. I know it might be difficult, but if you could tell us what happened to you..."

"I watched my son die of his injuries. No one would help him, no one," he said solemnly. There were no tears, no knee-jerk reactions. He was perfectly still, and he stared off into the distance as he recounted his ordeal. "We heard that the Sarai Rohilla Gurdwara was being attacked. My son and I ran to protect it, as did many others. We thought they were just trying to burn it down, who knew what they were really after? When the Railway Protection Force showed up, we thought we were saved, but instead of helping us, they too began shooting at the Gurdwara. The mob finally broke through. They beat my son so terribly. They broke every limb possible and even dropped him from the second storey. When they realized he was still alive, they set him on fire. He was alive, and they...somehow my son still survived. We ran and we ran, and we doused his flames. I took him to a hospital, but the doctors refused to treat him. Even the hospitals refuse us. He died yesterday. He died..."

"My sons are gone too." We turned around to find a grief-stricken woman behind us. She was heavily bruised but wrapped in a shawl. "All three of them, including my husband...gone...and I have nothing left of them, not even their ashes. They made me watch as they tortured my husband and children. Then they...they made them watch as the men took me and...and then they finished them off..."

I gasped as I suddenly realized what she meant. She gave in to her sorrow and wept uncontrollably as several other women joined in. The three of us looked on in horror as we listened to their cries. Every one had a similar story to tell. They'd had the same experiences. The process of torture and killings had been very much the same. Soon we realized it all appeared to have been very systematic. Whoever had made it to the hospitals was refused help. Every single one that we spoke to who said they'd called a police officer was insulted and given information that only endangered them more. Mobs had repeatedly visited their homes to ensure that they had found and killed every male Sikh in the household. Almost all had seen the lists that their assailants were carrying around. Several listed the names of high-ranking political officials, Congress members who had helped the men. Some recounted their efforts to plead with the officials to help save them, but they were kicked to the side.

One man told of how he had seen two boys run into the fields in Trilokpuri. Instead of following them in, the mob set the field on fire from all sides and burned the boys alive. Another large group of women described how they had all hid on the night of November first in another field in Trilokpuri, and men had come at night with flashlights. Many women were carried off, while others ran away or were caught and raped right there.

After hearing the last account, I stood up and walked away. I couldn't take it any more. It was worse than anything I had ever heard or read. I wanted to escape it all. Why was this happening? How could it happen? What frustrated me more was that no one besides a handful of people seemed to care. Where were the big relief trucks and personnel? Where was the aid? Why wasn't there any domestic media here? Why were there only international journalists in the camps? Where were the leaders of this state, this country? Where the hell was everyone?

"Esha, are you okay?" Angad asked, walking up to me.

"Angad, it's just too much. I can't listen to it any more," I said weakly.

"I know it is hard, but this is fact. If we stop listening now, then how can we expect the world to listen? This is how tragedies like this can be swept under the rug and treated like nothing ever happened. People do not have the stomach to digest the truth of such horror. We have to be strong." Angad was right. I had to be strong. I was a survivor now, and I couldn't let fear control me.

"I just want to be alone for a while. Why don't you help David and catch up with me later?"

"Sure," Angad replied as he walked back to the group.

I walked up to the higher levels of the Gurdwara and looked out over the vast forest beside it. It was the only beautiful sight left in all of Delhi. I opened my backpack and pulled out the green suede sack. The urn was still safely inside it. I took it out carefully. I couldn't remember the last time I had done so. I lifted it above my head and read the label at the bottom:

Remains Of:
DILAWAR SINGH SIDHU
Date of Passing:
May 05, 1984

"I bet you didn't expect this, Dad, now did ya?" I said, holding the urn close to me now. "What are we going to do, Dad? What are we going to do?"

I placed the urn back into the sack and zipped it up inside my backpack once again. Slipping it back on, I took a deep breath and tried to clear my mind as I concentrated on the view over the forest. I couldn't cry over Sumi and Daya any more. I didn't want to mourn them like this. I needed to feel like they were still with me; that Sumi was still my best friend, and she was still beside me. I needed to feel like she had never let go of my hand; that she was still here holding on. I needed to feel like I had protected her and not failed her. There was still the family. We still had to find the family. I wasn't going to fall apart like this, not now. I bit down hard on my lip and fought back the tears. No matter what, I wasn't going to cry. Not any more.

I still had my passport with me, and my ticket. I could still get out, but what was I going to do when I got back to Canada? How would I continue living like I used to? A revelation began to settle over me. I knew that I couldn't live in ignorance any longer. I didn't *want* to live like that. This trip had changed things. I had spent my whole life denying the label of Sikh, and now I had spent three days on the run, because to the world I was a Sikh. I understood now, though, that it wasn't just to the world. I felt it myself, and I accepted it. It wasn't about just being a Sikh. This carnage had proved that people can attack others for any reason. It just had to be organized enough. Whether someone was a black, a Jew, a woman, now a Sikh, different was different if someone chose to see it.

"Esha, there you are! I have been looking all over for you!" Angad shouted, running towards me.

"What is it? What's happened?" I asked, terrified of any further bad news. I expected him to tell me that another mob had shown up and that we would have to make yet another speedy escape.

"Your brother, Esha, your brother! Ekant is alive!" he cried out joyfully.

"What?"

"Ekant is alive! He is here at the Gurdwara. I just saw him!" I jumped into Angad's arms and screamed with joy. Ekant was alive, he was *alive*! *Thank you, God, thank you!*

"Where is he? I have to see him! Take me to him now!"

"Follow me!" Angad led me back down to the grounds. We walked over to a make-shift tent. People around us were lying on the ground, moaning in pain or still unconscious.

"Angad, what is this?" I asked nervously.

"This is where the injured are being kept. Do not worry, Esha, Ekant is okay."

We walked to the back end, and there he was, sitting up on a bench. I ran over and dropped beside him. His eyes lit up when he saw me, and a weak smile curled his lips. His turban had been replaced by a thick white bandage. His arm was also in a sling, but overall he looked okay. I desperately wanted to hug him, but I was afraid of causing more pain to his already fragile limbs, so instead I held his free hand.

"Ekant, I was so worried about you," I said tearfully. "I'm so, so happy you're okay."

"I was elated when Angad found me and said that you were with him, that you were safe. I saw you being chased by the mob. I could not do anything to stop them, Esha. I felt so helpless. I ran and I ran and I tried to find you, but I could not—"

"Ekant stop it. Let's not... Look, all that matters is that we're both safe, and we're together. I did just fine, and besides Angad found me when I needed him most. What about Dhadhi and them, any word?"

"I used the phones when I first got here. They made it to Dhadhi's sister's house in Chandigarh. Azfar got them out safely, and he followed the plan precisely. I owe him my life."

"Oh, thank God!" I said, letting out a huge sigh of relief. They were safe. They actually were safe. I felt a huge weight lift off of me. My family was safe.

"And Chotu? Where is he?" I asked, looking around frantically. He had played an immense role in saving our family. "Oh Ekant, is he..."

"Do not fear, my sister. Chotu is alive," Ekant answered with a smile. "He had some bad wounds, but he is being looked after."

"You see, Esha, I told you everything will be fine," Angad said, taking my hand. I patted it instinctively, forgetting for an instant that Ekant was with us.

"Anything you two want to tell me?" Ekant asked, raising an eyebrow. Angad quickly withdrew his hand and looked away, embarrassed. I guessed it would have to be me.

"Umm, yeah, there's something you need to know," I said, but my smile said it all, and Ekant nodded in approval before he began laughing. Angad and I both stood back in surprise as his laughter rang out. It truly was a miracle that between the heartache and the carnage, we could still find some joy.

TWENTY

One week later

O ne week had passed since the violence had broken out.
Since then, we had left Delhi and travelled to reunite with
the rest of the family. David had arranged for a car to take us
all to Chandigarh. Ekant and Angad were forever grateful for
his assistance, and he asked only that we allow him to tag along
a little while longer and speak with other victims of the Delhi
massacres. By now it was estimated that approximately fifty
thousand Sikhs had either left or were in the process of leaving
Delhi for Punjab. The violence had come to an end, but the
wounds hadn't even begun to heal. The country had started
to move on after the former Prime Minister's assassination.
A new, younger leader was in charge now, and all eyes were
on him. No one even mentioned the severity of the pogroms
against the Sikhs. It was being treated as though it had never
even happened. Our house had by some miracle been left
standing. It had been looted as expected, but it had escaped
any act of arson. It was one miracle in a sea of destruction.

The reunion with the family was bittersweet. Daya's parents
had gathered with Dhadhi and Jas, awaiting our arrival.
Dhadhi wouldn't stop crying and thanked God every second
for protecting her family. Jas couldn't find the words to express
her joy and relief that her husband was spared, something that

was very rare for any Sikh couple in Delhi that week. Bhagat beamed and jumped on top of us as we walked through the door. His dishevelled hair would take some getting used to, and it was a stark reminder of the trials we had faced. He looked like a brand new boy, but his eyes lit up as his father lifted him into the air.

"I love you, Papa," he said in his forever-sweet voice.

"I love you too, son," Ekant replied.

Daya's parents were completely shattered when I broke the news. Angad held my hand lovingly in support as I recounted their tragic fate, leaving out many details, of course. I didn't want to cause any more pain than they were already experiencing. It was then that I found out Sumi's family had never made it to Chandigarh as planned. That only left one explanation; they'd never made it out of their house. That day my family decided it would never return to Delhi again. Angad offered his home in Amritsar, but Dhadhi refused, saying that she would rather stay with her sister until they determined their future. It was also decided that we would travel to Kiratpur as soon as possible and finally put my father to rest. So on this day, Friday, November 9th, 1984, we all piled into two cars and travelled to Kiratpur.

It was a small village, nothing spectacular. Cows roamed the roads, and people begged in the streets. Small shops lined the main roads, but mostly it was farmland. The bumpy ride had taken a few hours from Chandigarh. I was more than relieved when the tall white Gurdwara came into view. Once we drove through the gates, I realized how vast the landscape was and how empty. There were hardly any people there. I had pictured it as being a popular and busy place. Nothing had ever suggested that it would be, but I had just always imagined it to be so. Instead it was very isolated. A few priests walked in and out of buildings, and a couple of low caste servants sat by the water, picking urns out of the river and washing them under the taps that had been set up in the complex.

The Gurdwara was situated at the front, facing the river. Between the main building and the river was a dining hall to the right and a large sacred pool on the left. We were told first to wash our hands and feet in the sacred pool, which we all carefully did. Stepping into the water instantly brought back memories of Sumi and Daya. I flashed back to the night we had visited the Gurdwara together when Sumi had pleaded with me to drink the water with her. Now it all seemed like a dream.

One of the priests asked who the widow of the deceased was, and I informed him that she wasn't present. He said then that the children, both Ekant and I, should take a dip in the sacred pool after the ashes were poured. We nodded then made our way barefoot to the river. It was an unusually warm day, and it was completely still, no wind, not even a slight breeze.

My hands shook as I took the green sack out of the backpack for what would now be the last time. I had become greatly attached to the urn during the past months, and now as the time approached to part with it, I felt something disappearing from within me. It was like I was about to cut off a part of myself. Noticing my anxiety, Ekant placed a comforting hand over mine then helped me in removing the urn from the sack. He opened it, revealing the plastic bag where the ashes had been stored. I took a deep breath and tried to calm my nerves as Ekant recited the final prayers. As we all bowed our heads after the final verse, I knew that this wasn't going to be as smooth as I had hoped. I felt as if I were at the funeral all over again. The ashes had been with me until now; my father had been with me. But after today, I would have nothing left of him. He would be just a memory. No physical part of him would exist.

Ekant led me to the edge of the riverbank, where he held out the bag and waited for me to join him. I took a deep breath and placed my hands over his. Suddenly a strong rush of wind blew around us. The women gasped behind us as their head coverings blew away. I looked up at Ekant, but he was already smiling down at me.

"Do you feel him?" he asked calmly.

I looked at him, baffled by his question, then closed my eyes. The breeze continued to spin around us. Images of my life with my father, the tender moments, even some of the chaotic ones all flashed before me. I felt his love, his guidance, and his presence. I felt Ekant tip the bag, but I kept my eyes closed. I wanted to keep seeing him, see his smile, hear his laughter, feel his warmth. I wanted it to continue. I wanted him to stay, but I knew he was already gone. I opened my eyes, and everything was still again. There was no wind, not even a breeze. Everything was quiet.

After we had taken a dip into the sacred pool, Ekant and I emerged as new people. I felt something lift out of me, but it made sense this time. I wasn't sad any more. The anxiety was gone, and in its place was a sense of peace and joy. My father's soul had finally been put to rest, and I had fulfilled his final wish.

After Kiratpur, Angad drove us to Amritsar, where we joined his mother and made our final pilgrimage to the Golden Temple. Security was still very tight, but they allowed us into the complex. We were told to proceed with caution, since a lot of reconstruction was taking place on the premises. Angad and I followed Ekant up the stairs of the main entrance. Apparently the Golden Temple was surrounded by a vast complex, and it sat below street level in the middle of the sacred pool of water. As we reached the top landing, Ekant stopped abruptly, and I stopped behind him.

"It was here, through this precise view," he said, turning to me.

"What was?" I asked, looking at him then at Angad, who was as puzzled as I.

"When I got over my pain and looked at life with new meaning all those years ago," Ekant continued. "You asked me a while back, remember? You wanted to know how I found God. Well, it was right here on these very steps, looking out over the beauty of this sacred abode. It was here that I found God."

I slowly took a step forward and walked out in front of him to see what he meant, then I understood. My eyes filled with tears as I looked out at our beautiful Golden Temple. It was beauty that only God could command. Even with the horrific damage it suffered in Operation Bluestar, it remained absolutely breathtaking. The destruction left by the Army's attack was still visible. The clean-up effort looked to be only in the very early stages. The Golden Temple itself stood marked by bullet holes, yet its magical allure still caught me. Looking at it now, I felt confident, confident about my purpose and my path in life. I was meant to be here, to see this. I looked up at Angad and thanked God that I was blessed to have him beside me. I adjusted my dad's kirpan that I now wore respectfully around my newly baptized body, and for the first time in my life, I felt not like Esha, but like a true devotee. This is *who* I am.

EPILOGUE

Five Years Later

I looked out the window and admired the beauty of the mountains. It had been five years, and still I couldn't get over them. I promised myself that I would never take such beauty for granted ever again. Bhagat screamed wildly as he chased after Mandy, Carrie and Reet with a water gun in the yard below as the rest of the family looked on and laughed at their craziness. He had come to love his new aunts very much, and they cared for him as if he was their very own. The whole family was finally together and happy. Naturally my mother fussed over me even more now, but for once in my life, I didn't mind one bit.

"Esha, dear, it's finally here!"

I turned around to see Angad walking into our bedroom. The sight of him still excited me. I wondered just how long it would take for me to realize that we were finally together, and that this was real. "What is it, hun?"

"Your law degree, it's finally official! Look, they've framed it."

"Oh, wow!" I said, taking it from his hands.

"So now you're not just my hotshot wife, but you're also a hotshot lawyer. Tell me, what are your plans now? Open a practice in the city or join the courts?"

"Now I head back to India," I said confidently. I had waited five years for this opportunity. The time had now come.

"India?" Angad asked with a puzzled look.

"We have a battle to finish, Angad. Justice still eludes those families who have lost everything. The world may have forgotten, but I haven't."

"Nor have I," he added. "But is this what you really want, Esha?"

"We need justice. Sumi demands it, Daya demands it, and humanity demands it. We have to do something before it happens to someone else. This wasn't about spontaneous communal violence. It was a manipulation of power and authority. It was an attack, a pogrom that had systematic qualities to it. In '84 the target was Sikhs. In the coming years it could happen again and to anyone, anywhere. It could be another religion, another caste. There are more reports of forced disappearances of Sikhs. Young men picked up off the streets, never to be seen or heard from again. The nightmare has not ended. Someone has to do something." Angad nodded. He knew I was right.

It had taken us a very long time to come to terms with what had transpired in the days following the prime minister's assassination. The nightmares still continued, and the wounds had not yet healed. I had spent the months immediately following the attacks trying to comprehend how being Sikh had qualified me as a target. I had spent sleepless nights trying to wrestle with this question, until one day I had finally realized the truth. Sikh was just the chosen target for a greater purpose. We had been pawns in the greater realm of dirty politics. I pored over reports, articles, anything I could get my hands on which could help me figure out what had happened in the years leading up to the events of 1984. I was appalled when I realized that the warning signs had been very much present, and nothing had been done to calm the situation. Friction between the Central Government and Punjab, particularly with the Sikh population, had been allowed to get out of control. I became terrified of the possibility of any other group meeting the same fate, becoming refugees in their own country. Even with the warnings and the friction, I still don't believe anyone could have imagined that such a violent attack on a single group could have taken place. The loss of life, the damage to innocent souls, it was still very unimaginable.

"It terrifies me to think that this could happen again, and God forbid, on a larger scale," Angad added.

"As intelligent people, we have to do something. What are those families going to do that have been completely shattered by what took place in '84? What about the grandmothers that are left destitute and responsible for their grandchildren, or the women who have been widowed, or the children that have been orphaned?"

"It will not be easy, and it will not be quick. Esha, are you sure?"

"Angad, I was sure the day we left Delhi," I replied without hesitation. It was true. The moment we drove out of Delhi, I took a vow that I would not stay quiet about what I had seen and heard. Every day for the past five years, I had heard Sumi's cries for help, and I had choked on the fumes of the kerosene that had devoured my friend and thousands of other innocents. But now the time had come. It was time to put the nightmares to rest.

"So, I guess now yet another journey begins for you?" he asked carefully.

"Yup, another journey," I replied, walking to the door. I stopped and turned back to face him again. "So, will you be a part of it?" I asked.

"I always am. You know that," he answered, flashing his still-perfect smile.

"I suppose I just needed to hear you say it," I said, smiling as the love of my life walked over and wrapped me in his arms. I closed my eyes and absorbed his warmth and energy, and a tear trickled down my cheek as I desperately wished my father had lived to meet him.

You would have been proud, Daddy.

Acknowledgements

A sincere acknowledgement to the victims and families that were touched by the events of 1984 in Delhi, India—your courage inspires me, and I hope we can all learn from it. To Professor Rusty Shteir, for pointing me in the right direction. Thanks to my grandfather, Prof. Kirpal Singh Sidhu, for all the references and being my strongest literary critic. Allister and Sylvia, thanks for believing. Thank you to Ensaaf and their continuous dedication to seeking justice for victims of the 1984 pogroms. Thank you to my beautiful family and friends, and those who were my very first readers. You all know who you are! Thanks to my loved ones who are closest to my heart. You helped along the way and made this journey absolutely incredible. And to Guru Ji, for His guidance.

Born and raised in Toronto, Nav obtained an Honours Degree in Political Science from York University, followed by law school at the University of London, in the United Kingdom.

She has been published in the *Toronto Star* and has also been featured in the same paper for her attempts to bring political awareness to the youth in her area. She can be visited online at navkgill.com